Sterling BRICK

L.B. DUNBAR

www.lbdunbar.com

Cover Design: Lori Jackson Designs
Photographer: Golden Czermak/FuriousFotog
Cover Model: Joey Berry
Editor: Nicole McCurdy/Emerald Edits
Editor: Gemma Brocato

Other Books by L.B. Dunbar

Sterling Falls
Sterling Heat
Sterling Brick
Sterling Streak

Parentmoon

Holiday Hotties (Christmas novellas)
Scrooge-ish
Naughty-ish

Road Trips & Romance
Hauling Ashe
Merging Wright
Rhode Trip

Lakeside Cottage
Living at 40
Loving at 40
Learning at 40
Letting Go at 40

Silver Foxes of Blue Ridge
Silver Brewer
Silver Player
Silver Mayor
Silver Biker

Sexy Silver Fox Collection
After Care
Midlife Crisis
Restored Dreams
Second Chance
Wine&Dine

Collision novellas
Collide
Caught

L.B. DUNBAR

The Sex Education of M.E.

The Heart Collection
Speak from the Heart
Read with your Heart
Look with your Heart
Fight from the Heart
View with your Heart

A Heart Collection Spin-off
The Heart Remembers

BOOKS IN OTHER AUTHOR WORLDS
Smartypants Romance (an imprint of Penny Reid)
Love in Due Time
Love in Deed
Love in a Pickle

The World of True North (an imprint of Sarina Bowen)
Cowboy
Studfinder

THE EARLY YEARS
The Legendary Rock Star Series

Paradise Stories

The Island Duet

Modern Descendants – writing as elda lore

Dedication

For small towns and first responders.

6

Chapter 1

[Halle]

The last thing I should have been doing at my mother's funeral was concentrating on *him*.

His dark hair was a little longer than the military cut he'd once kept. Gray hair tickled his temple and curled around his ears. His jaw held a circle of scruff around his full lips. His body had shifted from the lankiness of a teenager to the fullness of a man who now filled out a sharp, black suit rather nicely. His eyes were shielded behind shaded aviator-style sunglasses, but I recognized him.

Knox Sylver stood on the opposite side of my mother's gravesite toward the back of the congregation.

And he was watching me.

The flutter in my belly and wobble in my knees was the tell-tale sign. Once familiar only in his presence; long forgotten in his absence. The sensation recalled a school-girl crush, and I hadn't felt this unsettled since I was seventeen going on eighteen. Back then, it felt like we were the only two people that existed when he looked at me.

That was twenty years ago.

My current reaction might only be grief.

Snapping my gaze back to my mother's coffin, I quickly look away again, blinking at the dryness of my eyes. Crying over our final goodbye seemed wrong somehow, like I hadn't earned my right to take on the role of a grieving daughter, given that my mother and I had a tumultuous relationship. She was a difficult woman in the best of times. Difficult to please. Difficult to love. Yet impossible to hate. Leaving me behind with a mess of conflicting emotions.

For years, she'd wanted me to visit Sterling Falls, my teenage hometown. Her death was one way of making that happen. I'd avoided this place most of my adult life, despite the fact Knox Sylver hadn't been present either.

Which made it all the more puzzling that he was here now. At her funeral.

My mother hadn't approved of Knox or his family. His father had a bad reputation when we were kids. She'd feared Knox was the same, which hadn't seemed fair to my seventeen-year-old heart. She'd never seen Knox as I had. Sweet. Solid. Forever.

Then again, she might have been onto something because Knox turned out to be a liar. He'd proven he was unreliable. He'd been unforgivable but not unforgettable.

And the last thing I needed as I stood beside my two teenage children at my mother's funeral were reminders of how naïve I'd been when I was young.

With a shuddering breath, I wipe away all thoughts of Knox and return to the present. The minister is reading a prayer, but I'm still distracted. Birds chirp somewhere nearby. A soft breeze rustles the solitary tree closest to my mother's plot. My father's tombstone looks dull beside the freshly turned soil of my mother's final resting place, but the bright blue sky overhead causes the ache in my chest.

The desire to run overwhelms me. To feel the wind in my hair, oxygen pumping in my veins, and the strength of my legs carrying me away. But I can't run. Not today. Not any day. Not anymore.

I glance at a picture of my mother that somehow made it to the burial service. The image is from her wedding day more than forty years ago. She looks so young, so beautiful, but her eyes are as dull then as they'd been most of my life. She hadn't been a happy woman, and I'd borne the brunt of all her bitterness.

A gentle pressure comes to my lower back. As I turn in the direction of Jack, I flinch. He shouldn't be here. He's been absent for most of the major events in our fifteen-year marriage. His presence today isn't warranted, especially as our divorce is officially final. There's no need *for appearance's sake.* No ruse necessary for the media. We are no longer the picture-perfect image of a family that didn't exist behind closed doors.

"Would you like to say any final words?" The minister had approached. Jack's touch had been a signal I'd been spoken to but hadn't responded yet.

I shake my head. I don't want to talk. Not to more well-wishers. Not to old acquaintances. Not to anyone.

I just want to run away, but I can't.

The minister recites a final blessing.

"We'll give you a minute," Jack mutters to me as people pay their last respects and slowly meander off.

With my heels sinking into the grass under my feet, I remain planted. It hasn't sunk in that my mother has passed away. Between the week of her hospitalization and the days of preparation for a funeral, reality has not settled in.

I'm an orphan. *Can I say that at thirty-eight years old?*

Glancing up and over the casket, still above the earth, but prepped to be lowered, my gaze fixes on *him* again.

He'd been at the back of the gathering, but as funeral mourners stepped away, he came into view more clearly. Only the two of us remain.

Him standing there and me here, and it's all a reminder of who we'd eventually become. What happened to us.

Death had been the catalyst that tore us apart. However, I can't really blame fate beyond our control.

Knox made choices. And those decisions didn't include me.

+ + +

The local church ladies host the funeral luncheon in the church's community center, which is a glorified name for the basement. The meal should have been my responsibility, but I am no longer familiar with local catering companies or another place large enough to hold such a gathering. My absence from Sterling Falls is apparent when each and every elderly woman greets me with a tight, reprimanding smile.

"Your mother missed you so much."

"She was so proud of you."

"She talked about you all the time."

I offer a weary smile in return, knowing the truth. If she was proud of me, she had a strange way of showing it. If she'd been pleased with me, I might have come home more often. If she'd missed me, she shouldn't have pushed me away.

Forty-five minutes into the bombardment of well-intended women, I need a break.

After a quick check on Violet and Tim, my children, I head to the restroom, locking the door behind me. Crossing to the double sink, I lower my head and inhale. When I look up and into the mirror, I note the distinct differences in my face from the last time Knox saw me.

Lines mar the corners of my blue eyes. My mouth turns down in an almost permanent frown. My forehead holds a crease like a letter full of secrets folded in half.

A ghost of a memory hits me, plucked from my mind, and playing out as if on a projector screen.

I'm a senior in high school. I'm at the homecoming dance. I hadn't asked anyone as a date; still hopeful Knox would show up. After my emails and texts went unanswered, an old-fashioned letter was my last resort. He hadn't answered that either.

My foolishly childish heart believed begging and pleading would bring him back to me.

I'd slipped into the bathroom after shaking my groove thing to "Crazy in Love" by my then-girl Beyonce. The music had switched to a slower beat. A song about knowing someone has a new life, but still missing him. Couples had paired up on the dance floor.

While I stood in the bathroom, the door opened, and a man walked in. With a baseball cap pulled low over his face, I didn't see his eyes. A scream built at the back of my throat, ready to give him a piece of my mind, but my outburst remained locked behind my lips.

Because as his head lifted, his eyes came into view and instant awareness filled the space between us. His shoulders were broader. He stood taller. He looked harder. But I'd still recognize him anywhere.

"Knox?"

Was I dreaming? Maybe I was drunk. Only I hadn't been drinking.

Knox's index finger came to his lips as he'd shut the door behind him, locking us inside.

I should have been angry at his sudden appearance, at the months of radio silence, but I was so relieved to see him, I leapt for him.

And he caught me, like he always had.

The memory hits me so hard I suddenly can't breathe. I need to be outside. Even if I can no longer run, I need open space.

Turning toward the door, I grip the handle and twist. The metal lever pops off in my hand.

"What the hell?" Saying such a thing in a church basement is certain to send me to the fiery underworld, but I can think of lots of other reasons the devil and his pitchfork would welcome me down below.

"Hello?" I hammer on the closed barrier with the heel of my hand. "Is anyone out there?" The bathroom is tucked down a long hallway off the community room and it's doubtful my voice carries over the noise of the gathered crowd.

Unfortunately for me, my phone is in my clutch, somewhere on a table in the main room.

My breathing grows shallower as I fumble with the door handle, attempting to reset it. Jiggling it in place does nothing. The knob falls off once again.

"Don't panic," I mutter as my chest begins to tighten. A bead of sweat trickles along the back of my neck. I bang my palm on the door once more, my voice only a quiet shrill. "Help."

Crying out feels silly, but I'm stuck in the bathroom where my mother's funeral luncheon is being served.

Weeks without tears and reality hits like a mallet to my head.

My mother is dead.

I'm officially divorced.

I don't know what my next step will be.

And I'm currently locked in a bathroom during a funeral.

Chapter 2

[Knox]

I shouldn't be here.

Not at her mother's funeral. Not in the damn bathroom.

Compulsion to be present overrode sound logic. History and heartbreak propelled me to be here for Halle. To pay my final respects to a woman who hadn't ever respected me. I was present, if for no other reason than because she had been Halle's mother.

Anything for Halle.

Who shouldn't be in here either.

This is the men's room which must have escaped her attention despite the line of urinals along the wall.

As for me, after decades of communal pissing, I'd taken a stall for my personal business. When I'd opened the door, I was stunned to see her and quickly shut myself inside again.

I can't face her. Not yet.

She is grieving and this isn't the place to air *our* grievances. How I'd hurt her. How she'd wounded me. I didn't fault her. I'd tossed the first ax. She'd only buried the hatchet deeper when she married someone else.

So, here I stand, inside a bathroom stall waiting for her exit, until I hear her muttering to herself. Then comes the hammering on the door, and a soft cry for help. But the sound that draws me from my hiding spot is the soul-wrenching sob and the clatter of something metal against the tile floor.

Within seconds, I am out of the stall and clutching her to my chest.

Halle Reynolds hasn't changed one bit. Her hair is still dirty red, almost paprika colored. She is still trim with legs for miles, and she still fits against me like a missing puzzle piece.

"Shh, Sprint." I shush her, smoothing my hand down her hair and tightening my hold around her. "I've got you."

With her hands over her face, her forehead lands against my sternum. Her slim shoulders shudder with each gut-twisting cry. Leaning over her, I press my lips to her hair, lingering as I inhale a fragrance I haven't smelled in nearly twenty years. *Jasmine.* The scent tickles my nose, restoring memories of her tucked into me; us making out in my truck; her holding me when life felt hopeless.

She'd been my everything then, but I hadn't been good enough for her.

"It's okay, sweetheart," I soothe, tightening my arm around her back as I hold her head to my chest. I'd *never* seen Halle cry. Not once in that year together. Not once in our year apart. The only tears I'd ever seen from her were broadcast on national television for all the world to witness.

It broke my hardened heart.

Suddenly, two strong hands push on my chest. The unexpected pressure throws me off balance, causing me to strengthen my hold.

"Let go of me." Her grumble is muffled by the tears in her throat before she firmly presses at me again and I release her.

"Just what do you think you're doing?"

For the first time in twenty years, Halle gives me her eyes. The blue swims beneath lingering tears but they still glisten as bright as a summer day.

"I'm married," she blurts next.

My gaze drops to her left hand, naked of any rings. I saw her husband beside her, but I hadn't missed the distance between them. His lack of comfort. Her children surrounded her during the funeral service and the graveside prayer. When he'd touched her, just that once, she'd flinched away from him.

"Where is your ring, Sprint?"

"Do not call me that," she demands, pointing her finger at me as the old nickname tumbles out of my memory bank.

The corner of my mouth ticks upward and I bite my lip to prevent laughter. She's still cute. Cute *and* feisty. Despite mascara smudged around her eyes and lipstick smudged on her lips, she is as spellbinding as when I first gave her the nickname. Scowl included.

"What are you even doing in here?" She waves her arm outward, implying the restroom, before taking a closer look around the space. Realization slowly dawns and her cheeks brighten, the color restored after such a hard cry.

"Oh my God." She briefly closes her eyes, cutting off the blue beams I want aimed at me again. Even if she's only scolding me, I want her attention.

"It's the men's room."

"Thank you." Her lids flick open. "I see that now." Her terse tone doesn't surprise me. Her emotions must be all over the place. Her mother's funeral. Maybe my presence. And . . . glancing down at the floor I find the metal-against-tile culprit.

Bending down, I pick up the door handle and hold it between us. "Looks like we're stuck."

Halle tips her head back. "Perfect." Sarcasm fills her voice before her head snaps forward, mild panic suddenly etched into her beautiful face. Her eyes narrow, retrospective. "I can't be in here with you."

"What's wrong with me?" I pat my chest and give her a wide smile, knowing it once charmed her.

We had our differences but that was twenty years ago. Surely, she moved on. Actually, I know she did.

Jack Haskins is a state representative for West Virginia. He's also a total tool and her husband.

"What were *you* doing in here?"

"I thought it was the ladies' room." She lifts a hand to cup her forehead. The tension between us swirls like the water in a toilet bowl before disappearing down the drain. Then she lets out an awkward guffaw.

I match her sharp laugh with a light chuckle and keep my gaze on her. She didn't use the facility so what was she really doing in here?

Halle shakes her head, dropping her hand and lowering her gaze. "And, I was hoping to run away for a few minutes."

My shoulders loosen.

A memory hits. Halle running, full tilt and hellbent through the woods before colliding into me. Her lean body bounced back like she'd slammed into a tree, but I caught her by her upper arms before she fell. At first glance, I knew I'd always catch her. Or at least, I thought I would.

"You're built like a brick," she'd teased then.

"Always running," I joke.

Pain instantly etches her softened cheeks. She straightens her spine and shifts her eyes away from mine. "Yeah, well, not so much anymore."

I want to know what she means but my phone buzzes in my suit jacket pocket.

"You have a phone?" Her brows crease. *So cute.*

"Most people do in the modern era."

"Funny," she snarks as I pull the device forward to see I've missed a message from my brother Clay. Whatever he needs, I can call him back later.

When I glance up at Halle, she's watching me, eyes wide, brows lifted expectantly. "Well, call someone to get us out of here."

At her sharp demand, I lean my shoulder against the door holding us hostage inside the men's room. Crossing my arms, I give her another big grin. "You've turned into a demanding little thing, Sprint."

"I said not to call me that."

I arch a brow, noting how she's just proved my point.

"And I'm not demanding." She swipes a hand through her long hair, holding a clump at the back of her neck. "I just . . ."

"What?"

"I can't be in here with you."

So she's said. "Because you're married?"

Her brows hitch before she scowls at me again. "Because it's not appropriate. This *is* the men's room. And I don't want people thinking I snuck off in here with *you* after I literally just buried my mother."

Ignoring the wound her words were intended to inflict, my lip curls, confident and too cocky. "I don't know, Sprint. Grief makes people do the strangest things."

Her head is already shaking. "Nope. Not happening. Not today."

"Some other day perhaps?" I arch a brow, my smile still wide and teasing.

Halle glares at me, warning me with her hardened gaze she isn't in a playful mood.

Right. She's right. We shouldn't be in here together, but as long as I have her captive for another few seconds before I spring us free from the restroom, I have a question. A selfish one but one that's been burning in my brain for decades. While it might not be the best time to ask, there's an answer I need in order to walk away from her.

"Why'd you do it?" I tilt my head, watching her. "Why'd you marry the douche canoe?"

Her mouth falls open as her cheeks flame. Halle stands taller but she'll always be eight inches shorter than me.

"You have no right to ask me that." Her eyes are bright and penetrating, pinning me with years of built-up resentment . . . and hurt. The resentment I can live with; the hurt guts me.

I focus on those eyes, once so familiar, now so foreign. "I said I was coming back for you." Then again, I'm the one who'd taken too long to return. My hope that she'd still be waiting had been misplaced and I had no one to blame but myself.

"And your word meant anything at that time?"

The jab comes as intended, like an arrow through the heart. It hadn't been fair to make her promises, but I'd meant what I'd said. I was coming back. To explain myself. To right the wrongs I'd done to her. To us.

"Just answer the question."

"It's too late to ask."

The words come softly, like the energy to fight has been drained from her. Her arms band around her middle, as though to keep her insides from spilling out. Her emotions kept tightly wrapped within. Her head bows.

I hate seeing her this way. I hate her avoiding me. I hate the adverse parts I've played in her history.

Taking a hesitant step closer to her, careful with my large hand, I cup her chin, raising her head so her eyes meet mine. My gaze traces the slope of her nose, the curve of her chin, her tear-stained cheeks and tight lips, before returning to her ghost-filled eyes. Eyes that haunted me on lonely nights and saw me through dark times. This is a new Halle.

Fragile but not weak.

Strong but somehow delicate.

Her body language tells me to be gentle with her, patient even.

"It's never too late, Sprint."

She can run all she wants but I'm better equipped to chase her this time. And the truth she isn't telling me is as apparent as her naked left hand.

"And if you were wearing my ring, I'd be making damn certain you never took it off."

Chapter 3

[Halle]

Knox Sylver had some *fracking* nerve thinking he could say such things to me after all this time.

I didn't want to hear it. Not then. Not now. I just wanted out of this restroom and away from him.

"Get us out of here," I ordered, nodding at his pocket containing his phone and giving evidence to his claim that I'd become demanding.

If only I'd been more forthcoming, more honest, I might still be married. But that ship has sailed, just like the one that took Knox away from me. As a former naval aviator, he'd spent half his life at sea, or in the air, or wherever he'd been. His heroics had been retold to me by my mother of all people, who liked to keep me up to date on him, when she'd been the same person to tell me he wouldn't amount to anything.

As for my marriage, there wasn't anything left to salvage. Jack and I had simply fallen out of love on a slow fizzle, just like we'd fallen in love in the same manner. A kindle. A crackle, and then a brief flame. He'd moved on faster than me after our divorce. When he started dating a local schoolteacher, Peggy Montrock, suspicion quickly circulated that they'd been an item before the ink had dried on our divorce papers. Since our divorce has only been official for two months, I'd be foolish not to consider the rumors as truth.

The pain of their reality surprisingly only stings. The hurt wasn't that Jack had moved on but that he hadn't waited until we were legally over before pursuing someone else. For all the pressure from him to behave a certain way, act a certain way, appear a certain way, he'd broken our vows without regard for how his affair reflected on me.

Unfortunately, getting divorced didn't look good for a man with his sights on the White House. Being unhappy for another fifteen years wasn't a good look on me, though. Jack reluctantly agreed. He blamed a nineteen-year-old accident for our issues. He might have been right.

All this was to say, I was lost as I neared forty. But one thing I knew for certain at the moment was I had to get away from Knox. When his strong arms encircled me, tugging me against the firmness of his chest, the familiarity of his strength sparked more memories. When I was younger, he'd been the one person I thought I could lean on, who truly understood me, but I'd been wrong. I could only rely on myself.

My parents had proven it. Jack solidified it, but it all started with Knox abandoning me.

A bit dramatic for a woman almost forty. I should be over the pain he caused when I was eighteen. I *am* over it. But my current emotions are like the mountains around us, edgy and sharply peaked. I've shored up the walls around myself long enough, keeping up the pretense of *happy wife, happy life* but I'm no longer a wife and don't know where life will lead me next.

Least of all, I don't want to hear about promises and rings and Knox's failure to produce either.

Glaring at him, his eyes darken back. Then he huffs, presses away from the door, and sets the handle over the shaft jutting through the latch, and twists. The latch catches and the door pops open. Reaching toward the top of the barrier, Knox tugs it inward, keeping his arm extended.

"Thank you," I snap, stepping forward, attempting to exit by walking underneath his arm but he's quick to lower it, trapping me once more against the solid length of his muscular forearm.

"We aren't finished, Halle."

Oh, we are. He made that abundantly clear almost twenty years ago. What I don't recall is *him* being so commanding, and a strange ripple runs up my middle, faintly reminding me of the butterflies he once brought to my belly. He'd been my first love and my first experience with sex. I'd only ever been with two men in my life. The thought makes me . . . angry.

"Let me go." My teeth clack. Fists form at my sides.

Knox leans toward my ear. "Never, Sprint." Then he pushes off the door, pressing on it so it swings wide, and I can slip past him into the hall. He catches the door as is swivels back toward him, and nods once, implying I exit the hallway first.

As I do, I fight the urge to glance behind me. I learned a long time ago never to look back when it comes to Knox Sylver.

And true to his MO, he vanishes from the luncheon, just like he'd disappeared from my life.

+ + +

While Jack offers to stay the night, the truth in his eyes suggests he'd rather do anything but spend a night at my mother's house. Our former home in Charles Town is a five-hour drive away. Despite the late afternoon timing, he could make it before midnight if he left soon.

"I have loose ends to tie up here," I tell him, although it isn't his business. I simply mean I won't be returning to Charles Town soon. I don't have anywhere to go anyway. Jack got the house in our divorce because it's convenient to Virginia and Washington, D.C. for him. I still wasn't certain if I wanted to stay in Jefferson County, regardless of the kids and their social calendar.

Essentially, we're homeless.

Violet will be fifteen in two months, and she'll be entering her freshman year of high school. I've tried my hardest not to pressure her to be anyone other than who she wants to be, which changes as often as she changes hair styles and jeans preference.

Tim is a twelve-year-old middle schooler who loves soccer and video games. He's the lover of my two children, as Violet takes after me. A little steel-hearted. A lot stubborn.

When they learned we were staying in Sterling Falls for the summer, I braced for the push-back.

"But our house is in Charles Town," Violet whined, which was code for *all her friends live in that city*.

"I have soccer camp," Tim stated, a little less irritated, just curious how a five-hour commute would work.

"You're both going to stay with your dad for two weeks in July." *Jack* will have to learn how to balance Violet's social life and Tim's camp carpools.

A pang of guilt hits me, but my kids are old enough to speak up, which they've done often throughout the divorce process. They aren't small, incapable children. If they are resourceful enough to figure out how to get to a mall or a movie theatre, they can certainly help their father manage ride-shares.

Not my concern.

I'm not on strike as a mother, but I'm taking a hiatus. From the moment my children were born, I've embraced motherhood. Violet and Tim are everything to me. I'd give over vital organs for them, and I'd willingly become maid, chef, taxi driver, and teacher over the years. I'd thrown the best birthday parties and hosted amazing networking dinners for Jack. I volunteered as homeroom mother, scout leader, and team mom. But somewhere along the way, as I'd adopted all these roles and monikers, I became less me. Less Halle.

I love and adore Violet and Tim, but as my children age into middle school and high school, they rely on me less and less. It isn't that they don't need me, but their needs are different. Uniform laundry. Quick dinners. Homework checks. Gone are the nights of snuggling in their beds and reading books with them. Tim would rather curl up with his online video game buddies and Violet is permanently attached to her phone.

I don't begrudge my children growing up. I'm not my mother. I'd still sell my kidney for them, but for my own sanity, it was time to find myself again.

I needed to learn who I was beyond a wife and mother.

"Why do we have to stay with Dad?" Tim asks, concern etched in his tone. He knows the answer. The situation is part of our joint custody agreement. Plus, *we* don't live in his house anymore.

During the time the kids are gone, I plan to sort out my mother's place in preparation to sell it. I could use the cash to buy us a new permanent residence.

Maybe we'll stay in Sterling Falls.

The questionable thought is quickly erased from my mind. There would be no reason to stay here. The memories are old, dusty, and gray, and not ones I want to clear off or polish up. Broken hearts live within the bones of this house.

"Because five hours isn't a simple commute. Plus, Dad has you guys for two weeks every July." That's the new norm for us. Two weeks in the summer. Two weeks every other Christmas. Every other spring break, and every other weekend, provided it works with Jack's schedule.

No one takes into account *my* calendar. The days and weeks are filled with everyone else's activities.

The one endeavor I don't have is a paying job. As a stay-at-home mother for fifteen years, I'm not certain how to market my skills. Organizer? Time manager? Taxi driver? And at thirty-eight, I'm entirely too young to retire from a position that never paid anything except hugs and homemade cards.

Eventually, I'll need to find employment, but that's a thought for another day.

Tonight, my mother's house is quiet once Violet and Tim resort to their electronics, and I step onto the rickety front porch, taking a seat on a loose step. To save time, I brought the entire bottle of wine with me. Barefoot, I remain in my black funeral dress, curling my toes against the dirty wood planks. I wrap my arms around my middle, and dangle the wineglass beside me, staring into the weed-infested yard.

In the heat of late June, everything grows.

As the mountain air whispers, and the tall grasses dance, images of my teen years skip through my head. Or rather, race through my memory.

The first time I'd met Knox Sylver I'd been running through the woods just outside of town proper. There wasn't a specific trail. I just liked exploring the surroundings of my new home. I'd been seventeen and new to Sterling Falls that summer. And I loved to run.

Closing my eyes, I can almost see myself as I once was. Long legs. Lean body. Music in my ears; lost in my thoughts. Arms pumping at my sides as I raced beneath the filtered light of tall trees.

For some reason, I'd looked over my shoulder one day, simply a brief glance away from the path, when I suddenly collided with a hard form, solid and sturdy, like the trunk of a towering tree.

Strong hands caught my upper arms before I fell back.

"What's the rush, Sprint?" He was built like a brick. His voice as scratchy as the surface of one. His eyes were dark, earthy warm, and mesmerizing. And his hands on me were like a forest fire, heated and blazing a trail to a place rarely explored.

I'd been a virgin then. Knox accepted that gift from me, along with my heart, that year.

Lifting my wineglass to my lips, I take a deep drink, as if the peppery red wine could douse the memory. A memory so old I'm certain I don't remember it correctly. Time and age has only embellished the moment, making it into something more than it was meant to be.

Because from the second I met Knox Sylver, I thought he was my destiny.

And he turned out not to be.

Chapter 4

[Knox]

"Patios. This is Knox," I answer the call sent to me by the receptionist of Sylver Seed and Soil. The family business started with our parents before my oldest brother Stone was born. They had a nice little set-up going in our small town until my mother died and my father fell apart. In an effort to salvage the business and our family's name, my brother Clay took over, growing the Seed and Soil into a small empire with multiple divisions including my little corner of patio building and brick landscaping.

The job is a side-gig to my fireman position. With forty-eight hours on, and ninety-six off, there was no way I could sit around and do nothing for four days. Patio building involved sweat and labor, using my hands and keeping my mind busy, which meant I didn't have time to sit and dwell on anything.

Put out fires, build something, smile while I did both things.

Today happened to be one of those build something days.

And radio silence filled the phone after I'd answered. "Hello?"

A throat clears and a female voice speaks. "I was looking for the landscape division."

Leaning back in the office chair where I sit, I recognize the voice. *Halle.* Instantly, I recall sneaking phone calls to her, whispering late into the night when we should have been sleeping. When my dad was too drunk to know I was using the house phone and Halle was quiet, so her grandmother or mom didn't hear her.

A smile curls my lips at the memory and the sound of her voice.

"I can help you." Without waiting on her to acknowledge me, I ask, "What do you need?"

"The landscape division." Her voice is flat, cool with forced politeness.

"Need the lawn cut? Flowers planted? Shrubbery installed or removed?" I don't know why I'm asking. This isn't my department. We have a guy who schedules weekly lawn service and a team of landscapers who tend flowers, plant bushes, and handle spring and fall clean up.

Still, *I* want to know what Halle needs. And poking at her for a reaction becomes a mission. I'd rather have her spitting mad or reasonably agitated than devoid of emotion, like a perfect politician's wife.

"I need an estimate on yard clean up." Halle remains succinct and terse with her explanation, still acting like we are strangers.

"Ah," I tease. "And your address?" I tip forward, righting my position in the office chair and reaching for a pen like I need to jot down where she lives when I still remember exactly which house was her grandmother's place, and eventually her mom's.

"You really don't remember?" Her voice drops like a pebble plopped into a puddle. Confused. Concerned. Maybe even crushed.

"Yeah," I lower my own voice. "I remember, Sprint."

"Don't call me that." And there she is again. The new her.

I can almost hear her teeth clenching through the line. Ignoring the tension coming off her, I ask, "What day works best for a visit?"

"Just transfer me to the lawn service department," she demands.

I chuckle, knowing it probably pisses her off. I don't know when my Halle turned so demanding, or so distant. Maybe it has something to do with that asshat ex-husband of hers. I didn't even have to conduct an internet search to learn the truth—amongst the gossip—that Jack Haskins has a new woman in his life, only a few months after a very quiet and amicable divorce from his wife.

Dickhead.

Who divorces Halle Reynolds? Who leaves her? *Raises hand and volunteers to answer.*

Me. Another dickhead.

"Just give me a date and time." I fight the urge to clack my teeth. Smiling wide despite her not being able to see me helps. Smiling is how I get through most things: days, nights, and all the hours in between. A brave face and broad grin hides everything simmering inside me.

The loss of my mother. Then my father to alcohol.

The loss of a friend. Then my direction in life.

The loss of my heart to a woman going places when she was eighteen.

I had no direction then either.

"Fine," Halle grunts. "Tuesday. Ten o'clock." Then her voice softens, sounding vulnerable when she asks, "You're sure you remember the address?"

"I remember, Halle."

I remember everything.

+ + +

When Tuesday morning arrives, I try not to let my nerves get the best of me as I pull up before a house I haven't visited in over twenty years. Taking a second, I stare up at the window that had been Halle's bedroom.

Her father's mother owned the house. When Halle was seventeen and finishing her sophomore year of high school, her father had a sudden heart attack, and she and her mother moved to Sterling Falls after his passing.

According to Halle, at the time, the move was necessary because they had no other place to go. As perpetual renters, they hadn't owned a home and Halle's mother hadn't worked. Halle loved Gladys Reynolds, otherwise known as Gigi to her. Halle's mother wasn't half as enamored of her mother-in-law. Most days, Halle's mom didn't like anyone, especially me.

On that thought, I press open the door of a Sylver Seed and Soil truck and hop out, almost gloating that I'm openly walking up the cobbled path leading to the slanting front porch. I hadn't been particularly welcome here when I was younger. Not certain I was actually welcome now either, but I had more freedom to cross the cracks in the cement.

I didn't give a fuck anymore about a lot of things that bogged me down at eighteen.

With a sharp rap of my knuckles against a wood-framed screen door that had seen better days, I wait on Halle to answer, bracing myself for the shock of seeing her again.

Those blue eyes. That paprika-red hair. Hopeful for the smile I don't deserve. The one that lit a up a room when she entered, like she was the sun. The one she used to give only to me when she looked my way, as if I'd hung the moon.

As the front door swings open, my breath catches. Before me stands Halle at seventeen, which is impossible because she's aged like me. Being one year younger than me, Halle is thirty-eight to my thirty-nine. So, I blink to clear my vision. The image before me remains a slender girl with a red-haired ponytail and eyes that mirror . . . her mother?

"Hi. Knox Sylver to see Halle Reynolds." I point toward the truck. "I'm from Sylver Seed and Soil, here about the yard." Halle might have gone by Halle Haskins, but I wasn't ever going to call her that name. She didn't belong to him. She was still mine.

The young girl squints at me, probably noticing the use of Halle's maiden name, before she nods toward the yard. "Mom's out back. You can just help yourself." She hesitantly opens the screen door enough to slip her hand through and point toward the left side of the house. "There isn't a fence."

Without a glance, I know there isn't a fence present but something else is. Another memory.

I'd once promised Halle a white picket fence and a garden to raise our children in. It was going to be the perfect little house, full of love and stability, unlike the volatile existence I lived in with my younger siblings and my dad, minus my mother. The vow was idealistic eighteen-year-old talk about impossible futures. I was never going to be good enough for Halle. She had a plan. I didn't.

And according to my dad, I was taking up space he was eager to clear.

I clear my throat and rid my head of thoughts of my old man. "Thanks." I point in the direction the teenage version of Halle just did, as if confirming where to go when I know this yard and this house like an ancient map. Halle was my treasure buried within the confines of this place.

With a hop off the slanted porch, I round the house and find Halle sitting in the middle of the backyard. The grass is almost knee high where she sits in a red cedar lawn chair with faded green cushions. Her arm is perched on the thick armrest. Her chin rests against her fisted hand as if she's deep in thought.

Staring at her profile as I approach, I admire the column of her neck. The jut of her chin. The perky point of her nose. Halle is a study in beauty, and she's still the prettiest woman I've known.

And her face is too beautiful for such a pensive expression upon it. Selfishly, I want her thoughts to be plagued by me. I want to be the cause of her troubles and the solution to them as well. The only one to make her feel better, be better.

"Hey," I call out.

Halle flinches before dropping her arm and turning her head so she can glance at me over her shoulder.

"Knox?" Her brows pinch, forming a deep crease between them. Worry fills her eyes. Weariness covers her face.

"Hi. Knox Sylver from Sylver Seed and Soil," I tease.

"Where is the lawn service guy?"

"At your service." I'm not him, but I am here to offer Halle any service she wants with the friends-and-family discount we don't offer. Meaning, minus material costs, I'm free labor. I owe her.

"Knox," she groans, turning her face away from me and knocking her head gently against the back of the yard chair.

I help myself to a second chair near hers. In the silence that follows, I take in the yard. Overgrown flowerbeds. Tall grass. A sagging wooden stoop off the back of the house.

The space begs for a large deck or a brick patio with a low retaining wall, plus colorful flowers and a manicured lawn.

I could finally give Halle that long-ago promise of a white picket fence and a beautiful garden, even if it wasn't shared with me. I could make this yard comfortable, maybe even make this house appealing. I could show her reasons to stay in Sterling Falls.

"Knox, you can't be here." Her warning reminds me of the times I snuck over knowing her grandmother was napping and her mother was working. Back then, Halle would blush while she pulled me to her, taking my mouth with her hesitant kisses that quickly turned into heated make out sessions.

"Says who?" I dare her to name people who no longer exist. I double-dog dare her to tell me it's her. *She* doesn't want me here. If that's true, I'll leave and not look back.

The lie is one I threaten myself to accept.

Halle heavily sighs, cupping her forehead a second before scrubbing her fingertips over it, like she wants to erase a memory or thought. Like she wants to erase me.

That already happened once. I won't let it happen again.

"How are you doing, Halle?"

She lowers her arm, hand smacking on the wooden rest before she hits me with a glare that could incinerate a lesser man. I'm not that man, though, and something she sees in my eyes must tell her I'm asking in earnest. I want to know how she's really doing. Her mother's loss. Her divorce. Her return to Sterling Falls.

Halle looks away from me, staring off into the riotous yard. I silently wait her out, watching as her shoulders lower and her head gently tips backward. Her gaze aims at the sky above, a perfect match for the color of her eyes.

"I'm lost," she whispers.

She'd said the same thing during our first meeting when she was racing through the woods and collided into me.

I'm grateful I was the one to find her that day.

I'll happily find her again.

Chapter 5

[Halle]

I'm lost.

The mantra repeats in my head, and I don't know why I offer it to him. Of all people, he's the last person I want to know that I'm floundering.

Once upon a time, he was the first person I'd tell when I had a bad day. When I missed my dad. Or my mom was pissy. Or Gigi was tired, and I worried she was ill. When all I wanted to do was run, run, run, and lose myself in the pumping of my legs and beating of my heart.

"Let me find you," Knox whispers beside me, startling me, as if I'd somehow forgotten he was present, which would be impossible.

In a pair of jeans, work boots, and a tight tee with Sylver Seed and Soil embroidered over his left pec, he's a vision of manual labor. His forearms are covered in ink making me wonder what other parts of him have tattoos. My heart hammers at how hot he looks. His thirty-nine years have been good to him. Maybe it's been his military training. Maybe it's the yard work. Maybe I always knew the beautiful boy would become a stunning man.

I shake my head in response to his words. I don't want him to help me. He isn't dependable.

And what I need now is someone reliable. Someone to guide me through clearing out my mother's house, fixing what needs to be fixed, and mending this yard as best it can be mended.

"I'm selling the house," I blurt, staring out at the mixture of weeds and flowers, no longer able to distinguish which is which.

"Okay," Knox hums.

"I need to repair this yard. It's the first impression of the place." I turn my head and almost startle again at how intently Knox is staring at me. "I need to repair the inside, too."

God, the list is almost endless inside the house. My mother kept everything. The furniture is outdated. Most of the pieces are not old enough to be considered antique or interesting. The house has a funky odor. The carpet is the first thing on my list to remove.

"Okay," Knox mutters again.

I look away from him. "I need to get this place on the market and get on with my life."

A heavy silence falls between us before Knox leans against the solid armrest of his chair, coming into my peripheral view.

"And what is your life, Halle?"

How dare he ask? I want to rant and rave. My life is not his business. He made that perfectly clear when he enlisted in the Navy and left me behind, despite his promises, despite my dreams.

"My children," I state, without a second thought, glaring back at him, as if I can will him to remember something that never happened for us. Things that should have happened between us.

"She's your daughter," he states, not questioning.

"Violet. She's fourteen almost fifteen."

"She looks exactly like you."

The smallest curl of my lips gives away how much I enjoy that compliment. Not that I think I'm anything special, but Violet is beautiful. I wish I'd had half her confidence when I was her age.

"I have a son, too. Tim is twelve." Tim will grow up to look more like his father and be a consistent reminder of the man I briefly loved enough to make my husband.

Knox is quiet a second before he sits back in his seat, making himself comfortable like he'll be staying a while.

"Violet was my mother's name."

I twist my neck and gaze at him again over my shoulder. His profile is striking with the thicker, longer hair on top and scruff on his jaw accentuating the lushness of his lips. My memories of kissing him are a battle I can't seem to defeat.

And a puzzled look fills his expression.

"I remember," I softly say. He'd promised me a garden full of kids and we could name them all after flowers. He'd wanted a girl named after his mother, who died when he was six.

Knox sighs heavily and rubs his hand over his lips, before circling his fingers around his chin.

Sorrow and loss lingers between us. Lost dreams. Old promises. Time and distance. There is no point in turning back the clock on all that never happened.

"So, the yard." I clear my throat, gazing back at the out-of-control garden area. "I can't afford much. I was thinking of pulling up the garden and grass seeding the area. I need edging and lawn clean up. Once the outside is under control, I hope to have the interior of the house finished and be ready to sell."

"What's the rush to sell?" he asks, watching me.

I squint in the bright sunlight. *Because I need the money*. I need to move somewhere. I need a job.

Since I was a stay-at-home mother for fifteen years, I don't know that I'm very marketable. I also don't know what I want to do with myself. My college days earned me a basic degree I never used. My goal then had been one thing. The Olympics.

One leap. One hurdle. Dreams shattered.

I lean forward; my eyes avoiding Knox. "I need to find a place to live and a job." Dammit. I just promised myself I wasn't going to say anything personal to him. Yet, Knox always had a way of making me open up.

He's quiet for another second before stating, "I'm sorry about your divorce."

With the mention of my failed marriage, I stand, the desire to pace something I can't seem to contain. Seething, I stalk back and forth in front of him, fists at my sides. "You have no right to apologize."

My divorce wasn't his fault. My marriage wasn't either but there were days I cursed Knox Sylver for not upholding his promises. Silly teenage vows made in the heat of passionate kisses and tender touches when all we had were dreams.

Knox holds up a hand. Maybe as another form of apology. Then he slowly stands, unfolding himself in a way that I should not consider sexy. Those long legs, thick and solid. Abs I'm certain are still tight. Arms I can see are as strong as they are inked. At his full height before me, the pull I'd often felt as a teen is present. Like my heart is a magnet, attracted only to his.

What a foolish girl I'd been.

"I'll speak with our lawn division and get a crew set up for your yard."

"I need an estimate before I sign with Seed and Soil," I state.

Knox tips his head. "Halle, we're the only service in the area. You'll get a fair deal." He actually has the audacity to wink at me.

With a soft stomp of my foot, and my hands on my hips, I glare at him . . . and he freaking smiles. Lush lips spread wide. Bright white teeth on display. I'm blinded and that magnetic pull to him grows stronger. That delirious sensation only he could elicit in me tugging tighter. The draw to leap at him, like I'd done as a girl, where he'd catch me, laughing as he nuzzled into my neck and breathed me in, is fierce.

But that was then, and I hold my ground now, firmly planting myself in the yard as Knox quickly turns and walks away, giving me a good view of his ass in form-fitting jeans.

And his solid back, which I have imbedded in my memory from all the times he's walked away from me.

+ + +

With Knox gone, and my anger lingering, I tear through my mother's bedroom, easily packing up clothes and sorting through her limited jewelry. When I get to her wedding ring, I falter. I glance down at my own ring finger, now naked of the white-gold band and too-large-diamond Jack had given me.

I'd been training for my *second* attempt at the Olympics when Jack proposed. Prior to him, I'd told myself I didn't have time for romance. Dating hadn't been a thing with my hectic schedule. Falling in love hadn't been on my radar.

But Jack was sweet then, and persistent. As a new lawyer with his sights set on state politics, we met through a mutual acquaintance. Jack was a friend first, but he soon became the physical comfort I hadn't known was missing in my life.

We'd been good together . . . until we weren't.

With a sigh at the reminder, I glance back at my mother's wedding band placed with my father's in a segregated compartment within her jewelry box. She didn't want to be buried with her ring, convinced the mortician would steal it. She'd kept my father's ring for a different reason. She believed holding onto it bonded them together even when death had parted them.

Death hadn't parted Jack and I. Death had done that to Knox and me.

Closing my eyes, I shut out the pain the years have dulled to a whisper. The soft brush of sadness that never goes away. The achy pinprick of things that had never been. I count to seven, my unlucky number, and then release the memory.

With another heavy sigh, I get back to work at dismantling my mother's closet and drawers.

Chapter 6

[Knox]

"Vale, I need your help."

Valentine is the youngest in the Sylver clan, a brood of seven, and the only sister. She looks like the faint memories I have of my mother with straw-blond hair and summer-blue eyes like most Sylvers. And as the only woman in our family, she tends to have some of the sagest advice.

Vale skeptically eyes me over her shoulder, turning only her head in my direction as she washes dishes. We've just finished our weekly family dinner, mandated by Stone, our eldest brother, when we were kids. When we were young he used the time as a check in. Wanting to know what we had on our schedules for the week ahead. Poor Stone, he didn't have a clue how to raise a family, but he did. He stepped in when Dad failed. He took over when Dad—

"Does this have anything to do with Halle?" Vale hands me a large bowl to dry and I circle the outer edge before dipping the towel into the center.

"You heard she was back?" I don't meet my sister's penetrating gaze. Despite being the youngest, she's like a mother hen, knowing all the things. I suspect her knowledge comes from the book club she belongs to where the women share secrets and trade gossip like collectible baseball cards.

"*I heard* . . . you went to her mother's funeral." Vale is quiet a second. "How did that go?"

I sigh, pressing my hip against the counter as I set aside the bowl I dried. "It was a funeral."

Vale scowls, implying that isn't what she was asking, and I know it isn't what she meant.

"So, what do you need advice on?" she asks.

"Flowers."

Her brows lift while the corner of her mouth curls upward. "You don't know how to pick out flowers for a woman or you don't remember Halle's favorite flowers?"

Vale's tone is all tease, but it hits me she might be onto something. Does Halle still love daisies? Or have her tastes changed? Is she more refined? Did she receive dozens of roses over the years from that douchey ex-husband of hers? A thousand bouquets to apologize for cheating on her.

"Actually, I need help building a garden. I don't know what to plant."

Vale turns her attention to the window over the sink, glancing out into the backyard. The acre the house stands on has woods to the right and loads of open space before the stables off to the far left.

Currently, I live in our family home along with Stone and Vale. Stone inherited the place by default at our dad's passing. Vale moved in with her son, Hudson, shortly after having him. And I returned home last year after my twenty-year career in the Navy. The house has plenty of rooms to spare after raising seven children in it.

"Where?" Vale asks. She takes care of the smattering of flowers around the house.

"At Halle's."

Vale's hands still from scrubbing the grilling tongs. "Why?"

Because I'm selfish. Because Halle is back and I need to do something, anything, to right the wrongs I'd done to her.

"Just tell me what flowers to plant," I snap, not intending to be so harsh with her. Turning toward the countertop, I position both my hands on the surface, waiting on the next item to dry.

"What are you doing?" Vale lowers her voice, gentle, cautious, concerned.

I shrug. I don't really know. Maybe pursuing Halle again is a mistake. One I'm certain will burn me. But I also feel like I owe her. An apology. A peace offering. That garden I once promised her.

She named her first child Violet—my mother's name. *Why?*

Has Halle lived with the vows I made her flaming inside her all these years as they've singed and burned within me?

"I don't know," I softly admit. "But I want to help her clean up that place. She's going to sell."

Vale watches me. "It's a pretty house. Or at least it could be."

Sterling Falls has a series of Victorian homes one block from downtown. The dozen or so homes facing one another are separated by a tree filled island down the middle of the boulevard. The block is prime real estate. Halle's grandmother's house is one of several that need fresh exterior paint and some yard work, but the homes have potential for grandeur.

"You should ask Clay," Vale states, breaking into my thoughts of all the ways I'd improve Gigi Reynolds' old home.

"Yeah, about that." I side-eye Vale after she hands me the tongs to dry. "I'm trying to keep this on the downlow from him." I'm not stealing from the Seed and Soil. I'm just not giving the job to the family business outright. I'll personally pay any crew I need for projects and tackle what I can on my own. The work will be good for me. I love to be outdoors and using my hands keeps my mind occupied.

Although working on Halle's house is only going to fill my head with useless thoughts, like *what if* we'd inherited the house together? What if that place was ours? What if it was the home I'd promised her?

"Clay isn't going to mind. He loves a good romantic gesture."

I snort. As second in command of the family when we were younger, Clay loved a damsel in distress. Saving rabbits in the yard. Bringing home stray cats. But romance? I don't know about that from the all-work, never-play manager of the family business.

"No one's talking romance here." I swat Vale's hip with the towel in my hand. "I'm just helping an old friend."

Vale laughs, while dipping the pan she boiled potatoes in into the suds-filled sink. "Old friend, my ass."

Vale was around ten years old when I started dating Halle. I'd only brought Halle to the house once; a mistake I'd later pay for with my father. However, Vale met her when I used my sister in a ploy to meet Halle at the ice cream shop in town.

Halle and I didn't exactly sneak around. Most kids knew she was my girl, but her mom didn't want us dating.

Halle was too young, and I was a bad seed.

Halle shouldn't be so serious about me.

I was the kind of guy who would ruin her dreams.

That last one hit home the hardest. Halle had promise and I didn't want to be in her way. And at eighteen, that's what I thought of myself.

Dad said it often enough. *Get out of the way, boy.*

With reminders I don't want in my head, I gaze at my sister. As if she can read my mind, she shakes her head, silently telling me not to go down the random path my brain is skipping along.

"Okay." Vale sighs, but generously smiles. "Flowers. We talkin' wildflowers, formal rose garden, or something in between?"

Lazily, I mirror her grin. "Something in between."

+ + +

"What the hell are you doing?" Halle's voice yells over the hum of the lawnmower.

Almost a week has passed since I first visited Halle's house, and I have a mental plan in place.

Shutting off the mower's engine, I glance up at Halle and smile despite the scowl on her face. "Mowin'." I've been cutting the grass while two other men wade through the garden, pulling weeds and attempting to salvage flowers.

Halle steals my breath in a pair of denim shorts with a frayed hem and a form fitting tank top in deep purple. Her pretty blue eyes narrow and she tilts her head. Her glare is meant to intimidate but it's too cute. Her expression tells me to cut the crap, but I'm stating the obvious.

"I never received an estimate for lawn service and I'm not paying *you* to mow my lawn."

I nod. "That's right. You aren't paying me." Tipping my head toward the two men working the garden, I add. "And I'm paying them, so no fee."

Halle's eyes widen but her face doesn't soften. "That doesn't even make sense. You can't work for free. Plus, my lawyer says to keep records of everything regarding the estate sale."

I glance at the back of the house. I've been here about an hour and already plotted out the brick patio I plan to add to the vacant space. The front porch wraps around the side of the house and ends at the back corner. I'll remove the railing there to give an entrance to the future brick patio.

"Sounds smart," I mutter before pulling the cord to restart the lawnmower.

Halle steps closer to me. "What are you doing?"

Her eyes meet mine and if I didn't know better, I'd think she was asking a deeper question. Then again, maybe those are the questions rumbling through my own head in tune to the mower.

What am *I doing?*

I want another chance with Halle. Time to reconnect and ask for forgiveness. I want her to stop looking at me like I've cut out her heart. I want her to *love*— I can't go there. Too hopeful. Too selfish. But when it comes to Halle Reynolds, I've always been a selfish man. Wanting her as my own. Never letting her go; not really.

I cut the engine again. "Look, you need this yard cleaned up. Clay's team is booked for the rest of the summer. It's almost July. You can wait until fall, or you can let me take care of the lawn now."

Halle glances around my arm as she isn't tall enough to peer over my shoulder. "What about them?"

"Like I already said, I'm taking care of them."

"So, I owe you," Halle returns her attention to me, her tone makes it evident that she does not like the idea.

Actually, I owe her, but I don't mention it. "You don't owe me a thing."

"I'll need to pay you for your time." Her reply is more resolve than snark.

"Let's barter."

"Let's what?"

If I wanted a laugh from Halle with the term, I'd be holding my breath. She continues to eye me like I've suggested she eat grass clippings.

"Barter. A trade. My time for your time."

"No deal."

I should be offended how quickly she passes on my suggestion, but I'm not concerned. My time comes cheap. My patience free. I've been waiting twenty years for this kind of opportunity. The time to stand in Halle's presence again and breathe her in. The ability to look her in the eye. The chance to be this close to her.

Leaning for the pull cord on the mower again, I give it a yank, but it doesn't start. I bend forward again, hand at the ready when Halle says, "What kind of time?"

The pull handle falls out of my hand as I stand upright. "A hike." I have no idea why I say such a thing when I initially planned to suggest ice cream. We could re-enact our first date.

After Halle ran into me in the woods, I asked her out. I didn't typically pursue girls. Didn't want anyone exposed to the mess at home, but Halle was different. She felt right. She was also cautious, so I told her we could meet at the ice cream parlor in town. I thought I was so damn smooth, going to keep things casual, but the moment Halle looked me in the eye in those woods, I was already a goner.

She stole my heart like she took my breath during that first encounter.

"A hike?" Her sharp voice snaps me out of the memory of her licking blackberry cobbler ice cream.

"Yeah, a hike." The mountains around us are full of trails.

Halle sighs, turning her head away from me while shaking it, almost as if she was disappointed. Then, she briskly turns back to me, firm and resolved. "I can't hike."

"Sure you can." We took dozens of hikes when we were younger.

"I can't," she repeats, glaring at me as if I can read some secret inside her.

"You can," I state because I believe in her.

"I—" Halle waves toward her left knee. A giant scar runs over the joint. "I had an accident."

"I know."

"No, you don't get it. I fell in a race."

"I know," I repeat. *I know.* As well as the rest of the world.

In the pilot's ready room, the Olympics were telecast. My heart galloped in anticipation. There was my girl, only she wasn't my girl anymore. She'd been a sprinter when I'd known her, but she was on the hurdles.

"Knox," she drones. "You don't understand. I—"

"I saw you, Sprint."

Halle stares at me, recognition slowly dawning.

"You think I'd miss my girl finally getting her shot and taking it on the biggest track there is. My God, Halle. You were an Olympian."

"I wasn't your girl then. And I was never an Olympian. I failed."

"You *fell*," I remind her as if she didn't know. As if she wasn't aware her left foot hit the crossbar and she careened forward, foot entangled, and tore apart her knee.

In front of millions, Halle lay on the track in pain, crying tears I'd never seen her cry, not even with all we'd been through. And there wasn't a thing I could do for her from the middle of the ocean. At the time, I remember wanting to abandon ship and swim through shark-infested waters to get to her. I'd felt so frustrated and devastated not to be there for her. When I finally had shore leave, I was too late.

"I failed," Halle whispers, lowering her gaze and dipping her head, shoulders drooping as if with shame.

"Don't you ever say that," I snap, stepping up to her and gently lifting her chin. "You are not a failure, Halle. You are a champion."

"I wasn't." She stands taller, defensive and challenging.

"You *are*." I pause. "It doesn't matter how many times you fall as long as you stand back up. And you stood up." I gaze down her body, taking in the stiffness of her shoulders and the steel beam of her spine. Her long legs and pretty purple toenail polish.

"And if you fall again, I'll be there to catch you, Sprint." Just like I did the numerous times she ran at me, taking a leap of faith that I'd capture her when she sprang into the air toward me. And I always did catch her, loving how her legs wrapped around my waist and my hands fell to her ass to keep her attached to me. Our lips would meet, and we'd be in our own little universe buzzing through the wicked galaxy.

Halle lets her chin rest on my finger for a minute before lifting it higher and stepping away from me. "Well, none of it matters now. I don't hike."

"Don't? Or won't?" I hitch an eyebrow. "You can walk, can't ya? Then you can hike."

"I am not hiking with you."

"That's the payment for lawn service. A hike for cut grass." I pause, offering her a wide grin. "Unless you don't trust yourself to be alone with me?" I wink.

Halle glares at me, not understanding the more she aims her ire at me the more I want to pull her to me and kiss that scowl off her face. I want to know if her lips still taste the same, sweet with a touch of peppermint. If her tongue will chase my lead like she did when we first tangled them together. If she'll tug me close to her, like she often did when our kisses turned heavy and desperate, like she couldn't get me close enough and never wanted me to leave her.

Only, I did leave. Her. Me. Us. I had to get out of Sterling Falls.

But now I'm back and so is she.

"Fine," she huffs, stomping her foot once before placing her hands on her hips like she did the other day when I visited.

"Fine," I mimic, mocking her tone while giving her a big grin. I'm the champion of this round but I already know Halle isn't going to let me win in the future without a fierce race. "No excuses. Saturday. Ten a.m."

"I've never been the one with excuses."

The blow lands painfully, as Halle intended, but I force my smile to stay intact. Still, my sternum pierces, arrowed like a bull's-eye.

Maybe Halle doesn't remember. I did have reason to leave.

And it was never about her.

Chapter 7

[Halle]

On Saturday morning, I'm regretting that I said yes to a hike with Knox. Not that I formally accepted this date. Or hike. Or whatever it is he wants to call this mistake.

Time.

I'd said fine in the female equivalent for *I'll do it, but I won't like it.* I've been hoping he'd take the hint and cancel.

The hike itself isn't so much the issue as this nervous energy coursing through my body. For the seventh time, I smooth down my running shorts and light-weight racer-back top wondering if Knox will notice the physical changes in me, then mentally kicking myself for caring. What did I want? To impress Knox? I'm different than who I once was, but so is he, and that adds to my anxiety. Who is Knox now? Would he even like me as I am? Do I want him to like me?

When he arrives at my mother's house with four minutes to spare, I nearly come out of my skin. Violet is still sleeping. Tim went to the park to meet with a new friend.

"Good morning," Knox cheerfully greets me as I open the screen door and motion for him to step inside. "I brought reinforcements."

As he holds up a white bakery bag, my mouth salivates. Or maybe it's the look of him in a pair of hiking boots, knee-length olive green shorts with multiple pockets and a tight white T-shirt. Dog tags dangle around his neck. He looks like a hot and sticky delicacy bound to make a mess of my hormones.

Since returning to Sterling Falls, I've learned that Knox's youngest brother, Sebastian, owns the Curmudgeon Bakery in town and his berry scone has become a favorite of mine.

"If there's a blackberry scone in there…" *I could kiss him,* but I cut myself short before saying such a thing. I'm supposed to be angry with Knox Sylver. I'm supposed to be uptight about this hike.

But something about his smile, the pride in his expression while holding up that bag, and the way he's looking at me like *I'm* a bakery treat, cuts into my ire, warming the gooeyness still lingering inside me for Knox. When most people think of their first love, it's a dull ember of emotion, buried at the back of their minds. With Knox and I, it was a firestorm of emotions, one still blazing with fond memories of teasing kisses and erotic scents, warm words and pain-filled tears.

"I just need to grab my shoes." I don't own hiking boots but found an old pair of gym shoes in my former bedroom.

Sleeping in my old bedroom has been surreal. Memories swirl around me and it isn't just the faded wallpaper and numerous track ribbons and dusty trophies. Thoughts have filled my head each night of Knox. Him slipping through my open window. Him escaping out it. Him holding me in that ancient double bed.

As I slide on my shoes, Knox glances around the front room. The faded furnishings. The worn carpet. His smile dims. He wasn't welcome inside the house. Only when Gigi was napping, and Mom was still at work could I sneak him up to my room for afternoon make out sessions.

When Knox's gaze comes back to me, ancient history fills them. None of it matters presently.

With a more enthusiastic hop than I feel, I stand abruptly and slap my thighs. "*Welp*. Let's get this over with."

A hike for yardwork. Doesn't seem like a fair trade but I'll keep score and eventually learn what I financially owe Sylver Seed and Soil. I can afford the changes necessary to sell this place because I'm using my settlement funds from the divorce. My half of the house in Charles Town. The expenses here I'm considering an investment. I already have a handle on how much this house *could* be worth, if updated. The hope is to financially double what I put into this place and then decide afterward where to live and what to do with my life.

For now, my life is on pause, just like this hike is only a rest break from all the work that needs to be done.

This is *not* a date. It's a trade. Time for time.

Knox gave me a brief scowl at my declaration to hurry this along, but quickly schools his face into that bright smile. "Let's do this."

He holds the screen door open while I pull closed the front door behind me and lock it. I have a small backpack over my shoulders, and I tug it off my arms to sit inside Knox's truck. He takes it from me, slinging it over his burly shoulder. The leather sack is more fashionable than my old light purple Jansport and looks feminine against his broadness. He doesn't even blink at the move that's as familiar as when he carried my backpack in high school. He'd carry the bag out to his truck before giving me a ride home, when we would sometimes detour to make out for a bit.

I stop short looking up at the truck that's different from the Sylver Seed and Soil one he'd arrived in during his previous visits.

"Is that—" My tongue tangles as my eyes catch on a 1980 GMC Sierra Classic 1500 pickup truck in baby blue with a cream-colored panel along the sides. "It can't be."

Knox opens the passenger door and pins me with another wide smile. One full of secrets and old promises.

"It's her," Knox proudly states.

I don't know a thing about trucks, but I know the details of this one only because I rode in it numerous times during my seventeenth year on this planet. The worn leather bench seat with a rip in the center. The broken doorhandle. The fuzzy dice hanging from the rearview mirror.

As I step up to the open door, I notice the seat has been recovered in navy-blue leather and the new door handle gleams silver. Fresh carpet brightens the once littered foot well that held empty soda cans and other contraband. The fuzzy dice are replaced by actual dice hanging from a leather strap.

"It can't be her," I whisper although Knox just told me the contrary. Despite the newness, a wave of nostalgia hits me. The number of times Knox laid me back on that bench. The things he did to me. The way he touched me.

And then there was our final time together. I'd forgiven him for his absence. For disappearing on me with no communication. He was being shipped to Pensacola which wasn't exactly around the corner. He only had forty-eight hours before he was leaving again.

In the bed of this truck, the romantic stage was set with pillows and blankets. A canopy of stars overhead. We'd had sex several times by then, but this night felt different. Special. Solidifying. We were one.

"One last night," he'd said to me. The words as clear in my head now as the stars had been in the sky that night. I didn't read if for the prophecy it was. Our last night together. Forever separated afterward as Knox and Halle. No more Sprint and Brick.

My breath hitches as the memory crashes over me and I cover my lower belly, willing away the emptiness inside me.

"Knox," I whisper. I cannot climb into this truck, and I beg him to read the apprehension within my eyes.

Unfortunately, he misunderstands me, giving me another warm smile along with cupping my elbow and leading me forward. My breath shallows as I'm about to become a prisoner to memories. When my backside hits the fresh leather seat, I take a deep breath, reminding myself our history doesn't matter. As long as we learned from those mistakes, which I did, the past cannot touch me. With the repaired seat beneath me and an unscratched dash before me, I force myself into the present condition of this old beast.

Knox rounds the truck and hops in like our secrets don't sit on the bench between us. He sets my fancy backpack there instead and places the bakery bag in front of it, building a barrier. "Help yourself to the scone. We have about twenty minutes before we reach the trail."

"I'm afraid to get crumbs all over this new seat. Sierra looks amazing." Knox named his truck, keeping it simple by including part of the model.

He once thought Sierra would make a beautiful name for a daughter. The thought has me wondering if he has children. Did he once have a wife or currently have a girlfriend? There's so little I know about him now, purposely never asking for more details when information about him was offered.

Anxiously, I run my sweaty palm over the soft leather seat.

"Yeah, she's been a trooper, waiting for me."

I avoid the unintentional wound of his words like a pothole in the road. Then again, Knox never asked me to wait for him. He told me he'd return, the promise empty.

"Clay took care of her over the years and when I returned home, my first mission was restoring her completely." Knox turns the key and the engine roars to life.

While he reverses out of the driveway, I ask, "How long have you been home?" When Knox left for the Navy that final time, I didn't expect to ever see him in Sterling Falls again. I purposely didn't come here when I'd learned he was back.

"I retired last year. Put in twenty years before deciding it was time to come home." The brightness of his face tightens a little, like something momentarily mars his thoughts. "I'd been a little lost when I first returned. Didn't know what to do with myself. Every day I'd spend some time tinkering on Sierra until I volunteered for the fire department and started working for Clay again."

"Mowing lawns?" Curious that he picked up right where he left off, working for Sylver Seed and Soil. Back when we were kids, he did heavy-lifting jobs that involved slinging dirt and hauling gravel, thus building his teen body into a muscular machine.

"Actually, I run the brick division. We install patios and retaining walls."

"Brick?" I choke. "How appropriate." The smile curling my lips is one I can't fight. Knox was solid in stature when we were younger. He's just as firm now.

"Yeah." He chuckles, swiping his fingers through the longer pieces of hair on the top of his head. "I like to use my hands. Building things." He side-eyes me with the clarification, catching me as I glance at his broad hands and thick fingers, once powerful yet gentle when he touched me.

"So why are you mowing *my* lawn?"

"Because I want to." His statement suggests a finality. Like I should just accept his decision. The curtness is unsettling but then again being in his presence has me topsy-turvy.

"So you're a volunteer fireman and a bricklayer."

"Nothing wrong with helping my community and doing an honest day's labor."

My forehead furrows, quickly realizing he thinks I'm looking down on his career choices. I recall how Knox didn't know what he wanted to do with his future before he graduated high school. How he didn't see the years ahead as clearly as I did, and he worried he'd never be enough for me no matter what he did. As if his job somehow defined him. He'd make me so angry when he thought he was anything less than perfect.

"I didn't mean anything negative." I lift my hand as if to reach for him, set it on his forearm to reassure him of my sincerity, but I quickly retract my arm and set my hands beneath my thighs to keep them to myself.

"Bet you have a fancy job now."

I swallow hard and squint out the windshield, somehow feeling less adequate myself. "I don't, actually."

"Heard you live in Charles Town." The statement is said like he's impressed, like the location is some kind of accomplishment.

"I did." I swallow again. "But I don't live there anymore."

Knox remains silent and I offer an explanation. "Jack got the house in the divorce. I'm kind of homeless at the moment."

Knox's head swivels and he gives me a hard glance. "You aren't homeless. You have your mom's place."

"That isn't a home, Knox," I state, reminding us both of the prison the house had felt like when I was younger.

I didn't have it as rough as Knox, but I still dealt with mental entrapment growing up. My mother's push for me to do more, be more. She didn't want me settling in some small town, falling for a man who would die too young, and leave me living with my in-laws. She never understood how grateful I was to have Gigi in my life, serving as a buffer from my mother. Reminding me I could be whoever I wanted to be.

Mother or movie star. Wife or lawyer. Track champion or team parent. Nothing mattered as long as I was happy doing what I was doing.

"Is that why you're eager to sell?" Knox asks.

"I'm eager to sell because I'm dumping money into this place to fix it up and I need a good return on my investment so I can afford a new house. Somewhere else."

His brows crease. "Where are you moving?"

"I don't know yet." I squint toward the windshield, shaking my head at the emptiness of my future. The lack of plan and direction is unsettling.

Knox clears his throat. "So, what have you been doing all these years?"

Sharply, I turn my head toward him. "Are we really doing this?" Does he think we can cram twenty years into one short ride through the mountains?

"I'm a mom." Said with a little too much force, I clear my throat. "It isn't a job, and I certainly don't get financial compensation for the work, but it's what I've been *doing* for fifteen years."

Knox turns his head once more, his eyes brewing with a question he wants to ask but must decide to skip. He adjusts in his seat and drapes his wrist over the steering wheel.

"Honorable work," Knox says softer.

"Most days." Timidly, I smile.

Violet and Tim are taking our current situation in stride. More like a seesaw where one day they love our location and the next hate it. Tim is more the upswing, finding positives in where we reside. He can ride his bike to town and traipse the local woods. He found a pick-up soccer game on the green space in the center of town and made a new friend.

Violet, on the other hand, isn't adjusting so easily. She's given up babysitting gigs this summer and misses her friends, waiting out the days until school begins. Uncertain where we'll live, I haven't enrolled her in high school yet. She would have been going to a new school back in Charles Town this fall anyway, but her friends would have followed as the middle schools unite in one place.

"Your kids aren't liking Sterling Falls." Sarcasm fills his voice, mingled with a new sense of pride for his small town.

The contradiction has me questioning him. "And suddenly you do?"

Knox chuckles. "I've had twenty years to forgive this town for its transgressions and come to terms with a few of my own."

I snort. Knox gives me a sympathetic glance. But I don't want his sympathy, nor do I want to be one of the transgressions he's come to terms with. The slight makes me edgy, and I cross my arms, defensively sinking back into the leather seat and silently staring out the front window.

"What's suddenly on your mind, Sprint?"

I close my eyes at the nickname and internally seethe at the constant reminder of a lifetime ago. "I don't sprint anymore," I snap.

"And why's that?"

He already knows about the accident. That fateful fall in the hurdle trails where I tripped on the gate and tore up my knee. In many ways, I came back stronger, more determined than ever, in preparation for the next big games. Then Jack happened. And Violet.

"I got pregnant."

A rush of a memory hits me. *Knox standing inside that high school bathroom. My relief that he was alive and well and standing before me. My confusion that he'd been so absent, so negligent.*

"Halle, I'm sorry you've been worried. Leaving messages and blowing up my phone. I didn't have it with me." His head bowed, eyes cagey and avoiding. "It wasn't allowed so I didn't take it with me."

The explanation felt reasonable enough. The military had rules. I could respect them. Still, it would have been nice to know there would be this absence.

Rushing to him once more, I clasp his shirt in my fists. "It doesn't matter. You're here now." A wave of excitement rippled through me. "I have something to tell you."

"Me too." He still wouldn't look me in the eye. Hadn't kissed me hello. Hadn't mentioned if he'd read my letter or even received it.

"Let me go first," I'd teased, too excited to contain myself.

Knox closed his eyes. "Halle, I think we should—"

"I'm pregnant."

His face stunned, his eyes wide, he finally glanced up at me but quickly looked away, closing off those dark orbs once more. He swallowed hard, expressionless, emotionless.

He wasn't happy in the least.

The reminder solidifies why Knox and I were never meant to be.

A boulder of regret about this hike settles in my stomach. I don't know why I agreed to this. It's going to be a disaster.

But like any good sprint, the quickest way to the finish line is pushing forward.

As Knox pulls into a parking space in a lot near a public trail, let the stopwatch begin.

Race on.

Chapter 8

[Knox]

Unnerving silence filled the cab of my truck, until we finally parked. I don't know what happened in Halle's head after she told me she'd gotten pregnant, but she closed in on herself, wrapping her arms around her middle again and shrinking into the bench seat.

Like a thick twig, I want to snap and demand she talk to me. Then I remind myself her mind must be everywhere and nowhere at once.

Her marriage ending.

Her mother's passing.

The uncertainty her future holds.

Explaining how I came to terms with my father's death, as well as my separation from her, and the acceptance of my return to Sterling Falls, would take more than a simple hour-long hike. And I want to tell Halle everything, but not today.

Today is meant to spend time in each other's presence. I don't want to upset her or argue with her or even question her. I just want to know if that magnetic attraction between us is still present. For me, it's been sequestered in a compartment of my heart but sprang loose from its bindings the moment I saw her standing at her mother's gravesite.

For her, I'm not certain Halle holds any feelings for me other than as dust from her past.

The possibility stings but it's one I've been willing to accept. She moved on, as she should have. She fell in love, got married, and had children. All were part of the vision I'd had for her, only I'd hoped at one time that plan included me. I'm the one who burned the blueprint.

However, Halle is divorced now and has returned to Sterling Falls. This is my second chance to at least fulfill some of the promises I made her. A comfortable house. A beautiful yard. I want to make things easier for Halle. Dispel her sense of being lost and homeless. Help her find direction again. Be present for her in whatever manner she'll allow. Hoping we can restore what we once had feels futile, but maybe, just maybe, we can start again. Something new. Something different. *Just something . . .*

"You didn't eat your scone." She'll need the carbs and boost of sugar to tackle a hike. Then again, I don't intend to physically push her. I just remember her love of berries—blueberries, strawberries, and especially blackberries—and my brother makes an amazing scone with all three inside.

"I'm fine," she mutters, clearly not, but using that curt tone and sparse words like a shield. I didn't want Halle *fine*. I want her unhinged and open. I want her raw and reckless like she'd once been.

With a sharp nod, I motion to the small building housing the restroom. The trail I plan for us to take is a three-mile trek. Might be ambitious for a hike if Halle hasn't hiked in years. Sounds like she doesn't run either, even for exercise.

I got pregnant.

The words shouldn't have felt like a knife to my chest, but they cut deep, nonetheless.

Violet is a beautiful girl, looking just like her mother. If her heart and her drive are even half Halle's, I have no doubt Violet will be a successful woman.

I've yet to meet Tim but I'm curious about him. Does he resemble his father? Does he see his dad as a role model or a man after public popularity?

When I was a teen, I didn't want to stand out in a crowd. Our family already stood out enough with bruises we refused to explain, and the town drunk as our father.

Poor Sylver kids. They're mama must be rolling in her grave.

People had no idea it wasn't our mother we worried about. She was safer six feet under. Then again, our parents had a loving relationship while she was alive. They'd birthed seven children in twelve years because of their love. It was only when the last one came along, and Mom passed away, that our father dipped into the bottle and resurfaced a new man. A mean, devilish soul who despised his children, cursing most of them, especially the younger set. From myself downward, including Ford, Sebastian, and Vale, we bore the heavy-fisted brunt of our father's broken heart.

After using the restroom, I silently wave toward the trail and Halle leads on the worn path. I'm distracted by a view of her in bright purple running shorts and a racer back tank top that hints at a black bra underneath. The back of her is sexy as hell. Her legs are still toned. Her ponytail swishing. Her ass tempting in the best of ways. When I almost trip over my own booted feet, I glance away.

The well-traveled route is easy enough to follow and busy on a Saturday morning. While I'd wanted time alone with Halle, a mountain hike during summer months doesn't always allow for privacy. We travel the designated trail until I find the spot I want us to climb.

"Here." I stop Halle after more than twenty minutes of silent walking. She stops and glances around us, noting the wall of rock to our right. "We're going up." The incline is angled so the climb isn't steep but involves the skill of proper foot placement. A few hikers blaze a trail above us.

"I can't climb," Halle immediately states.

"You can." I don't remember her being so negative nor so quick to dismiss an idea without trying it first. Halle ran like the wind as a girl. She loved the exertion of a race, and I held my own with her, but running was in her soul. Hiking and climbing easily came in second. Halle was an explorer.

When did she stop? And why?

"I'll be right behind you."

Halle gives me a skeptical glare.

"What? You don't trust me?" I tease, a little worried she'll admit she doesn't. Poking at her remains my mission, though. Removing that scowl and winning a smile is my new challenge.

"Hmm, I happen to recall someone once telling me he was right behind me when he steered our canoe into an overhanging tree, and I was knocked into the river." Her eyes are narrowed slits, but they've lost their ire. Instead, a gleam flickers inside the blue rims.

I remember that date. A canoe trip down a local river. A picnic in the afternoon sunshine. Making out with Halle on a blanket in the privacy of the woods.

"Oh, my gosh. Your need to control everything had you steering us toward the embankment when everyone knows a canoe is best guided from the stern position." I laugh hard and rich at the memory of Halle going overboard in the shallow but frigid water, and standing up, drenched head to toe, threatening to toss me into the river as well, like she could budge a boulder.

While my laughter dies, the long-ago date lingers in my thoughts. I'd never let Halle sink or swim alone again.

Stepping closer to her, I tuck stray hairs from her ponytail around her ear. "I'll be right here, Sprint."

The nickname fires her up and her eyes narrow at me once more before she glares at the incline of boulders.

"Fine," she mutters, lifting her foot for the first layer of rocks. Her legs are shorter than mine, so without thinking, I place my hands on her ass and give her a boost to help her upward.

The scowl she aims at me over her shoulder could melt snowcaps, but I ignore her irritation and drag myself up to the same rock. The circumference forces us close to one another.

If we were twenty years younger, she might have made a comment about me touching her ass. I would have had a witty, sexual comeback. Then, I'd kiss her. I loved kissing Halle. Her mouth. Her tongue. The connection I felt to her.

Now, her lips are tightly pressed together, like she's holding back a snarky statement. More like, she's biting her tongue against lashing out at me for touching her backside. After another narrow-eyed glare, she turns toward the next level, and slowly we climb, with me occasionally taking liberties again to give her a push.

Halle's legs are still strong, her ass as fine as twenty years ago. The strength she displays doesn't suggest she's struggling but her face is flushed and her skin sweaty.

"Need a break?" We're almost to the top but we can pause despite the narrowing of the rock surface.

Halle shakes her head. Determination fills her eyes and a spark of the girl I once knew lights her up until she looks behind us.

She sways.

"Whoa." I catch her around her waist, tugging her to my side. Her breath becomes ragged as she purposefully faces the boulders again. Her shoulders hitch and fall as she takes calming breaths.

"What happened there?"

"Heights." Halle inhales. Exhales. "A perk of motherhood." Sarcasm laces her voice. "Phobias developed. Fears grew extreme."

"You're afraid of heights," I clarify.

"Deathly."

Holy shit. "Halle, why didn't you say something?" I wouldn't have pressed her if I'd known. While she'd been giving me all that crap about not hiking and not climbing, I'd assumed it had to do with her leg. A *false* sense of inability, not an immobilizing fear.

"I—" She takes a deep breath, eyes focused on the rocks before us. Her voice is whisper soft when she says, "I just wanted to try."

There she is. With relief flowing through my veins, I squeeze her to me and kiss her temple without thinking. "You got this."

Halle's head whips in my direction, eyes wide from my sudden action. Not wanting to address my slip-up, I encourage her, instead. "You're doing great. We're almost there."

Eyes that match the color of the filtered sky focus on mine for a minute. Sunlight flickers through the dark foliage overhead, hinting at the bright blue above. The dim lighting reminds me of our first meeting. Halle was a streak of brightness among the shadows. Not only in those woods but in my dark life.

Pulling her gaze away from me, she peers up at the remaining incline that grows a tad steeper but not impossible. She begins to scale the surface, watching her foot placement. I follow immediately behind her, struggling with my own concentration.

Her legs. Her ass. Her determination to make it to the top. That's what drew me to her when we were young.

Halle had big dreams. I wanted to be a small part of them.

Chapter 9

[Halle]

When we finally reach a plateau, I stand tall and stare out at the dazzling view of mountains and valleys covered in shades of green. West Virginia holds the title "The Mountain State" for good reason. The landscape can be breathtaking, and it's been a long time since I simply appreciated where I live.

With a deep inhale, I take in the freshness of summer sunshine, heated rocks, and oak trees. I also faintly smell water.

"Are we . . ." I glance at Knox beside me taking in the view as well. "Are we almost to Sterling Falls?"

The waterfall gives this area its name. The cascading river glows silvery when captured just right in the sunlight. Ancient settlers believed silver was hidden beneath the water but quickly learned the precious metal wasn't anywhere in these mountains.

Knox gives me a knowing smile, one that sends another wave of memory through me.

We lost our virginity at the top of the falls. Together.

Hard to believe the ever popular and extremely sexy Knox Sylver hadn't given up his virginity sooner. He waited until I was officially eighteen.

On the tip of my tongue is a demand that we turn around and head back down the boulders, but a stronger part of me wants to find the spot where I'd given my body to this man. Where we fooled around and fumbled, until we were one. I'd like to say it was magical. I'd like to claim I remember every tiny detail. But I don't.

The truth is twenty years, and another partner, overshadows that first encounter.

What I remember most was the setting. The too-hot sleeping bag. The buzz of a bug lamp to repel insects. The scent of firewood and perspiration mingling.

Decades of rock erosion and foliage growth would surely disguise the exact location. The only marker is the falls.

"Shall we?" Knox questions, giving me the out I want but I accept the challenge.

Yes, let's face the past and put it to rest.

Following his lead this time, we hop from flat rock to flat rock until a barely-there, narrow path leads to the silvery-colored falls. Ripples of cascading water sparkle and dance like a melting disco ball over a stiff ledge. The effect is almost dizzying.

Or maybe that's the overwhelming mountain scent of Knox too close beside me and the rush of memories from a simpler time in my life. When my dreams were big and my heart wide open. When I felt love like I've never felt before or since, and a connection to someone I thought was my other half.

"We should go," I immediately state, drawing my gaze away from the plummeting falls. My breathing becomes erratic and labored again. I can't seem to catch my breath and it isn't the climb that leaves me suddenly winded. Or my fear of heights. With a fist against my chest, I press at my sternum. The pain is almost suffocating.

"Halle?" Knox questions, brows deeply creased.

"Don't you remember anything?" I snap, furious that he could forget. Maybe he doesn't remember our first time any better than I do. Maybe he's brought others to this place, so it no longer holds meaning for him. Maybe—

"I haven't forgotten a thing, baby." He shifts to face me. His dark eyes soften while remaining firmly focused on mine, reinforcing the unspoken.

Certain I misheard him, I close my eyes.

I haven't forgotten the baby.

We can't go there. Not yet. Not ever.

"I lost someone, too," he reminds me, his voice hollow and distant, as if echoing upward from the canyon.

My eyes snap open. "Who?" I bark at him, angry and hurt, and awash with memories so old they're like a faded blanket. Still, the pain remains, sharp and stabbing and out of nowhere some days. Other times, I can pinpoint the exact trigger.

Knox suddenly crowds me, and I step back but he catches my elbows, tugging me toward him. Our noses practically touch as he growls at me, his own anger rising. "You."

We stand almost pressed together. A chasm rests between us while physically hardly an inch exists. With both our eyes closed, we breathe one another in. The heaviness of exhales. The depth of inhales. His scent fills my nostrils. Mountains, woods, and familiarity. His scruffy jaw gently scrubs against my cheek, tickling my skin, heightening my sense of him. My mouth salivates, filled with memories of his tongue dancing with mine. His teeth once tenderly scraping over my flesh. The memory isn't sensual as much as comfort, something feral and natural. A puzzling charge swirls around us, electric, magnetic, powerful.

I could kiss him.

Anger and lust. Regret and love. Frustration and confusion.

Grief makes people do strange things, he'd said.

My fist is tightly wrapped in his warm tee, his dog tags clutched within my hand as well. The metal is cool against my hot palm. I tug at the combination of cold metal and warm cotton as if I can bring him closer to me and climb within his chest. As if he could heat all my cold spots.

His heart hammers against my fist, matching the rapid thumping of my own. It's been a long time since our hearts beat as one. A long time since he kissed me with urgency and tenderness. Like when time passes too quickly and yet slows to a strange stillness. If only we could freeze time. Press pause on an instant.

But we can't.

With a strong shove at his chest, I step back, releasing myself from the spell of Knox. Spinning too quickly, I face the falls, dizzily watching them plummet into their counterpart pooled below. The river isn't deep enough to swim in. The rocks keep the water shallow and rough in some parts. Carefully placed steps might allow a traveler to cross the flow. However, there are legends of death and demise here.

There are also myths of eternal love for those who drink from the water.

Knox and I are proof the story is fiction.

With trembling fingers, I cover my lips where the ghost of kisses tingle against them.

Knox startles me when his arm snakes around my waist and he tugs me backward until I meet his chest despite the awkwardness of my backpack.

"You're too close to the edge." His lips press against the back of my head, and we stand on the flattened rocks for another silent minute while thoughts scream through my head.

"I'm sorry, Halle."

Twisting to face him, we stand nose to nose once more. Our breaths still jagged. His mouth moist while his nostrils flare. His gaze darts anxiously around my face. For the first time ever, raw fear exists in his dark eyes.

"I don't want your apology." What is he even apologizing for? Our history? Things that can't be undone?

"I almost kissed you." His voice isn't more than a whisper.

My eyes momentarily close and a fresh stab wound opens from this man. "Please. *Please*, don't say that."

A kiss would have been harsh and hasty, but it still would have been a kiss. Unwarranted passion rips through me, threatening to tear me in two. There's no doubt if his lips met mine, my desire to feel wanted would have overcome my resistance. I'd have pulled him to me, if for no other reason than to feel the thrust of him entering me, the thrill of connection, and the foolish sense that we could be more again.

"Tell me you don't feel it, Halle." Knox's eyes search mine, desperately seeking confirmation. His hands cup my upper arms and jostle me a little. "Tell me there isn't unfinished business between us."

My mouth pops open to deny him, yet how do I explain myself? All my emotions collide and conflict inside me.

I *won't* explain the loneliness of my marriage or the failure of it. Not to him. Not to the man I'd thought was my forever.

Knox said what matters most is getting up from a fall, and I'm standing. The ground is shaky and my future uncertain, but dammit, I'm still standing. And the last thing I need is to fall for Knox Sylver again. To believe he really cares about me.

I shake my head, unable to tell him that kissing him might hurt but it also might heal.

He lost me. And I lost him. And in the span of a kiss, I'm certain I'd be found. But I can't trust him to find me. This time, I need to find myself.

"Tell me."

Startled by his tone, his nearness overwhelms me. My fingers twitch, desperate to clutch his tee again and tug him to me, demand he kiss me like he had when we were teens. Make me lose my head and forget the past twenty years of disappointment. But that wouldn't be fair.

Not to him. Not to me. Not to my beautiful children.

"It can't." I whimper. "Nothing matters. Not the past. Not the present. My only focus needs to be the future." *My children and me.*

"Don't say it doesn't matter. It matters to me."

"Well, too damn bad," I grumble.

"Halle, talk to me." His voice strains, the plea thick.

"I . . . I don't know how."

His hands immediately release me and lift in surrender. His broad palms flat, fingers extended wide before curling into tight fists and lowering to his side as if defeated.

"Sprint?" The confusion in his voice is another wound to my chest. An icepick hissing from the pained heat in my nickname.

"We should go," I whisper.

"We aren't through here, Halle." He points between us like he did at my mother's funeral, standing taller with determination.

"We've been over for years, Knox. There's nothing left to say to one another."

He lifts his head higher, inhaling deeply before stating, "We were never over. We were on pause."

Chapter 10

[Knox]

What the fuck just happened?

When we return to my truck, my body still vibrates with the crackle of energy that surrounded us above the falls. Halle's nearness still hums around me. Her fist in my tee, and my hands on her elbows, holding her close to me. The familiar scent of jasmine on her skin. Her soft cheek, warm and comforting against the bristly hairs of my jaw. Her mouth, so close, so tempting.

I'd almost kissed her and that would have fucked up everything.

I'm walking a fine line with Halle. A line that I'll either get to cross one day or will denotate like a live wire. I can't risk an explosion.

Halle is too important to me.

Still, she's so fiery and snappish now, and I want her to turn that sizzling energy into something more constructive. Something flaming and hot, like we used to have.

I want her to feel me.

I'm here for you, Sprint.

Our past matters but the present is even more valuable.

Like I told her . . . we aren't finished. We were on pause, and the time is right to press play. Our song needs to continue.

A strange tension fills the cab of my truck as we drive back to Halle's place. I have questions but sense it's best not to speak as Halle stares out the passenger side window, caught up in her own reflections.

Speaking of songs, a new country hit plays on the radio. A melody that reminds me of Halle. One about watermelon moonshine and first times and giving away something special when you're young.

Dammit, Halle wasn't just my first love or the girl I gave my virginity to. She's been my only love, and she holds a special part of me. My heart.

I've been wanting a second chance with her for decades. Never hopeful it would happen but still wishing it could. I wanted time to bring us full circle. Maybe make us friends again if nothing else. Anything that could take away this emptiness in my chest whenever I thought of her, and the disappointment I caused her. The disappointment in myself.

I glance sideways at Halle again while I drive, feeling the chasm between us on this leather seat where she once sat pressed up against my side.

Can we really get that feeling back? Or is it just a fantasy I've concocted? Something my thick skull refuses to accept when I finally have Halle so close to me again.

Gotta walk before you can run, and I need to take cautious steps in letting go of who we once were and discovering who we are now. Because one thing I am certain of, I won't let Halle escape me again.

"What is he doing here?" Halle hisses, drawing me from my thoughts, as we pull into her driveway.

I park the truck and stare at the man suddenly standing on her porch, taking in his pressed pants and rolled shirt sleeves. He's too polished, too formal. And whatever the glare he's giving me intends, he can retract it.

He isn't getting her back.

Fuck Jack Haskins.

Halle is still mine.

Halle is quick to exit my truck, and I hastily follow her as she approaches her ex.

"Jack, what are you doing here?"

"Just passing through town."

Halle stalls and cocks her hip, crossing her arms as she stares at her ex-husband. "We live five hours apart. I doubt you were just in the neighborhood."

Jack smiles, mouth wide, teeth glistening. "Wanted to see the kids."

"So you drove five hours?" Halle's tone calls bullshit.

"Actually, I was on my way to Huntington for a meeting."

"And there it is," Halle mutters, her head lowering.

"Thought I'd take everyone out to lunch," he adds, eyeing me a second. "Unless you have other plans."

When Halle doesn't answer, I step forward, extending a hand. "Knox Sylver. I'm—"

"I know who you are. Thank you for your service." While he takes the steps to approach me and grips my hand in a firm grasp, his gratitude is sugar-coated. He doesn't give a damn about my service. He wants to know what I'm doing with his ex-wife. I'd want to know the same thing if Halle were once mine, which she was. However, she's not *his* anymore and he can fuck all the way off.

I nod as we shake.

"That didn't take long," he directs to Halle after dropping my hand.

"Don't," Halle snaps. "Don't you dare."

Jack turns back to me. "Violet tells me you're the lawn boy."

The insult is as clear as the sky above. I'm hired help. Despite his appreciation for my service to this country, I'm nothing more than a down-home local boy to him. I already disliked the man for marrying Halle; made even worse for how he treated her in the aftermath, but meeting him face to face, those feelings of disgust are like moldy cottage cheese in my mouth. I long to spit on his polished shoes. He's a douche canoe.

"Jack," Halle admonishes.

"So. Lunch?" He addresses her again. "I thought we could make it a family affair." His gaze travels to me again.

"I can't," Halle interjects. "But the kids would probably love it."

"I'm surprised you left them alone to go on a date."

"It wasn't a date," Halle argues. I ignore the sharp jab to my sternum while Halle continues, "And Violet is almost fifteen. She planned to babysit the Gibson's boys this summer. She's more than capable of looking after Tim for a few hours. Plus, he's twelve."

"When I got here, he wasn't home."

"Just what are you insinuating, Jack." Halle turns defensive and the tone I've heard too often from her lately returns. The barrier she's building between the two of them was learned by living with him. I don't like it. Not one bit.

"Being that my brother is the sheriff of this town, I can assure you of Sterling Falls' safety record."

"No place is immune," Jack argues.

"Guess that would be your job, seeing as you're one of the decision-makers in this state," I remind him.

Jack purses his lips and lifts his head. *Yeah, I know who you are as well*. Dickhead.

"I'm not having a pissing match with you, Jack. Do you want to take the kids to lunch or be on your way?"

Jack turns back to Halle. Maybe he's startled by the strength of her tone. Maybe he's attracted to the feisty sound of her voice. He watches her, eyes flaring with something predatory.

"How's Peggy?" Halle asks.

Hooking up with another woman is a sure-fire way *not* to get his ex-wife back. Not that he can have her back.

With Halle's question, the front door opens, and a dark-haired boy walks out with a striking blonde about ten years younger than us beside him.

"Mom," the boy—Tim— gasps as he approaches his mother. "Did you see that Dad's here?"

Halle's entire demeanor instantly shifts, like a curtain was drawn down but love rises up. She swipes a hand over her son's head even though he comes to her shoulder. "I see that. And he wants to take you out for lunch with Miss Montrock."

Halle glares at her ex. *So much for that family affair he mentioned.*

"Are you coming too?" Tim asks.

"I have plans." The lie falls too easily from her lips but gives me a thought.

"Halle," the younger woman pleasantly addresses her.

Halle tips up her chin without a verbal response. With another ruffle of Tim's hair, Halle leans in and kisses his head. "Go get Violet."

Tim disappears and the four of us awkwardly stand in the yard.

"I'm Peggy Montrock," the blonde enthusiastically introduces herself, holding out a manicured hand. Her voice is chocolate drizzle, matching Jack's sugar-coated tone like two sides of a KitKat.

"Knox Sylver." I shake her hand to be polite but have nothing more to say, especially when she steps back and slips her arm around Jack, as if making a statement. She's with him.

"Reunited once again," Jack adds, staring between Halle and me, and Peggy turns her head, adoringly glancing up at him while puzzled by the comment.

"Not that it's your business but Knox is going to be working on the place."

"How . . . convenient," Jack states. "When do you think you'll have it on the market?"

"I'm not sure," Halle admits, squinting in the direction of the house.

"Will you be home before school starts?"

"Home?" Halle blinks, glaring at her ex-husband. "I don't . . ." She pauses and takes a deep breath. "I am home, Jack."

"Are you thinking of staying here?" Disgust fills the question as he glances around the scraggily lawn.

"I don't have a plan yet."

Jack's head swivels back in the direction of Halle and I want to snap it right off his neck. He has no right questioning her, especially under these awkward conditions. His lover is underneath his arm. And I'm standing here. I don't care if Halle doesn't have a definition for me, but I'm not letting this asshat speak to her like this.

"I really think you should be—"

Halle holds up a hand to stop her ex from talking. "And I *really* think we should discuss this later. It's a family affair."

The words are more of a jab at Peggy than me, and Peggy weakly smiles, accepting her place. She's an outsider, like I am.

"Why don't you head to the car, darling?" Jack mutters, leaning into Peggy and air-kissing her blonde streaks.

Halle's hands fist at her sides as she straightens her spine.

"It was nice to see you again," Peggy addresses Halle. "Knox, nice to meet you."

I nod once, offering her an awkward smile. Peggy walks to the driveway and down to the street.

"No need to be rude," Jack says.

"Really?" Halle snarks back. "You really want to go there?"

Jack shakes his head, but a slow smile curls his upper lip. "It's been a long time since you've been this feisty, Halle. It's nice to see again."

Her mouth falls open then she slaps it shut. Without thought, I step forward, positioning myself just off to the side of her, but making my presence clear. Flirting with Halle is unacceptable. Not only because I fucking hate the prick and Halle is mine, but it isn't right that he wants to manipulate her feelings.

Thankfully, Violet and Tim exit the house. Halle sighs beside me and Jack turns in the direction of his kids.

"Ready to go?" His voice is too cheerful, too enticing.

Violet groans, "Sure."

"Yeah, Dad," Tim replies before eyeing his mom. "Are you sure you can't go? What will you do for lunch?" The concern in his young voice hints this boy worries about his mom. He'll protect her at all costs.

"Don't you worry. I'll figure something out." She ruffles his hair again and gives it a gentle tug, so he meets her eyes. When she smiles, he smiles in return.

"Violet, honey. Have fun," Halle says to her daughter.

"Right," Violet grumbles, ignoring her mother and stalking before her father.

Jack steps toward Halle and reaches for her arm. Halle lifts her face in a practiced move and Jack kisses her cheek, lingering on her skin longer than necessary. His eyes meet mine, flinty and narrowed, watching my reaction to this choreographed performance. I'd like to assume the action happens from rote, a familiarity between former spouses trying to be civil, but my fists tighten at my side, jaw tensing with a desire to push Jack away from Halle.

Get off what's mine.

"Knox." Jack holds out his hand and we shake again when what I really want to do is punch him.

Halle and I both turn in the direction of her kids climbing into her ex's car. With the clunk of their car doors, Halle raises a hand and waves. Only Tim waves back.

"I would have wished him luck, but he deserves the hell that meal might be."

I chuckle, and wrap an arm around Halle's shoulders, tugging her into me. "You okay?"

"Yeah." Her shoulders fall beneath my touch, but I keep her pinned to my side.

"I don't like that he kissed you."

She turns her head. Our faces are close. "I don't think you have a say in who kisses me."

"Really?" I arch a brow and the child inside me snaps. I lean forward and lick the side of Halle's face, washing her cheek clean of her ex's lingering kiss. I want all marks of him gone. "Now, what's for lunch?"

Halle stares at me, her hand hesitantly reaching for her cheek to cover where my tongue lapped over her skin. Stunned, her chuckle is staggered. "I'm not having lunch with you, Knox."

"Why not? You're free. I'm free. We both need to eat."

Halle sighs and shrugs out from underneath my hold. "Has anyone ever told you you're obdurate?"

"I prefer irresistible but throwing out the SAT word works." I swipe my finger down her nose and wink. "And as a matter of fact, yes. You."

Chapter 11

[Halle]

Obdurate.

The word defined Knox. He refused to do what other people wanted. Basically, he was stubborn.

"Although, I'd say I'm persistent," he corrects me. "Now. Lunch." He spins me toward the house, slaps my backside, and then helps himself through the front door.

What the hell is happening here? He licks my cheek. He spanks my butt.

Lifting my face to the heavens, I shake my head. *Men.* Or rather, not all men. Because no one pursued me like Knox did.

When we were younger, I didn't give him much of a chase. Right from the start, I'd wanted him as much as he'd wanted me. I'd hesitated to date him only because of *what* he was, not who he was. Popular. Friendly. Outgoing.

Growing up in a small town, it made sense that everyone would know him, and I was the new girl around here. I didn't want to be a novelty, and I worried Knox would grow bored with me.

He didn't. At least, not until his senior year ended.

As for Jack's current behavior, I have no idea where his snarky attitude came from. We eased out of our marriage almost as smoothly as we eased into it. Neither of us put up a fight when we ended, although Jack had been angry for a while. He needed the family image to promote his career. Public opinion favors a family man. The concept makes no sense to me. I've known too many husbands who were liars.

Proving my point, Peggy Montrock was an untold secret.

Dismissing thoughts of her, I lower my face and march into the house. Inside, Knox is busy rustling through my refrigerator.

"Get out of my fridge, you scoundrel," I tease.

Knox stands and faces me, a loaf of bread in hand. He gives me a wide smile and something inside me cracks. Maybe it's better that he's here, distracting me from the fact my ex-husband drove five hours with his girlfriend to take our children to lunch. There's always an ulterior motive with Jack, though, and I wouldn't have been able to stomach a meal with the happy couple, especially with my kids present.

Unfortunately, if Peggy is going to be in my children's life, I'll eventually need to accept her.

Hell, she has already been in their lives.

"You have no idea how happy it makes me to freely walk into this house and not have to hide in your bedroom." Knox watches me. "Although, I'll never complain about those moments in your bed. And I wouldn't mind if you suggested we head to your room again."

"Knox!" I admonish, although my voice lacks a true scolding. His flirty comment is the first reference he's made to our younger selves. That insatiable desire we had for one another. And a good distractor from the tension just moment's ago in the front yard.

He wiggles his brows and then holds up the bread. "Sandwiches or we can go out to lunch."

While keeping Knox a secret isn't something I'd ever do again, I'm not up for public scrutiny. Jack's comment hit hard.

That didn't take long.

Being married for fifteen years didn't entitle Jack to all my secrets, but he did know a major one and who that secret happened with.

I can still hear his voice in my head.

"Did you love him?"

"I did," I'd admitted.

Some people can brush off their high school sweetheart as young love, as someone not meant to be any more than timing and proximity in their lives. Knox had been different, or maybe that was just me. Either way, I couldn't lie to Jack. I'd loved Knox, but our time had passed.

"Give me that." Stepping up to Knox, I take the bread from his hands and set it on the countertop. "Sit down. I'll make sandwiches."

Scrounging through the fridge, I pull out ingredients and begin sandwich building using a baguette instead of sliced bread. Ham. Salami. Mustard.

Knox stares at me after I set his sandwich on a plate and deliver it to the small table.

"What?" I ask, setting it before him.

"You remember my favorite sandwich combination." He doesn't blink, eyes wide.

I shrug. "It's only a sandwich." However, without questioning if he still likes the combination, I'd made him what he called the Brick-special. The thing that made it brick-like were the layers of deli meat and a baguette. Knox's family rarely had 'fancy bread' as he called it, which was more expensive than a basic loaf. Once a week, I'd make him the specialty sandwich.

Returning to the counter, embarrassed by the memory, I cut a slice of bread in half and pile on turkey for myself.

"That's all you're eating?" He questions when I sit opposite him.

"Since Mom's passing, I haven't been terribly hungry. Too much work and immeasurable stress."

Thankfully, Knox doesn't comment. Instead, he lifts his sandwich, taps mine like we are toasting a special occasion and digs in. He eats fast and hums occasionally like the measly sandwich is the greatest meal he's ever eaten.

I laugh in spite of myself.

"It's so good," he mutters around a bite.

"It's a sandwich."

"It's the company."

I huff.

We aren't even talking to one another, but then again, for as much as we spoke when we were younger, we also didn't need to speak. We'd spend an hour in the back of his truck staring up at the stars or minutes lingering in my bed, watching the dark shadows dance across my walls. Conversation wasn't always necessary when you had an unspoken connection.

Knox pauses between swallows. "Tell me about Jack. How did you meet?"

How did I end up with *him* is the unasked question.

Since I don't feel I owe Knox an explanation, I flip the question. "You don't really want to hear this." I pick up my half-sandwich for a bite to derail the possible conversation.

"I do. I really do." Knox sets down his Brick-special, and crosses his arms on the table, giving me his full attention.

With the spotlight on me, I reluctantly begin. "When I fell in 2004, my coach said I had time to rebuild. I'd start a new training program. Relearn all that I knew and more." I pause. "All I ever wanted to do was run." And love Knox, but I don't add that part.

"I'd met Jack at a New Year's Eve party a few years later. He liked that I was athletic. Determined. Driven. Said he admired my spirit." I raise a fist for some reason, emphasizing Jack's compliments. "And he was charming."

There's no need to mention all the wining and dining Jack did. The months of friendship that lead to a physical relationship by the fall of that year.

"At first, I was standoffish. I didn't trust my heart." I gaze at Knox but quickly look away, staring at my half-eaten sandwich. "Nine months out from the Olympic trials, we made it official. Sex."

Knox winces at my directness as I recall my first Christmas at Jack's parents' house.

"That was the defining moment. I was his girlfriend." I swallow, remembering how Jack introduced me to his family as such because we'd had sex the night before. "In the beginning of 2008, I was training hard, but something felt off. I was easily tired. My legs ached more than normal. I couldn't keep anything down. And I'd realized I hadn't gotten my period. I was pregnant."

Beneath the table, my hands clench and unclench.

"Jack asked me what I wanted to do about *it*."

"What the fuck?" Knox barks, sitting upright in his seat.

I lift my head at his outburst and meet his eyes. "There wasn't a question in my mind." I stare at him, begging for forgiveness or maybe asking for his empathy. "I wouldn't be in the summer games. I'd be having a baby. Violet was born in September, weeks after the opening ceremony."

Knox sits back in his chair, bowing his head and swiping a hand over his face.

With his eyes aimed at the table, I rush to continue. "I stopped running. The doctors said my extensive training could be harmful to Violet." My voice trembles. "We now know an athletic woman is safe to continue exercising. But fifteen years ago, medicine still warned against intensive programs. Running was out of the question. I couldn't risk losing her."

Knox knows my reasons.

"Jack proposed and we married." I shrug as if it were that simple. When I decided to keep Violet, Jack suggested we marry immediately. The newspaper played it off as a love-match that couldn't wait. Anyone doing the math figured out the truth.

Knox finally looks at me. "Tell me you loved him, so I don't have to hate him."

"Loving him didn't make anything easier," I admit. "Did I love him like I loved you? Never." The confession is almost too much.

"Dammit, Halle." Knox stands abruptly and circles the kitchen. Hands behind his neck, he paces among the dark wood cabinets that make the space feel small, almost claustrophobic. A single window provides natural light to the room but it's not enough to brighten the sudden heaviness between us.

"Jack and I had been a slow burn. Friends to lovers. Then everything was a rush. The pregnancy. Our wedding. Suddenly, we were married. His career picked up. And my dreams faded." I sigh. "But without Jack, there would be no Violet and no Tim, and I'd never turn back the clock because of them. My children are my world."

"That's all I ever wanted for you." Knox stops pacing and faces me. "To be happy." He tilts his head, observing me. "But you aren't saying you were happy. And you aren't suggesting you married him for love."

"Love is perspective. Timing and proximity. He was there." *And you were not.*

Knox shakes his head. "When did you become so cynical about love?"

Glaring at him is my answer. He'd been the one to break my heart and change my opinion. Everyone who claimed to love me, left me. My father died. My mother withdrew. Knox abandoned me. It was safer to remain guarded with Jack. Or perhaps, I still ached from the loss of my true love.

"What about you?" The question comes sharper than it should. "You never married? No special woman in your life?"

"There'd only been one special woman for me." Knox's gaze zeroes in on me. "But yes, I married. Short and disastrous."

He sighs and places his hands on the back of the wooden chair he previously sat in. "We were both in the Navy. Proximity and timing as you said. She told me she was pregnant."

My sandwich rushes back up my throat, clogging off my airway, and forcing me to fight my gag reflex. I'm going to be sick, which isn't fair. I got pregnant and married another man. I had two babies with him. Still, every fiber in my being hates that Knox got someone else pregnant.

"We married hastily. It'd been a false alarm. We stuck it out for a few months, then I was shipped out on a mission. Divorce papers awaited me when I returned."

"I'm sorry," I say for some reason. Even a false alarm must have been conflicting.

Knox takes a seat again. "Don't be sorry, Halle. It wasn't meant to be."

He has no idea how strongly his words hit. So many things were never meant to be.

Thinking of Knox married to someone else is excruciating, but somehow knowing he hadn't found someone to love him the way he deserved makes me want to cry even more. Believing he had moved on and lived the life he'd always dreamed of, with someone who wasn't me, had made resenting him easier. To now know the truth—he hadn't found someone else—makes it that much harder to dismiss that we might be sitting here in this kitchen for a deeper reason.

Chapter 12

[Knox]

Hearing Halle talk about Jack stung, but I took some pleasure in her never mentioning love as defining their relationship. Not that I didn't want Halle to have all the love she deserved, but I wanted that love to only come from me.

I had so much to say and didn't know how to say any of it. To apologize for decisions I'd made when I was too young to think straight. To tell her how sorry I was about her missing out on the Olympics a second time. To beg her forgiveness for not returning sooner to her.

Halle always wanted to be a mother, so her disappointment in one direction only led to something greater in another. She had a daughter, and eventually a son.

It pains me that her asshat ex-husband is their father. It equally makes me want to smash his face when I consider he cheated on Halle. And he tried to play that flirtatious game on the lawn, like he held the upper hand with his ex-wife.

Fuck Jack.

His loss was going to be my gain because I'd already lost Halle once and I wasn't doing it again.

+ + +

Sunday is a family day for the Sylver siblings and involves a mandatory meal at the house. After Saturday morning with Halle, I'm out of sorts. The funk doesn't stop me from razzing my youngest brother, Sebastian, though. Watching him chase his tail as he falls in love is hilarious. Enya is the best thing to ever happen to him. Her baby, Adara, is part of the whirlwind around him. He didn't think falling in love could happen for him. He didn't know loving a baby could triple the size of his heart. Sebastian had it rough as we all did but he took a bumpy path before landing on a picnic bench in our backyard holding an infant and staring with heart-emoji eyes at the mother.

Watching him is a reminder of all I'd lost.

And I'm not thinking about Joanna. We might have married but our union was hasty and short-lived. Finding out she thought she was pregnant hadn't thrilled me the way I knew it would if the news had been from someone else. A certain someone who once *was* pregnant with my kid.

As my family cleans up from our afternoon barbeque, I sneak off to the stable, feeling a strange pull to a place I rarely visit. The barn door creaks as I roll it open enough to slip my body through the entrance and walk down the dirt packed corridor. There are only a few stalls, once filled with horses because my mother loved them. After her death, our father got rid of the animals. He couldn't face this building. As for the rest of us, it was the perfect place to hang a punching bag and take out our own aggression. Unfortunately, our father preferred to use a few of us instead of the boxing item for his anger. No one dared to fight back.

Until me.

Standing in the middle of the corridor, I consider how different things were for my older three siblings, Stone, Clay, and Judd. When our mother passed, Stone was twelve with Clay and Judd close behind him in age. Our father deteriorated before their eyes but not to the extreme he'd been once they each started peeling off from the family. Stone and Judd went off to college. Clay hid out in the family business trying to salvage what he could.

If there's a middle child in a clan of seven, it's me.

You're in the way, Dad told me. The words had more than one meaning.

I was taking up space in his house he wanted vacated.

I was going to leave anyway, so why not go sooner rather than later.

I literally stood between him and Ford or Sebastian or Vale.

Get out of my way. His voice rumbles through my head, sloppy and slurred as I stare at the crossbeams beneath the rafters of the stable.

The sound of the barn door rolling behind me doesn't make me turn my head, but the corridor becomes brighter.

"Whatcha doing in here?" Clay hollers as he approaches, his voice clear and cheerful, but I hear the underlying concern. He worries about me. They all have. Since I've returned, I see my siblings watching me, wondering if I'm really okay, despite all the proclamations that I am. I went to war but the biggest battles I faced were inside my own home.

Being that I work with Clay and he's my best friend since returning to Sterling Falls, he sees me the most and he's sensitive to my wavering emotions.

A joke or a jest assures everyone that I'm fine. Deep down, I simmer with anger at times.

Still staring at the crossbeam, I answer Clay, my tone more somber than the playful jabs of lunch. "You understand why I left, right?"

A firm hand claps my shoulder and draws my attention away from the rafters. "No one faults you."

"I do," I whisper.

Clay rubs my shoulder, gently jostling me. "He was an ornery bastard who made his choices. Poor ones at that."

"Yeah," I remind myself.

"Is this about Halle?" Clay should have been a social worker, always analyzing people. Instead, he runs Sylver Seed and Soil, giving us all a healthy dividend each fiscal quarter. "I worry she's a trigger for you."

"A trigger?" I snort. Then, I reconsider. Is Halle's return forcing me to face things I don't like to look at? Is Halle's presence the reason for so many haunting memories?

"It isn't Halle," I lie and Clay watches me, as if sensing the fib.

"You were only eighteen," he states. An age when we feel invincible and convicted. In our decisions. In our love.

Even though I loved Halle with everything in me, I didn't feel worthy of her. Her dreams were bigger than mine and while I wanted to be a part of her future, I also didn't want to hold her back. I couldn't do that to her. Or to me.

During the spring semester of my senior year, things happened in a spiraling progression.

Without telling a soul, I enlisted in the Navy.

Then my dad died.

And Stone came home.

When my brother was only twenty-two years old, he gave up his dreams to keep Ford, Sebastian, and Vale together. By the time I graduated high school, I had both feet out the door. Stone didn't try to persuade me to change my mind. He knew I needed to get out of this town. The air was my goal. While Halle liked to run, I wanted to fly.

"It's been twenty years, Brick." Clay affectionately uses my call name without knowing how the name actually originated. "It's time to let it go."

"I don't know if I know how," I softly admit.

"Forgive yourself," Clay suggests.

I huff, as if it's that simple. My dad. *My sister*. Halle.

"Sometimes, the only way to forgive yourself is to forgive him first." Clay pauses, letting the idea soak in.

I swivel my head in his direction and empathetic blue eyes meet my gaze. "Forgive him?"

"I'm never going to excuse his actions," Clay states, shaking his head in confirmation. "Never. But if you look at him as the man he was and the man he became, you see he was broken after Mom's death. He didn't know how to run a family. She did that. He didn't know how to love us. She did that. He was weak. She was strong. Again, not excusing him. Just trying to offer perspective."

"Yeah, well, I don't remember much of who he was with Mom. And his *perspective* preferred punches to hugs. He went after Vale." Venom fills my voice as I remind him our father hit a ten-year-old girl. His own daughter. That had been the final straw for me.

And the tipping point in dear old Dad.

"He didn't forgive himself," Clay softly suggests, offering misplaced sympathy. Truthfully, we have no idea why our father eventually killed himself in the stable, but circumstances coincide.

Dad and Vale.

Me interceding.

Him hanging from the crossbeam.

Clay was wrong. Our father didn't hate himself. He hated his children. And I never wanted to be like him. I ran away instead. Call me a coward. I've had years to beat myself up over my decisions and decades to build myself back together. I'm physically stronger, but my heart can still be weak at times.

Like when it comes to Halle. I didn't trust the love of a good girl or the blessing of a child.

"You ever talk to Halle about everything that happened?"

My head juts upward and I glare at Clay. "She had her own issues. I wanted to spare her."

"Maybe it's time to tell her everything and let her decide how she might have handled those extra details."

I can't. I won't lay my burden on Halle. I'd done enough to break her heart. She didn't need to know how much of our past had been a lie. And there were things my family didn't know about her as well. About us.

Maybe Halle was right. Maybe we needed to leave *our* past behind. But I preferred to think of her and I as on pause. We couldn't rewind, but we could press play to restart.

+ + +

The week starts out slow. The firehouse is relatively quiet, with no major emergencies during my forty-eight-hour shift, which means I have extra energy on my first day off to tackle Halle's place.

When I pull up before her house bright and early, and hop out of my truck, Halle is standing in her front yard with a man I recognize. Wearing a bright yellow sundress with thin shoulder straps, she appears surprised to see me.

"Hey." Her greeting is breathless, and dare I say, full of relief, like she didn't expect to see me again but here I am, dressed for a day's work in the hot sun in worn jeans, heavy boots, and a Sylver Seed and Soil tee. My dog tags dangle around my neck and a ball cap covers my head.

"Hi," I address her but shake hands with the man standing beside her. "How's it going, Clint?"

Typically, Sylvers don't speak to Havens. It's an unspoken rule after all that happened between Stone and Cortland, the eldest Haven, and once Stone's best friend. But I wasn't here during all that drama and certain times call for acting like an adult. Like when Clint stands in Halle's yard, staring at her house. He's a house painter.

"I forgot you two know each other," Halle says, looking between the two of us while Clint avoids direct eye contact with me. "Clint sure has grown up."

Halle's tease teeters on flirtatious. He's the same age as Sebastian, putting Clint three years younger than Halle. He is also the younger brother to Trinity Haven, and *I'd* forgotten that Halle and her were friends once I left Sterling Falls. Prior to my leaving, Halle and I were inseparable best friends.

Clint's face heats at Halle's compliment. Finally, he says, "I'm going to take some measurements and then I'll give you an estimate. Shouldn't take long but I can't get to anything until September."

Halle's shoulders fall. "That isn't great for me, but I'd still like a quote."

Silence falls between us as Clint continues to stare at the house before gazing at Halle "You should call Trinity. She'd be excited to hear from you."

"It's been a long time," Halle admits, suggesting the two hadn't kept in touch. "I'm just trying to get my head above water with all these projects. But I'll call. I promise."

Halle places her hand on Clint's forearm and gently squeezes, offering him a warm smile before releasing him.

Clint's face turns another shade of pink. *Does he have a crush on Halle?* He nods once and lifts a tablet in his hand. "Measurements."

As he walks off, Halle turns toward me. "I didn't expect to see you again."

"Today or ever?" I ask, surprised by the statement.

She shrugs. "I just didn't know." Her voice fades, hesitation evident.

Stepping up to her, I crowd her space and brush a loose hair around her ear. Crooking my finger, I tip up her chin, so she looks me in the eyes. "I'm not going anywhere, Sprint."

Sterling Falls is where I live now. As much as I once thought I'd retire by the beach and live in a flight zone, the mountains called to me, and I came back to West Virginia.

Maybe it was destiny telling me it was time to hit play on my unfinished relationship with Halle.

The slam of truck doors behind me alerts me my crew has arrived. "We'll be digging out space for the patio today. Landscaping will come afterward."

"Patio?" Halle huffs, eyes wide. "Landscaping? I only wanted the grass cut and the garden leveled."

Nope. I have a plan for this place.

"A patio isn't in the budget."

"There isn't a financial budget, remember?" I remind her.

"Well, there still isn't time or whatever for a patio."

"There *is* time." The finger that's been holding up her chin glides along the column of her throat. Her skin pebbles despite the summer heat. "Mine for yours."

Halle's lips twist. *Is that a smile she's fighting?* She chews the corner next. Definitely struggling not to smile at me.

"Now what?" There's no heat to her question, though.

"I'll think of something." I wink.

Before she can argue with me, I step away to greet my guys.

We have a patio to dig.

+ + +

"Whatcha doing?"

I glance up to see Tim standing only a few feet away from me.

"We're plotting out a patio." We've torn up the grass and dug down six inches. Next, we'll level the space, pour gravel stones, lay brick, and fill the seams with sand. The initial work is a three-day job, I'm trying to pack into two days. The brick won't be here for a week. The decision for what type of brick and what layout should have been Halle's, but I've taken the liberty to make a sweeping arc formation and selected a light limestone patio paver.

"Can I help?"

"Ever build a patio before?"

He laughs. "Never. My dad isn't the type to build anything. That's what service people are for." Tim catches himself and looks up at me, his young face full of embarrassment and eyes wide with remorse. "Not that you're a serviceman, but—"

"I get what you mean, and I am a bricklayer," I smugly state while chuckling. Seems dickwad Jack doesn't know how to use his hands for more than signing briefs and touching Miss Peggy Montrock. "I'm proud of what I do and that's all that matters."

"That's what my dad says, too." Tim hesitates. "Is it true you're a pilot?"

The question has me standing taller, leaning my forearm on the tip of the shovel's handle. "We're called naval aviators. We fly planes off aircraft carriers."

"Like that movie *Top Gun: Maverick*?" His gaze drifts to my dog tags which have escaped my T-shirt again and dangle against my chest.

"Yeah, something like that." There's a lot of fallacies in that movie, but, in general, it wasn't half bad.

"My mom says you're a hero."

Really? When exactly was Halle talking about me? How would she know anything about my career?

"I don't know about that," I admit, not wanting to discuss with a twelve-year old the woes of war.

After 9/11 happened in the fall of my senior year, I was more determined than ever to sign up and serve my country. I would have left high school if it hadn't been for Halle, and Ford, Sebastian, and Vale.

Not to mention Clay told me he'd kick my ass if I didn't at least graduate with a high school diploma. He didn't go to college, so he didn't argue with me when I said more schooling wasn't in the books for me. At least, not a university type of education at first.

"Did you have a code name, too? Like Maverick or Goose?"

Setting my hand on a hip, I turn my head to the side and sigh. "Yeah. It's called a call sign, and mine was Brick."

"Why?" His curiosity is endearing.

"Because your . . . an old friend called me that nickname. I'd told my new friends and it stuck." While Halle dubbed the name from our first encounter, and my family picked up the nickname as a joke about my being solid, my fellow aviators took on the name for what they considered my hard head. I can be stubborn. *Obdurate.*

I didn't know how to explain who Halle and I had been to each other to her son. I had no idea if she'd ever mentioned me other than apparently knowing I'd been at war. The hero part was questionable. Destroying bombs and losing a friend doesn't make someone feel heroic, even if the mission saved other people's lives. The coin of heroism has two faces.

"Can I have a call sign?"

"Sure." I shrug. "What do you want to be called?"

Tim taps his finger against his lower lip. "On Xbox, I'm TH11, but I'd like something more exciting."

"Call signs are earned and sacred. What kind of skills do you have?"

He lifts his thin shoulder. "I play soccer and video games."

"Let me see some of your soccer moves."

"Really?" His dark eyes widen and his brows lift.

"Maybe there's something special in your footwork," I suggest.

"My dad never wants to play soccer with me."

I shrug again, a bit saddened by what he said. I'm not his father. Not my dad either. "I've got time, bud." I pause a second. "Got a ball handy?"

"I can be right back with one."

"Tim, honey, you should probably let Mr. Sylver work." Halle's voice startles both of us and I spin to find her leaning against the porch railing that needs to be removed for access to the future patio.

Addressing Tim, I say, "Dear Lord, don't ever call me Mr. Sylver. Call me Knox. Or Brick."

"Brick," Tim utters in awe. "That's so cool." Then he's off to fetch a soccer ball.

Glancing at Halle, I meet her gaze. "This okay with you?" I'm not officially on any clock here. I can take a break whenever I need one. And I can spare some minutes to play soccer with her kid if she approves.

Halle gives a brief nod. "I'm certain you'll make his whole month."

Kicking around a ball for ten minutes? The feeling that suddenly overcomes me is strange but not unwelcome. To know I'm going to make that boy happy makes me happy.

I step closer to the railing. Being near Halle is making my entire year, but I only smile in response to her words. "It will be my pleasure. I'll let the guys have an hour break and then we'll be back at it."

"What about a break for you?"

I'm not certain Halle realizes what she's doing but she reaches for my hat, tugging it from my head and combs her fingers through my hair. Damn, that feels good.

I slip my arms through the wide slats of the porch railing and wrap my arms around the back of her legs. "I'll take one later."

Her eyes light up at she stares down at me, a foot below her. "So, your call sign was Brick. The Navy stole my nickname."

"You gifted it to me," I remind her. "Most of my team agreed, though, I am built like a brick." If only I could prove to Halle, I'm as solid as the nickname. Not just on the outside but inside as well.

Returning my ball cap to my head, she taps the bill. "How about a Brick-special then?"

"You know the way to a man's heart is through his stomach. You trying to get to my heart again, Sprint?" I squeeze at the back of her knees.

Halle's face flushes and I worry I've said too much, come on too strong. But she surprises me. "Do I need to work my way into your heart, Brick?"

Those blue eyes twinkle with the first spark I've seen since her return, and my chest inflates.

There she is.

The goofy grin heating my face can't be contained. "Nah, sweetheart. You've always resided there."

Tim quickly returns and I pull my arms back through the railing spindles. Halle breaks off the staring contest we were having, where the energy crackling around us was strong, and I almost leapt this railing, like Romeo climbing a trellis to get to his Juliet.

Written in the stars, Shakespeare had written of those fated mates.

I'm going to prove to Halle we're the same, without the morbid ending.

Chapter 13

[Halle]

Yesterday, Knox promised to return in the afternoon today. He also left me his cell number and told me to call him with any questions or concerns, or for any other reason.

The only concern I have is how often I found myself stopping at the window, staring into the yard to watch him work. Almost salivating every time I saw him thrusting the shovel into the earth and hauling up dirt, and wondering if he'd be bare-chested if he were working in his own yard.

So with a sense of urgency, I escape my home this morning before he arrives. As I walk toward town, I force myself not to imagine Knox Sylver sweaty and bare-chested and do a mental check of each room in the house. I've been making piles of items to dump, keep or sell.

Trudy Wallace is a local real estate agent and someone who advised me to hold an estate sale to sell items I don't want to keep. Also, during that conversation, Trudy let a personal tidbit slide.

Heard Knox Sylver has been hanging around.

Had there been a question in her comment? An appeal for more information? I hadn't responded, other than a simple nod, confirming Knox's presence.

But what did it mean? He was working on my yard but was it more than laying some brick and fixing the flower beds? What was he really doing hanging around my house?

Once I've entered the business district of town, I stop at the Curmudgeon Bakery, focused on a berry scone and morning tea.

Sebastian Sylver stands behind the counter and looks nothing like he did as a kid. A scrawny scrapper then, he's grown into a handsome, but hard-looking man. The scowl on his face is appropriate to the bakery name.

"Good morning, Sebastian," I greet him as if twenty-years hasn't separated me from his family. I've heard the gossip about his past from my mother. Drug dealer. Troublemaker. Jail time. None of that matters to me. Before me stands a respectable business owner.

He blinks at me before recognition slowly happens. "Halle Reynolds?" He sets down the tray of baked goods he'd been unloading from an oven and rounds the register counter. Stepping up to me, he gives me a hug I wasn't prepared for.

As one of Knox's younger siblings, I didn't interact with Sebastian often. He'd been in middle school around the time Knox and I dated, which was roughly Tim's age now, maybe. Knox had some serious concerns about his younger brother then.

"I'm sorry about your mom," Sebastian states, stepping back and giving me some space from the unexpected embrace.

"Yeah. Thanks." I reach for my ponytail and swipe my hand down the length, then reach for money stashed in my pocket.

"What can I get for you?" Sebastian says, walking away from me and back to his work behind the counter. "Anything you want, on the house."

A vibrant redhead with colorful tattoos down her arms gives him a scathing glance before looking at me.

Jealous employee? The effort is wasted on me. I only ever had eyes for one Sylver, and it's the same one as I've aged.

"I'll take a berry scone and tea, two lumps of sugar please."

Sebastian tips his head and arches a teasing brow. "Funny, my brother was recently in here and ordered something similar." He waves away the bills I hold out for my order.

"Funny that," I mutter, putting money back in my pocket. I didn't bring my purse, intending only to walk to town and home again.

However, I'm still restless once I have my breakfast treat and tea, and I head in a direction I haven't gone since returning to Sterling Falls.

I walk to the high school.

+ + +

As I stroll around the school, and see the track circling the football field, my heart thunders. The heavy thumping is like a funeral march as I process to the sacred space that forged my future. Here was where I pushed myself my senior year, breaking state records and winning the state title. Within a year after high school graduation, I was in college and had earned a spot on the national track and field team representing America. My coveted position had been a long shot, but I'd won over and over again at the time trials. Pushing myself. Proving myself.

I had nothing else in my life except running.

Once I near the old track, now updated, I walk through an open chain-link gate and stand among the six lanes. A man is running off in the distance, rounding the curve near the football goal posts.

Turning my attention to the equally divided lanes, I slowly walk between the bright white lines of the inside track, recalling how driven I once was to win. Determined to outrun my past. Hopeful of making a name for myself in the future.

The only name I'd made was Halle Reynolds, the girl who fell during the world's biggest competition.

Four years later, my name was Halle Haskins.

Thudding footsteps rhythmically beat behind me, and I step far right, allowing the runner to pass. I'm not in a race today. Just taking a trip down memory lane. As I cross to the outside track, the runner slows, and I risk a glance over my shoulder.

"Halle?" Arms swing before his broad body as his legs canter, slowing him down. His bare chest glistens with sweat and heaves from exertion.

It isn't fair how fit Knox Sylver is. His bulging arms inked. His abs a washboard of muscles. His pecs smooth; two slabs of perfection. I wasn't aware the artwork on his skin climbed up and over one shoulder, marking his left pec in an intricate design. His dark hair is slicked back from racing against the wind.

I remember the feeling, and I'm envious.

"Knox." His name is a sigh of exasperation. There's nowhere I'll escape him in this town.

"What are you doing here?" he asks, his breathing heavy from his abrupt stop.

"Just taking a walk," I admit, skipping over the reminiscence of being here. "Don't let me hold you back. Keep running."

"You'd never hold me back, Sprint." He takes long strides to stand beside me and waves toward the track. "Let's walk."

Knox's heavy breaths fill the space between us for a few minutes.

"You know, I never wanted to hold *you* back," he blurts, squinting into the distance.

He didn't. He left.

"That's one reason I left."

Has he read my mind? I nearly trip over my own feet. "Why would you say that?"

He turns his head toward me. "Because you were going places, Halle. And I was going into the Navy."

I huff and look away. The damn Navy. Honorable, but his decision deceitful. He'd always known flying in the Navy was what he wanted to do, but he'd never told me. Days before he left for boot camp, he announced he was leaving Sterling Falls.

Which was only days after he'd graduated from high school.

"We had a plan," I remind him. But did *we*? He was going to work at the Seed and Soil to save money. I would earn a scholarship. We'd go to college together once I graduated the year after him.

"Being a Navy wife was not your destiny, Halle. Your dreams were bigger than both of us." He waves a hand in front of him.

"Is that what you tell yourself to make you feel better? You blame everything on me?"

Knox stops short and I step forward before spinning to face him.

"I blame myself." He slaps a hand on his bare chest. "One thousand percent, the fault falls on me."

My mouth drops open and then slams shut. I didn't intend to lay all the blame on him. He'd had a lot going on in a short period of time. His dad. Graduation. Decisions for his future. I just thought I was a sliver of that future, until he'd cut me out.

And he didn't do it once. He sliced me twice.

"Look where you went without me, Sprint." His tone softens but I'm unaccepting of the praise.

I fell in the Olympics. Got pregnant before my comeback. Married for necessity, not love.

Unable to fight the truth, I admit, "I only wanted to be *with* you."

Knox shakes his head. "And it would have led you nowhere."

"You think I'm somewhere now?" I tap my chest with a fist. "I'm practically homeless. Divorced. And without a job. And I have two children looking up to me wondering when the hell I'm going to make decisions for them and *their* future. I told you I'm lost."

Knox stares, gaze hopping around my face. "You're home, Halle."

"I'm lost," I reiterate, the steam whooshing out of me.

I'm not sprinting with purpose. I'm flailing without direction. Tripping over that hurdle once again, foot tangled in the crossbar and headed for the rough surface of the track. I won't even land in one lane but extend into another, blocking other participants in the race of life— my children.

"Let me find you." Knox steps closer.

Find me? Those damn words again from him, that pinch, and sting, steal my breath. Words that make it sound so easy, like I'm simply misplaced car keys and he'll discover me in the bottom of my purse.

Knox had twenty years to find me. He had the chance to never lose me in the first place. Instead, he left me behind, discarded like an old chewed-up shoelace, that had seemingly tripped him and his life plans.

"How can you find me? *I* don't know who I am anymore." And I'm falling apart before the last man I want to be standing in front of.

"*I* know you," he responds, closing the distance between us, coming too close. "You're good and kind. A loving mother. A caring friend. You're full of determination and drive. You'd do anything for anyone you love, but you're uncertain of yourself. I can help."

He swipes a hand through his hair and holds it on the back of his neck. "We can figure out together what you want. What you can do. Where you'll go." His brows pinch on the last suggestion. His eyes soften to dark, stormy clouds full of concern but also rays of hope. He's willing to be here for me.

However, he left me behind before—*twice*— and I don't have it in me to let him do it a third time.

"I don't need your help," I blurt, still clutching a fist to my sternum where my chest aches.

He flinches at the sharpness of my words. His eyes blink a few times.

"Then help me get over you," he demands, his voice turning harsher, desperate and demanding.

His body language mirrors mine, a fist at his chest. Frustration and anguish mar his face. His jaw hardens as he practically begs me to let him go, as if some invisible force has kept him tethered to me all these years.

"What do you mean?"

"Night and day. Months and years, Halle. I can't get you out of my head or my heart. Let me help you move on, find some inner peace, so I can move on knowing you're well and healthy and happy." He waves up and down my body.

The implication feels like it refers to my leg and the fact I don't run anymore. "That's unfair."

"I mean, healthy in mind and spirit. You're sad, Halle. So fucking sad and it guts me. To know I'm a part of the sorrow in your eyes when I was once the reason they sparkled. I'm so sorry. So fucking sorry for the wrong I did in leaving you. And because I've never stopped wanting you."

He what? I close my eyes, shutting off his ability to look at me. I don't want him to see the sadness he mentions. The broken heart from his abandonment. The lingering ache from a failed marriage to someone else. The years of yearning for him as well.

"I've missed you, sweetheart," Knox whispers, too close to me.

With my eyes still closed, my other senses heighten. I inhale the manly scent of his run and the woodsy hint of familiarity. Him. Me. Us as we once were. With his closeness, his body heat emanates from his bare chest. I can hear his labored breaths that might not be from the exertion of his exercise.

"And you missed me." His broad hand covers my fluttering heart. His flesh is warm but causes my skin to erupt in goosebumps. Slowly, he glides his open palm up my chest, tracing my collar bone with his fingers, until his thumb and forefinger circle my throat like a loose-fitting necklace.

My eyes flip open.

"I'm sorry." His dark eyes focus on mine. "I'm so sorry."

Unwanted tears burn my eyes. It wasn't all his fault. It really wasn't. But it's been easier to blame him than accept the truth.

"I couldn't stop running," I whisper. I was young. I didn't know better, and I never stopped running.

"Shh." His hand coasts up to cup my jaw, stopping us from heading down the darker path of memory lane. "It's okay, sweetheart."

His lips touch mine, tenderly, sweetly, lingering. We meet and hold, but when he pulls back, I can't let him go. Not yet. I cup the back of his head and force his mouth to mine, kissing him with urgency like I did as a young girl. Desperate to keep the connection. Needing him more than air.

Knox Sylver knows how to kiss, and the slip of his tongue and the spreading of my lips proves he still kisses like he owns me.

The hand at my jaw slides down my neck again while the other fists my ponytail. I'm tugged closer to his body, but I'm not certain if he's drawn me forward, or I've stepped into him. I clutch his shoulders, then slip my arms around his upper back and hang onto him like if I don't, he'll drift away from me.

"God, I've missed you," he moans before moving his mouth to my neck, forcing me to tip back my head as he sucks along the column of my throat before rushing back to my mouth and capturing it once again. Over and over our lips move, swallowing desperate groans and gifting throaty whimpers. Joining our tongues isn't enough and my body presses firmly against his, slick from his run. My fingers glide back up his neck and into his hair, tugging at the longer length on top. I stand on my toes to bring my body flush with his.

If it weren't broad daylight, I might beg him to take me up against the fence. Or maybe in the middle of the football field where we once made out when the lights went off after a late-night track meet.

A lawnmower in the middle of the field fires up, a reminder that we're someplace very public. Knox breaks the kiss, leaning his forehead against mine, and I close my eyes again.

"I'm sorry I didn't have faith in *us*," he says, his voice low and strained. "I didn't believe in myself back then. And I wasn't strong enough for you."

He pulls back and stares at me, long and hard, eyes full of things I can't read. Then he takes a larger step away from me, arm extended to its full length as he cups my neck, keeping me distant from him once again. Finally, he turns, giving me his broad back and leaving me breathless, sexually frustrated, and wondering if there were things about Knox Sylver I didn't know when we were kids.

Chapter 14

[Knox]

As much as I want to prove to Halle that we belong together, I don't want to smother her now any more than I wanted to hold her back when we were teens. Like building a brick wall, the foundation needs to be sound, and the grooves filled with a substance strong enough the bricks hold upright. I don't want distrust crumbling down on Halle, crushing any progress I'm making with her.

Only she's toppling my resolve. Halle kissed me like she still owned me. Like she'd ruin me if I can't get things right this time. And everything in me wants me to rush to her side day after day, like that teenage boy seeking her out in high school hallways and sneaking into her bedroom late at night.

However, between waiting on her patio bricks, which will be delayed due to the holiday, and another forty-eight hours on at the firehouse, the time gives me space to practice patience. I don't regret kissing Halle, but I don't want to do anything to frighten her away from me.

And with The Fourth of July upon us, I'm in a conundrum. The pageantry of celebrating our glorious country doesn't bother me, but I'm not fond of the fanfare, honoring questionable heroes, like me. While I'm proud of being tapped to fly jets when I didn't have a college degree, and sent on a series of missions where bravery and skill were required, my military record has holes. Moments where I failed.

Namely, Rowan Lyons, my wingman.

In my small town, a parade committee exists, and insists on commemorating its hometown military personnel. For that reason, and much to my dismay, I've been talked into walking in the parade for the second year in a row. I hate having the spotlight on me in this manner.

Still, I march in my formal dress whites and wave like a trained baboon at the crowds gathered along the crossroads of Corner and Main Street. My family is somewhere among those collected on the sidewalk.

Vale originally met me at the line-up point. Probably to make certain I showed. Definitely to give me a pep talk.

"People are proud of you. Let them honor you," she'd encouraged. "If not for you, for them. Let them feel pride in their country as you strut down our streets."

"When did you become town cheerleader?" I'd teased, pulling her hair. She's dressed in a white tee with a giant star bedazzled in red and blue sequins. My nephew Hudson stood beside her, ready to march in the parade as well with his little league baseball team.

As I walk along the route, waving like I'm the freaking king of England, my gaze catches on Halle. She watches me, mouth firm, eyes focused. Her kids are gone for the holiday. When Tim and I were kicking around his soccer ball the other day, he told me they were going to their father's house.

Beside Halle is Trinity Haven, a petite, round blonde full of attitude and spunk. The two of them were thick as thieves during their senior year. The year *after* I left.

As I near Halle and almost pass her in the crowd, she lifts a hand and gives me a hesitant wave. For some reason, pride swells. I'd failed Halle but that doesn't lessen my need for her to be proud of me. I worked hard to prove myself in the Navy and become a highly decorated naval aviator. Eventually, I wanted to show her I was worthy of her.

I'd been too late, and I had no one to fault but myself. By then she was married to someone else.

That's where Joanna entered the picture.

Stoically, I salute Halle and continue walking, counting down the minutes until I can change out of my uniform. The parade funnels attendees and watchers into the town square, a patch of greenery just off the downtown business district. Food trucks line the square along with local vendors like a lemonade stand hosted by high school kids raising money. The space is a sea of people and well-meaning locals stop me every step I take to thank me for my service and congratulate me on coming home.

Alive, they mean. Some men and women aren't so fortunate. The day is a reminder of why I fought for this great nation and what I lost in doing so.

Time with family. The love of my life. And my best Navy friend.

Here and there, I glimpse Halle among those gathered for the community picnic. When I catch her looking at me, she glances away. If she looks up, when I'm watching her . . . she glances away.

We're playing cat and mouse today, and I let the game play out.

The Fourth of July messes with my head. I don't have the bandwidth to decipher Halle's questioning gazes or lingering stares, but I feel her presence. Even separated by the sea of people surrounding me, the pull of Halle is strong. If only she were a life preserver for my mind today.

Finally, I make my escape and head home for a quick change of clothes.

Once back at the picnic, I'm offered one complimentary beer after another. As Vale said, it makes *others* feel good to honor me. The pit in my stomach fills with the slosh of liquid barley and hops, and I muddle my way through small talk, feeling less and less worthy of each well-intended drink as the hours pass. Unfortunately for me, the beers added up, only aiding in my dismay over this day and the potential for a potent hangover tomorrow.

I've lost Halle among the masses and eventually stagger to Sebastian's bakery, which is within walking distance from the square, to seek refuge in my brother's apartment above the place. I'm too drunk to drive. Too melancholy to head home. Too desperate for Halle to be smart.

I want her. It's that simple and that complicated. We can't pick up where we left off twenty years ago. We're older, wiser, jaded and broken, but healing. I want Halle to be whole again. I want her to want me like I want her.

For every step I take to be closer to her, I feel her hesitation. She's skittish, like she's worried I have one foot out the door when, in truth, I'm ready to jump in with both feet. The only way to prove to her I'm solid is to be present every day for her.

But today isn't a day I can focus straight on anything.

Once I arrive at Sebastian's, the disheveled appearance of Enya, his beautiful acorn-haired new lady friend, and the pissed off expression on my brother's face suggests I've interrupted something, but I need a place to sober up.

"Aw, damn." I sway. I don't typically overindulge but today is an exception. My head hurts. My heart aches. "Why didn't you tell me you were busy?"

Ignoring my question, Sebastian asks, "Who are *we* avoiding?" Pausing to assess me, he adds, "Is this about Halle?"

"Who's Halle?" Enya asks.

"It's not Halle," I snap, struggling with the lie. "Just let me hang out with you guys."

Today, I'm a coward. I can't face Halle. Not like this. Not when my brain is buzzing with all the things I messed up at the same time as people praise me for situations that lack full disclosure.

Like my failed mission.

+ + +

Somehow, after a long nap and dinner made by Sebastian, I'm roped into babysitting while my brother hosts a romantic gesture for the woman in his life. I don't mind hanging with sweet infant Adara, Enya's daughter, for a few hours. She's too cute and coos at me while we dance around Sebastian's loft apartment to classic rock ballads.

Holding her reminds me again of what I've lost and by the time Sebastian and Enya return to his place, I'm a melancholy mess.

Thankfully, my brother suggests I crash here, and I accept the invitation, still desperate to hide my face and ignore the day. But no sooner does Sebastian leave, following Enya and Adara back to Enya's house, when my phone pings with a text.

Are you okay?

Halle? I'd put her number in my phone after she first called the Seed and Soil. Not exactly ethical, but I wanted a way to reach her. I didn't want to lose touch this time.

I'm good, I fib, and add a series of patriotic flag emojis.

Halle: **You missed the fireworks.**

Not really a fan of exploding lights.

Halle: **Where are you?**

The bakery.

When no response comes within seconds of telling her my location, I strip down to my boxer-briefs in Sebastian's spare bedroom and fall on the bed. The interior walls of Seb's place don't reach the full twelve-foot ceilings, leaving a two-foot gap around the enclosed spaces which includes two bedrooms and a bathroom between them. Mindlessly, I stare at the ceiling, thinking about Halle.

One minute I'm certain she'll never forgive me; the next she kisses me like she can't live without me again. Selfishly, I want option B. I'm not so arrogant to believe Halle needs me to live a full life, but I don't want a life without her. I don't know how we'll play out, or what a future looks like, and I hate that old feelings of inadequacy and doubt resurface on days like today.

Days when I'm hailed a hero but don't feel like one. Days when my cowardness rears its ugly head because I walked away from the love of my life rather than trusting her with my anger because of the situation with my father. Days when I was a ghost and slipped into the shadows, rather than accept responsibility and follow through on promises made to Halle.

When my phone rings, I almost jump out of my skin. Reaching for the phone beside me on the bed, I don't bother with the caller ID. I simply answer.

"Yo."

"Knox?"

Halle's voice has me sitting bolt upright. "Sprint?" I hold out the device to read her name lit up on the screen.

"Are you really okay?" she questions when I return the phone to my ear.

Falling back to the mattress, I rest my arm over my head, staring up at the dark ceiling again. "Yeah," I lie. "Why?"

"You looked . . . pained today. Like something was troubling you. Your smile wasn't real."

Funny she should notice. "You checking me out, sweetheart?"

"More like checking in on you."

Silence falls between us.

"Why?" I whisper.

"I don't know." Her voice sounds puzzled, and I can almost see the question on her beautiful face. A wrinkle between her brows. Her mouth pinched. Her eyes downcast.

Does she miss me? I accused her of such a thing on the high school track the other day, but I can't really be certain.

"Don't you worry about me." False cheerfulness fills my voice. "I'm good."

"But you're not." A rushing sound fills the phone, like Halle is rapidly walking somewhere, her breathing labored. "I know you."

Does she? Do I even know myself? I've been hiding so much for so long the edges of my life are blurred at times. Focusing on Halle grounds me, but do I even know her? Have I been living in this fantasy that I could win her back with a smile and some kisses? A chasm the size of West Virginia exists between us, filled with all the things we need to discuss.

A car horn honks through the phone.

"Where are you?" I ask.

The rumble of feet on wooden planks sounds next and Halle's voice is breathy when she answers.

"I'm outside Sebastian's apartment. Open up."

Chapter 15

[Halle]

This is reckless.

The statement plays on repeat as I stand on the landing outside Sebastian's apartment. The staircase off the alley leads to the loft above the bakery and as I wait, I question myself again.

What am I doing?

Yet, I haven't felt this alive in a long time. The three margaritas I had throughout the day might be the culprit, but the liquid courage helped me make a decision.

Knox looked miserable today and I want answers.

Since my return, I've been wrapped up in my own pain. My mother's death. My ancient memories. My uncertain future. But today, Knox is hurting, too.

What happened to him?

The door to Sebastian's apartment opens with a rush and Knox stands before me. Barefoot. Unbuttoned jeans. Waistband of his boxer-briefs exposed. No shirt. My mouth waters. He's the drink I need, more than alcohol. One look at his chiseled chest and broad shoulders, and I'm drunk on him.

But it's more than his damn physical appeal that draws me to him tonight. It's the sadness, palpable and raw, in his dark eyes which lessens a smidge as he looks at me. The lines of his face are more prominent, like he's hurting deep inside. Everything about him radiates darkness and dismay.

"Get in here," he whispers, reaching outward and pulling me forward by the hem of my stars-and-stripes shirt. Despite my feet fumbling, Knox tugs me into his chest and wraps his arms around me, inhaling at my neck.

"Southern comfort," he whispers.

While daisies are my favorite flower, jasmine is my favorite scent, and Knox used to tell me the scent brought him peace.

Without thought, my arms wrap around his lower back and squeeze. The warmth of his skin heats mine. I've been wearing the halter style top with stars and stripes mimicking our national flag and white shorts all day, but the mountain air has chilled this evening.

"Did you go to the fireworks?" Knox asks, releasing me too quickly and stepping back to give me space.

"I was at Milton Roadhouse. With Trinity." I'd run into Trinity at the grocery store the other day, and she demanded I hang out with her today after learning the kids were spending the holiday with Jack.

Jack and I had the arrangement scheduled before we realized that he'd be coming back in two weeks to pick them up again for their summer visit with him. However, he really wanted the kids for the nation's birthday as he walks Charles Town's parade, shaking hands and kissing cheeks, as politicians do.

Knox waves toward Sebastian's couch, suggesting we should sit. "Want a drink?"

"I think I've been overserved today," I admit.

Knox stops short and meets my eyes. "You drunk?"

"No."

I feel good, but I'm not so inebriated I don't know what I'm doing. Not that I *know* what I'm doing standing here, staring at my high school sweetheart, who has turned into a *fine* man and looks like he wants to devour me. But I'm cognizant enough to know I walked here with sound body and mind, prepared to ask questions. Only I can't seem to find my tongue right now with him staring at me like that and missing half his clothing.

"I'd love a glass of water, though."

Knox nods and helps himself to cabinets, removing glasses and filling them with ice water. When he comes to the couch which has an extension at one end, he folds into that corner. I've taken the opposite seat and he hands me a glass.

After a sip, I set it down.

"What's on your mind, sweetheart?"

"You." I meet his gaze and hold my ground. While my body hums and I want to leap across these cushions and devour his mouth, I fist my fingers and press my back into the corner to keep me still. "Why were you sad today?"

Knox tilts his head. "I looked sad to you?"

"You looked . . . tortured. Like you hated every minute of the attention people were giving you, but you smiled with a tight smile and acted like nothing bothered you." I pause. "I know you have that nickname, but you don't have to be strong all the time."

He snorts. "Pot meet kettle." He guzzles his water, eyeing me over the rim before setting the half-full container on the floor.

"I'm not strong," I whisper.

"You aren't weak, either."

I close my eyes and tip back my head a second. Then I lift it, and stare at him. "I'm not here to talk about me."

"Why are you here, Halle?"

"What happened to you?"

"When?" he coyly states.

"When you left Sterling Falls. When you were in the Navy. When you came back." *Take your pick, mister.*

Knox turns his head and swipes a hand through his thick, dark locks. His eyes avoid mine, aimed at the blank, flat screen TV on the opposite wall.

"That's a lot of time to cover. And I thought you didn't want to talk about the past."

There are so many things I don't want to discuss but just as many things we should. "Let's start with the Navy and the tension today."

Knox bitterly chuckles and glances back at me. "Damn, you *can* still read me." Spoken as if he's shocked, or questioning me, I focus on his eyes. The darkness is deep, shuttering to keep me out. I slip forward, crossing the middle cushion and sitting so I face his side.

"Tell me," I whisper.

"As you know, I enlisted in the Navy. My hope was to fly. Maybe supply planes or helicopters, but a pilot shortage at the time got me tapped for flight school as a naval aviator. It's a position typically reserved for officers and college graduates. I never saw college in my future." He sheepishly looks away, knowing we had tons of discussions about *us* attending college together. "The highly coveted situation was perfect for me, though."

Knox takes a deep breath and continues. "The long and short of it is I lost a friend. My wingman." He doesn't make eye contact with me, but I can't take my eyes off him.

"Rowan Lyons was one of Trudy Wallace's kids. I don't think you knew him. He was closer to Stone's age."

Trudy had a slew of teenagers come through her home. Some biological, like nieces and nephews, and others were foster kids. I hadn't known Rowan.

"Anyway, Rowan and I connected in flight school. He was a naval flight officer and training for WSO, weapon systems officer, which is not a pilot but serves as a wingman in a tandem seat plane."

I stare at him, trying to follow.

Knox soggily smiles. "We joked about being from the same small town and never being friends until we were stationed together."

He swallows and continues to avoid looking at me. I shift so my knees angle toward the back of the couch and my upper body can balance over his. My arm holds me off his chest, but I've drawn closer, sensing what he's about to tell me next will be difficult.

"It started as a routine mission, but something happened. We were forced to eject." With his hands on his lower belly, he rapidly twirls his thumbs like the spiraling of a plane falling from the sky. "To this day, the Navy isn't certain what happened. He should have angled for a clearing. Instead, his chute got tangled in a tree. He should have been able to cut himself free."

Knox lowers his head and stops the twirling of his thumbs. He shakes his head, and his hair falls forward, blocking out his eyes. "His neck snapped."

I fight a gasp. My imagination takes over, envisioning a poor man dangling from a tree.

"I'd been cleared of any wrongdoing, but it still fucked with me." His head slowly lifts. "And on days when we celebrate heroes I feel like an imposter. I'd lost my best friend. The man who had my back, literally, for years."

Knox heavily exhales. "His call sign was Raven. Perfect for a man in the air." His eyes finally meet mine. "I'm the one called Brick. Bricks don't soar, Halle. They fall. They land with a thud. Only with forceful impact can they break. But instead, this amazing man who had a name like a bird, who should have flown easily to the ground, got caught in a tree." The heaviness of his voice suggests incredulity.

I have no idea what the odds are of something like that happening. It doesn't change a thing. His friend is gone, and he somehow feels responsible.

"It wasn't your fault," I tell him, cupping the heavy scruff on his jaw.

"But I'm still to blame."

His counter-reasoning makes no sense, but I won't argue with him about things I don't understand. Instead, I lean forward and wrap my arms around him. At first, he's stiff. His chest heaving beneath mine. His breath is ragged near my ear. Slowly, his arms unfold from under mine and he circles my lower back, tugging me tighter to him. He inhales, as if not only drawing in the comforting scent of jasmine but grounding himself. In my embrace.

"I'm sorry that happened to you," I mutter to his temple, pressing a kiss against the graying spot.

Knox isn't crying. He's too solid but the sadness within him weighs him down like a bucket full of water. Heavy and hard to carry.

I pull back and cup his face again with both my hands.

Slowly, his eyes lift to meet mine again. "My brother isn't going to be back tonight. I know it's a big ask but would you stay with me?"

My hands slowly slip from his face, and I sit straighter. The position is still awkward as my hip rests against his. Knox catches my fingers and slides his thicker ones between mine, locking us together. "I'm not asking for sex or even to cuddle with you. I just want you near me. I won't dream if you're here."

Looking up at me with dark orbs that plead for me to stay close, my heart cracks open to the man I'm trying so hard to resist.

"Of course," I whisper. I'm suddenly bone weary from the long, hot day, and it's after midnight. Carefully, I unfold from the couch. "Mind if I use the bathroom?"

Knox hitches a thumb over his shoulder, pointing toward a wall with three doors. "Help yourself. Middle one."

I nod and use the facility, staring at myself in the mirror after I've washed my hands. My hair is in a messy bun, keeping the length tucked up from the heat of the day. My makeup is a mess. My skin sun-kissed. Using my finger and a dollop of toothpaste, I rub my teeth and rinse my mouth with a handful of water.

Opening the door, Knox leans against the doorjamb to a bedroom. With his arms crossed, he looks like a fitness model, not a man with a weight on his shoulders. His lids are lowered, and his eyes are sultry but tired.

"We'll be more comfortable if we're in here."

With a tip of my chin, I accept I'm about to sleep with Knox Sylver for the first time in twenty-years.

He might not dream with me beside him but I'm certain I won't even sleep.

Chapter 16

[Knox]

Strangely, telling Halle about Rowan has taken some of the tension off my shoulders and cleared my head. Then again, the relief might be from Halle agreeing to stay the night. My excitement wanes when I close the bedroom door, dousing us in darkness.

I'm going to sleep with Halle Reynolds again.

New anxiety settles in.

"I'll get you something more comfortable to wear," I say, then I remember I'm not in my room and have no idea what Sebastian has in the dresser drawers. Instead of rummaging through his things, I opt for my shirt which I'd dropped on the floor in my haste to undress earlier.

Swiping it up, I hold out the tee. "Sorry. It isn't exactly clean, but it will be more comfortable than your shorts and shirt." She's wearing this body-hugging shirt with red and white stripes around her stomach and white stars on a navy-blue background up top that ties behind her neck. The shirt has a V that accentuates her breasts and holds them pert and high.

I'd love nothing more than to pull the tie and free those luscious breasts. Lose myself inside Halle, but I promised no funny business. I won't even hold her hand if she doesn't want me to. I just want her close to me.

Halle doesn't respond to me holding out the T-shirt.

"I'll turn around," I add, although it's dark enough I can only make out the shape of her. A stream of light dimly glows over the top of the ceiling-less space.

She takes the shirt and I turn as promised. Slipping my jeans to my ankles, I step out of them. Sebastian's place has the air conditioning on but I'm suddenly too warm in the confined space of this bedroom.

When I hear the bed creak from Halle crawling on it, I join her on the mattress. We both lay on our backs, faces toward the ceiling.

In the dark, my senses are heightened. I can smell my shirt on Halle, mingling with the jasmine scent of her. The combination has my thoughts racing. The idea of her skin gliding against mine, and together we make a new fragrance. I'm also hyper-aware of how our arms align, less than an inch away from each. The coarse hair on mine faintly tickles the soft skin of hers. I sense Halle's hand near mine and practically come out of my skin when her pinky finger twitches, brushing mine before looping over it.

I take my first full breath all day and relax into the mattress. I close my eyes, content at least, while Halle's smallest finger faintly rubs over my pinky knuckle.

We're quiet for a long time. Long enough I think Halle might be sleeping when she says, "Can I ask you something?"

"Of course." I roll my head on the pillow and make out the outline of her face. Her pert nose. Her puffy lips. The jut of her chin. Her finger resting over mine is our only physical connection.

"Why didn't you ever take me to your house?"

I chortle. "Where did that question come from?"

"It's just something that's been on my mind since I saw you at the high school."

The other day when I kissed her on the track, wanting to lay her out, grind against her and bring us both to climax, like I once did on the football field.

This conversation is about to get as heavy as the one we had where I confessed to her about Rowan.

"Because my dad called you a whore, Halle. And you weren't." The memory bites.

My dad caught us in the stable and he said things that were so far from the truth I don't even know how he made them up. The names he used. The things he accused.

Dad never came into the stable and I thought we'd be safe in a stall, messing around, removing clothes, getting closer. We hadn't had sex yet. I'd been waiting for Halle to turn eighteen, but we were so damn close.

Rubbing naked parts against one another. Risking just the tip which drove us both wild.

That night we'd been half-dressed when Dad stumbled into the barn. I stood to protect Halle, pushing at my father to get him away from her. His insults were like a rapid-fire machine gun.

Whore like her will only get you in trouble.

Last thing you want is to be strapped with a load of kids.

Keep that dick clean.

I took the weak hit that accompanied his insults.

"I'd also been embarrassed that you were seeing that side of my life." My drunk father. The derogatory comments. The sloppy punches.

"Why?" I hear her head shift on her pillow and wish I could see her eyes in the darkness. That brightness that shines like a front porch light calling me home.

"I just didn't want you to be affected by him. I didn't want you to see *me* like that." Holding off my dad. Ducking his fists. "I worried you might think I'd be like him one day."

"Knox," Halle softly moans, rolling on her side to face me. "I'd never think that."

"I might have turned into him."

Halle props up on her elbow and I feel her gaze more than see it. "You would never be like that."

"How do you know?" It was one of my greatest fears and a reason I chased the sky. I never wanted aggression to become energy I needed to burn without a purpose. Flying gave me purpose. I could spread my wings and dog fight all day.

"Because I believed in you."

Her words mean more than she can know and hit me like a soft sucker punch to the gut. Had I been wrong about us when we were young? Had I mistrusted the feelings between us? I didn't think so. I loved her as much as she loved me, but I didn't *see* the future I promised her. Not really. I worried I wouldn't be enough, and I'd hold her back from being who she needed to be.

"Why didn't you ever talk to me about him?" Halle whispers, an ache in her voice, as if sensing I held back on her.

I had in some ways. "I just couldn't."

"You didn't trust me?" Deep hurt fills her tone and, again, I really wish the room wasn't so dark. I need her to look me in the eyes and read how much I believed in her. Wanted her. Maybe too much.

"It was never about trust, Halle." I sigh. "It was about not having faith in myself. My dad felt like evidence that I wouldn't be good enough."

I startle when I feel her forefinger trace over the scar on my left eyebrow. Hair won't grow through my bushy brow in this spot. A perfect slice of raised skin peaks through the dark tuft.

"You never walked into an open upper cabinet door, did you?"

I shake my head, feeling her finger against my brow. "He threw a beer bottle at me. I caught it with my face."

Halle gasps and her finger stops drawing over the pucker. "Knox." Her soft drone is full of sympathy. She surprises me further by lowering and placing a lingering kiss over the permanently marred brow. Like a mother would kiss away a boo-boo. Like a woman takes away the pain from a deeply scarred heart.

With the recollection of Dad catching us in the stall, I remember the remainder of that night. I'd snuck into Halle's bedroom after the fight with my dad and curled myself around her until she shifted and wrapped herself around me. She was my life-saving raft in a sea of uncertainty.

That's the night I told myself I only had to make it until graduation. Unfortunately, it meant I'd be leaving Halle behind.

"He'd tell me I was weak," I openly admit, never having confessed this to anyone. Halle's hand covers my left pec; my heart hammering beneath her touch. "Told me it was a waste of time to *moon* over a girl." I huff. "But he had no idea the strength it took to walk away from you."

The soft slam of Sebastian's alley entrance door stills both of us, abruptly ending the memories. As if we've been caught when we can't be seen, we hold our breaths a second.

Swiftly, I stand and peek out the bedroom door. Sebastian walks toward his room with Adara in her car seat. Something has happened and I should go to my brother, but Halle waits on the bed, and we've already had enough confessions for tonight.

"My brother is back," I say, crawling back on the bed.

We lay on our backs again in silence as the muffled, hushed voices of Sebastian and Enya swirl through the apartment.

"Should I leave?"

My head quickly turns on the pillow and then my body shifts as well. "Do you want to go? It's so late." And I really need her to stay, especially after the additional conversation about Dad.

"No," she quietly answers, and I release a breath I didn't know I was holding.

Within minutes, we hear the shower start, and I roll to my back again, staring up at the ceiling, wondering what the hell my brother and his girl are doing.

More minutes pass, and we have an answer when soft moans echo against the shower tile and vibrate upward, pouring over the ceiling-less walls.

Fuck me, I pray. As I'm certain that is what Sebastian and Enya are up to.

When a hard grunt ricochets over the open concept ceiling, Halle's warm hand clutches at my forearm.

"Are they—" her question cuts off when we both hear a strained whisper float above us.

"Oh God."

Halle's voice echoes Enya's like someone singing a round in a duet song.

I flip my hand and capture Halle's, entwining our fingers tightly together. I'm going to kill my brother. Right after I will away the hard-on that's arisen from hearing their moans but imagining Halle and me in a shower.

I'd press her against the tile and spread her long legs. I'd slip my hand between those sweet thighs and find her dripping for me. Then I'd thrust into her—

"Fuck," I hear my brother growl.

"Fuck," Halle softly repeats. Her fingers tighten in mine, holding on like we're both about to jump off a bridge.

While my chest lifts and lowers with breaths I can't seem to regulate, my dick is more the issue. *He's* rock hard just from holding Halle's hand and picturing all the things I'd do to her new body. Her older body. Her mom body.

Halle rocks a few more curves than her once lean figure. She's also a little thicker in areas and I'm not complaining about the fullness. Her hips are wider. Her shoulders broader. And I want to nip every inch of her skin.

"Knox," Halle whispers, strained and rushed beside me. "I . . ."

"What do you need, Sprint?"

"I need . . ."

"What, sweetheart?" Whatever she wants, I won't ever deny her.

"I just *need*," she whimpers.

"Get on top of me."

Halle quickly scrambles upright and climbs over my lap. As the heat of her covered center hits the solid shaft beneath my boxer-briefs, we both hiss. My hands catch her hips, a spot a little thicker than when we were young. I use the position to my leverage and rock Halle backward, dragging her warmth over my dick.

"Knox," she whispers again, anxious, or is that eagerness I hear?

"What do you want, baby?" I ask, bold and clear as I move her hips, gliding her back and forth over my stiff length.

Her breath hitches when the tip of my dick catches on folds pressed tight against her underwear. Her hands land on my chest, palms almost sizzling against my skin, as Halle takes over. Moving her lower half faster, grinding harder.

"That's it, sweetheart," I grit through clenched teeth as I try to keep quiet and stave off the rush happening within me. My balls drawing up. My dick hard as steel. Everything is happening too fast.

"Halle," I warn but she's lost in her head, rocking those hips and squirming along my thickness. Her wetness seeps through her underwear and saturates my boxer-briefs but it's not enough.

"I want to feel you, Halle. I want to feel you dripping on my cock, drenching me in your sweet juices."

"Jesus," she hisses. Her head lolls forward. Her messy bun bobbing. Her fingernails score my chest.

"Fuck. That feels good," I grunt, bucking my hips upward, catching the tip in her folds again. Her silky underwear and my cotton boxer-briefs aren't going to be enough of a barrier in another minute.

"Knox?" Her fingertips press harder on my chest as she rides me like a bucking bull. One hand slams at my left pec and then she stills.

Her head whips back and she bites her lip. I can see it all, eyes finally adjusted to the dimness of the room.

"You're so fucking beautiful," I tell her through my tight jaw, still fighting off my own release until she's drained.

Her head rolls forward and her eyes are a pinprick of light in the dark. "Knox." My name is a question and then she's shifting off me.

No, I want to yell but this wasn't about me. This wasn't the plan for this evening. I only wanted her close.

However, her fingers dig into the waistband of my boxer-briefs, and when she tugs them down before I can stop her, I choke on her next move.

Halle is kissing the seeping tip of my dick.

"Sprint," I practically cry. "It's been so long." So long since her mouth has been on me like this. So long since I've been wound this tight and desperate to burst. So long since anyone has made me feel like her.

Only she can do this to me.

Her mouth opens and I'm taken into the heat, her tongue swirling around my cock.

"Sweetheart," I grunt. "This is gonna be fast." Because I'm not going to last with the way she hollows her cheeks and sucks upward, drawing her tightened mouth along my thick length. "Fuck."

With my hands on either side of her head, I'm prepared to tug her off me as I reach my limit but Halle doubles down, cupping my balls in a titillating squeeze and repeating that upward suction that has me releasing like a private fireworks display.

Specks of tiny lights flicker before my eyes, as I lift my head and watch Halle take me deep and hungry. I open my mouth on a silent groan as I go off like the Fourth of July special.

Halle sucks and swirls her tongue until I can't take it anymore. "Enough, baby."

She pulls up my spent dick and pops off the end, giving me one more kiss and a lick across the seam of my tip.

"Damn," I whisper, tossing my head back to the pillow. My chest heaves as Halle sits upright. I haven't come like that in ages, if ever.

While Halle was eager to learn how to please me when we were young, she's improved over the decades, and I hate the thought of someone else teaching her how to give such pleasure.

"You need something," I whisper.

"I think I'm okay. But I'd love some water."

I'll climb mountains and bring her the sea to replenish her. Instead, I tug up my boxer-briefs, roll off the bed, and slip through the door for the bathroom. Finding the space empty other than steam, I take a moment to clean myself off before staring at myself in the mirror.

Who am I? And can that woman love me again?

Chapter 17

[Halle]

As Knox slips out the door, I fall to my back on the mattress and stare up at the ceiling before a giggle ripples up my throat. Swiftly kicking my heels and tossing my head side to side on the pillow, I'm giddy about what just happened.

Knox Sylver has the best dick, long and thick. He made me feel desirable with his commands. Rocking along his length drove me mad until I needed to taste his salty-sweetness. I swallowed everything he wanted to give me with pleasure.

Sucking him made me feel like a queen.

When he returns to the bedroom with a glass of water, I sit upright and down the refreshing liquid. After handing back the glass, he slides into bed beside me, opening his arm so I can place my head against his chest. His heart hammers beneath my ear and I absentmindedly trace over his sternum. Lifting my leg, I hook it over both of his. Knox wraps his hand around my thigh and tugs my bent knee higher against him.

Within seconds, my heart races again, and another place on me beats as well. Teasingly, I hitch my leg even higher, brushing over Knox's boxer-briefs.

His breath catches but I don't speak. Slowly, I relax my leg, dragging it back down his body but Knox tugs my thigh upward once more, rubbing my inner leg against the front of him.

As if I'm holding my breath, we silently continue in this pattern of him hesitantly pulling up my leg and me stroking over his growing length.

"Halle," he groans.

I hum against his chest, breathing him in. I don't know what's come over me, other than I've had a taste of Knox Sylver again and I want more. Like a sample of ice cream that leaves you craving the entire sundae.

We continue the quiet resurgence of sexual tension between us until I can't take it anymore.

"I need more," I mutter, almost embarrassed as the ache in my tone gives away my desire.

"Let me touch you," he commands.

"Please," I whimper.

In a move faster than I'd expect from him, I'm on my belly on the mattress and he's at my back, hiking up my hips while I keep my head on the pillow. His large palm slips beneath the tee I'm wearing and covers my bare stomach before slipping into my underwear, rushing to my center, and cupping where I'm overheated.

"Fuck, Halle," Knox groans before swiping his fingers through my throbbing folds.

I've barely caught my breath at the sudden touch and thrilling sensation when he slips his middle finger inside me. I gasp with pleasure then whimper again when he threatens to remove his finger, only to add a second.

My legs spread wider. His fingers are so thick. I'm so full. And I rock against his hand as he thrusts into me, simulating how it would feel to have his solid dick entering me.

"Knox," I groan. A woman out of control, I use his fingers as he winds me up again.

While his hand is wrapped around my front, the heavy length of him presses against my backside.

"Halle," he grunts. He needs me. He wants me. But I don't know if I can do more than what we are doing. Grinding against one another like we did as teens and yet everything in this moment, in this position, is nothing like we were twenty years ago.

This is raw, wild, desperate sex . . . without penetration.

Knox shuffles a bit, and then I hear the sound of skin against skin. Glancing over my shoulder, the best I can make out in the darkness is him clutching at himself, tugging at the firm shaft in his hand. He's jerking off while touching me and my body goes into overdrive. Rocking. Pleading.

Knox nudges me with his forearm around my waist, fingers buried within me, and I press up to my knees, my hands placed on the wall to hold me upright. Knox is on his knees as well behind me, stroking at himself while pleasuring me.

"Fuck, Halle. Do you have any idea what you do to me?"

I can feel him behind me. Hard and taut, and tapping against my backside with every swipe of his hand up his length.

"You're doing the same to me," I choke out as I reach my arm around his head, holding onto him in this awkward position but unable to release him. I don't want him to let go of me. Not yet.

As I ride his fingers, his thumb brushes my clit, and my breath catches. "Knox."

"Give me what's always been mine, Halle."

Eyelids blinking, mouth gaping, I falter. But Knox doesn't allow me to think. He doesn't break the rhythm. He doubles down and I hear my slickness on his fingers while the clapping of his hand around himself echoes behind me.

In tandem, we break.

A soft groan comes from him.

A silent scream fills my throat.

I come like I never have before, soaking his fingers and dripping down my thighs. Moisture hits the back of the T-shirt I'm wearing.

Our breaths are ragged and heavy as our hearts hammer. We're a tangle of limbs and a sticky mess.

Eventually, Knox presses a kiss to my covered shoulder and gently removes his fingers. I collapse down to the bed, spent.

"Let me get you something," Knox says, shuffling behind me.

"I think I'll just use the bathroom this time." I softly chuckle as reality seeps in. I've just come twice in a matter of minutes with Knox, and I haven't felt this blissed out in a long, long time.

Rising off the bed, I shakily unfold my legs and scramble to the bathroom without a glance at Knox. After I use the facility, I gaze at myself in the mirror above the sink. My hair is a mess, like I've rolled around in bed, which I have. Knox's shirt is askew, dipping to one side. My cheeks flushed. My eyes are brighter than I've seen them in years.

That's what good sex can do for you.

The thought is both scintillating and sobering.

What have I done?

And when can I do it again?

I exit the bathroom to find Knox leaning against the door frame of the bedroom again. His arms are crossed. His head leaning against the jamb. His eyes question me.

Do I leave? Do I stay? "I should probably go," I whisper.

Instantly, Knox presses off the frame and steps toward me. His fingers curl into the tee I'm wearing, and he tugs me to him.

"You're staying." He pauses. "Tonight."

Is this a one-night stand? I don't know how those work. My thoughts race until Knox tips up my chin and gently kisses me.

"Come to bed, Sprint," he whispers, reminding us both we aren't alone in the apartment.

I nod and walk around Knox, who follows me and then tugs on the back of my tee. "Let me get you something else to wear."

He blindly rumbles through a dresser in the bedroom and hands me a clean shirt. I give him my back to remove the one I'm wearing, suddenly sheepish and hesitant to expose myself to Knox although the dimness in the room would only provide an outline of my body. Not to mention, we've already gone two rounds with each other.

Knox doesn't say a thing when I return to the bed and lie on my side. He slips in behind me and wraps his arm over me, tugging my back to his chest. His hold tightens, keeping me in place.

"Don't think, Sprint. Not yet."

I sigh. He knows me so well. Too well.

And I try to ignore what he said in the heat of the moment.

Give to him what's always been his.

I don't know that my heart can handle Knox Sylver again.

+ + +

"Hey." Knox's groggy voice startles me in the morning light as I re-dress in my clothing from the day before. My white shorts and American flag shirt is a testament to my shame. I spent the night.

However, I'm hopeful the town will still be quiet this early, sleeping off the late-night activities of fireworks, summer celebrations, and reckless drinking.

"Hey," I mutter, fixing the straps around my neck into a loose bow. Swiping a hand through my wayward hair, I meet Knox's eyes as he watches me. "I need to go."

His gaze remains on me a moment, long and intense, and speaking a thousand things I can't read this early in the morning without caffeine and a decent night's rest. I didn't sleep well as my mind caught up to what my body had done.

I might as well have had sex with him.

Still, I can't take my eyes off him. His bare chest on display as he rolled to his back during the night and gave me some space. The sheet is below his waist, hinting at dark boxer-briefs, and nothing else on his body.

Proving my suspicion, he tosses off the sheet and sits upright. Then he stands and saunters toward me.

He catches my chin between his fingers. "Good morning." His eyes search mine a moment before he tenderly kisses me.

I could get lost in him again. I could never leave this room or return to my life as it is, but that isn't how I roll. My kids will be home later today, and I need to get my thoughts back in order. I can't get too wrapped up in Knox again.

Sensing my separation from the moment, Knox pulls back and stares at me once more before asking, "Where is your car?"

"I'm parked on the other side of the square." I'd driven into town yesterday morning for the parade and parked as close as I could get. Then left my car there as Trinity and I drank throughout the day and eventually ended up at Milton Roadhouse.

"I'll walk you to it."

"You don't need to do that." I dismiss the offer. Not that I'm trying to erase what happened last night, but I don't need to publicly announce that last night happened *with Knox Sylver.*

The scowl on Knox's face says he isn't having it. "I'm walking you to your car." Finality rings between us before he picks up his jeans and pulls them on. "Just give me a minute."

He steps into the hallway, closing the door behind him and leaving me to assess the room in the daylight. Rumbled sheets. Matted pillows. His worn tee on the floor beside the bed.

My face heats at the reminder of all we did. The way he touched me. The position we were in. The intensity of my orgasm.

My core pulses, as if I can still feel him. My heart is the logical part of me, though.

I should not fall for Knox Sylver again.

He quickly reenters the room. "Ready?"

Am I ready for another round with him? Could a third time be the charm?

"I think so."

+ + +

Knox silently walked me to my car, where he opened my door and pressed a kiss to the side of my head before I slipped inside and drove to my mother's house.

Once home, I showered although I hesitated to wash the scent of Knox off me so quickly. Still, logic said shower and change my clothes. After preparing myself some tea, I walked room-to-room, until ending up in my former bedroom, where I've stood quietly fighting the memories of last night mingling with the ones lingering in all the crevices of this space.

The trophies from high school. The ribbons from college. An article in a frame on the wall.

I've had my successes and my issues over the years, but I hadn't considered that Knox might have ones as well.

His own failed marriage.

The loss of his friend.

His return home after a long career.

I certainly didn't have the career he had. My accolades came in a different format. Handmade cards and macaroni necklaces. Hugs and handholding when my children were young. Rare moments of laughter as they aged.

I still have no direction for what I'll do next or where I'll move. And my thoughts return to Knox and last night once again. Could I stay in Sterling Falls? Would that decision be wise? What would that mean for Knox and me?

The second I hear car doors slamming in the yard, all thoughts of the future vanish, and I race down the staircase, eager to greet my children who might not be half as excited to see me. The holiday weekend was one of many we'll need to weather through in the future, and the days without them felt long despite all I'd achieved by boxing up items for Goodwill or storage.

"Hey," I cry out, opening the screen door before Tim and Violet reach the front porch. Tim steps up to me, falling against my chest as I open my arms to him. I kiss his head, having missed the pungent scent of his blossoming adolescence.

"Hey, buddy. I missed you," I whisper to his hair which needs a good washing.

Tim lifts his head, and affectionately smiles at me. "Missed you, too, Mom." Quickly he releases me and continues for the house.

"Violet, baby." I hold out my arms for her next and she leans into me, lingering longer than I expected. My brows pinch and I glance in the direction of my ex-husband who stands beside his car with his head lowered.

Did the kids even say goodbye to him?

Violet startles me when she pulls away, as if she suddenly realized she'd been allowing me to hug her. After she circles around me with her backpack dangling off her shoulder, I approach Jack.

"What happened?"

His head lifts. "What gives you the sense something happened?"

Mother's intuition. I stare at my ex, searching for what I once saw in him—a good man. A loving father. A decent husband. The last wasn't the best of accolades to give him. He deserved more, as did I.

"Let me help with the bags," I offer, ignoring his question while walking beside his car and heading for the trunk.

Our breakup hadn't all been his fault. He had aspirations. I hadn't by the time we married. Sure, I'd been a mom, and I loved it, but a part of me has been absent. A part I didn't know how to find now that my kids have grown more independent.

In an attempt to be pleasant, I ask, "How was the holiday?"

Jack sighs. "Good." However, his voice lacks enthusiasm or conviction. He squints up at the house after removing Violet's suitcase and I pick up Tim's duffle bag.

"How are things coming with the house?"

"Slow," I admit.

Jack remains behind his car, holding Violet's suitcase as he turns to me. "This drive is long, Halle. Ten hours round trip." He watches me as he reminds me of the distance I'm well aware of.

"You need to come home soon."

Holding my ground, I stare back at my ex. "Jack, I'm not certain what's given you the impression I'd ever return to Charles Town, but I'm not." I hadn't made that firm decision until this very moment. I'll never be returning to the town I once shared with this man. "I'm sorry Charles Town is five hours from Sterling Falls, but this is my house."

Maybe it isn't a home. Maybe I won't stay here, but this is still a house I own, and for now, I need to decide what to do with it. *Me.* I make the decisions. Not Jack.

Jack's mouth falls open, preparing to say more when a truck pulls up and parks on the street. Both our attentions turn in the direction of the Sylver Seed and Soil vehicle, and the man who exits it.

My face instantly heats. *Shit.*

"Interesting," Jack mutters, the weight of his eyes suddenly on me but I don't remove my gaze from the man sauntering up my driveway, looking damn fine and cocky in worn jeans and a tight tee, showing off his muscles and highlighting his ink. My face heats even more as I check him out, certain I'm turning a variety of reds, like broadcasting my guilt on my cheeks.

That man touched me last night, and I enjoyed every minute of it.

"He's working on the yard," I remind Jack when I can finally find my voice.

"Good afternoon," Knox states once he reaches us, offering me a wink like he hadn't already greeted me a few hours ago.

The screen door suddenly opens behind me, and Tim runs outside.

"Hi, Knox." My son eagerly waves, his smile bright for our visitor.

"Hey, Dash. Thought I'd get some more work done on the yard," Knox offers, addressing Tim.

"Dash?" Tim questions.

"Who's Dash?" Jack asks, his expression pinched.

Knox nods at Tim. "I thought of a call sign for you. Dash. Because you're quick on your feet with that soccer ball."

Tim's brows rise, wrinkling his forehead with excitement. "Dash. I like it."

"How does he know Tim plays soccer?" Jack mumbles beside me.

"He pays attention," I answer.

Jack snorts as if I've made a lewd joke, but then he watches Tim interact with Knox. The eagerness on his youthful face. The gleam in his eyes. He loves the new nickname.

"Dad, did you know Knox was a naval aviator? His call sign is Brick and now I have a call sign, too. Dash." Tim does a fast footwork improvisation like he has a soccer ball at his feet. "It's so cool."

"Yeah. Cool," Jack drones. "Dash." The name sounds bitter and tight on my ex's lips.

He takes our son's duffle from my hand and holds it out toward Tim. "Take your bag. And give me a hug."

Tim takes the bag and hugs Jack but it's stiff and quick. Then he is gone.

Jack hands Violet's suitcase to me, but Knox steps up to take it before I can, and awkwardness falls between the three of us.

"I got it," Knox states, removing it from Jack's grasp and heading toward the house.

"Making himself right at home, isn't he?"

"What's your point, Jack? I'm sure Miss Montrock has moved into ours." *His*. His house.

"*Peggy* does not live with me." He corrects both her name and their situation. Yet is the word he omits.

We stare at one another a moment before I look away. "I'll get Violet for you."

"It's fine. We said our goodbyes in the car."

Now that's interesting, but I don't press for information. I'll check in on Violet later, allowing her some space for now. I don't like when she goes quiet. God help Jack if he's done something to upset her or make her doubt herself.

As Jack enters his car, I stand guard, then watch him drive away. The porch door swings open behind me. Without a glance, I know Knox is standing on the front porch. He kind of has made himself at home.

And I don't know how I feel about either.

Knox. Or this house.

Chapter 18

[Knox]

My excuse was weak, but I had to see Halle. I had to know she wasn't overthinking everything that happened last night. And I especially wanted to check on her after hearing about the night Sebastian and Enya had. Someone had broken into Enya's house, and the situation left a bitter taste in my mouth.

I didn't like Halle being alone.

When I arrived at her place, her kids had just returned. That asshat Jack was standing in the driveway looking smug and debonair like he belonged there. Like that house was his. And Halle still belonged to him.

He'd have a fight on his hands because I wasn't letting her go so easily this round. Not after last night. The way she touched me. The way I touched her. There was no turning away from Halle again.

I'd clearly stumbled upon a tense discussion but decided it wasn't my place to intervene, thus taking the suitcase from Jack. My only concern was Halle *after* Jack left.

"He givin' you trouble?" I ask as she approaches her front porch.

She dismissively waves. "It's just Jack. And it's nothing." Halle pauses, looking troubled but freshly showered after last night's tumble in bed.

That bed. And her. Fuck, just thinking about it makes me want to ravish her on the front lawn.

"I'm worried about Violet."

Instant desire deterrent but a new concern rises. "What happened with Violet?" My hackles rise. Did Jack harm her? Did he touch her? *I'll kill him.*

"She just seems angry. Angrier than normal."

"Are you worried about her being alone with Jack?" Trigger warnings go off. Not every father is a creep but my thoughts flit to Vale as a child.

"No. Absolutely not." Halle's brows rise, her expression confirming my suspicions are not hers. Then her face softens, empathy filling her eyes, because of what she's learned about my past.

This moment isn't about me, though. "What would you do as a fourteen-year-old girl when you were angry?"

Before I finish the question, I know the answer.

With an understanding smile and a hint of what might be appreciation for my concern for Violet, Halle says, "I'd run."

"When I was a kid, I'd use the punching bag in the stable." Nothing cleared the head like some good, hard hits to the bag. I smile but watch as Halle's face morphs from concern to compassion.

"I'd have thought . . ."

"What?" I watch as she looks away, embarrassed by mentioning something sensitive. "That because my dad hit me, I wouldn't be prone to violence."

Halle's gaze shoots back to me.

"Not every person who finds release in a good one-two sucker punch means that person is violent."

"I didn't mean—"

I lift a hand. "I know."

"I just wish she'd talk to me. About the divorce. About her father. About whatever she's feeling."

"Sometimes talking doesn't always work. She needs something physical to release her anger. Like running," I remind Halle. "I have an idea."

Halle tips her head, a question written on her cheeks. "I don't think taking her to your stable so she can beat up a punching bag is the answer."

I want to argue. Instead, I say, "I have something better in mind."

+ + +

"Axe throwing," Tim reads the sign outside the warehouse.

"Is Tim even old enough to do such a thing?" Halle asks.

"I'm twelve," he proudly announces, and I smile to myself but I'm watching Violet through the rearview mirror where she sits in the backseat of Halle's SUV. Halle let me drive her car when I said I had a surprise for them.

For the past forty-eight hours, I've had to work at the firehouse, so I couldn't follow through on my plan until this evening.

Focusing on Violet, I watch as she scans the old warehouse outside of Sterling Falls. The place was recently turned into a pub and axe throwing experience. They have outdoor pits for summer evenings and enclosed cages inside for the cooler months.

"What do you think, Violet?" I ask.

"I'm game." Her eyes don't leave the side of the building, but I'll take her response. Halle isn't the only one I need to win over, although she's the most important to me. Her kids can love me or leave me, but I want them to like me.

"Let's go then." I pop open the driver's side door and round the SUV to help Halle with hers. At the same time, I reach for the back door and open Violet's.

"I got it," she mutters.

"He's being a gentleman," Halle explains.

Violet stares at her mother like the term is foreign.

I'm puzzled. "Guys don't open doors for women anymore?"

Violet shrugs. Maybe she isn't into boys yet. Or at all. There is still such a thing as manners, though.

"I want to be a gentleman," Tim announces, rounding the back of the SUV.

"Oh, you will be," Halle states, determined that her son will be respectful, as she reaches out for the back of his neck and gives it a squeeze before releasing him.

"You're only twelve," Violet teases. "You can't be a gentleman yet." She wraps her arm around her younger brother and tugs him to her side.

Tim pushes his sister away. "I can, too."

Halle laughs, and I smile at the ease with which Violet handles Tim. She isn't angry at everyone.

Once inside, we learn the rules of the game and get assigned a cage. Tim and Violet need safety gear because of their ages but the man behind the counter isn't too concerned. He's a fellow firefighter and knows I'll be watching both kids like a hawk.

"Let it all out, Violet," I say to her before she starts.

"I don't know what you mean," she says, narrowing her eyes at me.

"Yeah, you do." I match her glare with a knowing one of my own.

She has a bone to pick with the world and the best way to lessen the edge is to throw something.

Violet's aim is pretty good. Her speed is strong. She's a natural athlete like her mother.

"Play sports in school?" I ask Violet after her turn and while Halle coaches Tim.

"I was thinking of trying out for field hockey or lacrosse but since I don't even know where I'm going to school, I don't know." Irritation returns to Violet's voice.

Like Halle said, her kids are waiting for *her* to make decisions. The uncertainty of their future is a wobbling coin, and Violet isn't only angry. She's scared.

"Both sound like good sports." I nod toward the board that held Violet's axes. "You have good eye-hand coordination."

Her head snaps from the vacant board to me and back. "Yeah." The response is quiet, cautious, as if she doesn't believe me.

"If you end of going to Sterling Falls High School, we have both teams here." I expect it to be the wrong thing to say. It implies they might stay in Sterling Falls when Halle has been adamant, they won't remain here.

"Yeah," Violet whispers, closing in more, like a tortoise tucking into its shell.

"Well, wherever you end up, you're going to be great."

Her head lifts again and her eyes narrow, suspicious, and uncertain. "How can you say that? You don't even know me."

"Don't need to know you. I just watched you hit the mark and rack up points. Anyone can see you have focus and aim, both things needed for lacrosse and field hockey. Holding an axe is heavy work, so you have strength to handle a stick." Both sports require endurance and agility.

"My dad doesn't think I should play either sport. He says they're too violent."

I snort, disagreeing, but then try to cover the scoff with a cough. I'm not here to speak negatively about her father.

"Violet, let me tell you something. You can do whatever you want to do."

Violet huffs. "If that were true, I'd be back in Charles Town."

Point taken.

"Let me amend then. You can *be* whatever you want to be. Don't ever let anyone stand in your way. We all have dreams. Follow them."

Violet watches me and then looks away to observe her mother. "Is that why you left her?"

"What?" I choke.

"Yeah. I know you two were high school sweethearts and you broke her heart. Is that what you did? Followed your dreams?"

"I did." I admit, knowing it's more complicated than that. "But I also stepped out of the way to let your mother follow hers. And look where it got her."

"She wanted to be an Olympian." Her mother's failure is implied.

I shake my head. "She had you and your brother, Violet. I'd say that makes her a champion."

Violet startles a moment by my comment but then her cheeks pinken. She's her mother's winningest accomplishment, and somehow, I think Violet understands the value of being Halle's daughter. No one loves her more.

"Knox," Tim calls out and I turn to watch as he takes his first toss. Not a bad effort but he might want to stick to fancy footwork not games with sticks.

As for Violet, she could still use that punching bag.

+ + +

The evening ends with pizza and mounds of thank yous from Tim. Violet grumbles her own appreciation. However, Halle is the one I want to please most.

"This was really above and beyond," she says as we stand on her front porch. I've followed the family of three to the front door, where Halle and I linger.

"It was fun." I mean it. I had a good time tonight. Tim is a ball of energy and even sullen Violet perks up around him.

"You have a big fan in Tim."

I reach for her shirt and tug her toward me. "I want you to be a fan." I also want to kiss her on this porch like we've just shared a date but with her kids inside and time passing since our night together, I don't know if Halle would appreciate me kissing her here.

Then again, I'd made a promise to myself that I'd never let this house hold me back again.

Halle's hand comes to my chest and her gaze drops to her fingers curling into my shirt. If we were younger, her hand would fist, and she'd tug me to her.

My mouth moistens with anticipation. *Dammit. Kiss me, Halle.*

"I had fun tonight, too," she admits while ignoring my plea for her to be part of the Knox fan club. Instead, her eyes focus on my mouth, and a smug smile curls my lips. "The kids loved it."

I step closer to her, swiping her hair behind her ear and lowering my knuckles to brush the side of her neck. "But what about you, Sprint? Did you love it?"

Did she enjoy the four of us together? Did she see a future like I did? The one that popped into my head after talking with Violet, wanting to reassure her she could be anything. Or the moments where Tim's laughter felt contagious, and I just wanted to swallow the sound. He's so much easier going than I was at twelve.

"Yeah," she whispers. "I kind of did."

"Only kind of?" I playfully scoff. "I'll need to up my game then."

The way she suddenly chews her lip tells me she more than *kind of* enjoyed the night, especially when her gaze drops to my mouth again. The bloom of a sweet blush on her cheeks tells me all I need to know. She hasn't ruled out being part of my fan club and I want to pump my fist and let out a victorious *whoop*.

Instead, I reach for the plump swell of her bottom lip with my thumb, tugging at where I want to run my tongue. Want to slip my tongue inside her mouth and drink her in again. With every new taste I've had of Halle, I want more.

I want the entire dish of ice cream that she represents.

Smooth and creamy. Icy and sweet. Bad for my heart but oh so good to eat.

I grab her hand and lift her arm, pressing a kiss to her inner wrist while observing her face for more reaction. Scraping my teeth over her pulse point, I watch her mouth slightly opening, a perfect little O forming.

Yeah, Halle's a fan, and on that note, I need to walk away while I'm still winning the game.

"I'll see you tomorrow," I say, leaving us both a little frustrated but goofily grinning.

Because *I'm* her biggest fan.

Chapter 19

[Halle]

Knox works on my yard for nearly a week. Laying down the patio. Edging out flower beds. Removing the railing from the porch. And throughout the times he's present, he has a constant shadow in Tim, who Knox allows to place bricks, use a shovel, and even whack the railing during the demolition process.

As for me, I keep my distance but find myself drawn to the windows again and again, checking on both boys. Although Knox is so much *man*. I imagine again if my yard were his, he'd strip off his shirt as he works. However, he's representing his family's company, and the worn cotton of his tee plasters to his body, forming a perfect second skin that leaves nothing to the imagination. As my hands have recently touched that firm chest and those well-defined abs, I'm already familiar with what can't be seen.

Our night together has starred in my dreams every night since it happened, yet I've been questioning that evening.

Was it a one-night stand? Did we both get off—*twice*—and our heads are now cleared?

I certainly don't feel emptied of any desire for Knox because I can't seem to stop thinking about him. Perhaps it's the house, where every room holds a memory I'd once buried deep within me. Or maybe it's the box I found in my closet that I haven't had the heart to open yet. A treasure trove full of mementoes I'm not ready to face.

With that thought, I pull myself away from the second story window. I'm mostly finished clearing out the upper level. Only the furniture remains in each bedroom. Tim has taken over my grandmother's old room. Violet took over my mother's. Their modern things are slowly filling up the space around the antique furniture that doesn't fit either child's style.

With every room I empty, I'm reminded of my own anger when I first moved here. The unfairness of losing my father. The move to a new town, new school. The determination to run. To be the best I could be and get out of this place.

The ancient thoughts also remind me of Violet.

She's lost her father in a different way. And she's hostile about being in Sterling Falls but she only has a few more days before she and Tim will be going back to Charles Town for a two-week stay with Jack.

In some ways, I'm excited for the time alone. The vacant days will allow me to plow through more of these rooms and prepare the house for sale. On the other hand, I'm afraid of the loneliness I'm certain to encounter with my kids gone. Without them, I'm not always clear on my purpose.

I need a job. And even that's a daunting thought, as I don't know what I'd do.

My phone rings, rousing me from my weighty musings, and I chuckle when I see Trinity Haven's name on the caller ID.

"Hey you," I greet. Having turned away from the window, I exit the bedroom and head down the stairs toward the kitchen.

"Hi. I'm just calling to remind you about book club."

Last week, Trinity had invited me to attend. However, my kids were back from the holiday with Jack, and I hadn't accepted her invite. One thing I was learning about myself, though, was how often I'd decline invitations I wanted to take because of them. They were older now, needing my constant supervision less. When they each retired to their rooms, and I sat alone staring at the television set that night, I'd wondered why I hadn't taken Trinity up on her offer.

"I'll be there," I answer as I reach the lower level, grateful that Trinity had been persistent after telling me the invitation was open-ended.

"It's above the She Shed, remember?"

"I remember."

Trinity had explained how once a month the group met above the old yarn shop which used to be named Sheep Shed, or something similar, but was now called the She Shed and run by Meredith Mulligan.

"I'm so excited," Trinity states. "You'll be an official Sterlet by attending."

"Why does that feel like a secret club?"

"Because it is," she cackles. "Okay, see you tonight."

"Tonight, lady." Then I click off her call.

"What's tonight?"

The sudden gruffness of his voice has me turning to face a sweaty Knox, standing just inside the kitchen.

"I've been invited to attend a book club with Trinity Haven." I smile at the idea of hanging out with my old friend. I've missed the type of friendship I had with her, and we had a good time on the Fourth of July before I went to see Knox. Trinity and I melded together as if no time had been lost when there had been decades of absence from one another.

"A Haven, huh?" Knox teases.

I tilt my head. "Weren't your families thick as thieves? I recall Stone and Cortland, the oldest Haven, being best friends."

"Yeah." Knox scratches underneath his chin, itching the heavier scruff along his neck. "They had a falling out of sorts and a silent war began between the families."

"Really? You were pleasant to Clint the other day." The Haven's youngest son and a house painter will begin work in September. His schedule doesn't meet the speed with which I want this place on the market, but it is what it is.

"Sometimes you just have to be courteous and professional."

"Huh. Well, Trinity was a good friend. The best of friends." Unwarranted censure fills my throat. The insinuation that Knox hadn't turned out to be my best friend. Trinity had. And she'd been present during one of the lowest points of my life. She'd been a savior, actually.

Knox must hear the defensiveness because he stills, watching me as I smooth my hands over the countertop like I'm ironing out a wrinkle despite the solid laminate.

After a moment of silence, Knox says, "Sounds fun, but you know what that book club really is, right?"

"Trinity told me they call themselves the Sterlets. Like starlets, but for Sterling Falls."

Knox snorts. "Yeah, if that's what she says."

"What does that mean?" I shift, facing him across the kitchen.

Knox chuckles deeper. "You'll find out. Just promise me something."

"What?" My brows pinch, uncertain what all the secrecy is about.

"Whatever you purchase, you use alone and think of me. Or you use with me."

"What?" I'm completely confused. "It's a book club." And last I remember, Knox wasn't a reader.

+ + +

Upon entering Meredith Mulligan's second floor above the She Shed, I quickly learn the sixty-nine-year-old woman sells more than yarn and knitting supplies. She's a representative for Kringle, a line of women's self-pleasuring toys.

"I love this one," Trinity states, holding up a purple vibrator like she's examining the quality of an eggplant.

"Oh my God," I choke, having never attended such a party. The women in Jack's circle of friends were more interested in which flowers should be planted in the subdivision garden than which devices could pleasure your personal petals.

I've never owned a sex toy before and how naïve I am shows by the constant heat on my cheeks.

"I'd recommend this one," a woman says, pointing to a pink object that looks like it has lopsided bunny ears. She giggles. "It's kind of two for one."

"I'm going to pretend I don't know what you're talking about." Another woman laughs as she sidles up beside the first.

"Vale?" I haven't seen Valentine Sylver in years, but she looks so much like she did as a little girl. Her straw-colored hair set her apart from all her brothers with their varying shades of brown.

"Halle. It's so good to see you again." Her voice rings genuine then sobers. "I'm so sorry about your mother."

I weakly smile, never knowing how to respond to condolences. When Vale pulls me in for a hug, I'm even further surprised. Pulling back, she points to the woman beside her. "This is Enya. She's Sebastian's fiancée."

As Enya and I haven't officially met, but I'm familiar with her from the Fourth of July shenanigans in Sebastian's apartment, my face heats again. *I have got to stop blushing like a schoolgirl.*

"What?" Trinity squeals, interrupting my brief recollection of Enya and Sebastian's moans leading to Knox and I making our own sounds. She peers down at Enya's hand.

Enya holds up both hands, knuckles out. "I don't have a ring yet, but it is official." Her expression brightens the room. "I'm getting married to Sebastian."

"I'm finally going to have a sister." Vale sounds a bit star-struck by the possibility.

"I'm just glad he's making an honest *man* of himself," Trinity adds.

With that comment, I'm clearly missing something, but I don't ask for clarification. Instead, I let the excitement of someone getting married wash over me. Love truly is amazing and seeing it on Enya's face reminds me of when I first fell for Knox.

Those Sylver brothers are potent men.

Glancing back at the display of sex toys, Knox's voice whispers through my head. I'm only allowed to use something on myself and think of him . . . or with him.

"I thought this club was a secret," I state, interrupting the excitement of the wedding announcement.

"Oh, it is," Trinity confirms.

"But Knox said—"

"La-la-la-la-la." Vale places fingers in both her ears. "I don't want to hear anything my brothers say or do. I can't have that visual in my head."

My gaze falls to Enya who smiles wide and winks.

"So, the Sterlet motto is 'don't ask, don't tell'?" I ask, although it seems everyone is in on what is sold on this second floor.

Trinity lifts the purple dildo higher like a fist of solidarity and says, "The Sterlet motto is seek thine own pleasure and be happy."

We all laugh. She's made that up, but probably isn't wrong.

+ + +

When I return home later that night, I feel lighter, freer, happy even in some ways. The *Sterlets* were hilarious, warm, and welcoming, treating me like I'd always been one of them. It was so refreshing to be around encouraging women, and another reminder of how much I've missed real, honest, sincere friendships; something I'd sorely been lacking during my marriage as every friend seemed to come with an agenda.

And I'm not surprised when my phone rings.

"Knox," I groan upon answering it, already knowing why he's calling. He's in on the town secret.

"Am I interrupting something?" His tone suggests a salacious grin graces his smug face. "Because I gotta say, the sound you made with my name has me recalling a week ago when—"

"Oh, are we finally going to discuss what happened?"

"Do we need to discuss what happened?"

With reminders running on repeat through my mind, talking about what we did is the last thing I want to do. The fantasy in my head is more than I can handle some days. The one where Knox carries through on what he said that night. How he wants to enter me. Feel me surrounding him. Bring us both to a point where we can't remember. Our pasts. Our broken hearts. Our separate years.

"I touched you, sweetheart, and you touched me. And it was everything."

"Brick," I whisper.

"But what I'd really like to know, is if I interrupted something, and if so, tell me you were thinking of me?"

"Knox," I groan again, this time exasperated. "So, you knew the Sterlets were more like horny harlots?"

Knox chokes. "Are *you*?"

The question weighs between us. Am I horny? Do I want him to ease the ache? Do I want to use my new purchase with him?

"I don't know," I whisper, answering all the unsaid.

Because when it comes to Knox it's more than being horny for him. His new body. His new stamina. I'm struggling to separate the present man from the teenage memories, and those memories keep reminding me I loved him once.

Loving him again might be dangerous.

"I'm not going to pressure you, Sprint. Not for answers. Not for anything. But know that I'm here for you, for whatever you need."

What was he offering? That I could *use* him? I didn't like the thought. Knox wasn't some opportunity to rock my world. He was Knox. I wouldn't be able to separate the physical from the emotional with him.

And the other night had rocked my world *and* been emotional. The night was a reminder of what I'd lost when he left me. How we could have been. How we could have grown together as a couple.

Suddenly, my libido dial is turned down to a low simmer instead of a brilliant flame.

I need to follow the motto Trinity ad-libbed. Seek my own pleasure. Find out what would make me happy.

Knox clears his throat. "The real reason I called was to invite you to the house on Sunday."

"The house?"

"My house." He lives with his eldest brother and only sister in their family homestead, a house reminiscent of the Waltons. "We host a family dinner each week and I'd like you to join us."

"Family sort of implies it's private."

"Vale told me she saw you tonight. Said I should ask you to come, and I know the kids will be gone for two weeks so I thought you could use some company." Knox pauses. "Plus, you'll always be family to me, Sprint."

I snort, ready to mock the statement and remind him he left me behind, but something stops me. The tiny thrill coursing through my body. The twinge of hope that he might mean it. That we'll always be special to one another. There's still a place inside each of us that binds us together, like we could have been a family once upon a time.

Thinking of family, I will be alone for two weeks. "It might be nice to get out of the house for a bit. What can I bring?"

"Just you, sweetheart. Just you."

My smile uncontrollably grows. "See you Sunday."

Chapter 20

[Halle]

"Hey. You made it." Knox greets me as I stroll into the backyard of the Sylver family home. The white-sided house with a green roof and a long front porch looks better than I remember. Then again, I'd only been here once.

Knox approaches me, cups my elbow, and leans in to kiss my cheek. The greeting is sweet, cautious even.

"I wasn't certain you'd show," he adds, pulling back.

He sent me a text with the address and offered to pick me up which seemed silly considering he lived here. Plus, I wanted to drive so I had an easy escape if being around his family became too much. It's been a long time since I've seen most of his siblings, and many of them I only met in passing.

Like Stone, who I now know is the town sheriff. He'd been away at college when Knox and I began dating; however, the silver bearded man is the family's patriarch now and manning a grill.

"You remember Clay, right?" Knox re-introduces us. I'd met Clay on occasion as Knox worked at Sylver Seed and Soil, managed by his brother who worked for their dad at the time. A father who rarely showed up for the family business, leaving a younger Clay in charge. He's almost as silver haired as his older brother, having grown up equally fast when he was in his twenties.

"Of course." I offer a hand, but Clay stands from the picnic table and circles it to hug me.

"Halle Reynolds." He singsongs my name, which is actually Halle Haskins, but I don't correct him.

Clay scans my body but it's not salacious or threatening. "You've grown up very fine." With an exaggerated Southern drawl, I sense he's goading his brother more than inspecting me.

When Knox lightly slaps the back of his brother's head, my suspicion is confirmed. Clay only chuckles in response.

"Halle?" Vale's voice has me turning from the picnic table to the back porch where Vale is exiting the house. Her surprised tone makes me suspicious that Vale actually *didn't* suggest I be invited to lunch. However, she hands a bowl of something to her brother and approaches me, giving me a hug like Clay had. "It's so good to see you again."

I chuckle because I'd just seen Vale on Thursday at the book club, but we're under the *don't ask, don't tell* rule about the Sterlets.

"That's my son, Hudson." Vale points out a boy about nine years old, and I immediately miss Tim, although the kids have only been gone forty-eight hours. "I'm a single mom."

I'm not certain why Vale tells me this, as I already know from conversations during book club. However, I lean into the information. "I'm a single mom, too." This might be the first time I've said such a thing, and the reality hits hard again. While Jack and I will be eternally bonded because of our children, we are two separate entities now in relation to our kids.

Knox's hand comes to my lower back, startling me and when I glance at him, he's watching me. His brows don't pinch but his concentration on my face is hard, drawing me into his orbit.

"Is Judd finally going to show his face?" Clay asks.

Collectively, the Sylver siblings groan.

"What's that all about?" I laugh, breaking out of my melancholy about Violet and Tim.

"Judd is dating this obnoxious woman. No one likes her. We aren't even convinced *he* likes her. But he's always ditching family-Sunday to be with her family," Knox explains.

"Maybe he doesn't like us," Hudson calls out from his spot in a hammock.

"Hudson," Vale drones. She turns toward her brothers. "What did I say about this? Judd might very well love her, and if he does, *we're* going to love Heather Remington, too."

"Heather Remington? As in Remington Auto?" I remember her. The name is synonymous with a collection of car dealerships in the area.

"One in the same," Clay states, shaking his head.

"We made it," a male voice calls out behind me, and we all turn in the direction of Sebastian Sylver, who is carrying a baby. Next to him is Enya, his beautiful fiancée whom I met the other night.

"That's Sebastian's family," Knox whispers beside me. I'd heard the rumors about his troublemaking days, but I also knew he turned his life around and opened the bakery in town. Seeing him carrying a baby, though, is a shock. Especially, when grown men start fighting over who gets to hold her.

"Adara wants to come to Uncle Clay," Clay coos, stepping closer to his youngest brother and holding out grabby hands.

"She wants Uncle Stone." Stone's gruff voice softens as he eyes the baby from his position near the grill.

"Doesn't matter who she goes to, we all know Uncle Knox is her favorite, right, baby girl?" Knox double taps his chest and waves at the baby. Then, he sweeps in and takes the infant from his brother, holding her against his chest and kissing her little round head. When he turns to face me, positioning Adara in a way her tiny cheek pressing against his, something inside me breaks a little.

While I mentally made the connection between Knox and Hudson, being uncle to a nine-year-old boy, I hadn't considered Knox being an uncle to a baby. Or how sweet he is toward the cute bundle dolled up in yellow.

"Would you mind if I use your bathroom?" I quickly ask Vale while the men fawn over an infant.

"Sure." Her brows pinch, reading something in my expression, while quietly pointing to the house. "In through there, past the kitchen, down a hallway beside the fridge."

"Got it." The smile I plaster on is tight and fake, and I doubt I'm fooling Vale who is intently watching me. Without a glance at Knox, I rush to the restroom, closing myself in and taking a few deep breaths.

The visions in my head came out of nowhere. Graphic reminders of what my body went through when I was younger. The horrible pain and crippling emotions afterward. The unimaginable loss.

I'd just finished gym class and was on my way to English. Telling myself it was only a stomachache; I'd been having trouble keeping anything down for weeks as I headed to the bathroom. I already knew my condition and I was still processing how I was going to tell my mother. Waiting until Christmas and Knox's return was too far away. Still, I wanted him present when I shared my news.

I was having a baby.

We were getting married.

Rushing to the bathroom, I dismissed the pain in my heart every time I considered Knox's proposal.

We'll get married. *There'd been no emotion in the decision. I'd accepted that he was in shock. We were so young. I hadn't even finished high school, but we loved one another. He wouldn't possibly ghost me again, right?*

Reaching the putrid pink bathroom stall, I locked myself inside, finding nausea wasn't so much in my throat but a piercing pain in my lower belly. I spun for the toilet, lowered my jeans and underwear, and gasped.

What I saw lining my panties blurred in my vision. This was more than light spotting. With a shaky hand I covered my mouth, trying to contain the sudden sob. Seated, I wrapped both my arms around my belly, bending forward as something trickled into the toilet.

I didn't know what to do. There was so much blood, and I didn't have a pad with me. I hadn't needed one in almost two months.

The tears came fast—terrified and concerned.

"Halle?"

Trinity Haven's soft, concerned voice whispered over the crying I tried to silence. "Is it your period? I can get you something."

Already shaking my head, I didn't know how to answer her. Instead, I noticed the tips of her Converse shoes beneath the bathroom stall door.

"It isn't my period," I finally said, another sob filling my voice. "Please don't call my mother."

Silence fell between us. The stall door my only shield from the crippling pain both in my belly and in my heart.

"How can I help you?" Trinity asked, changing everything about who we were to one another.

"I think I need a doctor."

It had all been my fault. I couldn't stop running even though I'd known there were risks.

And until today, I hadn't allowed myself to imagine Knox with a child. How he'd react. How he'd behave. I might have pictured him, happy and healthy, in love with someone else and gifting her babies. But I didn't have a firm visual of how he'd act. How sweet he'd talk. The gleam in his eye. The love in his voice.

Taking a deep breath, I splash water on my face and stare at myself in the mirror.

What am I doing here?

I'm a fool to think Knox and I can go backward. Or take steps forward to be friends. I'm not staying in this town, and I shouldn't be entrenching myself with his family. I need to get on with clearing out my mother's house and finding a job. Moving on with my life.

With that thought, I open the door and find Knox standing outside of it, arms spread wide, holding either side of the frame.

"You okay, Sprint?"

"Of course." I shake my head and straighten my spine but avoid eye contact.

"Don't lie to me, Halle. That's not what we do."

I huff, ready to argue that telling the truth isn't something we always do either, but I hear voices down the hall from the bathroom.

"Take a walk with me," Knox quietly commands.

"Let's just have lunch," I counter, but Knox isn't having it. He grabs my hand, entwining our fingers, and leads me through the house and out the front door. Once outside, I remove my hand from his and we avoid where the family has gathered by rounding a free-standing garage and walking down a path toward the infamous stable. The place where his father caught us.

The last thing I need are more reminders of my youth.

Crossing my arms, the sound of gravel beneath our feet mixes with the harmony of crickets chirping and trees rustling in a light breeze.

Those woods are where I met Knox.

More reminders. More memories.

Suddenly, I stop walking. "I should go."

"I think we should talk." Knox takes another step forward then spins to face me.

Glancing away from him, I stare at the vacant field beside us, once possibly a penned area for horses, now overgrown as a meadow. "I don't think there's much to say."

"There is. And we need to get it out of the way."

"Out of the way," I bitterly stammer, turning my attention back to him. "Like something inconvenient? Like the baby we lost?"

Knox's dark eyes widen and turn to coal. "I never said the baby was an inconvenience."

"You didn't have to," I yell. "Your disappearance said it all." While I should be storming back toward my SUV, instead, I stomp around Knox and head for the old stable. The dirty-brown barn door is partially open, and I slip inside the coolness of the dark space. Inhaling deeply, I swipe a hand into my hair and still.

"I didn't disappear, Halle. I was at sea." His voice is as hollow as the emptiness around us.

I spin to face him. "You ghosted me."

The summer between my junior and senior year, when Knox had gone off to boot camp, he returned only once to see his family before shipping out. And as mad as I was at him then, I'd slept with him again, after his simple explanation that he wasn't allowed communication during training.

"More emails and texts. Another godforsaken letter." I pause, inhaling deeply. "I was alone, Knox. Alone. You can't imagine what I went through. My head and my heart." I clench a fist near my lower belly. "My body."

Knox lowers his head, contrite, and somehow aware he'll never understand. The loss. The ache.

"I thought I was doing what was best for you."

"Bullshit. You did what was best for *you*."

Knox swipes a hand over his face, knowing I'm right. For all his platitudes that he left me so I could advance in life, he also left me crippled under the loss of him. The sheer abandonment in my biggest time of need.

"I would have married you."

I choke. "That pathetic proposal." *We'll get married.* There'd been no emotion in his response to my telling him I was pregnant. A weak promise he'd return for me by Christmas, and we'd get married.

My romantically twisted heart at eighteen was so clouded but it became abundantly clear that Knox hadn't returned because he read a letter I'd sent where I told him I was pregnant. He'd returned to break up with me. To tell me to leave him alone and get on with my life.

I'd lost the baby, and Knox had gotten his wish. I went on without him.

"I didn't ghost you, Halle. I just . . ." He sighs, slipping his fingers into the longer portion of his hair before cupping the back of his neck. "So much happened so fast."

"We dated for a year," I remind him, my voice rising. The time marked how well we knew one another, or so I thought. How we should have been able to trust one another with the truth.

"It wasn't about us." His voice rises as well, and I stand taller, watching as his eyes drift to the rafters above me, avoiding me.

"I wanted to marry you," he starts again, lowering his tone and returning his gaze to me.

I huff, cross my arms, and look away from him.

"Look, I take the blame for everything. The fact I left. The fact I didn't respond properly. But it wasn't about you. It was about me." With the sound of his hand slapping his chest, I glance back at him.

"My dad was a royal fuck-up, Halle. And it scared the shit out of me that I might one day be like him. He changed. With our mom gone, he loved booze more than he loved us kids."

My mouth falls open, prepared to argue that I didn't believe he'd ever be like his father, then I clamp my lips shut and wait him out.

"When you told me you were pregnant, it was a shock. We were both so young. And we both had dreams."

The truth in his remark stabs me in the heart. Our dreams were separate, not together.

"You were going places, Halle. I mean, you made it. You went to the biggest fucking arena there is."

I don't need to remind him I fell. My failure is constantly present in the scar across my knee and the twinges of pain as I age.

"And you flew away," I mutter.

"Damn right I did. I needed to get out of this town, Halle. I needed to spread my wings and forget." He opens his arms wide.

"Forget me," I whisper, raw from his admission.

"Not you, Halle." He steps closer to me. "Never forgot you." He sighs. "I just didn't want to hold you back any more than I wanted to hold myself back."

"And a baby and a wife would have done that."

"I didn't say that." His voice lifts once more, filled with frustration. "I wanted to marry you but marrying *me* would have meant you'd settled."

Shaking my head, I fight the urge to argue. The need to point out he's turning things around as if he altruistically did me a favor. He made decisions for us without consulting me. "I wouldn't have considered it settling. I thought we were in love."

"We were," he insists, stepping even closer to me and re-emphasizing the past tense. "We *were*." His hand cups the back of my neck, and although I try to look away, he holds firm, forcing me to face him. "I'm sorry, Halle. I'll say it a thousand fucking times. I'm sorry. But it's never going to take away the pain I caused or the loss you experienced. It's always going to haunt us. *We* lost a child. And I lost you."

I'm not certain when the tears began to leak but Knox brushes his thumb over my cheek, making me aware of the wetness.

"My leaving had nothing to do with you, sweetheart. It was all me. My dad's death. Stone coming home. We—you and me, had this miracle in between, and I just didn't know how to handle it."

He squeezes my neck again. "Forgive me." His plea is full of yearning and a deep desire for me to free him from his guilt. He was young. He was selfish. He was lost even though I was standing before him willing to find him.

"Please, Sprint. Please forgive me." Knox exhales heavily, his shoulders rising and falling as punctuation of his plea. Then he closes his eyes a second. "My father's death was my fault, and—"

"Why would you say that?" Placing my hand on his warm chest, I feel his heart racing.

"We'd had a fight. The biggest fight of them all." Knox swallows hard. "It was one thing when he came after us boys, but this was Vale. Only ten and his own fucking daughter. She should have been the apple of his eye." He shakes his head, closing his eyes in pain once more before opening them and staring directly at me. "I hit him harder than I've ever hit anything in my life. In the midst of our fight, I told him he was despicable and disgusting, and we all wished he was dead instead of our mother."

"Knox," I whisper, reaching for his jaw.

His eyes have gone cold. His head certainly full of visions. Then his gaze lifts to the rafters over my head again. "He hung himself in here. I'm the one who found him."

I'd known Knox found his father's body. I'd even known the details of his death, but I hadn't known this backstory.

"Why didn't you ever tell me?" I whisper, shocked and hurt all over again.

"Because it was just . . . unthinkable." Knox shivers, tilting back his head. "I was embarrassed. And I blamed myself."

"Knox, your father's decisions were not your fault."

"I know." He huffs, tipping his head forward again. "But I was messed up then. And you . . . you were this good, pure light in all that darkness. I couldn't taint you with all of it. I didn't want to tell you about it."

Knox's voice cracks. The weight of what he's carried. The blame I've put on him as well.

He's right. We were young. It was twenty years ago. That doesn't lessen any of the pain. The absence that will haunt us the rest of our lives, but that heartbreaking loss didn't define us either. He had his career. I had my family. Violet and Tim are my treasures.

I didn't know the depth of Knox's story. The darkness of his home life. I'd known things were rough, but I hadn't known how rough. I hadn't questioned him like I should have. I hadn't encouraged him to seek help, or request it from his older brothers, two of whom were in college. I was starry-eyed and in love, and believed all the things he told me about marks on his body, black eyes, and the cut on his brow. I trusted that he'd tell me if there was more to tell.

"I'm sorry," I whisper.

"Me too." His voice cracks.

He'd made decisions for us, about us, and it hurts but I understand a little bit better. It wasn't me he was running from. It was himself.

Suddenly, I'm drained. I'd like to say I felt lighter or better, but I'm simply exhausted by the confessions. My loneliness. His guilt. Either way, the truth is out, hopefully, eventually, cathartic for being aired, but for now I just cannot define my feelings. I've loved Knox Sylver my entire life. Once actively as a teen; for decades secretly in my heart. I can forgive him. I can believe he never meant to hurt me. I wish he'd been open with me when we were younger. However, I have a better understanding now. I'm ready to move on.

A throat clears near the entrance to the stable. "Don't know if you two are making out or making up, but food is ready," Clay says, his strong voice echoing down the corridor.

"We'll be right there," Knox addresses his brother over his shoulder before turning back to me and leaning his forehead against mine. His hand still cups the back of my neck and mine still holds his jaw, and we stand in the cool shade of this old building filled with ghosts we might finally be able to let rest.

Chapter 21

[Knox]

After our moment in the stable, I'm wiped out but put on a brave face for my family for the remainder of the day. A joke and a smile covers the ache simmering beneath my skin.

I'd hurt Halle. I'd hurt myself. And I could only blame my youthful age on both counts.

Being older and wiser, I've accepted the mistakes I made. I should have told Halle the truth. I should have been more honest when I left. I shouldn't have slept with her that final time. I'd been selfish then, wanting a last chance to sink into her before giving her up for good.

Hindsight is twenty/twenty, though. I hadn't predicted the baby. Or the loss of her. She had been a girl.

Watching Halle eventually interact with Adara and then ask if she can hold her, I see what my future could have been. This beautiful woman would have been my wife for twenty years by now. We would have had a girl as special as Adara, and probably a few more children.

But that hadn't been our fate. Halle became someone else's wife. She'd had someone else's children, too. Her blessings are still great.

And the misfortune of her divorce, I've flipped like a silver coin. I'm winning the toss this time. This is the second chance I desperately want with her. I can't get back twenty years of absence. I can only hope for twenty years in the future. Time to make things right between us.

As I'd told Halle when I first saw her again, we aren't over yet. We were only on pause all these years. We had things to say and discuss, and the attraction is still simmering. The chemistry. The pull. The desire. All ready to boil.

We were in love, as I confirmed in the stable. What I didn't say is that we still are. We wouldn't be fighting over ghosts and loss and absence if there wasn't something solid beneath the rubble. A foundation that started when a girl racing through the woods ran into me like a bolt of lightning in a storm.

Halle was a beacon then, but I'd been lost for a while.

Now, I'm back and so is she. And I envision the path before us more clearly.

+ + +

Once Halle left, Clay suggests I hang out and watch Ford's baseball game—he plays for the Chicago Anchors—I ask Halle to join us. Unfortunately, she used the excuse of working on her house as a reason to leave. Deciding to give her some space, I let her go when I really wanted to leave with her.

Throughout the game, which I am hardly paying attention to, Clay keeps watching me. His mouth drops open like he wants to say something then decides against it and clamps shut.

Halle's words come back to me. *That pathetic proposal.*

She'd been right. The emails. The text messages. They'd been too much. Reminders of what I'd left behind. The bad and the good. When I'd come home on leave that first time, I was selfish once more. Seeing her, I didn't have the strength to tell her what I should have said. How I should have set her free. Instead, we had a romantic night underneath the stars where I made love to her as my final farewell.

Halle hadn't so easily let me go, and when I slipped home between Pensacola and shipping out on my first mission, I had a plan. I had practiced what I'd say. I'd steeled my heart, knowing if I only avoided her eyes, I could get through my speech and then she laid the bomb on me.

We'll get married. I'd blurted out the first thought that came to me, still struck numb by what she'd told me. But I remember thinking I couldn't be a father. I was still reeling from the negative relationship I had with my own, whose death had been my fault. I didn't know how to be a father. I hadn't had a guide.

I'd stared at her then, suddenly numb and cold all over.

Nothing in my bald statement told Halle how much I loved her. How much I wanted to be with her forever. How happy I'd be to father her children. But not yet. I needed to get away and she had plans.

I didn't have to break up with her. I'd killed our relationship.

Eventually, I can't take the pressure of Clay watching me. "She was pregnant."

His mouth falls open.

"The summer after my senior year. I'd been home on leave between boot camp and heading to Pensacola. And we . . ." Clay can fill in the blank.

He lifts his head, rolling his lips inward to prevent him from speaking.

"She lost the baby sometime in the fall. I wasn't here for her." I pause, scrubbing at the sudden sting in my eyes. "She never forgave me for leaving her alone."

The explanation is too short, too simplistic for the pain I'd caused Halle. I wasn't here for her, and she had deserved better from me. If she never forgave me, I'd deserve it.

That pathetic proposal.

I'd wanted Halle to be my wife. Even my young heart knew one day I'd make her mine, just not at nineteen. Not when she had a future. And I was escaping my past. But someday . . .

Clay remains quiet. The man full of advice and analysis, lover of a damsel in distress, has no words. He can sense my failure. Again.

"At some point, we have to stop beating ourselves up for mistakes in our past."

Ah, there he is.

"Sometimes, they aren't more than that. They're just mistakes. Other times, they are silent blessings."

I lift my head and glare at him. How can he say such a thing about the loss of a child? It had broken my heart to learn Halle had lost our baby. Still, I hadn't been invested yet, hadn't wrapped my head around what that would mean for us. What the loss meant for her.

He immediately shakes his head, sensing my interpretation. "You misunderstand me. You and Halle weren't meant to be together then. You had other paths to travel and things to accomplish, separately."

"Like her falling in love with another man? Having *his* children?"

"Possibly. And you saving lives in Afghanistan."

"That was penance," I argue. For the lives I'd lost. My father's. My child's. My friend's.

"No, it wasn't, Knox. That was your calling." He pauses to let that sink in. "Just like Halle's was to run."

I don't want to remind him she didn't pass the biggest trials that exist. And when her second chance arrived, she was pregnant again. Motherhood had been her destiny.

"You need to let go of the ghosts," Clay adds. "Live for them. Or in spite of them. Or because of them. But not *with* them."

I catch Clay's eyes as he stares at me, willing me to understand.

"I get it." I nod, not confirming or denying I'll take his words of wisdom, though. With a heavy sigh, I add, "And I've got to get out of here for a bit."

I know exactly where I'm going.

+ + +

Standing outside her house, I'm eighteen all over again. With a fist full of pebbles, there are certainly better forms of communication. I could just call her. Or text her. Hell, even knock on the front door despite the late hour. But standing here, like this, rolling the small stones between my fingers feels right.

I toss one at the second story window. Despite the glass being old, the velocity of my throw won't break the pane, only clatter against it.

I toss a second one and then a third until a light flicks on behind the sheer curtain. The outline of a female form darkens the middle of the glass before the sash is lifted.

"Knox?" Halle whispers in the darkness. "What are you doing?" Her voice rings with a cross of incredulity and laughter.

"Let me in," I command, the statement heavy with more than one meaning.

Fear took over once Halle left the house earlier this evening. *She'll be the one to disappear this time.* When I've finally gotten her back, she'll be the one to leave me in the dust. I'd deserve it, but I don't want it.

Halle stares down at me long enough that I'm tempted to scale the house like I used to do when we were younger. The old tree that stood off the corner of the front porch is now gone, which means I'd have to shimmy up the column post to reach the lower roof below her window. Still, I'd climb any structure, any mountain, to get to her.

Pressing off the windowsill, Halle disappears into the room. The light on the front porch blinks on. Racing up the porch steps, I tug open the screen door just as Halle opens the front door. We stare at one another a beat. My heart hammers, trapped in a rib cage too tight to contain all the feelings I have for her. My sorrow. My regret. My love.

I want to reach for her. I want her to reach for me.

Instead, we stand opposite one another as if time stands still. *Paused.*

"What are you doing here?"

"I had to see you." I had to make sure she hadn't left town, which is silly because she has unfinished business with this house.

Halle leans against the front door. Her body covered by only the slip of a night dress that hangs just below her knees and curls over her shoulder with thick straps. Every hill and valley of her form is outlined. She isn't even trying to be seductive and yet I'm seduced.

"Let me spend the night," I beg.

"Why?"

"So I can hold you."

A heavy pause fills the distance between us before Halle steps back, widening the space to allow me entrance. As she closes the door and turns the lock, I toe off my shoes. Halle silently leads me upstairs like the house is full of others when she's alone here. Without a word, we enter her old bedroom and the memories slam into me.

Climbing up to her window. Sneaking into this room. Crawling into her double bed.

The old wallpaper. The bulletin board, now empty of ribbons. The shelf once heavy with trophies.

Halle takes a seat on the edge of her bed. Only a single lamp illuminates the room. I flip the switch preparing to undress in the dark and slip into bed beside her, eager to hold her like I should have done years ago, like I should have been doing for decades since.

To my surprise, Halle reaches out and flips the lamp back on.

"I'm not hiding in the dark with you anymore, Brick."

Slowly, she stands, approaching me with cautious steps before reaching for my shirt. Methodically, she unsnaps each pearl snap, separating the front panels then shoving the material over my shoulders.

My breathing comes ragged and rushed. "What are you doing?" The question is no more than a choked whisper. Her touch is too much. Too sensual and invigorating. I promised to hold her, but I want to touch her.

Halle reaches for the waistband of my jeans next, popping the button and lowering the zipper. My body screams to toss her on the bed and dive into her. With a determined shove, my jeans drop to my ankles, and I step out of them, standing before this woman who has owned me heart and soul for almost twenty years. Who has made every woman pale in comparison to her. She could crush me, and still, I'd never resist her.

Stepping back to the bed, Halle sinks down like the seductress she's become, then scoots back, leaning against the pillows. I crawl over her, balancing on all fours before skimming my hand around her throat and down her chest. Her heart hammers beneath my palm, a steady rhythm that beats *mine, mine, mine.*

Halle tips up her head. "I need your mouth."

She's stolen my words. Words whispered in the dark on reckless nights and even demanded in broad daylight in the woods.

As I lower to kiss her, everything clears. This is what she did for me. She wiped away the fog in my brain and filled the darkness with her light for a while.

As our mouths meet, tongues quickly seek, and I lower over her. We kiss like the once-eager-teens and the adults-we-now-are, hungry all the same. I move from her lips to her jaw and over her chin, before sucking at her neck. My hand wanders down the curves of her body and settles on one breast.

Halle sighs, arching as I palm her, silently begging me to take more. I squeeze the ripe swell covered by silky material. Then I pluck at her nipple, sharp and peaked, straining against the soft fabric. Lowering my head, I nip her through the silk, leaving a wet mark where I've bitten her.

"Brick," she groans, using my nickname in a way I haven't heard in years.

Halle reaches for the edge of her night dress and slowly tugs the material to her waist, like a curtain lifting to expose her long legs and her bareness.

"No underwear?"

Halle rolls her lips inward, suppressing an explanation.

"Were you . . . touching yourself?" I lift my head and search the room. "Were you using a Sterlet toy?"

Still clenching her lips closed, Halle shakes her head back and forth.

"But you wanted to," I confirm, narrowing my gaze on her. "Tell me you were thinking of me."

"I was thinking of you," she whispers, ragged and low.

"I'm here now, sweetheart. Tell me what you want me to do to you."

Her bright eyes meet mine, but she holds back on speaking. I take my cues from her body instead. As I drag a finger up her thigh, Halle spreads for me. "Good girl."

As I draw closer to her center, she closes her eyes and tilts back her head.

I swipe over her damp heat. "Baby, you're sizzling for me."

Halle turns her head to the side.

"Look at me," I demand, needing her eyes. Needing her permission to go further. "Let me taste you."

My finger presses right where I want my mouth and Halle arches into my touch.

"Please." The plea in her voice breaks me.

She'll never have to ask me twice. I scoot down her body and hitch up the nightgown to fully reveal her to me. Spreading her thighs wider, I lower and inhale. She's sweet intoxication everywhere.

When I lap along her slit, she practically hovers off the bed then chuckles as she drops down. "I'm sorry. It's just . . . been a long time."

I don't want any details. This is *our* time.

With another swipe, Halle hums and then I'm feasting. Tongue splitting her open. Mouth sucking at her readiness. She's a peach, ripe and juicy, refreshing and sweet, as she coats my lips. Her fingers delve into my hair, grasping at the short pieces on the back of my head. Her knees bend and lift, caging me in as I savor her.

"Knox." Her breath hitches. Her voice a warning, but there's nothing to warn me about. I want her to break. I want to taste every drop and swallow every hum. I want to please her, so she'll never doubt me again.

I love her as I always have.

And I want us. Again.

"That's it, sweetheart," I mutter against her lower lips. "Give me what's always been mine." Her orgasms. Her pleasure. Her heart.

Halle breaks, lifting her hips and pressing her core tighter against my mouth. I clutch her firm backside, holding her up like a cold man sipping from a warmth-filled mug. Needing comfort. Desperate for something that will revive me and make me whole again.

Halle is my other half and I've been separated from her for too long.

As the tension in her legs lessens she floats back to the bed, and I slow my pace offering soft kisses and short, quick licks before she begs me to stop.

Climbing back up her body, I kiss her again, making her taste herself on my tongue. Halle wraps her arms around my neck and hooks a leg over my hip, tugging me down to her.

I grind against her wetness, seeping through the front of my boxerbriefs. "What are you doing to me?" I groan, knowing exactly what she's doing. In this position, I'm going to come in my shorts like I did as a randy teen.

Halle's hands skim over my shoulder blades as she wraps her other leg around the opposite hip, locking her ankles at my lower back. My body has a mind of its own and I rock against her soaked heat.

"Halle," I grunt, wanting to be closer. Wanting to enter her. But we aren't there yet. "Baby, I'm gonna come."

"Yes," she hisses, eyes widening and latching onto mine. "Come. For *me*."

Fuck, she's become more demanding, more needy as we've aged, and I won't deny her anything. I rock faster, press harder, and drive at her entrance as the cotton-covered tip begs to be allowed inside her.

"Sprint," I grunt, knowing I'm close. My lower back tightens. My balls rub against her and then I'm coming. "Fuck!"

For the first time ever, I'm loud and proud in this room, wanting the entire neighborhood and the ghosts within these walls to hear me. I'm back on top of this girl and I'm not leaving her ever again.

We won't be quiet. We won't hide.

I'm going to love her in the light.

Chapter 22

[Halle]

I'm breathless as Knox collapses over me and I hold his weight like a beloved blanket, keeping me warm and cozy beneath its heat.

He startles me when he pops up on his hands, caging me within the columns of his strong arms. He glances down at where we align, and says, "I'm a mess."

I start to giggle and Knox laughs, lifting his head to look me in the eyes. "There she is," he whispers, watching as giddiness takes over. No one has done what he's done to me in a long, long time.

"There might be an old pair of your boxers in the bottom drawer," I eventually offer.

One of his brows arch, questioning me, before he hops off the bed and heads to the lowest drawer of the dresser. I hold my breath, knowing he'll not only find an old pair of his loose-fitting boxers but also an ancient Sylver Seed and Soil shirt and the box. The one containing mementos of us. Photographs. Receipts. Pressed flowers that have probably crumbled to dust. I moved the box from the closet to the dresser when I took down all the trophies and ribbons hanging in the room.

Knox only hesitates for a moment before lifting a pair of paisley briefs. He laughs at the loose material before nodding toward the door. "I just need a minute."

I do as well. His arrival was not what I expected after another heavy confession and lunch with his family. Nor was this interlude.

Slowly, I swipe my hands down my belly and lower my nightdress. My core still pulses, sensitive and sticky. *How does he do this to me?* Then again, he's the only one to make me feel this restless and reckless.

Knox quickly returns, and I snatch my hands upward as if he caught me touching myself. He almost did as I'd been laying on my back before he arrived at my house, trying to find the courage to use my new toy.

Knox stands at the side of the bed. His eyes narrow, watching, observing. "Where is it?" he finally asks.

"In the drawer," I timidly answer, not needing him to define what *it* is.

He tugs open the bedside drawer and holds up the purple vibrator Trinity recommended. When he flips it on, I close my eyes. This is so embarrassing.

I sit up and reach for his arm, but he holds the thing higher. "Lay back."

"Knox," I warn. He doesn't have to do this. In fact, he probably shouldn't. I've never used something like this before and I don't want to share my inexperience with him.

"Lay. Back," he commands, leaning forward, holding the vibrator between us like a wand casting a spell.

I heavily sigh. With my legs off the side of the bed, I lean back, balancing on my elbows.

Knox lifts one of my feet to the edge of the bed and then the other. My nightdress slips to my hips, exposing me once again to him.

"Ever use one of these before?"

I shake my head, before dropping back on the mattress and throwing an arm over my eyes, as if that will hide my embarrassment. I'm almost forty and I've never done something like this.

Knox rustles around in the bedside drawer once more, finding the oil Trinity also recommended. The cap flips open and then the telltale sound of liquid spurting from a tube happens.

As Knox leans over me, his hand comes to my lower belly, and I sense the vibrator between my thighs. "Tell me how this feels."

"Clinical," I rapidly state, based on my position and his question.

The vibrator goes off and my eyelids spring open. Knox is suddenly a man on a mission. Before I know it, I'm shoved further across the bed and then he's strapping my thighs together with his belt. There's only enough give to move my legs apart and allow the vibrator between them.

"Gah," I groan as he flips the switch to *On* and vibrations hit my inner thighs. Then Knox slides the purple pleaser forward, inward, and I gulp. "Oh my God."

It's more than I can handle, but I also don't move, overwhelmed by the sensation.

"Fuck, sweetheart. This is hot."

"Knox," I whimper, uncertain how to respond to the look in his eyes, or the feeling between my thighs. I reach out for him, and he straddles my upper legs.

"Sprint," he groans. The thickness of his dick edges out the loose opening of his old boxers. His gaze is hyper focused on where the toy enters me.

"Let me watch this time." My voice is raspy, stammering.

Knox's head lifts, his eyes wide.

"You were behind me last time. I want to watch." I don't even know what I'm saying but I want to see him pleasure himself. I want to know that looking at me makes him so hard, he has to get off.

Knox lowers his boxers, allowing his stiff length to spring free. Solid. Firm. Long.

All things sweet and sinful, he's more glorious than I remember.

He curls his fist around himself and bends to balance on his other arm. As my hips start to rock, moving with the vibration between my legs, Knox glides his hand up and down his shaft, watching as I squirm.

I watch him as well. Magnificent and broad, tight and powerful, pleasuring himself over me, because of me.

"That's hot," I murmur, copying what he said.

Quickly, I'm losing control as my hips lift, my lower body seeking his. I want him between my legs. I want that masterpiece gliding into me. I want to feel how full he'll make me. I want—

"Knox!" I scream, going off like a rocket, propelling toward the heavens and bursting beneath the stars. I've reached a new level of release, one I've never crossed before, and silvery dots prickle my vision as I ride out the blast.

As I come down from the high, the sound of skin on skin fills my ears, and I glance at Knox, tugging, swelling, needing relief. He stills, jetting off himself, and covering my lower belly in his own starlight.

"Oh my God," I praise, as he spills on me.

We're both breathless and in awe. We were never like this as teens. Never so reckless, so raw.

Knox turns off the vibrator and slowly removes it. Next, he loosens his belt around my thighs and massages my legs.

"Did I hurt you?"

"That was incredible," I counter, dispelling his concern.

"You're incredible," he says, leaning over me and kissing me hard and deep, his tongue thrusting into my mouth and taking my breath. I clutch at his biceps with the minimal strength I have remaining.

I never want to let go.

Too quickly, he pulls away. "Let me get something to clean you up."

He disappears toward the bathroom but returns with a warm washcloth to swipe my belly. Then he kisses me there, peppering me with tenderness over my marks of motherhood.

Eventually, I right myself on the bed, and Knox lies down beside me. We face one another, simply staring into each other's eyes. I should feel awkward after what we've just done, but I don't. This is us. We shared many firsts. And when he looks at me like he is, I feel like the only woman in the world.

And it's dangerous for my heart to consider I might be the only one to matter to him.

Chapter 23

[Knox]

"You okay about last night?"

It's early morning and I've slipped from Halle's bed. While I've been dressing, she's been watching me in silence, and I wasn't able to read her expression.

I'm here for the long haul. But, I'm not so certain Halle doesn't have both feet out the door, ready to sprint when she no longer runs.

She nods and I brush back her vibrant hair, admiring how it looks spread over her pillowcase in the dawn light filtering in through the window. Something like pride fills my chest that I'll be walking out the front door, not sneaking out that window, to leave her house.

"I'd like to take you somewhere. Tonight at six."

Her mouth twists, a smile slowly forming.

We said a lot to one another yesterday. We did a lot last night. I don't want there to be any confusion in her mind, which I could see happening while I dressed.

"We good, Sprint?" I ask, not wanting to bog down this morning with more heavy confessions and revelations. I don't have anything left to tell her other than I still love her. I'm afraid that might be more than she wants to hear right now.

"Six works. Where should I meet you?"

Not willing to let her have an easy out again, I say, "I'll pick you up at five-thirty."

+ + +

I'm pretty certain the last place Halle thought I was taking her was an art studio.

"This is Art Simms, owner of Art's Studio, and a fellow veteran." While I introduce Art to Halle, he extends a hand and shakes hers. Watching her, I see what she sees. A man with a scraggly white beard, threadbare in a few spots, and skin wrinkled like a rumbled blanket. His eyes are kind but watery. He sits in a wheelchair, two legs missing below his mid-thighs.

"Nice to meet you," Halle says, keeping her eyes firmly on his face.

"Haven't seen you in a while, punk," Art teases me.

"Been busy, old man," I dish right back.

"This guy." Art hitches his thumb at me. "He acts like I'm antediluvian, when I'm proudly an octogenarian."

"Antediluvian?" Halle mouths at me.

"From before the Flood." I shake my head while broadly smiling. "Art likes big words." And he'd loved to toss them out like an SAT lesson when we'd met.

"So, how'd a pretty woman like you end up here with this ugly mug?"

Halle sweetly blushes, peering at me before looking back at Art. "History."

"Ah." Art's open mouth exaggerates his answer while he glances between Halle and me. "I knew a red head once. Only once. Girl broke my heart, but she was worth it." Art dreamily admires Halle.

She brushes her hair behind one ear and softly smiles. "We're a feisty bunch."

I chuckle and grip the back of her neck, giving it a gentle squeeze.

"Quit flirting with my girl, Art, and give us a project."

With that comment, Halle turns her head toward me. "A project?"

"Art offers painting, pottery, and sculpture here. He's not classically trained, so he doesn't encourage staying within the lines. In fact, he recommends that you *don't* stay within them." I pause, glancing down at someone I consider a friend and mentor. A man who helped me adjust to civilian life and accept a few of my demons from the past, suggesting I work with my hands to ease my mind. He epitomizes the saying: *idle hands are the devil's workshop.*

Art waved a hand in the air. "Take a look around the room. See if there's something that strikes you. You can paint. Or make pottery. Or sculpt."

Halle slowly travels the room, taking in the sketches and watercolors in a variety of images hanging from clips off a wire. Her gaze falls to the pottery wheel in the corner of the room and some of the work waiting for the kiln. Finally, she stops to inspect unusual sculptures highlighted on a shelf.

"These are different," she says, hesitantly pointing at something that looks like a bird with wings made from metal, with corkscrews for legs, and a miniature, red clothespin for a beak.

"Trash to treasure, I call it," Art proudly announces. "It's kind of like recycling, only better. You take what someone considers old and useless and make it into something beautiful and unique."

Halle hums, softly agreeing with him. "I wouldn't even know where to start. Doesn't it take a sort of vision to create art?"

"That's the beauty of beginnings. The canvas is blank. In case of sculpture, you might have all these bits and pieces, but it's how you arrange them that sparks an idea." Art's eyes sparkle with the endless possibility in creativity.

"Art used to tell me to arrange and re-arrange. When it starts to feel right you know you're onto something." I point at a 3-D image that looks like the face of man. As Halle inspects the image, she sees the material of the structure. Broken wire. Torn paper. Cardboard container scraps. Plastic pieces. "Basically, it's garbage."

"That's incredible," Halle marvels. "I don't think I'm that creative."

"We're all creative. It's perspective. And you don't have to start with something as ambitious as this," Art explains. "What are your interests, Halle?"

"I used to love to run." Her gaze drops to Art's lap. He's missing both his legs from a mission overseas. Quickly, her eyes lift, sympathy and pain filling them.

This is why I brought Halle here. She feels broken, but she needs to see the blessings she still has. Art is the best of men, and he embodies gratitude. He's happy to be alive and able to create. His chair is an extension of him, and he'd be the first to tell Halle her legs are still an extension of her. Her fall didn't cripple her, it changed her—arranged and re-arranged her. Her energy and enthusiasm for running just needs to be repurposed.

"We all deserve to be free," Art says, sounding philosophical and hippie-ish, like he can be, wearing his army jacket in the heat of summer with smiley face patches and rainbow hearts sewn onto it. "Creating art can do that."

Art pantomimes with his hands, molding something round yet unstructured between them and then tugs his hands apart like a magical explosion. He might seem kind of out there, but no one has a better heart. And his message became evident to me after my first few visits here.

Working with your hands can clear your head. I'm hoping for Halle it can open her heart. She still has endless possibilities before her. She's just stumped on where to start. A bit metaphorical, but Art's Studio is a good place to begin.

"Consider this place art therapy," I state.

"Or therapy according to Art," Art adds with a laugh at his own joke.

Halle smiles and her gaze returns to another bird made from chicken coop wiring, legs from giant screws, and bright paper scraps within the outer structure.

"I think I'd like to try something like that." She points at the bird.

"Have at it." Art smugly grins.

"Where do I begin?" Halle asks.

"In that garbage can." Art laughs again. He doesn't actually mean the bin is full of trash, but it is a sturdy garbage can, full of cleaned bits and pieces, just waiting for someone with an idea to make a masterpiece.

Halle wanders over to the bin.

"Thanks for letting us in on your day off," I address Art, lowering to a chair.

"Anything for my star student."

I chuckle. "You say that to everyone who comes here."

"And I mean it." Art's eyes hold on mine, emphasizing he'd do anything for anyone that came to him. Offer them an art lesson. Teach them a life skill.

"She put that sparkle back in your eyes?" He turns his gaze to Halle, already knowing the answer.

"Been the light of my life. I let that flame flicker to an ember but I'm stoking the fire again. Smarter this time."

Art turns his attention back to me. "There are those who are none the wiser as they age. And then there are those who are downright genius at a certain point." Art reaches over and pats my thigh like a loving father. "I knew a redhead once," he repeats. "Biggest mistake of my life was letting her steal my heart and never chasing after her to get it back."

"Don't plan to make that same mistake twice," I admit.

"Always room for error in our lives. That's why erasers were invented. And Wite-Out. But when we take those mistakes and create something better from them, well, that takes skill."

I stare at Art.

"You have the heart to make a masterpiece, punk." He nods at Halle. "Surpass the master."

Art warmly smiles and then rolls away. He'll leave Halle and me to our privacy, having opened his studio tonight just for us. I wanted to bring Halle somewhere special to me and give her the freedom to explore herself without pressure.

Maybe she'll find answers in this studio like I once did.

+ + +

By the time we leave the studio, Halle has a good start on her creation, and Art suggests she return on Thursday night when the studio is open for public work versus his official class offerings. Halle eagerly agrees to come back and I'm happy to see a genuine smile on her face.

"Did you have fun?" I ask once we leave Art's place and head back toward town in my truck.

"That was amazing." Awe fills her tone. "Thank you for taking me."

"My pleasure, Sprint." My smile is twenty-fold from the delight in her voice, and I sneak a peek at her beside me.

Halle looks right sitting over there. Her straight hair blowing in the breeze through the rolled-down window. Her hand outside the open frame, bouncing up and down with the velocity of our speed on the highway. For the first time since I've seen her again, she looks content. Happy.

I slow as we reach town and park along Corner Street.

"What's this?" Halle ducks her head to read the sign through the windshield.

Sterling Falls has two crossroads centering town, thus the street names of Corner and Main. On each of the four corners is a store with a front entrance angled toward the intersection of the two roads. On this corner, the original apothecary shop for the town combined with an ice cream parlor which eventually took over the store. The space is complete with countertop seating and traditional parlor-like tables among rows and rows of wooden shelving and square-shaped drawers in the lower portions.

Frederick's is a staple in this town and the place where Halle and I had our first unofficial date. I also kissed her for the first time outside it.

"Ice cream for dinner," I state, opening my door before Halle can object. We should probably eat something healthier, but we spent two and a half hours at Art's and it's late. The diner closed earlier this evening, and I'm not ready to share Halle by taking her to Milton Roadhouse for a burger.

Halle helps herself out of my truck before I round the hood.

"Are you sure this is a good idea?" Her expression has morphed, wary and uncertain. Another memory from the past stands before us, but I don't want our history hurting us anymore.

"Blackberry cobbler ice cream is never a bad idea."

Her smile slowly returns, tipping up the corners of her mouth. I hold out a hand, asking her without words, to follow me.

Chapter 24

[Halle]

"My, my, isn't this cozy?" Emory Milton coos, tilting her head, and shrugging her shoulders in a way they dip toward one another. She has so much hair spray on her brassy-blond hair that not a strand falls out of place as she does a double-take standing in line in front of Knox and me. The town's biggest busybody was also one of my mother's chastising friends during her funeral and a person I've tried to avoid since my mother's passing.

The Miltons come from the founding family of Milton Peak, the mountain Sterling Falls rests on, and Emory Milton devours the idea of her family's legacy. With five daughters, she also loves that her eldest is now the town's mayor. Rumor has it that eldest daughter is also a friends-with-benefits of Stone Sylver, the town sheriff.

"Ladies." Knox salutes with two fingers above his scarred brow at both Emory and Trudy Wallace, the realtor who has given me advice about the housing market and estate sales. Trudy offers us a honey-sweet smile with bright white teeth contrasting the depth of her dark skin.

"What kind of ice cream are *we* getting tonight?" Emory shimmies her shoulders again.

"Emory," Trudy chides. "Let them be."

"Just want to know what flavors they're interested in?"

"Vanilla," Knox deadpans.

Trudy lets out a sharp snort. Emory wrinkles her nose at the simplistic taste.

"It's good to see you again," Trudy addresses me. "How is the house coming along?"

"Slow, but the yard is improving." Thanks to Knox, the patio is complete, flower beds are laid out and the lawn is under control. "I couldn't secure house painters for the exterior until September, though."

Trudy nods, understanding the limitation.

"I'd sell as is. Let someone else pick the colors for the house," Emory suggests.

Trudy is already shaking her head, knowing if I want top dollar, I need to fork over pennies first. Curb appeal is everything in selling a place.

As the line moves forward, Knox remains quiet. For some reason, I place my hand on his lower back. Emory notices. So does Knox, who stiffens a moment. Immediately, I remove my hand, but he quickly grabs it, setting it back in place just above his backside. He even holds my hand there, as if keeping me in position to make a bold statement.

I'm with him. He's mine.

"Well," Emory sighs.

"Emory," Trudy warns again as if she knows her friend is dying to make a comment and grateful it's their turn to order.

Knox's fingers entwine with mine over his lower back as we wait out Emory and Trudy.

Once they've finished, Emory turns and wiggles her fingers at us. "You kids have fun tonight. Don't do anything I wouldn't do."

"Well, that closes the door pretty quickly," Trudy mutters, giving Knox a wink before they move down to the register.

"Blackberry cobbler for the lady. No cone." Knox tells the young girl behind the counter, surprising me that he remembers I don't like cones. "And vanilla on a sugar cone for me, please."

I laugh and Knox turns to me with a wide grin. "What? I really do like vanilla."

+ + +

Knox suggests we eat in his truck to avoid more prying questions from Emory and Trudy who took a seat on a bench outside the parlor. However, our position doesn't stop their questioning eyes from scanning the front of the truck as we sit inside it.

To avoid what's going on outside the truck, I ask Knox a question after a large spoonful of blackberry cobbler ice cream melts on my tongue.

"Why did you take me to Art's Studio?"

Knox sheepishly side-eyes me as he licks his vanilla cone. "Art is a great man who has an even better outlook on life. He helped me when I first came home, a little lost, a lot uncertain about what to do next with myself. Returning to Sterling Falls was the right move, but I didn't know *what* to do when I got here. Art helped me see that using my hands would keep my mind occupied and working at the firehouse fulfilled my need to provide service to others."

"A true hero," I tease.

Knox snorts before shifting toward me and turning serious. "Sprint, you're dealing with a lot. And I know what it's like to struggle with loss and change."

"We both lost our fathers," I remind him, as if there is a comparison. We've also lost our mothers.

"The difference is you cared. I didn't."

"You don't mean that."

"Yeah, I do." He sighs, swiping his tongue around his ice cream before it drips further down the cone. The skill of his tongue does not distract me in this conversation.

He clears his throat. "But I'm talking about other losses. You lost your original career, your marriage, and your mother."

He suspiciously leaves himself off the list and the miscarriage.

"I want to help you find yourself. And forgive yourself."

"Forgive myself? For what?"

"For thinking any of it is your fault."

I scoop a bite of blackberry cobbler ice cream into my mouth and ponder what he's said. It had been my fault, though. I'd lost our child because I couldn't stop running. And then I lost my career *while* I was running. My marriage happened and I lost it because I was never able to let go of the losses behind me. My mother and I didn't have the relationship I wanted, and while her loss leaves a hole, the ache is different.

I wanted her to be more understanding, more sympathetic and less judgmental. She hated that I ran while at the same time pushed the sport because she saw the financial gain I could accumulate. She loved my marriage to Jack even when I wasn't happy in it, and she faulted me when I walked away. My loss of her began long before her passing. It was the absence of a positive, healthy relationship.

"A bit of the pot calling the kettle black here," I state, knowing he's put blame on himself for things that weren't entirely his fault.

Knox huffs. And I don't want to talk about my life status. Instead, I say something else. "Violet told me what you said to her. About how she can be anything she wants to be."

"Hope I wasn't speaking out of turn."

"No, I like that you are so encouraging. Sometimes, I worry I haven't been a good role model for her."

"Why would you say that?" Knox asks before biting into his ice cream cone, the crunch resounding between us.

"I just don't know that I'm always *showing* Violet how to follow her dreams, especially when I no longer know what mine are."

"Why'd you stop running, Sprint? I mean, I understand the fall, but you were making a comeback. Having a child shouldn't have stopped you from chasing the wind again."

"I was just scared. Running had already taken so much from me." I leave the miscarriage unsaid. "When I was pregnant with Violet, I didn't want to risk losing her. And then Jack was there, and I worried my pursuits would jeopardize us. I just pulled back. From everything."

Knox hums. "That's not really the Halle I remember."

I turn my head toward him. "But I'm *not* the Halle you remember. I'm this new person. Mother of two. Divorcée. Orphaned adult. With no job and no home."

"You have a home," Knox sternly states.

"I have a house." I pause, aggressively scooping up a spoon of ice cream and filling my mouth. Once I swallow, I continue. "When you left and I'd lost the baby, even though running had been the reason for that loss, I threw myself into the sport, determined to earn a scholarship and get out of Sterling Falls." I sigh. "I didn't want to be here anymore than you did by then."

"Halle," Knox warns, as this conversation could turn to another heavy confessional when our night has been so pleasant.

"My point is, I gave it my all, and then my all disappeared. And right now, I need to look forward not back." I'm drowning in the tide behind me when I need to wade to the shallow and catch my breath.

"And that brings us back to Art's place. I want to help you. Or let him help you."

"How is making art going to help me?" My tone is harsher than necessary, and I swallow down a big scoop of blackberry cobbler, but hardly taste the delicious combination.

"You'd be surprised what it can teach you." He gives me a knowing grin, instantly melting away the mounting tension between us.

I relax against the seat and tell myself what I already know. It's time to let go of the past. While I've lost races along the way, there's always another race to complete. Running involves a forward motion, not backward, and I need to stop looking behind me, which only slows one down in a marathon.

I need to keep my eyes frontward, focused on the finish line.

Finding myself.

+ + +

The kiss in Knox's truck in my driveway starts out innocent enough.

I lean over to give him a peck and thank him for the evening. But Knox is quick to catch me by the back of my neck, hold me in place, and give me a moment to tell him I don't want more. When my fingers fist his shirt, tugging him to me, he has my answer. Within seconds, I'm climbing over his lap and he's pushing back the seat as far as it will go, so I can straddle him.

Our mouths are hungry, open and wet, kissing and licking and sucking at one another. Knox scraps his teeth over my chin. I nip his lower lip. He sips at my neck, and I tug open snaps on his shirt. With my center over his hard length, we grind against one another like randy teens. There is too much clothing between us.

My hands hit his bare chest, while his hands slide beneath the back of my T-shirt. My skin sizzles from the electric contact and I break our kiss, tilting back my head as I rock over him.

"Halle," Knox groans, before licking up the column of my throat.

"Why haven't we had sex?" I blurt.

Knox abruptly stills.

"Don't you want to have sex with me?" The question comes out ragged and strained, puzzled and concerned. Why has he held back? And why do I sound so desperate?

Leaning back, I cup his shoulders. Have I made another grave mistake with him? Have I misinterpreted what we're doing? Are we only scratching an itch that won't heal until we stop picking at it?

Knox's hands flatten against my lower back, burning against my flesh.

"No, Sprint," he says. "I don't want to have sex with you."

"Oh." I lower my hands to his chest and attempt to push back from him, but he tightens his hold on my back, sliding his hands further inside my shirt and keeping me firmly in place.

"I want to make love to you, Halle." His words are a trigger to the past. My seventeen-year-old self nearly begged him to take my virginity, and he told me he wanted to wait. Our age wasn't the issue as much as our emotions. Knox wanted to love me first.

"And that's only going to happen when you trust me again." His eyes search mine. There's something he's left out of that statement.

Only going to happen when I love him again.

My hands drop to his waist, and I bow my head. I don't know if I've ever stopped loving Knox Sylver, but that trust part is the issue. Maybe it's more that I don't trust myself. I could too easily be sucked into him again then lose myself when he walks away. Only I'm the one leaving this round.

Slowly, I nod, disheartened but realistic at thirty-eight. I'm not a casual sex kind of girl. If I don't trust him, I can't love him the right way. Plus, I'll be moving once I figure out my mother's house.

I fumble with the snaps of his shirt which I've opened down to his waist. Knox removes his hands from my shirt and straightens the material.

"Halle." He cups my chin forcing me to look at him. "It's gonna happen. You and me. We just need more time." His eyes say otherwise. *I* need more time.

Quietly, I nod again and retreat off his lap, hitting my good knee on the steering wheel before almost falling on my backside onto the passenger seat.

"Thank you for tonight," I whisper, opening my door. As I slide out, I hear the soft click of the driver's door closing. Knox rounds the hood of his truck and stops in front of me when I shut my door.

"I'm not leaving, sweetheart." He points to the truck seat. "That was only pushing pause. We're going upstairs and we're getting in your bed, and I'm going to do other things to you to show you how much I want you."

His fingertip trails along my throat, causing a shiver to race up my spine. I chew on my lower lip, thinking I should tell him we shouldn't while grateful he's telling me what will happen next.

I won't be wandering around lost tonight. Knox won't let me.

+ + +

When I wake in the morning, tangled up in Knox, I slide out of his grasp and take a moment to admire the view. His strong nose. The scar on his brow. The mess of his hair on top of his head. The graying shortness around his ears. He's perfection.

I want what we once had while at the same time I want something new.

But the first thing I need to figure out is how to love myself. Knox might be a brick in my rebuilding process, but I need to be the one to stack the layers.

Climbing out of bed, I quietly sneak downstairs and stare at the front room. The ancient musty carpet. The antique furniture that holds no sentimental value to me but might have financial worth.

Two warm hands cup my shoulders, startling me. "Whatcha doing?" he quietly asks, as I stand in the middle of the room in my nightgown. He caresses down my arms before wrapping around my middle and placing his chin on a shoulder.

"I'm not certain I have a right to ask this, but you mentioned before that you wanted my time."

"I do," he says, turning his head into the crook of my neck and inhaling before placing a kiss there. "What did you have in mind?"

"I was thinking, if you helped me rip out the carpeting, you could have a date of your choice with me."

Knox chuckles, lifts his head, and spins me to face him. "I thought last night was a date."

"Was it?" I tip my head but keep my tone teasing.

Knox twists his lips, fighting a smile. "So *another* date, huh? For ripping up the carpet."

"Not much of a trade, I know."

"But it'd be my choice." A wickedly pleased gleam comes to his dark eyes.

I swallow, knowing I might be in over my head with the commitment. "Yep."

"You got yourself a carpet remover," he teases, leaning forward. "Now kiss as a contract."

I laugh, before throwing my arms around his neck and kissing him like I didn't just get the better part of this deal.

Chapter 25

[Halle]

Because Brick has patio jobs, two days pass before he brings Clay and Sebastian over in the late afternoon to rip out the carpeting throughout the house. The three men take turns pulling up the threadbare covering, removing old tacks, and discarding the carpet in manageable rolls. I'm pleased to discover relatively unscathed hardwood floors beneath.

Clay offers a suggestion as I stand in the dining room among their finished work. All the furniture has been moved into the front room. "A little floor polish and some fresh paint and this room will look brand new."

He isn't wrong. Minus the antique furnishings and musty dated carpet, the room has so much potential. It's just a room, not the space in which silent meals were endured between my grandmother, mother, and me. Happier memories of when my father was alive, and we visited Gigi are rare. Almost absent in my mind, as if removed like the discarded carpet.

Envisioning white painted trim work, brightly polished floors, and dove-wing-colored walls, I know I could have the dining room of my dreams. One with warm lighting and comfy chairs, inviting and encouraging people to linger through dinners or dawdle after breakfast. The rush to eat would be erased by the comfort of the room.

My heart aches from the absence of Violet and Tim even though I spoke to each of them only this morning but this vision of us becomes clear. Happy and laughing, having pancakes for dinner, something Jack hated. We'd be a new version of ourselves. The three of us.

Only the dining table seats four, and Knox drifts into the image.

"Halle?" Clay's voice jars me out of my fantasy.

"Yeah," I softly respond, giving him a grateful smile. "How about a beer? I'll order pizza."

"Never say no to free food from a beautiful woman."

Knox happens to enter the room as his brother flirts, and he claps him on the shoulder. "Don't hit on my girl."

My mouth falls open, prepared to dispute that I'm not his anything, but when his gaze meets mine, my lips shut. Did I want to be his girl again? Is the future where we are headed or are we tangled up in the moment?

Watching Knox Sylver, he is giving me that look. The one that says *I'm his*. The one that lights me up inside and makes me feel like I'm the sun in the sky to him. And if we were alone, we'd be against the wall, making out, grinding against one another, and chasing orgasms.

I shiver at the thought.

Because it's something that feels a little more realistic than Knox joining my family.

A thought I'm not ready to allow myself to consider.

+ + +

I feed the guys pizza and beer for their hard work but can't hang out with them as I have plans to return to Art's Studio. Knox had been right. Working on a creative project sparked something inside me. I wasn't going to suddenly be an *artiste,* but the concentration needed for creativity took away all my other concerns for a little while.

Art's Studio is a bustle of energy. Music plays overhead. The pottery wheel whizzes. Soft chatter comes from two people standing in front of their easels, commenting on each other's paintings. The vibration of innovation hums silently within the room.

Art greets me and allows me time to find my started project and gather the supplies I'd collected and left in a small storage bin a few days ago.

Eventually, he wheels over to me, inspecting my work without a word.

"What?" I finally ask, unable to contain my concern that he thinks my product is shit.

Art introspectively hums at first. "I notice your bird doesn't have visible wings, like they're clipped." His watery eyes meet mine. "I have to wonder if the artist believes *her* wings are constrained."

He mimics his musings by tucking his arms tightly against his side.

"Or perhaps, it isn't your wings." He slowly releases his arms, spreading them dramatically wider until they extend like a plane. "But your legs that make you feel confined."

My gaze falls to his lap but quickly lifts, full of chagrin. Art appears comfortable in his chair as an extension of who he is. Proud. Content. Inspirational.

I bow my head, ashamed of myself. "More like a cheetah trapped in a cage." I swallow hard after the admission. "Like I'm ready to roam but I'm trapped, only pacing back and forth."

"Ah," Art acknowledges, his eyes gleeful with the analogy. "Then we need to break you out of the zoo, my new friend, and return you to the wild."

"I don't know how to do that." My shoulders sag, my heart weighted like a stone.

"Yes. You do." Art taps his heart. "The answers are inside you, as natural as running comes to a cheetah or flying is to a bird."

"But I don't run."

"And why is that?" Art tips his head, thoughtful and questioning. Not like Knox asked and I'd answered with the truth. I'd been scared. Afraid to miscarry Violet and even possibly lose Jack. But the deeper truth. I'd been afraid to face myself again. To focus on a dream one more time that wasn't going to come to fruition.

Fall down seven times. Get back up eight, the Chinese proverb goes. I'd fallen down twice. I don't feel strong enough to face a third.

"Did you know that Halle means army general," Art interjects. "You're a warrior, a fighter, and I can see why Knox would be drawn to you."

"I'm not certain I put up much of a fight for myself."

"But haven't you?" Art questions as if he knows the difficult decisions I made, to leave my marriage because of my personal unhappiness.

"Did you also know that Knox means hill?"

Something in the back of my mind tells me I did know this tidbit. All the Sylver siblings were named for something natural. Fitting for the children of a couple who owned a seed and soil company, and whose names had been Violet and Flint.

"The upward climb always feels daunting until you reach the top. Then, it's as if the struggle is forgotten. There's no better feeling. You've accomplished something." He lifts his arms as if in rousing victory. "But we can never stay at the top, my warrior friend. We need to come back down in order to be *inspired* to climb again."

As we're talking in riddles, I say, "What's that saying about the grass is always greener on the other side . . ."

"Sometimes, it is." Art smiles. "If growing older is climbing a hill, and one day, we are considered over it, what a surprise when we find the grass is just as green if not greener when we are *wiser* on the descending hike. Ever hear the saying 'don't give a fuck'?" He chuckles.

I match the sound.

"That's the greener pasture, my dear."

His jovial expression softens. "Do you think running is the only way to stand up again?" He waves at his amputated legs then lifts his arm to gesture at the room. "It's not, Halle. What matters isn't *how* you stand, not what you stand on." Art smiles, warm and encouraging. "When we stand still in here"—he points to his temple—"and here"—he taps his chest over his heart—"That's when we are stagnant. That's when we are broken."

It was as if he'd peeked into my heart and knew my fears.

"You might be broken in body, but not in mind," he continues, pointing to his temple again. Then he clenches a fist at his chest, leaning forward and sobering his expression. "Not in spirit, little warrior. As long as we create, we stand tall. We are still alive."

Art nods once, giving me a firm, friendly smile before rolling away, and only then do I realize I'm crying.

For clipped wings and fallen dreams, and the overwhelming desire to stand back up and start over.

Chapter 26

[Knox]

After returning from Art's, Halle was quiet and somber when she finds me waiting for her in her new bed.

With the removal of furniture from one room to the next to rip up the carpeting, Halle made the switch to her grandmother's room for herself, moving Tim's belongings into her old bedroom. The antique four-poster bed had a new mattress that she'd ordered and had been delivered the other day, and with my brothers present, I took the liberty to set up the room.

Bed frame. New mattress. Fresh sheets. And me.

The newness of the mattress and the move to the larger bedroom has me wondering if Halle might be staying. Is she subconsciously setting down roots? Rearranging the pieces before the vision for a masterpiece occurs, as Art might say.

To my surprise, Halle climbs onto the bed fully dressed in a flouncy skirt and tee, crawls over my lap, and curls into my chest.

"Want to talk about it?"

Art has a way of getting to people, and I sensed he'd gotten to Halle as only Art Simms can. The wily veteran was full of keen perspective and a no-holds-barred advice that he delivered with directness.

Halle shakes her head against my chest, and I stroke my fingers down the length of her hair, combing through the paprika-colored strands.

"You okay?" I cup the back of her neck.

Halle wraps her arms tighter around me. "You know . . . I think I will be." She shifts to bring her face level with mine. "Thank you for being here."

Her mouth gently covers mine but when my hand squeezes her nape, Halle adjusts again, deepening the kiss while straddling my lap. I've been with Halle every night so far this week and we haven't been able to keep our hands, or our mouths, off each other.

I meant what I said the other night about having sex. I wasn't looking for some short-term fling. I was looking for the long-haul with her. Until she trusted my intentions, I wasn't crossing a line. Didn't mean I wouldn't enjoy the interim. My hands covering every inch of her body. My fingers exploring every dip and curve. My mouth following any trail I blazed with my touch, needing to taste her as well.

This night would be no different as Halle rocks over my boxer-covered dick and I pull up the sides of her flouncy skirt to expose silk panties, damp in the center.

"Ready for me, sweetheart," I tease.

Halle hums against me.

"Let's lose the clothing," I murmur against her neck, tugging at her panties while she pushes at the waistband of her skirt. Within seconds, Halle is naked above me, tempting me as she has since the moment I saw her again.

"God, you're so beautiful, Sprint." I marvel at her, outlining her shape with my palms along her sides before cupping the swells of her breasts and pressing them together. I suck one before moving to the other, watching as her nipples harden to sharp peaks. "Want to fuck you here one day." I run a finger through the valley between her luscious breasts.

Halle gasps. "I've never done that."

I hum in appreciation. "Always going to be your first, Halle. And I'm going to make damn sure I'm the last to explore this body, love it right, worship it, and never let you go again."

Halle gasps, and I'm quick to distract her further, coasting my hand to her lower back and sliding my fingers through the crease of her ass. "What about here?"

Halle shutters, closing her eyes and breathlessly admitting, "Never."

For someone who laughed at my selection in ice cream, seems her sex life has been rather vanilla, and I plan to change that. I want *our* lives to be every flavor on the menu.

"One day," I promise, kissing her breasts. "But first, you're going to ride my face."

+ + +

Sleeping naked with Halle would be dangerous. Too much risk of just-the-tip, which we played often as teens. Knowing full well that she could get pregnant with only the end of me inside her, we'd taken the chance on occasion, especially before we lost our virginity together, which took the strength of a mountain *not* to surge forward and fill her. And then even afterward, when we'd only take a moment of bare connection before condoms were in order.

I wouldn't say I was a man who couldn't control himself, but the struggle was real around Halle. So it was a good thing she dressed in that sexy night dress she didn't consider seductive and I returned to my boxer-briefs each night as some semblance of deterrent.

Still, Halle and I sleep huddled together, facing one another before she rolls over and I pull her against my chest, spooning us together like a perfect set.

On Friday when I wake, my excitement for the day is difficult to contain. The date of my choice is on today's calendar.

"Get up." I wake her with a slap on her ass before kissing her shoulder and rolling from bed.

"Too much enthusiasm," she grumbles into the pillow, but I hear the smile in her voice.

"We have plans today."

Halle flips to her back and brushes at her wayward hair. "We do?"

"Yep. Date day."

She sits upright. "The entire day?"

"All day, Sprint. Now get up. We leave at seven. It's a two-hour drive."

Halle scrambles from the bed while I reach for my jeans. "What are we doing? What do I wear?"

Turning I appraise her body in that damn nightdress. She can wear that all day for all I care but we'll be outside, and I'd never share with others how good she looks in only a slip.

"Close-toed shoes. Jeans. Maybe a T-shirt to start but bring a sweatshirt."

"Mysterious." She smirks, giving me a look that has me crossing the room and kissing her.

"Shower quick. Or we shower together." The intention would be to speed things up but if I had her naked in a shower there's no doubt we'd be slowed down.

Halle runs her fingers along my collarbone and down my sternum, spreading her fingers through the hair on my chest before lowering her knuckles to the finer hairs leading into my waistband. Her gaze follows the trail she blazes over my skin. Feasting. Appraising. Wanting.

"Together it is, then." With my resolve snapped, I bend at the waist and pick Halle up, hitching her over my shoulder in a fireman's hold. She squeals at my back before slipping her hands in my back pockets and squeezing my ass.

Inside the bathroom attached to the new-to-her bedroom, I set her on her feet, keeping a hand on her belly as I reach inside the shower and turn it on.

Twisting back to Halle, I pull her nightdress up and over her head, getting another full drink of her lush body. Most of our nights together have involved some level of clothing remaining on us but last night was different. I don't want any parts of us hidden from here out.

I tug down my boxer-briefs and hold out a hand to lead Halle into the shower stall. In this old house, the upright shower is an addition to this poorly laid out space. If it were my place, I'd rip out the bathroom and start fresh. But renovations are not on my mind as Halle and I take turns spinning in the shower spray, keeping our eyes locked on one another.

Within seconds, my mouth is on hers again and we're kissing like ravished voyagers. Our hands wander, feeling places and parts we've been reacquainting ourselves with over the last week. Eventually, Halle is flat against the tile wall and I'm holding my dick outward, sliding it between her thighs and along slick folds.

Both our gazes fall to where I drag my stiff length between her legs until Halle is panting, fingernails digging into my biceps.

"Just the tip," she begs.

My head lifts. Her head is tilted back. Her eyes half-lidded. Had she been reading my mind earlier?

"Sprint," I groan, recalling the teasing risk.

Halle's head straightens. Her eyes widen. "Please." Her breath hitches as the crown of my cock catches on her clit, and I rub against her in a teasing swirl.

"Halle," I warn again. My heart racing, blood coursing, I hate denying her.

Both our gazes lower once more to where I'm sliding between her thighs, stroking against her clit. Halle widens her stance.

"You're so much bigger than I remember," she whispers as if lost in a memory, watching me, watching us.

"Still going to fit." The response has memories flipping through my head. Me surging into her. Me filling her. When it was difficult to know where Halle ends, and I begin.

"Just the tip," I mutter, like I'm recalling the game. "It won't be enough."

The warning is clear. I'm a man about to break my own oath and I won't do that to us.

Only Halle grips my biceps harder and lifts a leg, agilely wrapping it around my hip, opening her up.

She whimpers, desperate, pleading. "Just the tip."

The crown of my cock breaches her slick seam, gliding into tempting warmth, eager to thrust forward and fill her.

With my fist cuffing my cock, I hold myself steady so I can't slide any deeper and Halle rides the tip. *Fuck!* With my other hand balanced over Halle's head, fighting against the strained patience, Halle lowers her fingers for her clit. Watching her touch herself, my dick jolts like a restrained colt, eager to be set free and surge.

"That's fucking hot, sweetheart."

Her fingers slip apart, whether intentional or not, and spread to encompass my dick perched just inside her. She squeezes her fingers together, pinching me between them, and I hiss.

"Hanging on by a thread, Halle."

A mischievous grin curls one side of her mouth as she watches where we're entangled by hands, fingers, and my dick.

Her fingers retreat, back to rubbing herself but occasionally sneaking out to circle my shaft. She rocks forward, desperate for more, and I want to give it to her, but not yet.

"Knox," she whimpers, riding the tip faster, her fingers working harder until her back arches, her lower half surges forward. She stills but I feel her clenching around me.

"That's it, baby. Mark what's always been yours."

Her eyes pop wide. "Yours?"

"Mine, Sprint. Always mine."

Fingers cupping my jaw, her mouth crashes on mine for a hot, swift kiss while I squeeze at my tortured cock, jerking fast and hard between us. Halle breaks the kiss and slowly glides down the tile wall until her knees spread on either side of my legs. She cups my balls, squeezing once before brushing my hand away to take my thick length between her lips. She looks up at me, eyes innocent and wide, before leaning forward and taking me deep.

Fuck! She's a dream come true.

My hand on the tile wall turns into a fist, fighting the urge to thrust forward, and tap the back of her throat. Instead, we go at Halle's teasing pace of long sucks and short licks across my slit before opening and taking me deeper. Her hands cover my ass, holding me tight to her face as she sucks me like she's on a mission.

She's out to prove I belong to her, but she doesn't have to worry. I never left her behind, not really.

Halle has always been a part of me. And she always will be.

I'm hers.

+ + +

We finally hit the road for our date after a brief stop for a berry scone, tea for her, and coffee for me at Curmudgeon Bakery.

"You're so fortunate to have siblings," Halle states as we hit the highway heading east, referring to my brother who still has a gruff demeanor somedays, despite having Enya in his life.

"Yeah. I don't begrudge them all the time," I joke, knowing Halle is an only child and always wanted loads of children. "How do Violet and Tim get along?"

I'd had a small taste when we went axe throwing, but I haven't had any additional interaction with the two kids together.

"Violet really is a good big sister, looking out for Tim. I'm worried she's playing mother hen at Jack's, scheduling activities and such."

"He can't handle his own kids' activities?" He probably has a personal assistant who tackles his calendar.

"He can but he won't if someone else will do it for him. If Violet could drive, he'd probably buy her a car so she can cart Tim around. Instead, she's probably organized all the carpools for Tim's soccer camp."

"May I ask something about Violet?"

"Of course."

"Why did you give her my mother's name?" I side-eye Halle, wishing I could watch her face while I drive. Instead, her head bows, and she plucks at the denim covering her thighs. Silence fills the cab for a moment.

Halle eventually sighs. "I guess it was just one of the names in my list of flower children." She cautiously laughs. "A top name we'd selected."

I clear my throat, suddenly finding it rough and clogged. I could ask if she had other names in mind for her first girl child. I'd have even thought she might have used the name for the child we lost, tossing away the use of such a name once our child never was. But to think Halle held onto that name, my mother's name, and used it on her own girl . . . I shift in my seat, blinking at the burn in my eyes.

"Tell me more about Violet. What is she doing for herself? Other than scheduling Tim's carpools and playing commander-in-chief when you aren't present."

Halle watches me, slowly smiling. "She's been hanging out with friends." Her brows pinch, and she looks away. "She's really closing off, not overly sharing the details of who she's with or where she's going." Halle pauses. "She reminds me of myself when I was just a little older than her. Without my dad around as a buffer between me and my mother, I didn't offer more than the basics."

And those basics were to cover up her dating me. I don't need to question how much Halle's mother disliked me. The fact was confirmed when I never officially met her. Halle didn't bring me to the house when her mother was home, and the times I had been present were after dark and late at night. If we were in public, and her mother walked into the diner or down the street, Halle had us ducking around corners to hide from her.

I could have been upset, but I often used the time to distract Halle by kissing her.

"She really hated me, didn't she?"

"I don't think it was ever about you. It was all on her. She'd lost the love of her life, according to her, and she was so miserable, she didn't want anyone else to be happy. Especially me."

"Halle," I groan. "I'm sure she loved you." While her mother might not have been my fan, she worshipped her daughter, or at least that was the gossip around town whenever I heard about Halle Reynolds upon my return two years ago. Married a fancy politician. Had two perfect children. Was the best mother. Halle's life sounded like a dream.

She squints at the windshield. "She loved the idea of me, but not me. Not who I was but who she wanted me to be. The perfect wife. The perfect mother. A martyr for them both."

Surprised by her tone, my brows lift.

"Don't get me wrong. I love my children. I'd do anything for them but sacrificing my life wasn't teaching them to be independent or to follow their heart."

I remain quiet, letting Halle talk.

"I wasn't happy with Jack. I was content, for a while, and that isn't enough." Her tone turns defensive. "It wasn't fair to either of us."

"Are you trying to convince me or yourself?"

"I tried to convince *her*." Halle exhales. "And I think, that despite all the love-of-her-life stuff, my mother wasn't happy with my father. She'd wanted her own out at some point but never took it. And she blamed him for dying on her, and me for living."

"Sprint," I snap. "That isn't true."

"I'm not saying she wanted me dead, just that she didn't like her life, and she hated that I had the courage to change mine."

I chew my lower lip, wondering if she heard what she said. *She had the courage.* She had the fight. "And there she is," I murmur.

With another side-eye glance, I see Halle watching me. Her eyes wide. Her mouth agape.

"I'm a warrior," she whispers. "Art told me that."

"That you are." I chuckle. "Told you he's a smart man."

Halle settles back in her seat but reaches for my hand.

All her strength isn't going to keep me from wanting to be beside her, supporting her, holding her hand, through the future.

Chapter 27

[Halle]

When we pull up to the small hangar and air strip, I'm confused. Seated in Knox's truck, I take in our surroundings. The emerald mountains stand as centurions on either side of the black strip that glistened under the sun's glare. A series of small hangars line up, one open with a propeller plane inside. As I stare out the window, puzzled by our location, another plane whizzes down the tarmac and gracefully ascends into the sky.

"What are we doing here?"

Knox puts his truck in *Park* and cuts the ignition. "This is our date."

"Are we going on a trip?" There's another plane with a propeller parked just outside the hangar on a second runway, and a glider-looking plane several yards behind it.

"Kind of." Knox chuckles, lifting my hand and brushing his lips over my knuckles. "Trust me."

He isn't asking, but he's still questioning me all the same. There are several things I would trust Knox to do. Take care of me if I fall. Help me with manual labor. Stand by me in a fight. But I'm unclear what we're doing here.

"We're going flying."

"What?" I drag my eyes away from the prop plane and glare at him. "Knox, you know I'm afraid of heights."

"And you know I'd never let anything happen to you. Ever. I'm a damn good naval aviator." He proudly states, smiling with ease. "This will be fun."

As he presses open his door, I don't move. Knox exits the truck and circles to my side, opening the passenger door for me. Holding out his hand, I extend mine, which is already shaking.

"I can't do this," I whisper.

"Can't? Or won't?" He'd asked me the same question once before. "Come on, brave warrior. You *can* do this." Teasing fills his encouragement, but the verbal support does not ease me.

Hiking with him. *Fine.*

Art making and ice cream. *Good.*

Sexual exploration. *Excellent.*

Flying. *Not so sure about this.*

However, Knox has my hand in his and my sweatshirt over his arm, leading us toward the propeller plane.

"Knox," a man calls out, coming around the back of the small aircraft.

"Hunter," Knox greets him.

As we near the tall, broad-shouldered man, Knox clasps his hand and leans in for a chest-bump hug. Hunter wears aviator glasses, blocking his eyes from the bright sunshine, but the rest of his face is hard and tight despite the cordial greeting.

"Hunter, this is Halle." Pride fills Knox's voice and hints that Hunter has already heard of me.

"Nice to finally meet you." Hunter reaches out a strong hand, shaking mine firmly once. It takes me a second to realize he said *finally*, and I should ask what Knox has said about me, but I'm too focused on ascending to the sky in a small plane piloted by Knox.

"Ready?" He turns toward Knox again before gazing up above us at the blue canopy overhead. "Gonna be a perfect ride."

"Counting on it." Knox draws me before him and rubs his hands up and down my arms. Hunter walks toward the glider and just when I think we're headed to the plane, Knox leads us toward the glider as well.

"Knox?" I shakily question.

"We're gliding."

"What?" I stop walking and Knox bumps into me.

"Gliding. Hunter will take us up and then we'll coast back down."

I stare at the glider, a slim aerodynamic machine that looks more like a go-cart with bent wing tips.

"That's very Christian Grey of you, but no thanks." I hold my ground, but Knox is rubbing his hands up and down my arms again while leaning into my neck and kissing me.

"You can do this, Halle. It's going to be amazing." He spins me to face him. "Just how I'd never let you stay lost; I'll never let you fall. Trust me."

My heart hammers but my head says I can trust him.

Still, with deep and trembling sarcasm I say, "Yeah but tripping over my feet isn't the same as dropping from the sky."

Knox chuckles, tugging me back to him, kissing me, deep and reassuring. His tongue thrusts into my mouth, sweeping around, distracting me, before he pulls back, sucking on my lower lip and releasing me with a seductive gleam in his eyes.

"You cannot kiss your way into convincing me," I warn him.

"Wanna bet?"

Actually, I don't want to bet, because I'm becoming too familiar with the reminder that when Knox kisses me, I'm a pile of goo, and I'll do whatever he wishes.

I shake my head and Knox laughs harder. "Come on." He wraps his arm over my shoulder and tugs me forward.

Hunter opens the top of the glider, explaining various parts, and then holds out a hand to help me into the single back seat. Knox takes his position in the front seat where he'll be piloting us. The men exchange jargon I don't understand as I settle into my position but still uncomfortable with this decision.

Within minutes, Hunter runs through a battery of checks with Knox and then closes the clear lid over our heads. Inhaling and exhaling slowly, I talk myself through the panic.

"Hey, Sprint," Knox says to me through a special headset we each wear. "Remember when I promised you that we'd see the world together?"

"No," I admit as we jolt once before the glider moves forward over the pavement. Knox and Hunter communicate, and I stare out the glass enclosure as nature whizzes past us.

"This is only the beginning of that promise, Halle. Even the sky won't limit us." With that, the propeller plane before us lifts and then we do as well, rapidly drifting upward and over the mountains.

Taking deep breaths, I glance out the window, watching as Knox's truck grows smaller and smaller. Next, I focus on the evergreen and emerald mountains, rippling and flowing like giant waves beside us. A blue cast gives these mountains their name as they reflect the brightness of the sky above us. In the distance, a cloud floats in mid-air, suspended in nothing, looking soft and comforting.

No longer concentrating on my sweaty palms or my racing heart, I'm still terrified but at the same time absolutely exhilarated. From the breathtaking view. From the weightlessness. From the freedom.

"You okay?" Knox breaks into my thoughts.

When I glance forward at the back of his head, the plane that dragged us into the air peels off to our left, having dropped its connection.

Knox is now in control of our flight, expertly guiding us over the rumble of mountains and a river that glistens below us.

"It's so beautiful," I shout, although the raised voice isn't necessary with the headset.

As we coast, I close my eyes a second and imagine myself running. The brilliant sunshine overhead. The swift wind on my face. My feet carrying me over the ground as if I'm flying.

My eyes slowly open and I realize what's happening. If I'm not going to run on my own two feet, Knox is going to carry me. He's going to give me the sky to spread my wings and . . . sprint.

My heart bursts at the thought. He really wants to give me the heavens with no limits.

"How fast are we going?" I question, as it feels like the world is standing still, and we are a feather drifting above it.

"About sixty miles per hour."

I can drive faster than that and the thought makes me snicker. Then I laugh harder until I'm almost crying.

"Sprint?" Concern fills Knox's voice, and he shifts but he can't turn around to face me.

"I'm good," I holler.

"You sure?" His tone still rings with worry.

"I don't think I've ever been better," I admit, relaxing into my seat and enjoying the view. I'm gliding over the mountains I love, spending time with a person I used to love.

Immediately, I amend my thoughts.

I don't know who I think I'm kidding. I've always loved Knox Sylver. Despite everything, I've never stopped.

+ + +

When we finally reach the ground, Hunter greets us as Knox unlatches the lid. I'm working at unbuckling myself when Hunter reaches in to help with the harness. My hands are still trembling although I'm not frightened as much as exhilarated.

Knox hops out with ease while I'm not quite as graceful, still a bit shaky from both the initial fear and the adrenaline high.

"Halle?" Knox questions, once my feet hit solid ground.

Despite Hunter's presence, I leap for Knox, almost knocking him over with the sudden burst. He catches me by wrapping his arms around my lower back. But I'm not done climbing him, hitching my legs around his hips, and tightening my arms around his neck. His hands come to my ass, and he hikes me higher against him, laughing as I bury my face in his neck, inhaling his mountain air scent.

Knox squeezes at the underside of my thighs while I cling to him.

"You okay?" he questions again.

"That was amazing." As I sip at his neck, Knox carries me as I am, a koala wrapped around a tree.

We enter a hangar and I lower my shaky legs, but my feet don't hit the ground. Knox sets me on a desktop, and then his mouth is on me.

"God, I fucking want you," he growls before dropping to my neck, sucking my skin.

"Where's Hunter?" I groan when Knox nips me at the juncture of my shoulder. I'm not one for public affection, let alone voyeurism, but I need Knox's hands on me.

"He's giving us privacy." Knox cups my backside and drags me to the edge of the desk, spreading my legs around him again. He leans forward, forcing me to my back, and grinding the undeniable ridge in his jeans against me.

One of his hands cups the back of my neck, while the other glides down my body and snaps the button of my jeans.

His fingers quickly dip inside my pants, finding me wet and pulsing. "You excited by that flight?" he breathes at my ear.

"Excited by you."

Knox was in his element, soaring through the air, and gifting me this thrill. The rush has released endorphins in each of us.

His fingers curl inside me, finding that spot that causes my breath to hitch. His thumb flicks my clit, and within seconds, I'm flying once again, flitting like a bird among blue skies.

"Knox." Surprise hits me at how quickly he's taken me over the edge.

His mouth returns to mine, swallowing the last of my cries as I float back to earth, and remember I'm teetering on the edge of a desk in a wide-open space.

I press against Knox's chest, the reality of our position and location catching up to me.

Knox only chuckles, slowly removing his hand from my jeans and sucking on his fingers. "More of this later." He winks, and I hate to admit my libido soars again.

I want this man more than I should.

"What are you doing to me?" I groan, unable to fight a smile and the heat on my face.

"I'm helping you fly, Sprint." He pauses while his gaze dips to my mouth. "Thank you for trusting me."

I shouldn't trust him. Not with my heart, but I don't want this sensation to end. This floating, drifting, easy-going feeling I have around him. Like he'll reach for the heavens for me. He'll let me spread my wings or find my feet.

And I'm not certain I ever want to come back to earth

Chapter 28

[Knox]

After the high of gliding with Halle, I take her on a picnic, in a quiet, deserted field beside the river we flew over. Our meal includes Brick-special sandwiches and cold beer finished off by completing what I started in the vacant hangar. Halle is my dessert.

Since my first taste of her again, I can't get enough of her. I'll never be full.

Later that night, I spread her out on her bed, arms wide and legs clamped together like my personal glider. I need to check switches and buttons which is a metaphor for all the sensitive places on her body. Taking my time, I kiss her from fingertip to fingertip. Then work my way from forehead to toes. We still didn't have sex but loving every inch of her like that felt like we had.

When we were young, we explored one another as fumbling, hungry teens. As adults, I've been even more turned on by the rediscovery of our bodies, taking time to find what makes her tick. What *we* like together and separately. I love how her breath hitches with the first lap of her slit or how she moans when I first press against her clit. How her legs automatically spread to invite me in. How her kisses feel like yesterday and tomorrow as we enjoy them in the present.

Yet time feels like it's ticking faster with each passing day and before I know it the second week of her children's absence is almost up. Between catching up on brick patio work, hours at the firehouse, and projects at Halle's house, time speeds by.

Halle decided to start the daunting task of painting every room, beginning with her grandmother's room, now her bedroom. I'm hopeful the change will bring her further closure from the difficult history of these rooms and open her up to future good times in this house.

Before her kids return, I have one final date planned for her. A night out and away from the house and it's endless projects.

"Where are we going?" Halle asks in that tone that's both eager and curious, especially when I turn onto the drive for my house but bypass the garage and drive past the stable.

"When I first returned home, I needed something to do. Anything to keep my hands busy and my mind at rest. On top of working on this truck, Stone had a slew of projects around the house. Small repairs here and there, and then he brought me here."

I pull up before a small structure with one window, a low roof, and a short door. Parking, I turn off the engine and stare at the place that was both a pain in my ass and a labor of love.

"Stone thinks the original structure might have been from great-grandparents or something. Surprisingly, a portion of the house was still intact." I point out the windshield at the stonework along the side that wraps around the back of the place. "We had one solid wall to work with and the rest we built as a replica."

The front façade of the cabin-like house is now brick. We found old images of the place and laid it out as best we could to match the original. We could have built something out of logs, fitting for early settlers, but we decided stone and brick was more permanent and telling of the modern builders.

Stone and Brick.

"Stone and I are really the only ones who come out here. Not that we don't have tons of space and solitude in the main house, but it's just nice to feel like you've gotten away from everything out here in the middle of this." I wave at the green waves of dry grass floating around the structure.

"Shall we go in?" I ask, turning to Halle who stares at the place. She isn't going to need an extensive tour. The space is one room with exposed stone on the back wall and brick around the rest. Instead of building a new hearth, which we believe the original home had, we put in a wood-burning stove. The furnishings are sparse with only a double bed and one rickety wood chair. Camp lamps are needed to illuminate the place. A slab floor was poured but a large rug with padding beneath it covers every inch and offers comfort.

Leading Halle inside, she gasps as she takes in the dark quarters. On the bed is a sleeping bag, opened to expose the red-and-black-checked flannel interior.

"That . . . can't be," she hesitates, pointing at the item on top of the comforter covering the bed.

"It isn't. But it's close."

The sleeping bag is exactly like the one we used on our first night together. Also similar to our last time before I shipped out.

Halle glances around the room, the viewing brief. "All we need is a fire, some stars, and lots of bugs," she giggles.

I step over to the wood-burning stove and open the front grate. "Might be warm for a fire but I can build one."

Next, I step over to a battery pack and flick the switch which causes soft lights to project against the ceiling, imitating stars overhead.

"And just because you're a smart ass." I pull out my phone and find a chirping sound, although the singular window is letting in the natural noise. A screen protects us from actual insects, though.

Halle laughs, covering her mouth as her eyes rapidly flit around the room again.

"What is this?" she finally asks, although not really asking about the location but the meaning of this night.

I could say something cheesy, like it's time. Or tell her outright my plan to make love to her, but Halle doesn't need my words as much as my actions.

I step over to her and cup her jaw, kissing her slow and sweet. When I pull back, it's as if she read my mind and knows my intentions.

"We can walk back out that door, if you want. Or we can stay and see where the night leads. We'll only go as far as you're comfortable but make no mistake about how much I want you, Halle. All of you."

When Halle grips my shirt in her hand and tugs me to her, causing our mouths to bump against one another rather than kiss, I have my answer and we both chuckle.

"I'm nervous," she whispers. "It's been such a long time."

"We don't have to do anything you aren't ready to do."

Her surprised gaze searches my face. "That's not what I mean."

Not understanding, I tilt my head. We've already covered some of the basics. It's been almost a year for her. She's not on the pill but has an IUD. For me, it's been six months and I've been checked out since then as having regular physicals is routine for me as a veteran.

"What then?" I ask.

"It's been a long time since someone has loved me."

The quietness of her voice nearly rips my heart out of my chest, but the hammering within also prompts me to take her face again and bring her to me, kissing her, touching her.

Because tonight, I'm going to show her how much I love her.

I had the evening planned with wine and charcuterie, but we skip the appetizers and head to the main course . . . slowly.

I take my time to remove her shirt and then her bra. Halle undoes the snaps on my shirt. For a long minute we stand chest to chest, letting our hands roam over shoulders and down our fronts. I drag a fingertip along one breast and around her nipple, watching it peak, then I do the same to her other breast. All the while, Halle's palms coast over my pecs and down to my abs, fingers shakily tracing over the ridges above my waistline.

When I dip to take one of her lush breasts into my mouth, Halle's breath hitches and she cups my head, holding me to her as I suck and lave at the firm swell, twirling my tongue around her pert nipple before moving to the other breast and paying it the same homage.

Halle's body is kryptonite. I can't get enough of her skin, of her scent, of her sounds or her taste. She's every sensation on high-definition and I welcome the overload.

While I ravish her breasts, she unbuttons my jeans. When her fingertip finds the moist slit of my tip, I pull back.

"We aren't rushing tonight, Sprint. There's no race this evening." Still, I'm eager to see her naked and feel all her warm skin against my flesh.

I take my time to pull down her shorts and underwear, sparing extra minutes on my knees to inhale between her thighs and then tease us both with a lick. She's already wet and we'll have more time to play later.

When I stand back up, Halle works at my jeans, shucking them off me. Again, we stand before each other, inspecting, exploring, discovering all the ways we've changed and yet all the ways we are exactly the same.

Her reddish hair. Her bright blue eyes. Her tender smile. "You're the most beautiful woman I've ever known."

A soft blush creeps over her skin and her eyelids lower a second before her hands land just above my dick, making me suck in my abs and my cock jolts. She lifts her hands, swiping up my chest while her eyes meet mine. "You're the one who is stunning."

My own face heats at the compliment. Then I'm kissing her again, melding our lips together and bringing our tongues into the mix. We kiss and we kiss and we kiss, until we're moving toward the bed.

I pick Halle up in a cradle-hold and she squeaks from the sudden movement, but then I'm lying her on the soft flannel and climbing over her body.

"I promise this time will be better." When we were young, we fumbled at bit even though we knew where all the pieces fit. I'd also hurt her that first time as we both expected. The moment wasn't terribly romantic, with, as she reminded me, the incessant bugs that night.

But here, underneath projected stars and surrounded by solid walls, on top of a cushioned mattress, I'm going to make love to Halle Reynolds like I should have the first time.

With every stroke of my fingers against her skin and every flutter of hers over mine, we grow more insistent in our touches, hurried for more, until we're finally a tangle of limbs.

With my dick in my hand, I swipe against her slit. Foreplay isn't needed. Halle is drenched and I'm stiff as the bricks around us. We'll play more during the second round, because there will be more than once tonight, but this first time is the pinnacle we've been waiting for, denying ourselves what has only been on pause.

"I've loved you all my life, Halle Reynolds."

I don't expect her to say it back but when a stray tear leaks from the corner of her eye and her lips start to quiver I have a response. She never stopped loving me either.

As I balance on my elbows, I kiss her tenderly, and slide into her. Our mouths pause and quiet gasps of relief echo between us as she stretches to accommodate me, and I fill her until there's no end or beginning to either of us. Taking a minute to adjust, we kiss again until Halle's hips rock upward. From there, we're a series of slow glides and rushed slides until we're both panting.

Halle's legs are wrapped around my lower back, and I cup her ass to hold her close to me as we roll together.

"Need to feel you, sweetheart. Want you to come on my cock."

Halle rolls her head on the flannel, ready to deny that she can't like this, but my hand is between us and I'm rubbing my thumb where she needs me until the telltale signs begin. Her mouth pops open. Her head tilts back. Her legs stiffen. She lets go.

"There she is," I groan. "Take what's always been yours."

Her eyes flicker open, and she stares at me as she comes apart, clenching my dick like it's the first time all over again. The first time I entered her, feeling her surround me, wanting me.

"I love you," I whisper.

Halle's eyes widen, then she licks her lips. "I love you, too. I always have."

Never in my wildest dreams did I imagine being this close to Halle again. Never in those dreams did I dare hope to hear her say these words to me again. Yet here they are, spoken with heart and honesty. She still loves me. The feeling is more than words can explain and everything I've ever wished for. Like the stars have aligned, and the moon finds its reflection in the sun.

With her hands skimming over my back and my hips rocking faster, I kiss her, swallowing her words. She draws me deeper into her, and I let go. I jet off like never before, filling this woman with all that I have.

My heart. My soul.

For the first time in years, I feel like I've truly come home.

Chapter 29

[Halle]

Knox Sylver has definitely improved since our first time. Not that I didn't already know it, but he made *the love* out of me. And my response was to spill those three little words I've been holding back for nearly two decades.

Although I'd loved another, we rarely said the phrase. However, I was someone who needed to hear it. I needed to feel it and Knox made certain I felt the emotion everywhere.

As we lay beside each other, spent and sated, the heat of the late-July evening swirls around us. We're both sticky and sweaty despite the initially slow pace.

My thoughts should be on what I said to him, and in some manner, they are. I never want to leave this little cabin or the sensual bubble around us. But my mind eventually flips to Violet and Tim, who will always be my number one priority.

"It's a little hard to run away with two children."

Knox rolls to his side to face me. "I'm not asking you to run away, Sprint."

I turn my head toward him. He isn't asking me to stay either, but that is a concern for a different day.

"I'd never take you from them or ask you to leave them behind. I only want you to carve a little time out for me." He sounds vulnerable and sweet, and I roll to mirror his position, placing my hands together and slipping them beneath the pillow.

"I want to give you all the time," I whisper, admitting another truth now that the first has escaped. "But Violet and Tim will be back on Sunday."

Knox nods. "I know. And I'm here for it. For you. For us. For them."

No sweeter words have been said. He's open to my children, to learning who they are and supporting them.

"Would it be selfish to admit I wish I never had to leave this bed, though?" I keep the question quiet, afraid of karma or jinxing myself or some other bad juju for admitting how much I want to stay right here with Knox.

"Not selfish, sweetheart." He reaches out and brushes my hair behind my ear. "Just honest. You're allowed to have time for yourself, too."

"Everything I've always done was for them." For Jack, too. "I'm no further ahead than when I got to Sterling Falls."

Sure, I've been fixing up my mother's house and making it appear more like a home, but I haven't made any final life-altering decisions. I'm still unsettled whether I'll sell or stay. Where the kids will go to school. What job I'll take. I'm still failing myself and my children because I haven't made any concrete choices. Like sand slipping through an hourglass, how much time do I have before I'm buried by my indecisiveness?

"But you aren't any further behind either, Halle. It's perspective. You still have time. *We* have all the time."

But did we? Perhaps now wasn't the time for such thoughts. Not when I am comfortable and relaxed, feeling desired and well-loved, staring at the man who has stolen my heart again.

"Let me clean us up and then we'll eat. No heavy stuff tonight, alright?"

I nod to agree.

Knox climbs off the bed, pulls a cloth from a bag beside it. He pours water from a bottle on the scrap over a basin I hadn't noticed in the corner. The place is rustic without running water or electricity, and yet I meant what I said. I could live here with him in this little one-room cabin, in our own cocoon of space, if it weren't for outside responsibilities.

My stomach rumbles after Knox hands me the cloth, and he chuckles. "Need to feed my woman. Be right back."

He tugs on only his boxer-briefs and exits the cabin, returning in seconds with a cooler. "Fuck, the mosquitoes are bad out there."

"Better out there than in here, though."

Knox gives me a warm smile and opens the cooler to remove wine and a charcuterie board with an array of meats, cheeses, and fruits.

"Wow," I mouth at the spread while Knox joins me back on the bed and we have a picnic on the sleeping bag.

I slipped on his snap-button shirt, enjoying the cool material against my skin, as we talk and laugh about everything and nothing. Music. Movies. Books.

Knox *has* become a reader, and he explains a mystery he'd recently read. With him propped back on the pillows, casually holding a glass of wine on his stomach, I get distracted by how handsome he is. He could be an underwear model in his laid-back position and with the way his boxer-briefs dip, exposing more of the trail leading south on him.

"What?" He chuckles, taking a final sip of his wine and stretching to place the glass on the floor.

"I got distracted," I admit as he rights himself.

For a long minute, he lays still and lets me admire him. My fingers trace over the intricate tattoos covering his left peck. The artwork is like a mural of images. Pieces of his life perhaps. Interests. History.

Leaning closer, my gaze catches on something. In the mix of ink are two tiny feet, not more than the size of navy beans. They tuck together as the heels touch and vaguely form the shape of a heart.

"Are those . . ." *baby feet?* I can't seem to form the words. Are they for ours or the one he never had with his wife? Then I see the feet appear to be on the trunk of a tree with bark-like etchings behind the small toes. Within the feet are two letters. H + K.

My eyes tear up as I glance up at him. I don't know how I missed it. Why I didn't notice it before during all the other times I've seen his skin? Perhaps because I was too wrapped up in him and how he made my body feel to really inspect his.

"Forever," Knox whispers. He'll remember her. Us.

He reaches forward and removes my wine glass from my hands, plus the charcuterie board, and returns to his lazy lean against the pillows.

I climb over his lap, clutch his jaw between my thumb and forefinger, and stare into his eyes.

God, I've missed him.

"I love this," he says, eyes wide and watching me again.

"I need to hear it again," I whisper, playfully squeezing his jaw in my grasp while hating how needy I sound.

His brows pinch for a second before he says, "I love you?"

Instantly, I sit back, withdrawing my hand, but he catches my wrist and tugs my fingers to his jaw again, holding his firm hand against mine to keep me in place.

"You questioned it," I whisper, avoiding his eyes and staring at his bare chest.

"Halle. Look at me."

My eyes flit upward.

"I love you." Slowly, he releases my hand, but I keep mine in place beneath his jaw.

"I need to hear it every day." While some women might find it tiresome, even annoying to hear the phrase day in and day out, when your entire marriage rarely consisted of those three words being said, you crave hearing the daily confirmation.

"Such a demanding little thing," he teases, having said it before about me now that we're older. Maybe in some ways I am bolder.

"Every day," he adds. His grin speaks volumes, like he knows a secret. His hands come to my hips, and he rights me on his lap, placing his hard length directly beneath my bare core, letting me know he's ready for round two.

And I'm just as eager for every round with him.

+ + +

Although we spend the night in the rustic cabin, the twelve hours went by too quick and soon we leave for my house. Knox has a shift at the firehouse, and Violet and Tim are due home later today.

I spend the day cleaning up the rooms I can. The dining room has the table and credenza back in place, although both are too antiquated for my taste, and will be added to the assortment of pieces I have an antique appraiser scheduled to assess.

My bedroom consists of my grandmother's original bedroom set, including a four-post bed, low dresser with mirror, and matching nightstands, which I don't mind. Tim will be in for a shock when he finds himself in my old room but before I redecorate that space I want his input, just as I want Violet's opinion on how to redo my mother's former room for her. Their decisions will make the rooms more their own, a permanent statement as to who they are, leading me to wonder why I'm asking for their input at all, if I wasn't going to stay here. However, deep inside I know the answer.

My thoughts flip back to Knox. He told me he loved me before he left this morning, and the words bolstered my confidence.

We actually might work this time.

When the sound of car doors slamming perks my ears, I push away all thoughts of my future with Knox and race for the front porch.

"Hi, guys." My voice is too high, my eagerness to hug my kids uncontainable.

Tim sluggishly walks into my open arms. He looks exhausted.

"Up late playing video games?" I question, fingering his hair and clutching a clump to tip back his head.

He nods. "Fell asleep in the car."

Five hours *is* a long drive.

When I release Tim, he heads for the house, nearly dragging his backpack on the ground. I chuckle at the sight of a tired twelve-year-old and turn back to Violet who stands a foot away from me.

My brows pinch with concern, questioning the expression on her face. She lunges for me, almost knocking me over.

"Hey, baby," I whisper to her hair, stroking my hand down the length. I meet Jack's eyes across the yard where he stands beside his car like he did the last time he dropped the kids off. His head lowers, shaking back and forth.

Now what?

"I missed you," I say.

Violet nods against me and then pulls back. She doesn't respond other than to swipe at a loose tear.

"What's this?" I brush her cheek. Did she miss me? Does she really miss Charles Town that much? Does she really hate it here?

For a brief moment, I ponder how Violet and my history parallels. I'd lost my dad, and my mother moved me here. Her father and I are divorced, and I moved here with her and Tim.

For now, whispers through my head but then I think of Knox.

I'll make it work.

"Later," Violet says, glancing over her shoulder at Jack before heading to the house with a large tote in hand.

As both kids have disappeared, I approach Jack. "Hey."

"Hi." He sounds contrite and beat up.

"What happened?"

Jack squints toward the house. "When are you coming home, Halle?"

"Jack," I begin. "We've been over this. I don't—"

He raises a hand and I hate how I stop speaking. "We can find you a place closer to me."

I'm already shaking my head. "There is no we, Jack." I point between us. "*You and I* are over. And you and I are just going to have to figure this out." I take a deep breath. "Because I'm staying."

"You're what?" With one hand on the roof of his car and the other on his open door, like a shield between us, Jack straightens.

"I'm staying." I turn toward the house in need of exterior paint and possibly a new roof. "The house is mine. I won't have any expenses and I've done a lot of work inside. It's becoming a home."

I swallow hard around the words. For all the years this place didn't feel that way, the changes I've made are improving my opinion.

"Halle, you cannot live here."

My spine tingles and I stand straighter, turning back to him. "And you cannot tell me what to do."

Jack sighs, swipes a hand through his stylish haircut, which already looks a little mussed up.

"What's going on with the kids? Why is Violet crying?"

Jack shakes his head. "The past two weeks were . . . difficult." He exhales, offering me a weak, sorrowful grin. "I didn't realize how much you do for them."

Summer camps. Carpools. Carting kids around. It's a lot, and I'm happy he's acknowledging how tough it is to be a parent, but he's fifteen years too late.

"Thank you," I mutter, not certain he's complimenting me, but I'll take his appreciation all the same.

A beat of silence fills the space between us.

"What about the kids' schooling?"

"I'll register them here."

"And I'll need to drive five hours two ways to see them." Disbelief laces his tone.

My shoulders rise and fall, as I exhale on a heavy sigh. "I guess so, Jack." I hold my breath waiting for him to tell me I'll hear from his lawyer, who happens to be a good friend of his. Instead, his shoulders lower and he swipes through his hair again before eyeing the house.

"They hate it here," he tells me.

The jab stings as he intended, and I have my own barb to toss. "And they always look sad and forlorn when you drop them off." The implication is clear. It isn't the return to the house that upsets them. It's the time spent with him.

I sigh after the retaliation. "Let's not do this." We promised to remain civil, for the sake of our children. "They'll get used to Sterling Falls."

"Like you did," Jack counters, knowing how I always felt about this place. How I couldn't get away fast enough and hardly ever returned. He doesn't know all the reasons, but he knows the most important ones.

I got pregnant by a boy who ghosted me.

"Times are different," I state, defending my hometown.

"Really? Care to expand," Jack drawls.

"How is Miss Montrock?" I counter, realizing playing fair might not be in Jack's repertoire after all.

"*Peggy* is well."

Not really a raving review, especially in a tone that bites. I don't actually care about his new girlfriend. The poke was more a reminder that Jack moved on before I did, before the ink dried on our divorce papers, maybe even before we had them drawn up. He has no right to question my decisions or offer judgment on them. I am no longer his wife or his concern.

We glare at one another a long moment before I clear my throat. "Let's just get the bags so you can get back on the road." I'd offer him a drink or ask him to stay for dinner, but I don't want him here any longer than he'd like to linger in Sterling Falls.

My ex-husband sighs as if torn, defeated even. He closes the driver's side door and rounds the car for the trunk. Removing two suitcases for Violet and one giant duffle bag for Tim, I take Tim's bag and Jack carries Violet's to the house.

"Guys," I holler outside the screen door. "Come get your bags and say bye to Dad."

One set of feet thunders down the staircase while another thuds like she's wearing weights on her ankles.

"Mom, you changed my room," Tim enthusiastically says, suddenly restored to his energetic self.

"I did, buddy. We can talk more about it later, okay?" I'm not discussing all the changes in front of Jack.

Tim steps over to Jack and hugs his side. "Love you, Dad."

"Love you, too, pal." Jack looks almost stricken by how quickly Tim steps back with his duffle bag in tow and disappears into the house again, thundering in reverse up the inner staircase.

"Love you, princess," Jack says to Violet who steps into his open arms next but hugs him just as quickly as Tim. Pulling back, she doesn't respond to what Jack said, instead picking up both her suitcases. I hold open the screen door, and Violet silently steps inside.

For half a second, I almost feel sorry for Jack. Living five hours away from our kids, he'll miss out on so much, but then again, he was rarely involved. He'd show up last minute, take calls during activities, smile and talk to other parents, and leave events as soon as they finished. He'd be visible but not present. Still, he wasn't a terrible man or a bad dad.

"They'll see you in two weeks," I remind him.

"Maybe you could drive them to me?" The question doesn't sound reasonable, but I don't argue with him. Because I'm staying we might have to share in the every-other-weekend driving.

"We'll talk." But we won't. We didn't during our marriage and that lack of communication led to our end.

Jack juts up his chin, as if agreeing with me. *We won't.* Then, as if by rote, he steps up to me, presses a quick kiss to my cheek, and struts down the porch stairs.

Somedays, it's difficult to believe I loved a man like him.

Then I hear Tim call out, "Mom."

And I know the two reasons I stayed too long with Jack.

Chapter 30

[Halle]

The discussion about bedroom changes and staying in Sterling Falls goes over . . . weirdly.

Tim isn't argumentative, which surprises me but shouldn't. He's affable and has friends in both towns. He also is excited about decorating his new room.

Violet is a different story. "But why? Why would we stay here?"

Despite my explanation about the house, and how I won't owe any money on it, or the argument for a fresh start, Violet isn't interested in remaining in Sterling Falls.

"Why can't we live somewhere else?"

"Like Charles Town?" I counter.

"No," she snorts, which has me questioning her again.

"Then where?"

"Just anywhere but here."

"What's wrong with here?" I ask, brows rising as I stand in the kitchen, leaning against the dark cabinets. With the living room furniture jumbled like an antique showroom in the front room, the kitchen is the only space to gather besides the dining room. I had hoped food would ease this conversation.

A bag of chips and a jar of salsa sits on the round table.

"You said yourself how much you hate it here," Violet reminds me, waving out at me.

"You're right. I did say that, but I've changed my mind." And my heart. I chew on my lower lip, holding back thoughts of Knox. He's giving me this night with my kids, but he wants to have dinner with us here at the house in two nights. I'm nervous and excited, and concerned with Violet's vehement arguing.

"What happened at Dad's?"

"Nothing," she snaps.

And we're back to single word answers. Giving her a look that says I don't believe her, I cross my arms and wait. She mirrors my position, leaning back in her chair with her arms folded over her chest.

Tim lowers his head, as Violet and I stare each other down.

"Seriously, what's going on?"

Violet immediately stands. "You wouldn't understand." Then she storms out of the room.

My mouth falls open. *What's happening here?* While I accept that Violet is growing up, we've always been close. I don't want her shutting me out and I prepare to follow her when Tim speaks up.

"Violet and Dad fought almost every day."

"Why didn't someone tell me?" I lower onto a chair across from Tim. Every phone call was rushed but the kids seemed happy, busy.

"Dad didn't want you to know," he innocently admits, before reaching for a chip and dipping it in the salsa.

"Still, Violet should have told me." And not my twelve-year-old son.

Tim shrugs. "She didn't want you to worry about us. *She could handle it.*" Tim rolls his eyes before chomping on the chip, crunching away as I process what he said. Their visit was exactly as I imagined. Violet played second in command . . . to me . . . in my absence.

"I'm sorry, buddy. Was it rough?"

He shrugs again. "Dad was Dad. And Miss Montrock was around a lot."

"I'm sorry," I say again, uncertain how to respond regarding her presence.

He shrugs once more, reaching for another chip. "You won't ever fall in love again, though, right, Mom?"

I stare at him, wondering how I'm going to explain that I never fell out of love with a certain man.

Instead, I grab a chip from the bag, fill it with salsa, and stuff my mouth.

+ + +

"How was tonight?" Knox asks when we're on the phone later that night.

"Well, Violet and I got into it within fifteen minutes of her being home. Tim told me she did everything, as I suspected. And she fought with Jack every day she was there."

Knox is quiet for a second before stating, "I don't know Violet, but I know you. You raised a responsible girl and while it shouldn't have been her responsibility, she did it. She handled it."

"That's exactly what Tim said with a giant eyeroll, and he's not the eye-roller. Violet is."

Knox chuckles. "What was the fight with you about?"

I swallow, glancing out the living room window. I'm standing in the middle of the dark room, wondering what to do with all this furniture I don't want.

"I'm thinking of staying in Sterling Falls."

"Really?" Knox's voice cracks, and I hear the sound of a blinker clicking on.

"Where are you?"

"Let's get back to what you just said. You're going to stay in Sterling Falls?"

"I said I'm *thinking* about it." But despite the defensive words, I can't fight a smile. Since last night, I've been on a high I hadn't anticipated upon first seeing Knox Sylver again. I could blame it on the sex. For a woman who hasn't had any in a year, the connection was unprecedented. But the truth is that connection wouldn't have happened with anyone other than Knox.

However, I don't want him thinking I'm staying for him alone. It wouldn't be fair to put that kind of pressure on him. I meant what I said to the kids, staying would be a fresh start for them, for me, for us.

"Let me convince you to move from the thinking stage to the doing stage."

"How?" I laugh.

"Come outside."

I rush to the window, glancing up and down the street, but I don't see his truck.

"Go around the back of the garage."

Spinning toward the back exit of the house, I giggle, still clutching the phone to my ear. When we were younger, under the guise of taking out the garbage, I'd meet Knox behind the free-standing structure late at night for a few stolen moments and some heavy kisses.

Pushing through the back door, I step onto the patio Knox built and rush behind the smaller building. Knox catches me as I leap for him. With my arms tight around his neck and his banded around my waist, we stand in this embrace.

"God, I didn't know how badly I needed a hug," I mutter to his neck, inhaling his mountain scent.

"I'll be here to give you as many hugs as you need." Knox tightens his hold and I kiss his neck. The movement has Knox releasing me a little, but only enough to pull back and kiss me, hard and fierce, as if imprinting on me.

If I'm staying, I'm his again.

Rushing into another relationship after my divorce might not be the best idea, but Jack and I were separated long before we legally divorced.

And this is Knox. We've been a slow burn for twenty years.

+ + +

On Tuesday, Knox arrives at exactly six for dinner. He holds a bouquet of daisies in his hand and presents them to me with a kiss to my cheek.

"You look beautiful," he mutters, before pulling back.

Wearing shorts and a loose-fitting top, I brush off the compliment. My bedroom is a disaster as I didn't know what to wear, until I finally reminded myself this wasn't prom. It's simply dinner. And I'm not serving a five-course meal. We're having tacos. The meal is a favorite of both kids plus they can be actively involved in preparation, selecting whatever toppings they'd like which typically means opening the package of cheese for Tim and dicing up peppers and onions for Violet.

"Come on in." I'm nervous but it's not like Tim and Violet haven't met Knox before. We went axe throwing together. Tim already thinks Knox hangs the moon, or at least a few stars. Violet is indifferent, orbiting only her world lately.

"Hey, Dash." Knox lifts a hand to greet my son.

In response, Tim steps up and high-fives him before returning to the counter to pour the cheese from the package into a bowl. The layout of this kitchen isn't conducive for multiple people working on the limited counterspace. If I stay, one thing I'll need to budget for in the future is a kitchen remodel.

"Violet," Knox addresses her.

She lifts her chin, tipping it upward at him with a soft, "Hey."

I don't care for her sullen attitude, but I need to pick my battles, and this cool greeting isn't one of them.

"What can I do to help?" Knox claps his hands before affectionately squeezing Tim's shoulders.

Tim glances up at him and smiles. "I've got the cheese." He proudly holds up the bowl.

"Looks great. How'd you cut every piece so perfectly?" Knox teases.

"I *didn't* cut the cheese," Tim replies.

"You didn't?" Knox tips a brow, smiling at the implication, knowing Tim walked right into that set up. Little boys only grow up to be immature men at times.

"Sure smells like you cut the cheese," Violet adds, the first hint of a smile in forty-eight hours curls her lips. Then she quickly straightens her mouth, as if momentarily forgetting she's mad, and returns to the task of slicing peppers.

"Whoever smelt it, dealt it," Tim counters, sniffing the air.

"Okay, guys. We are not discussing farts." Still, I laugh.

"Who said anything about farts?" Knox chuckles. "I was only talking about cutting the cheese."

Tim laughs harder, reaching up to fist bump Knox.

"You," I mutter, pointing at Knox with the wooden spoon I was using to stir the ground beef and seasonings in a skillet.

Knox takes a step forward, but abruptly halts. I predict what he intended to do. He was going to come up behind me, wrap his arms around my waist, and kiss my neck. I might have added that last move into the fantasy, but his quick stop and eye-shift to Violet terminated any action.

"Dinner in ten," I call out. "Tim, set the table. Knox, would you like a beer?"

"Sure," Knox replies.

Typically, I'd have a margarita with tacos, but tonight, I reach for two beers in the fridge and hand one to Knox. He twists the top on the one I offer him, and hands it back to me, suggesting he opened it for me, and then he takes the second one I hold.

"Cheers." He taps the neck of his bottle against mine and drinks.

I take a sip of mine as well. I haven't had a beer in a long, long time.

"Since when do you drink beer?" Tim asks, returning to the kitchen for silverware.

"Since it's hot and I'm thirsty," I say, leaning forward to rustle his hair. When I stand upright, I catch Violet glancing from me to Knox and back.

"Seems Mom is full of surprises lately. Maybe she *changed her mind* about liking beer."

"Violet," I grumble in warning.

"A woman has a right to change her mind, right, Mom?" Tim says.

I glance at Knox before looking at Tim. "Who told you that?"

Tim shrugs. "Dad."

"Why would he say that?" I hesitantly chuckle, knowing it isn't like Jack to make such a comment. The statement implies women are fickle instead of complimenting them for being intelligent, introspective, and reflective in decision making. Not to mention, the comment lumps women together in a derogatory way compared to men who are just as opinion-flipping as women can be. Sometimes even worse.

"He says you'll change your mind and move home."

Knox stiffens, pausing his beer half-way to his mouth. Violet hisses Tim's name but my son doesn't hear anything wrong in what he's said.

"We talked about this the other night," I remind Tim before shifting my gaze to Knox.

"I know." Not a hint of concern is in Tim's voice as he repeats what I said to him. "Home is wherever the three of us are. You, me, and Violet."

"And *our* home is going to be here. In Sterling Falls," I state as a reminder.

Tim purses his lips in a knowing smirk and nods once to accept the statement.

"For now," Violet mutters. "Until you change your mind again."

My mouth pops open to reprimand Violet for her tone and her comment, but her phone buzzes in her back pocket. She quickly reaches for it, reads the screen, and mumbles, "I'll be right back."

While Violet rushes out of the room, Knox glances at the peppers and onions in a state of mid-chopping.

"She's almost fifteen," I comment to Knox as if that explains anything.

"Practically a woman," he states, before taking a long pull of his beer and nods at the cutting board. "Has the right to change to her mind."

I laugh, shaking my head at the nonsense Jack spewed. I'm not moving back to Charles Town, Jack's house, or any other implication my ex might consider the term home means.

Violet and Tim are my home, and the three of us are here. Would Knox be willing to join our little triangle?

With Violet's sudden disappearance and Tim returned to the dining room with silverware, Knox steps up behind me and presses a quick kiss to my neck.

"It's going to be okay, Sprint. You. Them. Us." He pauses, meeting my eyes and holding his gaze steady. "You aren't changing your mind, are you, though?"

The vulnerability in his tone melts my insides. "You might be stuck with me this time, Knox Sylver."

Slowly, a grin curls his mouth and I want nothing more than to tug him to me and reassure him I'm not leaving Sterling Falls.

"Not stuck," he clarifies. "You never left me, sweetheart." His thick hand pats over his left pec.

And I'm leaning in for that kiss I desperately want when Tim reenters the room, jabbering away about how he's decided to try out for the local soccer team. If he noticed anything, he doesn't mention it, and I return to stirring the sizzling ground beef, feeling happier than I've ever felt doing such a mundane thing.

Chapter 31

[Halle]

The following night, it's almost eleven o'clock when I hear a light rapping on my bedroom window. I nearly scream when I see the outline of a man crouched outside the pane.

Knox?

"What are you doing?" I snicker while opening the window. I glance around him for evidence of how he got onto the awning roof that overhangs the front porch. Even though I've moved bedrooms, one window still faces the front yard.

"Scaled the porch column." He's a little breathless, and a vein on his neck throbs, but he appears unfazed by the fact he climbed up to my bedroom.

"What are you doing *here*?" I question, glancing over my shoulder to my open bedroom door. When Tim falls asleep, he's out. As the saying goes son up to son down, he's a busy boy, but once he closes his eyes, he's down for the night. Violet is a lighter sleeper, but she's also in her room, certain to have headphones in her ears and watching something on her phone.

Still, I rush to my bedroom door and close it before returning to the window.

"Let me in," Knox mutters.

"You shouldn't be here like this," I say. At the same time, I lift the screen, and he clambers through the window, knocking his foot against the lower sash and banging the side of his head on the upper one.

"Ow," he whines, rubbing his temple as I reach for his hair. Lifting my arm gives him the advantage, and he wraps his around me, capturing my mouth and tackling me to my bed. The old frame squeaks as it scraps against the hardwood.

"Knox," I warn, tipping my head to glance at my bedroom door.

"I know. We need to be quiet." His lowered tone and that phrase draws me back to him, catching on his gaze as he slowly smiles. "I had to see you. Needed to kiss you."

I hum to agree before his mouth is on mine again. "This is so risky," I whisper against his lips.

"Just like old times," he states, reminding me once more of us as randy teens.

"It's a little different this time. My *kids* are down the hall."

"Then you better stay silent." He nips at my breast through the night dress I'm wearing and covers my mouth with his thick hand. "I need to be inside you again."

My eyes widen, mouth still covered, but I nod to agree. As if I need to feel him again to remind myself what happened in that cabin on his property was real and not a dream.

Quickly, Knox lifts my nightgown and removes my underwear, dipping his head between my thighs. I cry out at the first lap and Knox lifts his head.

"Shh, Sprint, or we're going to get caught."

The way he's looking at me, the chance sends a thrill through me. Not that I want my children to walk in, but I'm thrown back in time to the risk of rushing, quiet and hurried.

Knox returns between my thighs, swiping at my slit with his thick tongue before focusing on my clit. Between the panic of Violet and Tim down the hall and the fear I won't orgasm in rapid time, I freeze up. Only Knox reads my body and doubles down. His fingers join the mix with his mouth, easily sliding into me, filling me while the tip of his tongue flicks at my sensitive nub.

I grip the sides of his head, lifting my own to watch Knox devour me. To my surprise, he's watching me in return, eyes dancing with delight and hunger. He curls his fingers inside me and sucks my clit hard.

Digging my teeth into my lower lip, to suppress a groan of relief, I break. Like the haste of a race, a sudden jolt shoots through me, then a rush down the middle, and quickly I'm crossing the finish line, victorious and out of breath.

Within seconds, Knox stands, unbuckles his belt, shoves down his pants and underwear in one move and kicks off his shoes. He struggles with his socks and then stands tall to remove his shirt, giving me a momentary view of his sculpted body. I shouldn't have been surprised that he could shimmy up a porch column and scramble onto a roof. He's been trained for such things through the firehouse, or maybe even before that, through the military.

I don't have time to ponder or admire his physique long before he grips my ankles and flips me to my belly. With a sharp squeal, thankfully aimed at the mattress, I'm suddenly face down with Knox crawling over my back.

"Gonna be fast, sweetheart. Stay quiet."

Wishful thinking. Knox tips up my hips, forcing me on my knees and slides into me with one thrust. I turn my face to the mattress again, fighting a yelp before placing my cheek to the rumpled surface. The bed creaks with each energetic thrust. While the mattress is new, my grandmother's bed frame and four-posts are not, and the frame needs to be tightened if we plan to do this again.

And God, do I hope we do it again in here.

Noting the noise, Knox wraps an arm around me and lowers us to our sides, never separating from me. I open my legs, prepared to slip one over his hip but Knox brushes it back, forcing me to clamp my legs together. I'm bent in half with him tightly secured behind me, hammering into me with the tilt of his hips.

"Nothing has ever felt better than this. You. Us." Knox mutters to my neck as he moves faster, causing the bed to shift. With my arms near my head, I clutch the pillow, silently agreeing with him.

This. Us. Home.

Knox stills and I feel him pulsing inside me, filling me, making me whole. I relax into our position, still breathless from my own orgasm and the energetic rush of Knox's.

He lets out a huff behind me, placing his face in my hair, and chuckles. "Jesus."

"Nope. Just Halle."

He laughs a little lighter, but still quiet. "You've never been *just* anything, Halle. You are my heart and my soul."

I melt into his words before swiftly spinning to kiss him, being a little less hurried.

And content with my decision to stay in Sterling Falls so I can spend more time in this man's arms.

+ + +

[Knox]

"I wish I could stay," I eventually mutter, with Halle still wrapped up in my arms. However, I won't ask because I don't want Halle's kids to find us like this.

"I know," she whispers, silently agreeing I need to go.

Slipping from her bed, I quickly dress, staring down at Halle mussed up and gorgeous. A soft, sleepy smile graces her face. Leaning in for a kiss, I whisper, "I love you."

"I love you." Her eyes light up before I return to the window and slip out the way I entered.

It's after one o'clock in the morning when I land with a thud in front of Halle's house. Having slid down the column and then hopping off the edge of the porch, I stand upright and catch my balance with one foot behind me and abruptly pause.

"Violet?" I narrow my eyes in the darkness at the girl on the front porch, stepping back from a taller, male figure, as if caught in an embrace. *Was she kissing him?*

"What are you doing out here?" There's an edge to my voice, fatherly and concerned, that has no business being present.

"What are *you* doing here?" she counters, quickly wiping the guilty expression off her face and stepping closer to the porch railing.

Ignoring her question for another of my own, I ask, "Does your mother know you're out here? Who's up there with you?"

She's fourteen going on fifteen, and while I have no reason to judge innocent actions like kissing on a front porch, I'm still worried. It's the middle of the night.

"It's no one," Violet says at the same time a male voice guiltily croaks, "Hey, Knox.

My eyes squint as if that will help me recognize the voice better. "Barnett?"

Barnett Matthews works for my brother at Curmudgeon Bakery. A little over a week ago there was an issue with him, but Sebastian made a deal with Barnett in hopes to keep him out of trouble and headed to college this fall.

"Dude, she's fourteen," I scoff, stalking closer to the front porch.

Barnett's head whips toward Violet. "You said you were sixteen."

It shouldn't matter. Barnett recently graduated from high school. He's leaving in a few weeks for WVU.

Violet's mouth pops open as if about to correct Barnett, then she turns on me. "You ruin everything." With that, she spins toward the front door, opens the screen, which screeches through the quiet night like a howling coyote, and then slams the solid door.

Instantly, the light in Halle's room flips on and I move closer to the house, prepared to storm the porch and intercede between mother and daughter.

But first, I need to talk to Barnett. "I can pretend I didn't see anything, but this is the last time you contact her." I stand my ground as the lanky teen bows his head.

Barnett is a good kid who's had a troubled past, but his aunt has raised him better than this. He's the legal age for trouble with a girl younger than him. One *not* even officially in high school yet.

"She said she was sixteen," he repeats, slowly stepping down the porch stairs.

"Well, she's not," I remind him. "How the hell did you even meet her?"

Halle's been concerned that Violet hasn't made any friends in Sterling Falls, keeping to herself when she first came to the house.

Having only been back a few days from her father's, she hasn't gone anywhere.

"Online."

Ah, the internet. The new era of next generation connections.

"Risky business, man," I warn him. "Especially when it turns out like this."

"She said she was a junior."

I tilt my head, staring at him as best I can in the dark yard. "And you just graduated. Do yourself a favor, be the man I know you are," I state reminding him again of his eighteen-years. "Walk away before you break her heart."

Before she loves you and you have plans to leave. Even if this were only a summer fling, one destined to end soon, their age difference has legal implications for Barnett.

He turns toward the house where there's evidence of yelling somewhere inside.

"Sounds like you might have already done that," Barnett chides, without malice in his voice but my anger is growing.

"Get out of here, Barnett."

His shoulders droop. "Are you going to tell Sebastian about this? How I fucked up again."

Slowly, I shake my head. "I'm hoping you've learned your lesson faster this time around."

I'm not certain how long the relationship has been going on between Barnett and Violet, or whatever the heck kids call it these days, but I'm giving him the benefit of the doubt that it's over now.

"Noted," Barnett offers, before quickly crossing the lawn to a truck parked in the street.

For half a second, my heart hurts for the kid, as I recall sneaking into this house for a girl. However, *that* girl was closer to my age back then. I face the house, and almost chuckle when I consider I'm thirty-nine and still sneaking into this place for the woman inside.

A woman whose voice carries, and a girl's responds.

I'm torn between intervening or letting mother and daughter hash this out like Halle had to do with her own mother when she was young. Instead, I take a seat on Halle's front steps, knowing I've already stirred up enough trouble being caught dropping from the roof after escaping through Halle's window. *And* catching Violet making out with an eighteen-year-old boy in the middle of the night on the front porch.

Taking out my phone, I text Halle, telling her I'm right outside and waiting to hear from her. I'm here when she's ready to talk or whatever else she might need because I'm not slinking from this house again.

And I'm not letting another mother and daughter inside it be divided.

Chapter 32

[Halle]

"What the hell was that?" I storm from my bedroom at the sudden slam of the front door. Only seven minutes have passed since Knox left my bedroom through the window. I'd watched him disappear from my view. He hadn't fallen or hurt himself. In fact, I saw him standing upright in the yard before I stepped away from the window, leaning against the wall and covering the smile on my face.

Knox and I had sex again. In my bed. In this house.

I felt alive. Like every fiber of my being is wired and tingling.

After we had our quick minutes together, Knox lingered, and we talked. I told him about my plans to auction off the furniture in an estate sale and finish fixing up the various rooms. For the first time in a long time, I was excited about the future.

Then I heard the *bam*. A vibration that made this old house rattle despite its solid foundation.

Racing from my room, I find Violet stomping up the staircase.

"Were you outside?" I'm puzzled by the time, by Violet's stricken face, and by the angry vibration humming around her.

"It's because of him, isn't it? It's all his fault we're staying."

"Violet, what on earth?" Flabbergasted by her outburst, and the tone and volume of her words, I blink several times at her.

"I saw him." She stops halfway up the staircase and points toward the front door. "He just left your bedroom through the window." Her face wrinkles in disgust.

History has flipped upon itself. Now *my child* is upset about Knox Sylver being in my bedroom versus the haunting memories of my mother's ire.

"Violet—"

"I know who he was to you. *Your first love*," she mocks. "But he left you. He ran away and broke your heart. And now you left Dad."

A heavy exhale releases. "Who told you about Knox? And your father and I divorcing has nothing to do with him." My rapid heartbeat has transformed from fluttering fright to thumping anger.

A weighted pause fills the distance between me and my eldest child. One where I'm pissed at my ex-husband for being the one to tell Violet about my history with Knox, and fury at the same man for making it appear that my reunion with Knox has anything to do with our divorce.

Violet already knows the simple explanation. Her father and I fell out of love, and while we will always love one another for the time we shared together, which brought us our children, it wasn't good for either of us to remain in our marriage.

For half a second, it occurs to me that leaving Jack was similar to Knox leaving me all those years ago. Our goals were different. And like Knox once said about me, Jack's dreams were bigger than us.

But none of that is important at present.

"Violet, I don't appreciate your tone or your insinuation. You know darn well why your father and I divorced, and it had nothing to do with Knox Sylver. He wasn't even in my life before we returned here."

"And that's why we're staying. Because *he's* in your life now, right?"

Now isn't the time to counterargue my daughter and confirm that Knox is a sliver of the reason I want to stay. I want *him*.

Violet is also a child, and I don't owe her this explanation yet.

"You still haven't told me why you were outside at this time of the night or why you slammed the front door. What were you doing out there?" I gaze toward the glass-paned barrier as if I can see through it from my position at the top of the stairs. Then an incredulous thought occurs. "Was someone else outside with you?"

Had she left the house under cover of darkness? Was she sneaking around to meet someone? I'd laugh at the irony if I wasn't so agitated by her sudden outburst.

Crossing my arms, I glare down at my child who remains halfway up the staircase. She still hasn't answered me, avoiding my stare, and lowering her head a bit.

"Is this about a boy?" The moment I ask, I flinch. I sound just like my mother. Not teasing or sympathizing, but irritated and accusatory. Violet and I should be sharing this moment to talk about what happened. What upset her. Who hurt her. Instead, it's a showdown of wills and *I'm* the one who had been interrogated first.

When she still hasn't answered me, I have my answer.

"Go to your room." I unfold my arms and step back, waiting for her to complete the climb up the staircase. When she reaches the landing, I hold out my hand. "Phone."

"What? Mom. No." Her expression is one of horror as if I've asked her to cut off a limb, and in many ways, I'm certain she feels I have.

"Give it to me."

"I'll tell Dad."

"*I'll* tell Dad." I sound as petulant as her. "You were sneaking out of the house. Meeting who knows whom. You've proven you can't be trusted, and a phone is a privilege at your age."

"Mom." Her plea almost sounds like pain, but my hand is out and I'm holding firm.

Violet hands me the phone but not before her final display of defiance which is to power it off as if I can't power it back on. Swiftly turning, she stalks away from me, but I'll have the final word.

"Oh, and Violet, the next time you try to pull this *I'll tell Dad* bullshit, just remember which parent has been the one there for you."

The words are spiteful, bordering on mean, but my fourteen-year-old daughter needs a reminder that I'm her mom, and in that case, it means I'm the parent who will always put her first.

+ + +

When I return to my room, I'm still shaking with ire and fall onto my bed, knowing I won't sleep. Not even the scent of Knox on my sheets can settle me and I reach for my own phone to see a message from him.

He answers on the first ring, keeping his voice low with a rugged, "Hey."

"Hey. Did I wake you?" Holding back my phone, the time reads almost two in the morning.

"I haven't left your front porch. You okay?"

Closing my eyes, I pinch the bridge of my nose, desperately wanting to ask him to come inside and knowing I shouldn't. "Violet saw you leaving."

"Yeah, she saw me." He chuckles but the sound is bitter and strained, just like I feel.

"What was she even doing outside this late at night?" I lower my hand and stare up at the ceiling.

"Didn't she tell you?"

My head rolls toward the window, knowing he's still outside on the front porch. Also knowing he knows something he isn't telling me.

"Knox. What was she doing out there?"

He's quiet for a second. "I don't think it's my place to say."

"You're taking her side." I rub my forehead, a sudden headache coming on.

"Side?" he huffs. "There aren't sides here. Just let her tell you why she was out here."

"I'm asking you to tell me."

"If I did, you'd only have my observation which might not be the full story."

"Knox, this is my daughter," I remind him.

"And because she is, I'm respecting her privacy and allowing her to tell you why she was outside at one in the morning."

"I really don't like that answer. As my . . . you should be telling me."

"As your what, Sprint?"

Boyfriend? Lover? I wasn't in the right frame of mind to define him.

"Rule number one of parenting, Knox. United front. Parents do not keep things from each other regarding their children."

Silence falls between us until Knox quietly states, "Violet isn't my child, Halle. She's yours. And as such, I don't want to come between mother and daughter again."

"You already have." The words are out faster than I can consider how they might sound. How they might sting.

Knox isn't holding back on me. He's giving Violet the benefit of the doubt, trusting her to be mature enough and responsible enough to tell me the truth. Something Violet should be doing. If she had been up to something harmful to herself or someone else, I'm certain Knox would be telling me what he saw. Still, it hurts that he's holding back.

"I'm sorry," I mutter, knowing my accusatory words were unwarranted. "I'm just worried about my daughter."

"I'm going to head home, Halle. Get some sleep."

Remorse hits me. We'd had such a good night together and I hold my breath, waiting for words he promised to say every day. Words he texted me this morning and said earlier tonight before leaving. Still, I need to hear them to know we are solid.

But they don't come and inside my head whispers, *Go. Leave.*

Knox might not know my children yet or have a relationship with them, but at the first hint of trouble with Violet, he's seemingly pulling away. My children will always be in first place with me which is upsetting when I consider Knox is leaving when it gets to be too much.

Like he did before. Like he's good at.

I hate the malice in the thought and the hint of truth.

Knox Sylver was always going to leave me again. Better to rip off the bandage sooner rather than later and let the healing of my heart begin.

Chapter 33

[Knox]

For twenty-four hours, I'm surprised and a bit hurt—no, a *shit-ton* hurt—that I don't hear from Halle. I'm at the firehouse, having taken a shift for a fellow firefighter. And as soon as my shift ends, I'm determined to face her.

Her words the other night were harsh, and her apology for them weak. I wanted her to understand I wasn't trying to come between her and Violet, but rather allow Violet the grace to explain herself. I also wanted Halle to come to me with a more heartfelt apology or at least talk to me about her concerns with her daughter. If Parenting 101 was a united front, Halle had to unite with me.

The thought of sharing Halle's children with her does strange things to me, further solidifying my fantasies about us as a family. I have no uncertainty about Halle and her children being a package deal. One I'm willing to accept and embrace, but Halle has to accept me into the fold as well. She had to see that Violet and I have to forge our own relationship. And that relationship had to start with me trusting that a teenage girl would tell her mother the truth.

My thoughts flit back to sneaking into Halle's room, though. How that might not have been the best decision, but I had to see her. Had to kiss her, touch her, be near her, like that crazed teen madly in love with her. My excuse now is that I'm a reckless adult, equally mad about a woman that I want to go to bed with every night and wake up next to every morning. I've had that experience for nearly two weeks with her children away, and I missed Halle next to me. I equally missed her after a day of silence.

We spent twenty years separated over a conscious decision on my part, when I purposely set out to hurt Halle, push her away. However, there was no way in hell I was letting our second chance at love and a life together implode due to one little argument.

Halle's feelings were valid. She was worried about her daughter. But my feelings matter as well. And if we want a future, we have to communicate.

I'm standing outside the firehouse, checking my phone for the millionth time to see if Halle might have messaged me, responding to my daily text that I love her, when I hear my name.

Glancing up I see a dark-haired boy on a bike riding up the drive, hitching one leg over the middle of the wobbling frame, and tossing himself off the thing while it is still in motion. The bike clatters to the cement, while Tim is running toward me.

"Hey, buddy." I crouch to halt him, catching his upper arms when he nears me. His hair is wild, his breathing ragged. His eyes are wide as he tries to catch his breath.

"Where's the fire?" I tease.

"Knox." He exhales heavily. "You got to stop it. I'm trying out for the soccer team."

"The soccer team? That's awesome, buddy." I hold out a fist, hoping to bump his for good luck, remembering the tryout is in a little more than a week. I'd promised Tim I would practice with him, and I feel bad that days have passed since making that vow.

Tim doesn't tap my fist back but bends at the waist instead, hands on his kneecaps, still trying to catch his breath.

"Stop what?" My playfulness morphs to concern. "What's wrong? What's happened?" Immediately, I'm scanning his thin arms and long legs for scratches or bruises.

"Did someone touch you?" I slide my fingers into his hair, tipping back his head to better inspect his face. "Someone hurt you?"

Shaking his head under my examination, he exhales. "No. Mom. And Violet."

I fold to my knees. "Someone hurt your mom and Violet." I'll kill whoever did it.

Tim shakes his head harder, standing upright while clutching at his sides. "No. Them. Fighting."

Oh. "They're still fighting," I clarify.

Acid fills my belly. I've come between mother and daughter again, as Halle said. Her accusation hit like a sucker punch at the time and for hours I stewed that she might be right. I'm causing a rift in her small family. Then, I reconsider. Halle and I just need to talk.

"Violet is always crying and yelling at Mom, and no matter how calm Mom tries to stay she eventually loses her temper. It's like they're both on their periods."

I roll my lips, chewing on the bottom one to prevent a smile. I could question how he even knows what periods are but he's twelve and he has a sister and a mother.

Strengthening my tone as best I can, I say, "Tim. Word of advice about women. Never, ever accuse them of being on their period during a fight."

Suddenly, the alarm goes off in the fire station behind me and I stand to my full height. "Shit." I glance back at Tim, whose bright eyes widen at the sound and the sudden rush of people within the open garage.

"Tim, I've got to go."

"Can I go with you?"

I shake my head. Ride-alongs need to be pre-approved and kids need to be sixteen or older.

"Move your bike," I yell over my shoulder while racing for my turnout gear before heading for the truck. Once I've climbed into the second set of seats in the fire engine, I glance out the window for Tim. He's already back on his bike, moving over to the side of the drive but exiting into the street.

We pull into the road, and I give a wave out the window as Tim races alongside us. I have no doubt he'll try to chase the engine, and I smile to myself, hoping this is only some routine call.

A cat stuck in a tree. Meredith Mulligan abusing our services by calling in some disaster at the She Shed only so she can ogle firemen.

But when I hear the location, my heart catches in my throat.

The house is on Halle's street.

+ + +

Fire licks above the roofline of the two-story home. The air is heavy with the scent of charring wood and cloying smoke. The guys and I rush for gear and then race around the house. Between the hot tub, a smoker grill, and an outdoor fire pit, any one of these items could have been the origin of the angry flames licking up the back of the structure and threatening the roof.

As my team holds the hose, dousing the affected structure, I circle the house, inspecting lower windows for signs of life inside. As the call came from a guy walking by with his dog, the assumption was the home is vacant, but we always check. I've rounded to the side yard when I see a kid pressing his face to the glass on the second floor. Running back to the front of the place, I call out to the chief.

"Kid. Second floor. Right corner room."

With Zane Hendricks at my side, we bust through the front door and hit the staircase, working our legs double time to reach the upper level. Dense smoke and flaming debris floats from the ceiling, proving the roof has been hit and is at risk of collapse.

We need to find this kid.

I make it to the bedroom first but don't see him. *Fuck.*

Lowering to glance underneath the bed and then looking in the closet, I still can't find him. Hiding is the last thing anyone should do in a fire situation.

"He's not in here," I call out to Zane through the thick facial mask I wear for protection.

We separate to investigate the remaining second floor rooms. The fire has engulfed the back wall up here and wraps around the side of the house, like a threatening embrace. The heat is intense. Walls bubble. The risk of collapse grows with every second we don't find this kid.

We search every room. Beneath beds. Inside closets. Even in a wardrobe. Anywhere a small child might try to cover himself.

Finally, the master bathroom disarray is a clue. Bottles of shampoo, shaving cream, and cleaning supplies litter the floor, suggesting a cabinet has been hastily emptied. Cautiously opening the sink cabinet door, I find a small child curled into himself with his head tucked between his knees, which are bent up to his shoulders.

"Hey, buddy. We need to get out of this fire."

The blaze outside the window means the fire has reached this room, and any second now, flames will burst through the swollen wall, the pressure too great to be held off. There isn't time to negotiate with this kid. Scooping him up in my arms, I stumble over the collection of bottles and jars, tubes, and containers, some of them lethal if exposed to flames, and exit the room.

I call out to Zane again, and we make our way to the lower level as quickly as we can. Zane breaks off to investigate the first-floor rooms now that we've found the kid and I nod, suggesting I'll return shortly to help him once I pass the kid off to the paramedics.

As I near the front door, sharp popping sounds resonate behind me, like fireworks going off in a string of flares, and then an explosion occurs.

Chapter 34

[Halle]

Like a true nosy neighbor, I stepped out of the house at the sudden appearance of a fire truck on the other side of the island dividing the boulevard. Admittedly, I haven't gotten to know the neighbors around me. The older couple next door waves when I'm in the yard, and the people two houses down and across the street are friendly when they walk their dog. The only person I'd officially met was the woman directly across the street when she brought over a casserole and offered condolences after my mother passed. Although Mom mentioned her often, I couldn't remember the woman's name. She was more around my age than Mom's and had a little boy. That's all I knew.

When a second truck arrives, I finally see the flames leaping above the roof from the back of the house across the way. I'd smelled smoke in the air but assumed it was someone burning leaves, although a bit early for leaf cleanup.

Watching the rush of firefighters spill from the trucks like ants, I Hold my breath knowing Knox is one of them.

Suddenly, Tim appears on his bike. "Mom. Do you see it?" He hops off his bike while it's still moving forward and gracefully lands on his feet.

"I see it," I reply, holding out my arm so Tim can step into my side for a half hug. I send up a prayer for the family across the boulevard, hoping the woman and her son aren't home during this tragedy. I also wish for safety for Knox and his fellow firefighters.

Tim straightens and stares across the street. "Knox is over there."

"I know," I whisper, afraid to admit my fear. *Please be safe.*

The blaze is dancing above the roof and visions of the entire backside of the house in flames heightens my concern for him and his team.

"He was so amazing, Mom. Jumping into fireman mode. Running for his gear."

Quickly turning my attention to Tim, I ask, "How do you know?"

Tim sheepishly lowers his head. "I went to see him. He promised to practice with me for the soccer tryouts."

My shoulders drop. *Soccer*. Tim wants to try out for the middle school team, and I told him he could. The other night, Knox did promise to help Tim, and the undeniable guilt gnaws deeper at me that Knox and I haven't spoken. In twenty-four hours, we haven't talked but he hasn't let his words be absent.

I love you.

The words came through in a daily text as a reminder of the promise he made me. The one I demanded of him. Every day, I had to hear the phrase in order to believe him.

But words are just words. And I'd said hurtful ones the other night. Knox isn't coming between me and Violet. Violet and I are coming between each other.

My children are such a contradiction—one hopeful to stay, the other desperate to leave. If I do right by one, I'm certain to do wrong by the other. The past twenty-four hours have been a whirlwind of conflicting decisions among the yelling from Violet and the quiet of Tim. If I allow one child to be excited for the future, another child's heart will break with my choices.

My thoughts are quickly restored to the present situation, though, when two fireman barge through the front door across the street and rush inside the house.

I'm only half-heartedly listening to Tim who is still rambling as I watch for signs of Knox. Was he one of the firefighters who entered the house? My focus remains on the flames licking up the house and swallowing the roof of the home, crackling and popping into the air. A thick halo of smoke lingers above the house like an ominous cloud. Then, a massive explosion goes off, the sound nearly deafening even at a distance.

My heart stops. Eyes wide, hand to my mouth, I hold my breath as my lips wobble in dismay.

"Oh my God." Everything in me says to run. Toward Knox. Toward the fire. But my feet keep me planted, clutching at Tim beneath my arm.

"Mom," Tim whispers, having the same fear as me.

"I'm sure he's okay," I say, squeezing Tim tighter to my side. Although I'm not certain of anything anymore.

Tim and I remain focused on the house across from us, collectively letting out a sigh of relief when one man exits the building, holding a small child. Quickly carrying the tiny body to a waiting paramedic, he then turns back toward the house, rushing inside again. The flames lick around the side of the building and the crumbling of lumber resonates through the air. Somewhere a wall is collapsing or maybe the roof.

Get out of there. Whoever went back inside, I want him safe. And where is Knox? I can't recognize a single feature of the men in their gear.

Tim and I hold our breaths again until the man who rushed into the house returns outside, alongside a second firefighter. Between them, they carry a woman.

Handing her unconscious body over to the paramedics, one firefighter whips off his helmet and mask.

Knox.

Relief rockets from my heaving chest to my heavy feet. I squeeze Tim tighter, as if he's an anchor holding me at bay, so I don't rush to the savior across the street.

The damning fire and display of heroism reinforces how dangerous Knox's job can be. How dangerous his life must have been in the military. In our current time together, Knox has only briefly mentioned former missions or the people he'd known. He only spoke of Rowan Lyons that one time.

The house fire is a reminder that in an instant, life can change. Someone can be taken from you. And the thought of losing Knox in a life-threatening situation has my heart thumping once more.

After what feels like hours, the blaze is down to sizzling embers and the firemen mill about, picking up hoses and gear. Concerned neighbors have moved closer to the scene.

"I'll be right back," I mutter to Tim as my feet finally move when Knox rounds one of the fire trucks. "Knox!"

He turns in my direction as my legs pick up steam and I run for the first time in fifteen years, straight to the man who holds my heart. I leap for him, and he catches me despite the bulk of his fireproof jacket.

"Halle, baby, I'm all dirty." He smells like charred wood and smoky vapor.

"I don't care. I'm just glad you're safe."

Slowly, he lowers me to my feet, and we stare at one another. His face is streaked with dirt and ash, but he's never looked sexier. Or so exhausted.

"I need to go," he hitches his thumb toward the truck. "But I'll—" His eyes narrow as his gaze catches on something over my shoulder. His expression hardens and the filth on his face only intensifies the edge.

"You're moving?" His sight doesn't leave the sign in my front yard.

"Oh, I wanted to talk to you about that."

He finally glances at me, eyes alight but hardened like coal before burning. "When?"

"Today." Today when he was done at work. Today when the sign went up in the yard. Today when Trudy Wallace worked faster than I'd anticipated. I'd only given her a call this morning.

Sidestepping me, Knox begins crossing the street toward my house. Within seconds, his longer stride brings him before the sign. COMING SOON, like an announcement that the house will shortly be on the market.

Tim stands nearby, mouth agape, eyes wide, as Knox kicks at the post with the inside of one booted foot and then kicks the other side with the inside of his opposite foot.

"What are you doing?" I holler at Knox, but his concentration is on each foot, side-kicking the newly planted post which easily loosens under his aggressive attack.

Eventually, Knox wraps his large hands around the support and yanks the entire sign upward before dropping it on the ground with a heavy thud. His chest heaves. His shoulders rising and falling from the exertion.

"What the hell?" I snap.

Knox's head whips upward as if finally remembering he's in my yard, in front of my house, and I'm present.

"*What the hell*, is right," he counters. "Two days ago, you told me you were staying."

"We're moving again?" Tim's small voice catches both mine and Knox's attention.

"I—"

"You said I could try out for the soccer team." Tim's voice is full of questions and wobbly concern.

"I did, buddy, but—"

"What are you thinking?" Knox interrupts me again, the question asked as if I haven't been thinking. As if my thoughts haven't been a constant battle for two full days. Stay or leave. Please Violet. Break Tim's heart. Break Knox's. Wreck my own.

The fight with Violet rushes back to me. In another battle of wills between her demands we leave and my desire to stay, I finally gave in.

Want to go home, Violet had whined, and the plea broke me.

You win, I conceded to my child, with the overwhelming sense that I'd become my mother. I'd ruined Violet's life. But had the original move to Sterling Falls really ruined mine? I'd met Knox. I'd fallen in love for the first time. I had not hated this place after all.

Still, I didn't want to be my mother. I didn't want to hurt my child.

"I'm thinking . . . that I need to do what's in the best interest of my children. I'm their mother." I point a finger at my chest, glaring at Knox.

"A mother, but not a martyr."

"It's the same thing," I yell.

Knox is already shaking his head. "It doesn't have to be, Halle. It shouldn't be." He glances over at Tim before turning back to me. "What about us, Sprint?" His voice falls lower, quieter. "I love you."

The phrase is filled with every emotion. Infatuation. Sorrow. Awe. Concern. Adoration. Anger.

"I—" My response clogs in my throat, like I'm the one who fought a blaze and inhaled too much smoke. My gaze catches on Tim. "They'll always be in first place."

Knox's gaze doesn't leave my face. "It isn't a competition, Sprint. I told you I'd never ask you to put them any less. But us,"—he points between us—"we deserve this chance. *You* deserve it."

In my heart of hearts, he's right. I deserve this second chance with him. I want this, but I can't reconcile my desire for him with the pain I'm causing Violet. The way her life parallels mine when I was roughly her age. I won't let history repeat itself.

"I can't stay," I whisper. "They want to go home."

"You're running away," Knox counters, anger laced in the words.

"That's . . . unfair."

Tim remains close by, his head twisting from Knox to me and back. Questions fill his soft expression. "I'm trying out for the soccer team," he repeats, though not strongly, still puzzled by what's happening.

After the impulsive concession to Violet, I'd called Trudy Wallace this morning to inquire again about selling. She told me the sooner a sign was out front to build anticipation, the better the likelihood there would be for immediate interest upon officially listing the house for sale. While I hadn't made a firm decision, the sign was suddenly in my front yard, and I hadn't had time to question its mysterious appearance before the chaos of the fire across the street began.

With my heart hammering, I stare at Knox. I'm devastated by the possible turn in events, the possibility I might have to move to put my children first. I've made so much personal growth in Sterling Falls, reigniting a friendship with Trinity, finding comfort in Vale, even attending art sessions with Art. Sterling Falls feels like home again, not the cold, plastic existence of living in Charles Town.

And most of all, I'd fallen in love all over again.

The idea of moving was tearing me up inside.

Still, Knox had no right to accuse me of making this decision on a whim. I'm being pulled in so many conflicting directions. Violet and her desire to leave. Tim and his hopes for the soccer team. And Knox, my heart bursting and aching all at once over him. I'm tormented by the thought of leaving him. But I love my children, and I'll always put them first, even at the expense of my own happiness.

As the three of us remain in the front yard, a man hollers for Knox. "Sylver. Get your ass over here."

Knox glances upward, his expression briefly filled with surprise, as if he'd forgotten he just fought a fire and stepped away from the scene of the crime.

The fire chief stands with a deep scowl on his face, apparent even at this distance. Knox immediately matches the edgy stance but turns back to me.

"This isn't who we are anymore, Halle. We aren't pulling crap behind each other's back. We—"

"You did it first," I snap, cutting him off and punching him once again with my words. I sound like a petulant child. I sound like my teenage daughter.

Knox straightens, swiping a dirty hand over his sweaty face. "And it is the biggest regret of my life." He swipes a hand through his sweaty hair, frustrated and rightfully upset.

"You said you'd stay." His rough voice grates over my skin, leaving me feeling as dirty as he looks. The guilt crawls over my skin, cloying and revolting.

"Don't go," he begs, stepping closer to me. "Please. Don't leave me."

"I can't stay." I pray for him to understand but he's already shaking his head.

"Can't? Or won't?"

"I won't." I won't disappoint my child. I could lie and say there isn't anything here for me, but the truth is swollen and achy inside me. He's here. And I want to stay but I want to please my child more.

As if reading all my thoughts, Knox turns away from me, crossing the street, giving me his solid back.

"Mom?" Tim's small voice draws my attention back to him. As he stands there, staring at me full of his own inquisition, Violet rounds the house and I instantly wonder where she's been during all the commotion of the fire across the street and the scene in our front yard.

"What's going on?" A smile graces her face. The first one I've seen since her return to Sterling Falls after her two-week stay with her father. The first I've seen since giving in to her.

Before I can answer, Tim turns on her. With a sharp finger pointed toward the sign lying flat in our front yard, he yells at his sister.

"You said Mom ruins everything. But you ruined it. Not Mom."

With sudden tears in his eyes and a short sob, Tim takes off for the house, rushing past his sister and leaving her stunned.

Despite brother-sister ribbing, Tim worships Violet and I don't think he's ever raised his voice at her.

And my heart breaks in a new way as I watch my son's shatter.

Chapter 35

[Knox]

What the hell?

A blazing house fire was better than what went down in Halle's front yard.

She's leaving after only days ago swearing that she'd stay.

Her argument that her kids come first is valid, and I meant what I said that I wouldn't ever expect her to put them in any other position. What puzzles me, though, is that her kids don't seem to agree with her decision. Or specifically, Tim doesn't. He appeared as shell-shocked by the sign in their front yard as I was.

That leaves Violet. Did a fourteen-year-old child have that much sway over her mother? I get wanting to protect Violet or spare her feelings. *But moving?*

Or was there something else? Something I'm missing?

I'd been so hopeful that with Halle's property coming together, despite the house still slightly in a state of chaos, she'd find staying in Sterling Falls a positive step forward. A toe-tip in the direction of being found. She'd made the decision to stay planted, erasing the homeless sensation she feels. She'd accepted that I was here, I love her, and *we* are headed into the future together.

I'd been so wrong.

As I sit in the second seat behind the engine driver, arms crossed and mind stewing with this new development, I brace for the verbal-lashing I'm going to receive once we return to the fire station. Chief is going to rip my ass for stepping away from the final business of that house fire, but nothing compares to the flame in my chest, burning my heart to ashes.

How could Halle do this to me? How could she not give me a little warning?

You did it first.

She wasn't wrong. The situation reminds me of when I finally told her I'd signed up for the Navy.

You what? The betrayal in her voice. The hurt in her soft face. The piercing of my own heart despite thinking I was doing the right thing. For me. For her. I needed to get out of her way. I wanted to get out of this town.

However, I wasn't standing in Halle's way now. There was nothing that pointed to me holding her back. Her children would always come first, but that didn't mean Halle had to put herself second.

She'd made the decision to leave this time without talking to me.

Again, the irony isn't lost.

Maybe she wanted to get me back at me for the pain I'd caused her when she was eighteen. Maybe she still doesn't understand how much it hurt me, like severing a limb, to walk away from her. But like I've already told Halle, my leaving was bigger than us. Bigger than our love was then.

Is our love now still not enough?

My head tips toward the window of the fire engine. The adrenaline rush of chasing a blaze, finding a hiding child, and yanking that damn sign out of Halle's lawn slowly dissipates. I'm crashing like a thick piece of wax dropping off the side of a candle.

My insides are melting at the prospect that I'm losing Halle Reynolds all over again.

+ + +

The next night, I'm practically kidnapped by Clay and Sebastian, who demand I go to Milton Roadhouse with them for a beer. The three of us used to spend every Friday night in this bar, but it's been weeks since we were last here. I'm not up for company but I also know it isn't smart for me to be alone. I'm not ready to face Halle.

My conflicting emotions have me in an emotional tailspin.

"Okay, spill," Clay demands once our beers are delivered. Sebastian doesn't drink anymore but he's good with a non-alcoholic brand.

"Spill what?" The innocent question is full of guilt.

"You've been a pouty puss for days," Clay explains.

"Pouty puss?"

"He's trying to politely say you've been a grumpy ass," Sebastian clarifies.

"And how the fuck would you know?" He's so wrapped up in Enya and Adara, he's the one who doesn't know his head from his backside. Still, my anger isn't really aimed at him. I'm envious of his situation.

"Because this small town has big mouths." Sebastian narrows his eyes at me. He once accused me of being the know-it-all in the family, hearing the latest gossip and easily sharing it with others. I couldn't help it that people liked to talk to me, tell me things, but being on the receiving end of any speculation doesn't feel so grand.

"And what are people saying?" I drop my gaze, staring at the condensation rolling down the side of my glass. "On second thought . . . fuck 'em. I don't care about the talk."

When I was a kid, it bothered the shit out of me that people spoke ill about our family. Rightfully so, they'd been accusatory of our dad turning into a deadbeat, but it still stung that the community had words for our situation.

Trudy Wallace had been someone who tried to help dispel the rumors, even offer assistance when we were younger. She taught Stone and Clay how to change a diaper since Vale was a newborn when our mother passed. She tried to take Ford and Sebastian in on occasion to lessen the burden for our dad who blatantly boasted his children had become *giant pains in his ass*. Then he chastised Trudy for trying to intercede, claiming she had enough concerns with her own brood of nieces, nephews, and foster children.

Trudy was one of those women with eyes and ears everywhere but never a negative opinion.

Why the hell was she encouraging Halle to sell so quickly? Did she need the commission? And why was I wondering these things, as if it was a personal slight on behalf of Trudy, when the decision ultimately landed on Halle.

She'd decided.

So had you, once upon a time, asshole.

"Good God, if your brain starts spinning any faster, you're going to steamroll out of this bar," Clay teases, tightly clasping his hand on my shoulder.

"I'm not spinning," I lie.

"Then what *are* you doing?" Sebastian asks.

"I'm—" My answer falters when Halle walks into Milton's with Trinity Haven behind her. Just seeing Halle takes my breath away and scatters my thoughts.

How did things get so fucked up so quickly?

Maybe that had been the issue. Too much happened too soon. I'd told myself I'd be patient with Halle. She had so much going on between her mother's loss, the inheritance of the house, and the questions about her future. But Halle had me wound tight and every time she looked at me, I'd thought she wanted me. I'd been certain she was ready for us to take things to the next step. A step toward our future.

"A little birdy told me she's moving," Clay softly states.

"Well, fuck your little birdy," I mutter, lifting my beer and guzzling the remainder. Slamming down the thick pint glass, I force myself to focus on my brothers and not the redhead across the bar.

"Wow," Sebastian exaggerates.

"Wow what?"

"I wouldn't take you for a quitter."

"I'm not a fucking quitter," I sit up straighter, glaring at my younger brother. He's asking for a headlock and knuckle-rub to his skull.

"Then go talk to her," Clay states.

"She made her choice."

"And you didn't once upon a time?" Clay arches a brow, his expression answering his own question as if I need the reminder.

"Really? So that's it? Fuck her?" Sebastian counters.

"Hey," I bark, not liking his tone or the strong accusation. "Look, it's not like she needs me. She's an independent woman with two children to consider in any decisions she makes." Jesus, now I sound like I'm justifying Halle's choices.

"Well, do something about that," he adds.

"Like what? And since when are you a love therapist?" I growl.

Clay's brows rise. "Oh, are we admitting we love her again?"

I ignore Clay, having a stare down with my younger brother.

Sebastian doesn't look away from me when he answers. "A bit of advice. An independent woman will never need you."

"That's reassuring," I mutter. "You're fired as my therapist."

Sebastian lowers a hand to the table with a hard smack. "She *wants* you, dammit. There's a difference, and that's the secret to love. When she fucking wants you, Knox"—Sebastian blows out a breath—"you're the luckiest son of a bitch in the world."

My brother tips his head in the direction of Halle.

I won't look. I won't look. I won't look.

"And that woman over there isn't glaring daggers at you like she can't wait to get away from you. She's staring at you so hard her eye-fucking is making *me* horny."

"Well," Clay chuckles. "That's graphic." Then he narrows his eyes. "Think if I eye-fuck that brunette over there, she'll come to me." His gaze is aimed at a woman standing at the bar.

"Dude," Sebastian groans.

"I said come to me, not come for me." Still, Clay salaciously wiggles his brows. Although he isn't typically the dirty one in the group, his comment breaks the tension at the table.

"I can't believe I'm going to say this," Clay begins, turning back to me. "But Sebastian is onto something. If Halle wants you, as much as you want her, don't be the one to walk away. Again."

Clay continues to give me a pointed look, having already told me once Halle deserved to know all my reasons for leaving way back then.

And now, I deserved answers as well.

Sliding off my stool like a chastised child, I straighten my spine and cross the bar, determined that Halle and I aren't leaving this place without words.

+ + +

[Halle]

"Don't look now, but here comes the best kind of trouble," Trinity teases.

I chuckle as I sip my margarita. With a will of their own, my eyes glance upward despite Trinity's warning. Still focused on him, I ask, "What kind of trouble is that?"

"The kind about to stake his claim and then ravish you in his truck out back."

I snort, choking on a second sip of tequila heaven. From the moment I entered Milton's, I felt the pull of him. His presence across the space causing my heart to hammer and my mouth to dry. Everything in me demanded I go to him, but I held back. His typical look, narrowing in on me and making me feel like the only woman in the room, was dim. An aura around him warned me to give him space despite how much I wanted to enter his orbit.

Tonight, I'd been the one to reach out and invite Trinity for drinks. I desperately needed to get out of the house. When she asked me how things were going, I only had one word. *"Knox."*

"Have sex and move on," had been her advice. I hadn't told her we already had sex, and moving was part of the issue.

I didn't want to move. I also didn't want to traumatize Violet. She'd already been through enough. And me falling back in love with Knox Sylver had been too much too soon. Like that youthful girl racing through the woods, lost and not paying attention to her surroundings, I'd run into a situation I wasn't prepared for. The hard-bodied boy—who was now a sexy man—had caught me once again with firm hands, holding onto me like he could be a hero. My *Brick*.

However, it was more than me who needed saving this time.

"Hey," Knox greets Trinity as he nears our table. "Hi," he addresses me.

Our eyes lock like they often did when we were young, and the world around us faded away. Only, I can't ignore that my world involves more than me this round.

I clear my throat and drag my gaze away from him. "Hello." My voice is low, almost timid, and I hate the sound. I want to be strong. I want to be firm. I want Knox to understand.

"Can we talk?" he asks, keeping his gaze on me.

On the tip of my tongue is a snarky remark, questioning that now he wants to talk after almost two days of silence. He hadn't reached out to me. But I hadn't reached out to him either.

My house has been meltdown-central. Violet was constantly crying because Tim wasn't speaking to her. And Tim was crying because he blamed Violet for us moving. And I'd been crying because my children were both unhappy and my heart was breaking once again over Knox.

"I think I'll go order another drink," Trinity states, despite having a full margarita before her on the table. Slipping from her stool, she picks up her salt-encrusted glass, taking a sip to prove how filled the container remains. Still, she steps away, offering Knox and me privacy.

He slides onto her stool and clutches his hands together on the high-top table. Awkward silence filters around us, louder than the chatter of the bar crowd.

"The sign wasn't a FOR SALE sign," I state, which immediately sounds like the worst lead in.

"Does it matter?" Knox counters. "You're still going to sell eventually, aren't you?"

"I hadn't decided," I admit. "I called Trudy on a whim and before I knew it the sign was in the yard."

Knox narrows his eyes. "That doesn't make sense."

I shrug. "Well, that's all I have." I hadn't been able to reach Trudy after Knox pulled up the sign and I dragged it to the garage.

"Are you moving because of Violet?"

"My children come first," I remind him.

"And I'd never doubt that, but you're using them as an excuse."

My mouth falls open, ready to defend myself.

"And that's a lot to put on your child, Halle."

Sitting straighter, hackles standing at attention, I prepare to argue that my child is not the cause of my decisions, but something in his eyes has me holding my tongue. He'd been blamed for loads of things by his father when he was younger. Then he'd put pressure on himself. He took responsibility for circumstances out of his control. Adult decisions that had nothing to do with him as a teenager.

"It's not only Violet." I sigh, defeated and worn. "Maybe we moved too fast. Maybe I'm getting ahead of myself."

Swiping my hand through my hair, I exhale again. I still don't have a plan. A job. A future. Like I'm standing on the track, but I don't know which direction to run. And a relationship might be the last thing I need right now. "I'm still kind of a hot mess, Knox. My future is undefined, and I can't make decisions for what happens next solely about me." I'm still as lost as I was the day of my mother's funeral.

"Who else should it be about?"

My brows lift and I peer up at him, the defense of my children on my lips but Knox holds up a hand.

"Violet and Tim are the most important people in the equation, but they can't be the sum of all your choices. You need to make some decisions for yourself this time."

"What do you mean *this time*?"

"You didn't love Jack. You settled for him because you were pregnant. And you stayed with him out of ease. Comfort. Contentment. But you couldn't have been happy. If you made the decision to leave your marriage, it was because you weren't happy." He pauses. "Is that the issue here? You aren't happy? You aren't happy with me?"

The questions weigh heavy between us and tears instantly well in my eyes. Rapidly blinking them away, I sit straighter again, holding back my shoulders. "I've been happier with you than I've been in years."

Knox's hands unclench and lay flat on the table. His nostrils flare.

I want to reach for him but the tension around him says *don't*.

"You said we were on pause, but what if we weren't? What if this,"—I wave between us—"was just an attempt to rewind when we can't really go backwards?" I soggily smile. "I have children, whom I can't ignore. I need to think of them. I can only go forward."

"Then move forward *with me*," Knox counters.

"I want you," I whisper. "But I don't know how to keep you." Knox blurs in my vision and I blink again, willing away public tears.

"And I imagine that's how you felt about me once upon a time." He loved me but he couldn't keep me. As he said, being a Navy wife wasn't what *he* wanted for me.

"Moving away isn't going to help," he softly chides, anger lacing his words.

"Leaving is what we do, I guess." He left me once for the same reason I'm going now. I don't know how to stay and do what's best for me and my kids.

"Violet is miserable," I add.

"But Tim isn't."

Tim is as crushed by the potential of leaving as Violet is at the thought of staying. I can't seem to do right by both of them equally.

"She still hasn't told me what she was doing on the front porch at one a.m."

Knox's head pops upward, his eyes catching mine briefly before looking away. He doesn't want to betray her. It's admirable in some ways. Protecting her. Preventing me from being angry all over again.

"It was a boy," he finally says, his voice low. "Just like her mother," he softly adds, his tone warmer but still sad. "Seems that house can't keep them away."

"What boy?" My hackles rise but the hint of my mother has me cringing inside.

"Doesn't matter. I set him straight. Told him Violet was off limits."

I scoff. "You scared him off."

"I protected what could have been mine."

The idea of Knox claiming Violet as his girl has my breath catching. He would have been the best father. Loving. Protective. Devoted. Sweet.

"Knox." I reach out for his forearm but he's quick to retract his arms, tucking them beneath the table.

His head shakes. "I can't do it, Halle. I can't pretend the past few weeks hasn't felt like something special, something *building* toward a future. I can't pretend *we* don't exist. I love you. I always will."

He straightens on the stool, hands coming to the edge of the table like he's bracing himself against a fight.

"I've been chasing ghosts my entire life, Halle. My dad. Our baby. Rowan. You."

"What do you mean *me*?" My brows pinch.

"You weren't dead to me, but you've haunted me. And I came back to find you." He slowly lowers his head. "Went to see you in Virginia after your fall in the Olympics. I was home on leave and had twenty-four hours. One full day to get to you. See that you were physically okay and then explain myself. Apologize for being selfish and immature. Beg for your forgiveness." Knox shrugs. "But you were with someone else."

My eyes widen. *Who? Where? How?*

"And you looked happy." His brows crease and he tilts his head, reflective and confused. "But I'm not certain I interpreted that moment correctly because I've seen you happy, Sprint. You've been happy here. With me. You light up the fucking world. Turn night into day. Turn darkness into sunshine. And that's typically when you're looking at me."

He softly chuckles, vulnerable and raw. "I walked away then, thinking I was doing the right thing. Again."

"When did you see me?" I demand, angry that he'd been so close to me, and I'd missed him.

Knox squints. "Christmas 2004."

He'd been two years late from the date he'd promised to return. I can hardly remember any boy between Knox and Jack. I didn't date. He had to have been mistaken. "It couldn't have been me."

Knox bitterly chuckles. "Oh, it was. Same red hair." His gaze roams my head. "Same lanky body." His eyes lower down my form before he glances across the bar like an image is on the opposite wall. "And a tall guy with jet-black hair whose arm you were underneath, smiling up at him."

"Jet-black hair? That had to have been Paolo, my coach. You saw me with my running coach." Exasperated, I glare at him. "Why didn't you approach me? Why didn't you say anything?"

"Like I said, I thought you were happy, and I didn't want to get in the way. But I also made a promise to myself, that if you were ever free again, I'd be there for it. And here you are. And here I am."

Knox stretches out his arms, imitating a plane's wings. "You can duck and dodge *us*, but I'm not going down again. And neither are *we*. I can dogfight all day if I need to, Sprint. I'm fighting for us." He slips from his stool and pauses. "I'm solid, Halle. And I'm here for you. For your kids. The decision is up to you this time. Whether you want us to work or not. Don't be the fool I was. Don't take decisions away from me, from us."

With that, Knox crosses the bar and I watch him drop bills on the table where his brothers sit.

Then he exits Milton Roadhouse. And I'm left breathless by his disappearance, like he took all my air with his exit.

He could have been mine again. He still is mine, and I'm just sitting here watching him go, heavy with sadness and weighed down by confusion. My heart is an organ of contradiction. To do right by myself, I'll have to hurt someone. Knox. Violet. Tim. Or me.

And yet, Knox just told me how he's here for us. All of us. He's willing to fight for our future.

Art Simms told me I'm a warrior, and it's time I learn to fight, as well.

Too often I've braced for Knox to leave me again, but he's not walking away.

I'm running away from myself. And what I really want. *Who* I want.

It's always been Knox. H+K carved into a tree. Forever.

And forever starts now if I'm willing to fight alongside him for it.

Chapter 36

[Halle]

Outside.

The text the following morning is succinct and that one word so sharp I don't question him. Despite it being broad daylight, I round the corner of the garage and almost collide with Knox. Instantly, I'm tugged into his chest and held against him. His heart hammers beneath his warm shirt.

While I appreciate the hug, badly having needed one from him especially after all the emotions of yesterday, this is different. Something is wrong.

"What's happened?" I mutter into his neck because, of course, I can't resist his clean mountain scent.

Knox squeezes me a little tighter before setting me down and stepping back, as if he's suddenly remembered he's very upset with me and doesn't know why we were hugging.

He swipes a hand through his hair, glancing toward the side yard before looking back at me.

"You cannot tell a soul what I'm about to tell you. But being that Stone is the sheriff, he had some news on the fire across the street."

"Okay." I nod, having thought our embrace was about us, but shifting gears at the concern on his face.

"The wife had Rohypnol in her system. The sheriff's department believes she was roofied in her own home."

I gasp and cover my mouth with my fingers before asking, "What? How?"

Knox shakes his head. "Stone didn't say. There is definitely an ongoing investigation, but I guess the husband and wife were having issues, and she'd asked him for a divorce. Said she wanted to sell the house. The husband said he'd burn the place to the ground before he'd sell."

"Oh my God. Does this mean . . ."

Knox is nodding once more, his hand on the back of his neck. "It could have been arson. And he could have intended to kill his wife and son in the fire."

"That's awful." My heart races with the news but also pierces with pain. That poor woman. Her poor son. "Are she and the boy okay?"

"She's still in the hospital. The boy was picked up last night by a family member."

"And where is the husband?"

Knox's gaze narrows in on me. "Stone doesn't know." He blows out a heavy exhale. "Halle, I want you to be careful. You and the kids. He could be dangerous."

He could be and it's certainly frightening to think my neighbor might have attempted to burn down his house with his wife and child inside. But a crime like that usually sticks to the family.

I almost feel guilty I hadn't known there were issues across the street. I've been too engulfed in my own drama but nothing in my house compares to that kind of threat. Jack isn't vindictive or cruel, and Violet and I will work out our differences.

"If she hoped to sell, do you think—"

"The sign in your yard might have been intended for hers. Just a simple miscommunication on the address."

A change from an even numbered house to an odd one. An easy error but I still shiver. If that yard sign was supposed to be a target, perhaps for a hired arsonist, my house could have been destroyed by a blaze.

Knox watches me, almost reading my thoughts, and reaches for me again, tugging me to his solid chest.

"I'd never let anyone get to you. Not you. Not to Violet or Tim. You're *all* mine."

The conviction reinforces what he said last night. He's not letting us go without a fight.

Not any of us.

+ + +

On Monday evening, I cautiously enter Violet's room. We've called a silent truce over the weekend, giving each other space to cool down after days of arguing. However, I'm determined we talk, calmly, tonight.

As I sit on the edge of her bed, Violet tucks up her knees allowing me more space.

For a moment, I take in my beautiful girl. She's changing before my eyes both physically and mentally. She'll be turning fifteen in September and starting high school somewhere. She's on the verge of womanhood and the time has gone too fast.

Since returning to Sterling Falls, I've often wondered what my mother thought of me at this age. Being the mother of a teenage daughter is daunting. Being a teenage daughter is terrifying.

"I know you're disappointed in me," I begin. Immediately, Violet's brows rise. Blue eyes that match mine stare back at me. "But I'm disappointed too."

Violet scowls and I brace for another fight. But I have things to say and then we have somewhere to be.

"You never told me a boy was with you on our front porch after midnight."

Violet's eyes widen, shock written in her expression. "Didn't Knox tell you?"

"Not at first, he didn't. He didn't want to betray you, and he believed you'd tell me immediately. But you didn't, did you?"

Violet lowers her gaze, her head bowing as well.

"Who was he and why was he out there?" I don't need to ask *what* they were doing. I was a teenage girl once.

My daughter shakes her head. "He doesn't matter anymore."

"Because Knox scared him away?" I hold my breath, waiting for my daughter to blame one more person for something gone wrong, in this case Knox, but whoever was outside was a choice within her control. She met him on the porch.

"Because he was too old for me," she admits. "And he's leaving in the fall."

"How old?"

"Eighteen."

I sigh. My daughter is a beautiful girl who looks like a woman, and while age is relative, there's still a huge difference between fourteen and entering high school, and eighteen and graduating from one. However, my heart does ache for her. At least she has been able to let this boy go before she was entangled in his love and the hope of a future with him.

"Do you understand that you have years ahead of you to fall in love with someone who better fits your circumstances?"

Her head pops up. "Like you fell in love with Knox?"

"Possibly. But yes, when I was in high school, he was my sweetheart."

Violet cringes. "No one calls it that anymore."

I don't even want to know what the kids call their partners, boyfriend/girlfriend, or whatever. "My point is, Knox was a year older than me. Only *one* year, and we were in high school at the same time."

"And you broke up."

Heavily, I sigh again. "Yes. Because . . . life got in the way." His father. My mother. His plans. My goals.

Violet stares at me for a long time.

"My mother didn't like that I was dating Knox. I dated him anyway." My shoulders drop. "I don't want that kind of defiance between us, Violet. If you're dating someone, I want to know who he is, and I'll try to be objective and accepting."

Violet shakes her head again. "We wouldn't have worked. He's going to college next month."

I could ask how she met him or what happened, but she seems resolved that he was only temporary. As I said, she has years ahead of her to fish the sea of love.

"I can't say you lied to me, but you omitted the truth. I love you, Violet, but I don't want you sneaking out of the house like that ever again. I won't tolerate lies."

With eyes wide and earnest, she defends herself. "It was only to the front porch. I swear. And only the one time."

"Do you understand my trust is broken, though?"

She nods.

"I suppose I've broken your trust, too. I promised to love your father forever and I didn't. I still love him *because* he's your father but not as a man I wanted to stay married to. Does that make sense? It's like you realizing that boy wasn't right for you."

"Because Knox is," she counters.

"Violet." I exhale. "Knox isn't who we're discussing. We're discussing you and me. How I feel about him doesn't matter because you and Tim come first for me. Always."

Violet continues watching me.

"When I was a little older than you are now, my dad died. You know this. And my mother moved me here to Sterling Falls. I was scared and lonely and missed my dad terribly." If Violet misses Jack, she has a strange way of showing it, always returning sullen and irritated after her visits with him. But she still might miss the concept of him being her father. "I didn't want to be here anymore than I suspect you do. But then I met a boy, who became my best friend." I can't help the smile that crosses my face. "And he changed my opinion about this place. This move. This town. Love changed my mind."

I reach for Violet's knee. "But I don't want you to think boys are the answer. And I'd like to hope I showed you that staying in an unhappy relationship isn't healthy. Sometimes you need to burn things to the ground before you can build them back up again. Stronger. Better. Happier." I tap my fist to my chest. "Happiness needs to come from within first. Externally second."

"Are you happy, Mom? Does being here make you happy?"

I glance around the room; the space once belonging to my mother, but slowly filling with Violet's personality. "When we first returned, I was resentful again. I didn't want to be in charge of this place. Especially when everything else seemed to be falling apart. But, I think coming here was exactly what I needed."

I don't think I'd even realized this truth until telling it to Violet. I needed to return here. I needed to fix what was broken. The house. My history. Knox. And I haven't given Violet an answer because I don't have one. I'm not unhappy, but I could be so much happier, if we stayed.

"My mother liked to claim she didn't have any choices other than to move herself and me here. But I do have options, right? So, if you're truly unhappy here, we'll find another place to live. Another town. But globe hopping isn't going to bring happiness, Violet. We need a home. A solid place to live."

I gaze around us again. I never thought I wanted this place to be *the* house, but I've changed my mind.

Love had done it again.

My love for Violet is stronger than anything, though. For her and Tim.

"I need to know if your desire to *leave*, has something to do with this boy. The one going to college."

A heavy silence falls between us. Violet's gaze remains suspiciously lowered. "It doesn't matter."

"It does matter because you clearly had feelings for him. And it matters because he somehow hurt your feelings."

Violet covers her face. "It was me. I might have fibbed to him about my age and then I was embarrassed when Knox called me out, telling Barnett I'm fourteen, like I'm a child."

She is a child, and the rebuke is on the tip of my tongue, but I hold back. "And this happened when Knox caught you on the front porch."

"Knox told Barnett he couldn't see me again, like he's my father or something." Violet scoffs.

"And does your Dad know you were sneaking out of the house, meeting a boy on our porch after midnight, and kissing him?"

"Mom!" Violet glares at me.

"I was a teenager once, Violet. I'm not stupid."

She glances away from me again. "It was just so embarrassing."

"So, if I have this straight, you'd like me to move our family because of a boy."

Violet whips her head back to face me. "Because Knox embarrassed me."

"Because you embarrassed yourself by lying to a boy and then got caught." I let the truth simmer between us. Maybe she thought Barnett would never know the truth. I could question what a college-bound boy was doing with a not-yet-in-high-school girl, but as I said, I was a teenager once. Violet could pull off *saying* she's sixteen, but she lacks the maturity and wisdom that two more years would bring. And her decision to lie and sneak around was childish.

But once again, I'm reminded of myself. I did the same things. Snuck around to see a boy. Kissed him on my front porch. Met him late nights and in the dark. I'm no better than my child, but I am older, and maybe a tad wiser. I don't want to see her hurt. I also want her to accept where blame is due.

Violet lied. Knox protected her *from herself.*

"If Barnett is important to you, and you're important to him, you'll reconnect at some point. When you're older. When you're on more of a level playing field." Like when she's thirty.

"Is that what happened with Knox? You've reconnected."

Exhaling first, I hope to explain without all the details a mother doesn't need to share with her child. "Here's the thing. Knox and I were . . ." I still. I resort to his words. "On pause. We were always meant to be together, and twenty years later, we've found one another again. That's how it works when the right person comes along, gets lost, and circles back." *When you come home to that person.*

"Am I making any sense?" I squeeze Violet's knee.

"Yeah."

"So, it isn't really Knox that you're mad at. And maybe you're mad at me only a little bit." I tease. "But I think you're more upset with yourself, am I right?"

Violet falls back to her pillow and stares up at the ceiling. "Yeah."

We're both quiet for a minute.

"Tim is still upset with me, too," Violet states, lowering her gaze once more and looking directly at me.

"He wants to stay. He's made friends. He's gotten involved in soccer. Other than this boy, have you made an effort?"

Violet looks toward the wall, knowing she hasn't.

I hadn't either when I first arrived in Sterling Falls at seventeen. I ran around the town and through the woods, alone and sad. In some ways, I didn't know myself then any better than I know myself now, but I want to change. For both of us.

"I have somewhere I'd like to take you tonight. Just you and me. A date with Mom."

Violet's gaze comes back to me and widens. We haven't had a mother-daughter moment in a long, long time, and we're overdue.

+ + +

Thankfully, Tim is able to go to a friend's house for the evening while Violet and I head out on our date.

"Art's Studio," she reads the sign while exiting the car. A snicker fills her voice.

"I came here while you were at your dad's." I'd also been back the past week, finding that visiting two times a week has really helped me forget all the outside forces and just be me for a little while.

I'm not terribly creative but I'm learning that working with my hands helps settle my mind.

"Hello, ladies," Art greets us once we enter. Monday nights he's typically closed but I'm calling in a favor as Knox did that first time I came here. Art doesn't seem to mind the intrusion on his day off.

"Art, this is my daughter, Violet."

"ROY G. BIV." *Red, orange, yellow, green, blue, indigo, violet.* "Did you know that violet is the color of royalty? Are you a princess, Violet?" Art asks.

Violet sourly giggles. "My dad calls me that."

"Hmm. You look like royalty. Powerful, noble, and ambitious." Art winks. "Are you ambitious, Violet?"

Violet shrugs but she's already glancing around the room. She loves to sketch although she isn't trained at it. Her hope is to take art classes in high school.

Art wheels himself around the room, following Violet and explaining the various stations. Painting. Pottery. Sculpting. Violet's eyes widen as Art details the trash to treasure possibility, but her eyes wander back to the painting area. The stacks of sketch books. The blank canvases.

"I think I'll draw," Violet finally says.

"Don't say it like you're put out. You're going to create." Art says with a flourish including the wave of his arm for dramatic effect.

"I'm going to create," Violet copies.

"Come on. You can do better than that." Art waves his arm above his head again. "You're royalty. Add some flare."

Slowly, Violet smiles, tossing her arm up in a zealous arch before her face. "I'm going to create," she says with a little more enthusiasm.

Art narrows his eyes. "See? Powerful. A masterpiece awaits you." He points at the blank sheet hanging on an easel.

As Violet heads toward the stool before the stand, I mouth to Art, *Thank you.*

"Roses are red," Art begins. "But she's a Violet."

I smile, not certain I understand him but feel a compliment all the same on behalf of my daughter.

Then, I head to the pottery wheel having tried it last time I was here. I'm determined to master making a bowl.

Art follows me to the bin with clumps of clay. "How are things going for you?" he asks like a knowing father and a worried friend.

Glancing at Violet and then back at Art, I say. "I've fallen down again, but I'm standing back up."

"That's all we can do. Over and over."

I nod to agree and then take a seat at one pottery wheel. As the wheel spins and I work with fingers slathered in water and clay, I mold the beginnings of a bowl when I hear Art cursing. "Dagnabbit."

I chuckle at the word but note Art's frustration as he sits in front of a computer. If I stop the wheel, I'm going to lose the form I've started but Art's scowl has me pausing my project. Dipping my hands back into the murky water and then reaching for a rag to wipe them clean as best I can, I cross the studio for Art's corner desk.

"What's the trouble?" On the screen are the beginnings of a flyer, advertising a fundraiser for the studio. The image lacks artistic pizazz, considering the brochure is for this creative space, and it looks like Art is having trouble manipulating the computer program to move around the text.

"Damn computers. They're sucking the creativity out of this world."

I chuckle, disagreeing but understanding a man like Art still wants to work with paint brushes and pottery clay.

"I can help." To my surprise, Violet stands behind me. "We used this program in school."

Art wheels backward and waves toward the machine. "Help yourself. And if you can help the looks of that flyer as well, I'd appreciate it."

Violet steps over and within seconds has text moved and images added, increasing the font size, and emphasizing the special nature of this place.

"I don't mean to pry but are you low on funds?" Glancing around the room, I note that the pottery wheel and kiln couldn't have been cheap. The art supplies, including paints, pens, and paper also add up. While the trash bin might be full of free, potentially artistic treasures, it still costs Art something to keep the lights on in here.

"Just thought I'd try to get a little help. Never hurts to ask." He nods toward Violet.

I agree, although I haven't been one to ask for much help over the years.

Within minutes, Violet has a much better design completed and prints the flyer to inspect the final product.

"A masterpiece," Art pronounces, holding the printed paper out to Violet. The design highlights how Art wants to host ARTFest in September. He's inviting people to visit, create, and participate in activities to raise money for his place. The event encourages family fun and community gathering. There will also be local artists present to sell their creations.

"Too bad we won't be here," I admit, then instantly clamp my mouth shut. I wasn't ready to say goodbye to Art. He's been an inspiration for me. But if Violet gets her way, we'll be moving.

"Leaving so soon?" His brows hitch. "That punk run you off."

"Afraid I'm doing the running this time," I admit.

Art watches me, observing my face a moment. "It's only when we're out of breath, that our heart tells our legs to stop running. Then it's time to change direction."

I weakly smile before glancing at Violet, who continues to stare at the flyer while no doubt listening to our exchange.

"Thanks for your help, girlie." Art holds out a hand for the paper. "I'm going to have that printed and distributed around town. Maybe you could do the leg work for me, Violet, the color of royalty?" He pats his thigh, and then winks at me.

Somehow, I'm not certain he needed help from Violet to create that fundraising invitation after all.

He was trying to help her.

Chapter 37

[Knox]

I'd been driving back late from a patio job outside of town when I see the lights on at Art's Studio and a familiar SUV in the lot. As much as my brain says *don't do it,* my hands have a will of their own, and next thing I know I've turned the wheel and am parked beside Halle's vehicle.

The silence between us is almost maddening and I've had time to reflect and accept that this burning sensation inside me must be how Halle felt when I'd left for boot camp with no communication. I'm lit on fire with no hope of being extinguished.

Pulling open the door of Art's Studio, calmness instantly settles over me. There's just something about this place that eases me a bit each time I enter. Maybe it's Art and his crazy philosophical comments. Maybe it's the creativity and hum of music within. Or maybe it's just the combination of everything, giving this place an atmosphere of no judgement here.

Be who you are.

Halle looks up and our eyes meet across the studio. She's sitting at the pottery wheel, working her hands over a clay creation, and the naughty ideas flitting through my thoughts should not exist. I'm a damn randy teen again when I have no right to imagine what won't ever be.

She loves me. I love her. But something is in the way.

My gaze falls to Violet, although I'm not blaming a child. Halle is the adult. She's also the parent. In some ways, I love her more because she's putting her kid first, but I don't like that Halle isn't considering herself in her decisions. Her happiness is getting overruled again.

"Hey, punk," Art greets me.

"Hi yourself, old man." I step closer to him, leaving Halle to her pottery and Violet to whatever she's creating behind an easel. Glancing from woman to girl and then at Art, I joke. "You sure are a sucker for redheads."

Art chuckles. "Knew one once. Biggest mistake of my life was letting her steal my heart and not chasing her to get it back."

I've already heard this story from him.

"Gonna make the same mistake, boy, or are you going to catch the thief?" He nods toward Halle. Art isn't one for town gossip, but news must have traveled fast of Halle's decision to leave.

"Not the sheriff in this town," I tease, trying to avoid an answer. I'm not making the decision this time. Halle is.

I don't think she's purposefully punishing me for taking away her decisions when we were younger, but the hurt of our current circumstances is a reminder I did her wrong back then. If Halle and I had planned a life together, we should have made choices *together*.

Instead, I made the decision to join the Navy and leave Halle behind.

Then again, I'd told Halle I'd be back for her, and when I returned, I was too late.

"Gonna create tonight?" Art asks.

"Nah. Just saw the light on and wanted to check that the place wasn't burning down."

"Because an arsonist always turns on the lights first before he starts a fire, right?"

I chuckle. "Yeah, something like that."

"Speaking of arson, I heard about that house on the boulevard." The house on Halle's street.

"Damn sad story."

I glance at Halle, grateful that her husband, while still a douche canoe, isn't a spiteful person. When I'd heard the news from Stone, I had to see Halle. Had to make certain she was safe, she was informed. I also needed to feel her in my arms to know both things. I didn't want to let her or her kids out of my sight if a mad man was on the loose in the area, but I also knew I couldn't force myself to be a houseguest in Halle's home. I didn't want to be a guest. I wanted to be a resident. Forever.

Art reaches for a flyer on the low table near him. "Look what Princess Violet made me. She's going to have copies printed for me and then distribute them around town to help me out." Pride fills Art's voice. His tone also reflects something all-knowing, like a sneaky secret. I know this man well enough to know that Violet probably didn't willingly offer her help but was *voluntold* by the owner without her even knowing she'd been bamboozled.

I glance up at Violet after scanning the paper to find her watching me.

"Says your fest is in September." Halle and Violet might be gone by then, but not if I have my way. "Let me know what you need. I'll be happy to help."

"I'll need those bulky muscles of yours," Art admits. "And maybe a few of those brothers, too."

"We'll be here." My family knows how important Art has been to me. "Maybe I can convince Sebastian to donate some kind of treat."

Art purses his lips, pleased with the suggestion.

I glance over at Halle again, whose hands struggle to remain steady on the creation on the wheel. Her gaze is on me as well and I offer her a weak smile before lifting a hand. Her bowl or vase or whatever it was intended to be collapses before her.

"Guess I'll be getting home, seeing as your place isn't on fire."

"Isn't it?" Art asks, glancing from me to Halle and back.

I snort and turn for the door. I've almost made it to the exit when I hear my name.

"Knox." A throat clears. "I mean, Mr. Sylver."

I turn to face Violet, who looks so much like her mother it's uncanny. She's just as shy as Halle had once been, cautious in some ways, contrite in others.

"I just wanted to . . . um . . . apologize for the other night. On the front porch." Violet glances over her shoulder at her mother, who remains seated before a lump of clay on the stilled pottery wheel.

"And . . . I, um . . . wanted to thank you for not ratting me out to my mom at first."

My attention comes back to Violet.

"I told my mom everything. She knows about Barnett. Him being too old for me, and how I won't be seeing him again."

Uncertain how to respond to this news, a twinge of relief blends with acceptance of her apology, and I nod. "Plenty of other fish in the sea."

Violet tilts her head. "Only I don't like fishin'."

A second passes before it registers that Violet was trying to make a joke.

I offer her a small smile. "Apology accepted, Violet."

She clears her throat and glances back at her mom again before looking at me once more. "And I'm sorry if I ruined things between you and Mom." Her lower lip quivers before she bites it hard to stop the shake. "She could really use a new friend. Well, you're kind of an old friend. I mean, you aren't old . . . just someone she used to know, and—"

"I get it," I chortle, holding up a hand to stop her. "And what about you? Could use a new friend?"

Violet's bright blue eyes well with tears but she blinks hard like Halle does. "You can never have too many friends."

I chuckle and slip my hands into my jean pockets. "You've been hanging out with Art all of five seconds and you already sound like him."

Violet giggles, gazing over at the old veteran. She shrugs while teasing, "He's alright."

Art's face pinkens a bit, but he brushes Violet off with a wave. "Girl, I'm damn near perfection."

Violet laughs outright and I look at Halle again, who has been watching us. Shock fills her face, and I'm wondering if she's thinking the same thing I am.

I hadn't heard Violet's laughter before. She laughs like her mother, along with so many other traits.

The sound is amazing.

+ + +

Later, I'm surprised to receive a text from Halle.

Tim wanted me to remind you he has soccer tryouts soon.

Thoughts race through my head. Does this mean they are staying? Does Tim want me at the tryout? Then, I remember my promise.

I said I'd help him train. Does that still work for you?

Balls in her court, or in this case, the net. I don't want to press if Halle doesn't want me involved with her kids, but my dogfight mentality is taking over again.

I made Violet laugh.

Tim's already in the Knox fan club.

I just need Mom to get on board.

Maybe you could come over tomorrow night. It's taco Tuesday again.

Quickly, I lose the battle to keep the ear-to-ear grin off my face. Halle Reynolds is locked and loaded in my sights, and I'll be coming in for the kill.

More like kisses.

Four days of relative silence has been hell. I'll be damned if I know how I went twenty years without her.

Tim trying out for soccer feels like a positive sign, like a plus in the staying column. Has Halle changed her mind? *Please, let her have changed her mind.*

However, at the same time I want Halle to stay, I've come to a conclusion of my own. A decision that didn't come lightly, but came about because I vowed I wouldn't lose Halle again.

I can't change the past. I can't predict the future. But I can control the present. And the choice I've made is to leave Sterling Falls once more.

This time, if Halle does choose to leave, I'll be going wherever she goes.

+ + +

When I arrive at Halle's house, I'm nervous but my anxiety quickly dissipates when Tim rushes out the front door, soccer ball under his arm.

"Are we really doing this?" His enthusiasm mixes with hesitation.

"We're absolutely doing this." I glance up to see Halle standing on the porch. "I'd like to take him to the field, if that's okay with you. More space."

Halle nods, wringing her hands together. "Tim, you listen to what Knox tells you. Dinner at six, yeah?"

"Sounds good, Sprint."

Tim's eyes widen. "Does Mom have a call sign?"

"All the best people do." I place a hand on his shoulder and guide him toward my truck. Helping him hop in, he buckles his belt, and I round to the driver's side.

"Violet doesn't," he states once I'm seated.

I start the ignition and peer at Tim, wondering what he means.

"Violet doesn't have a call sign."

"Does she need one?" I ask.

Tim lowers his head. "She's still a best people, even if I am mad at her."

"Why are you angry?" My brows hitch.

"She made Mom cry. Dad did that too much before."

Fuck. I hate that Halle cried because of Jack. "But things are better now, right? Between your mom and Violet?" And without Jack.

"She's definitely smiled more being in Sterling Falls than she smiled at our old house."

"Good." Backing out of the driveway, I decide not to question a twelve-year-old about his mother. "So, tell me what we need to work on."

Within minutes, Tim is restored to his excitement for our impromptu practice.

+ + +

At the end of an hour, Tim is beat, and we head back to Halle's. He's been a trooper, working hard, following every direction I gave although I'm certainly not a soccer aficionado. I know some moves, but I'm not a pro. When we were on the field, Tim regaled me with team names and famous players, and fancy footwork he hoped to master.

But once we hit the truck, he sobers again. "Thanks for helping me."

"Whatever you need, Dash."

He smiles softly. "My dad doesn't like that name. He also doesn't think I should try out for the team."

What a dick. "Why not?"

"He says if we move closer to him, making the team here won't matter." Tim squints out the windshield. "But I don't want to move closer to him."

I don't have words for his father. At least not ones appropriate for his young ears. "What does your mom say about trying out?"

"She said to be brave and give it my all."

"Sounds like good advice." More positive than his dad's bullshit. "What did you say to that?"

"I told her I'd be brave if she'll be brave."

My brows lift and I sneak a glance at Tim before pulling into Halle's driveway. "What does your mom need to be brave about?"

"Mom says trying new things can be scary. Change, too, like coming here. I told her if I was brave enough to try out, she should be brave enough to stay here forever."

And just like a graceful glider, hope rises.

+ + +

"I hope I make the team," Tim exclaims around a mouthful of ground beef and cheese, after an exaggerated recounting of our practice together.

"Why wouldn't you make it?" Halle asks. "You're a star on the field."

Tim shrugs. "I wasn't a star at soccer camp."

Halle gently clutches at the mop of hair on Tim's head. "Well, this isn't soccer camp."

"What happened at camp?" I question.

Tim only shakes his head, dismissing whatever drama occurred. *Good boy*. He should be concentrating on future accomplishments.

"Well, congratulations. Trying out is half the battle," I add.

"What's the other half?" Tim asks, serious and poised for a deep answer.

"Making the team and continuing to work hard while you're on it."

Tim nods, as if I've just imparted the wisest wisdom. "I can't wait until the tryout. Can we practice again tomorrow?"

I glance at Halle for permission. "I have to work the next two days at the firehouse, but I can do Thursday evening when I'm off. Or anytime Friday or this weekend."

"Yes. To all of it," Tim enthusiastically answers, pumping his arm at his side.

"You're going to your dad's this weekend," Halle reminds him.

Instantly, Tim's face falls. "Do we have to go to Dad's?"

Halle gives him a sympathetic gaze. "Yes, baby. Dad wants to see you."

Tim lowers his head and I glance at Violet who has remained quiet throughout most of the meal, although she isn't as sullen or sarcastic as she'd been before her apology. Violet and I seem to have come to a silent agreement.

Friends.

"I'll be driving you part of the way," Halle adds, as if this is some consolation for her son.

However, I don't like that she's driving her kids for Jack's turn to see them. Something in my expression must show my displeasure and when she glances at me, she says, "I'll be meeting him near that airstrip where you took me."

"What airstrip?" Tim inquires before taking another large bite of taco, the sauce dripping down the side of his hand.

"Knox took me gliding." Halle's voice softens and her face blushes, possibly recalling the same thing I am. The thrill of the sky. The joy of touching her on Hunter's desk. The picnic afterward where we made out under the afternoon sun.

God, I want to kiss her.

So much happened so fast but it's always been like that between Halle and me. We're flint and rock. Sparks fly when we're together.

"That sounds so cool. I want to be a pilot like you when I get bigger," Tim states, swinging his legs beneath the table, proving he's still a little kid.

"The other day you wanted to be a fireman like Knox, too," Violet teases.

"Boys can change their mind." Tim's declaration reminds me of the other night we had tacos and he awkwardly announced how women change their minds.

I don't want Halle to change a thing, other than her heart. I want her to love me like she said she does.

"Next you're going to say you want to be a professional soccer player," Violet jokes, balling up her paper napkin and tossing it at Tim.

He swats it away.

Halle mutters, "Hey."

Tim shrugs. "Maybe I will be. I can be anyone I want to be, right, Violet? You said Knox told you that."

Halle's head lifts, her eyes meeting mine. Certainly, Halle's told Violet the same thing. But somehow, pride swells in my chest that Violet took my advice and passed it on to Tim.

Halle clears her throat. "Okay, let's finish up, guys. Tim, you need a shower. Violet, dishes."

Groans rumble all around. Tim doesn't budge, still lingering over steamed corn on his plate. "Do we really have to go to Dad's?"

Halle sighs. "Buddy, we talked about this. Two weekends a month, you go to your dad's place."

"It's so awkward, especially since camp."

Instantly, I'm worried he was bullied or picked on or just made to feel less than he is—a great kid.

Violet is watching Tim, as she hasn't moved from the table either.

Halle glances at me and back at Tim again. "What happened at camp that has anything to do with your dad? You told me camp was just hard."

Tim snorts. "If you call kids teasing me for my dad fucking my teacher . . . hard."

"What?!" Halle shouts.

Violet sits forward. "What did you say?"

Holy shit. *What?*

"I don't want to go to Dad's. Miss Montrock will be there, and everyone knows Dad is having sex with my old fifth-grade teacher."

"Tim!" Halle bellows again, shock and confusion on her face.

I watch as the wheels spin in her eyes. Hell, they're spinning in mine.

His teacher? From last school year? Is sleeping with Jack?

"Why is no one addressing that he just dropped an f-bomb?" Violet questions, but Halle and I are both still stunned by Tim's revelation. The other kids were picking on him, because of Jack's affair. *With Tim's former teacher.* It appears Halle didn't know about the teasing; however, she must have known Peggy was Tim's teacher. Surely, she met her at parent-teacher conferences or something. Is that where Jack met her as well?

"Oh my God." I start to chuckle, almost unable to control myself. It's wrong and priceless at the same time. *Jack.* What a fucking asshole.

With my laughter, Tim starts to giggle as well, and eventually Violet is guffawing, too. The situation isn't exactly funny but humorous, although we all seem to be laughing for different reasons. Only Halle isn't chuckling, staring at her son, clearly having misunderstood the difficulty he had at summer camp.

Abruptly, she stands and exits the room, and I try to contain my laughter, coughing into my fist to control myself. I point at Tim. "Shower, like your mom asked." Then I glance at Violet. "Dishes."

"On it." She scrambles from the table, and I get up as well, seeking Halle.

Chapter 38

[Halle]

I didn't find anything funny about the situation although the laughter certainly helped ease the tension at the table.

Still.

It was difficult enough to accept that my ex-husband might have been sleeping with my son's teacher before we were legally divorced, but the fact that other kids were picking on Tim because of it seemed to drive the proverbial knife deeper.

The divorce, the temporary move, the changes in general have all been hard enough. My kids did not need to bear the brunt of adult choices.

Fuck.

Fisting my hands at my side, I stare out the back kitchen window, while not focused on any one thing in the yard. I haven't been out there much despite the patio Knox installed and the new flower arrangements. I've been so focused on the interior of the house and improving myself that I've missed another child's trials.

First Violet and the front-porch-boy.

Now, Tim and the kids at summer camp.

"Hey," Knox says, covering my shoulders with his hands.

I should flinch out of his touch. Should reject him for laughing. Instead, I lean into him, resting my head on his shoulder. "It isn't funny."

"You're right. It's not. He's a dick. Other kids are assholes. And Miss Montrock, just what the fuck?"

I scoff at the verbal layout and scrub at my forehead. "How does Tim even know what sex is?"

Knox snorts behind me. "He's twelve. I don't think he's had it, but I bet he knows a little bit about it."

Knox is right. Sex education was taught last year in school. By the same teacher *fucking* my ex.

"Oh my God," I mutter at the realization. The situation isn't humorous, but I start to chuckle myself, covering my mouth to hold in my pained laughter.

Knox remains behind me until the riotous guffaw has turned to shuddering sobs. I spin into him, tipping my head into his chest. His hand covers the back of my head and I sense him bending to whisper against my hair.

"Tim will be okay."

I nod. But it's still upsetting that kids hurt Tim's feelings because of Jack. Because of me. I'm the one who instigated the divorce.

"You told him to be brave for the tryouts. I bet he was brave during camp, even without the encouragement."

I lift my head. "Still, I don't want kids to pick on him."

Knox gives me a sorrowful grin. "If it isn't one thing, it's another. Like I said, kids can be assholes."

"Jack is the asshole," I whisper.

"Damn straight." Knox squeezes the back of my neck and our eyes lock.

We're so close our noses almost touch. I could kiss him, and my gaze falls to his lips. Licking my own. I want him to kiss me. I want *us*. Moments like this where he comforts me, makes me laugh, and eases my upset. I'm never going to have that with anyone other than him.

Fresh tears well in my eyes.

Weeks after my mother's death. Months after my divorce. I'm still a mess. But dammit, the only right thing in my life is Knox.

He swipes at my cheeks. "Shh, baby," he soothes. "I'm here. And I'm not going anywhere."

He isn't. He's never going to leave Sterling Falls, but I *might*, and the thought breaks my heart into more pieces when I didn't think it could be shredded any further.

I don't want to leave him.

"I'm sorry there's been so much silence between us. And I'm sorry I accused you of coming between Violet and me, and running away first, and I've just been so harsh, and rash, and—"

"Hey. Shh, sweetheart, it's okay." He smooths over my hair and tugs me to him, holding me tightly to his chest and I melt into this embrace. No one hugs me like this man.

Too quickly, a throat clears to my right, and I turn my head to see Violet watching us.

"Dishes." She holds up the plates stacked on top of each other.

The sink is behind me. "Right." I step away from Knox and brush at my cheeks, before stepping closer to Violet. Rubbing a hand over her shoulder, I say, "I'm going to check on Tim."

I need a moment alone. A moment to collect my thoughts and settle my racing heart.

"Your mom is one brave woman," I hear Knox tell Violet as I exit the kitchen.

"The bravest. She burned down her world and she's rebuilding it brick by brick."

And somehow, I smile despite the pain in my chest and the tears still floating in my eyes.

I'm trying to rebuild.

God, I'm fucking trying.

+ + +

After dropping the kids off with Jack, exchanging them like a backwoods drug deal near the airstrip, I spent the day organizing for an estate sale planned for tomorrow. Initially, I intended to take a bath in my quiet house but decide to hold off and head outside to enjoy the peaceful late-summer evening. After Knox laid the new patio and planted an array of flowers that won't bloom until next year, he placed the set of two red-cedar wood chairs on the patio. The contrast between the older wood and the new limestone patio is striking but the chairs are one more thing that looks outdated about this house.

Tomorrow much of that datedness will be gone and I'm more reflective than melancholy about the pieces leaving Gigi's original home. Strangely, it feels good to consider the empty rooms. Blank canvas. A masterpiece awaits. Art's voice ripples through my head and I chuckle to myself.

But perhaps that blank canvas is me. I'm a blend of colors but the image is becoming clearer with every stroke, every change. A new life begins soon, and here. The decision has been tough but not difficult; not as hard as I thought it might be. I'm not leaving Sterling Falls. It's my life, and I'm taking charge of it. My children will always come first but they also need to follow my lead. This is home—or it will be once we add more of our personalities to the bare walls and fill the rooms with things that express who we are. Who we want to be.

In the midst of thinking these things, my phone lights up the dark patio. Along with my wine, I brought my phone outside in case one of the kids called or sent a text.

Outside?

I laugh for two reasons. I'm home alone and we don't need to sneak outside to meet, and I'm already in the yard.

Already there.

Leaning back in my chair, I expect minutes to pass before Knox answers or arrives, but he steps out from behind the garage within seconds.

"Why are you in the dark?" he asks.

"What were you doing back there?" I counter.

Despite the darkness, I can make out the outline of his body. Broad shoulders. Tall stature. Thick legs.

Knox shrugs. "Just thought we could talk."

Because that's what we always did behind the garage? Talking was never on the agenda when I snuck out to meet him.

"Have a seat." I nod toward the chair near mine.

Instead, Knox lowers to the base of the free-standing fire pit in front of the chairs and turns on the gas-fed flame. Instantly, blue flames illuminate before turning to a vibrant yellow and angry orange. The glow is beautiful and lights up Knox's face.

"I wouldn't think you'd like to sit before a fire, being a fireman."

"I love a good fire, and patio fires are the best. The object is to be aware of the danger while respecting the flame. Kind of like love," he adds.

"What do you mean?"

"It can burn but the truth of love is in the warmth."

I smile, gazing up at him as he remains standing. "That was rather poetic."

"I'm a lover of words."

Is that all he loves? I don't ask. He's been telling me every day how he feels about me, and it might be time to *show* him how I feel about him.

"I like what you're wearing," Knox says, while reaching for my phone.

"Hey." I stretch to retrieve it from his hands but he's quick to type in the code. "How do you even know my password?"

"It's *my* birthdate." He arches a brow, challenging me to prove him wrong, or to explain why I've been using his birthdate for years as the passcode for my phone. "Just like your birthday is the code for mine."

"You're joking."

Knox holds up his pinky finger and his forefinger, curling his middle fingers to his palm, and forcing his thumb out to the side. "On my oath."

I laugh again. His finger display isn't any pledge combination I've seen before. "You're ridiculous."

"I prefer risible."

I laugh harder. "What?"

"Another SAT word. To provoke laughter. I love your laugh, Sprint."

Slowly, my shoulders loosen, and my laughter subsides.

I love *him*.

He taps at my phone a few more times and suddenly the entire patio is lit. I'd been aware that Edison-bulb lights hung above the patio, but I hadn't known how to turn them on. Nor had I been outside in the dark to experience them. However, it isn't just lights overhead that are lit but an array of smaller lights around the flowerbeds, giving the garden a fairy-like effect.

"It's so beautiful," I whisper, awed by the layout. "And you did all this?" Knox never consulted me once about the design of the patio or the re-creation of the flowerbeds, but it's breathtaking.

"I promised you a house with a garden full of kids one day, Sprint. At least I could make good on the garden part." Knox lowers to the chair beside me. Casually, he leans back, stretching his legs forward and crossing them at the ankle.

"I only ever wanted your heart." I softly admit. "And you've given me more now than you know. I don't need the rest." I have my mother's house, my own children, and this beautiful garden. It didn't all come from him, but it didn't need to, either.

"What have I given you?" He moves only his head, glancing at me over his shoulder.

I swallow, hesitant to expose myself but knowing he needs my answer. "Hope."

Knox watches me, waiting on more explanation.

"I didn't think I'd ever love again like I loved you when we were younger. Or ever have sex again, like I've had with you. But I *wouldn't* have ever had those things without you. And now you're here."

Knox continues to stare at me, his dark eyes glowing in the firelight.

I wave at his posture while leaning over the armrest of my chair. "You've been through so much. I'm not downplaying any of my tragedies, yet, you came back here and embraced Sterling Falls. You made peace with your demons or buried them, and I hadn't done that. Like you said, you've been chasing ghosts all your life, and I've done the same. I missed my dad. I wanted more from my mother. And I faulted you for not loving me."

"Halle," he groans.

"But I'm tired of running." I bitterly chuckle, "And I don't even run anymore."

"What are you saying?" Knox stiffens but he doesn't move from his laid-back position.

"I'm saying . . . I want what I want, and that's you. Us. I don't know how, but—"

Instantly, Knox is over me, hands braced on the armrests of my chair, body caging me in. "I want it, too. I want you permanently. I want the kids as well. I want this house and new memories here. Or . . ." He takes a deep breath. "Or I'll leave with you. Go wherever you go."

Startled, I stare up at him leaning over me, breathing him in. His mountain scent. His confident air.

"I can't ask you to do that," I breathlessly counter.

"Can't? Or won't? Because here's the thing . . . I want you to ask me. And then, I'm going to say yes. Yes to it all. You aren't really making any decision. I am."

"Always deciding things for us," I tease.

"Tell me you don't want me to go where you go, and I won't. But you're going to have to prove to me first that you don't want this second chance for us."

I chew my lower lip, shivering at the gleam in his eye. "And how exactly would I prove it to you, if I *did* want it?"

"Your time for mine." The corner of his mouth slowly ticks upward.

"What kind of time are we talking about?" I lean forward, tipping back my head, because I know *how* I want to spend time with him.

"Forever."

The term is so strongly stated that I flinch but not from fear. A thrill runs through me.

"If you don't want that, don't want a lifetime with me, I'll walk away right now." Still, he hovers over me, so close I could kiss him. I could clutch his shirt and draw him to me.

"And if I want it . . ." I pause, allowing him to spell out more.

"I'm all yours, as I always have been. No more pause, Sprint." He lifts his hand like he's holding a stopwatch and clicks his thumb. "Pressing play."

"Race on?"

"No race." He stands taller and holds out a hand. "Now we slow dance."

I place my hand in his and he tugs me upward. I collide with his chest, giggling at the awkward stumble, but true to who he is, Knox catches me by slipping his arms around me. Without any music, other than the gentle breeze and cool mountain air, we sway in a circle like teenage lovers.

"I'm not really dressed for a dance," I jest, glancing down at my attire. I'd put on my nightgown, although a bath was coming later in this evening's plans. However, with the warm days of August turning to cool nights, hinting that a seasonal change was coming soon, I'd slipped into a pair of cabin socks and tossed on a flannel shirt over my pajamas.

"You're beautiful in everything. And nothing." Knox winks before spinning me out from him and then tugging me back into his arms.

"I'm sorry I didn't take you to your senior homecoming dance," Knox whispers, reminding us both of the dance he stole into to break up with me.

I shake my head, dismissing his apology, while running my hand over his hair and gently tugging at the short ones on the back of his head. "No more going backwards."

"I think this dance might be our true homecoming, Sprint." Knox gazes at the lights overhead and the stars even further above them.

Homecoming. Not an SAT word but a sentimental one instead.

Because I'm truly home in his arms.

Chapter 39

[Knox]

After a few more spins, holding Halle in my arms, I step back and lower next to the fire pit, turning off the flame. Halle's gaze never leaves me as I reach for her phone next and shut off the outdoor lights. Standing in the dark, my eyes take a second to adjust, but I don't need to see Halle to sense her.

Her jasmine scent. Her shallow breaths. Her comforting warmth.

A fire that could burn but instead heats me from within.

Reaching for her hand, she holds out hers, and I turn, walking backward toward the house.

"Where are we going?" Her voice is flirtatious. She must know where I'm leading her, but I'll spell it out.

"I'm taking you inside. No scaling up columns or sneaking through windows. I'm walking in through the door because I can." As I reach the back entrance, I twist the knob and press it open. "What I *won't* do any more is hide us."

We both pause. The moment feeling monumental.

There's no one inside to stop me from entering. No one that forces me to be stealthy and quiet if I do slip in. Nothing will stop me from loving this woman right here. Right now.

Swiftly, I bend and scoop Halle into my arms, like a bride. She squeals as her arms wrap around my neck and she tugs herself tighter to me.

"What are you doing?" Laughter fills her voice.

"I'm carrying you over the threshold." I don't care if she owns this house already. I don't care that she has children of her own. I didn't really need to give Halle a garden. She has my heart and soul.

With giggles still in her throat, I enter the house and kick the door shut. I don't release Halle but twist, so she can lock the door while still in my arms. Then I strut through the god-awful kitchen and the furniture packed living room to the staircase.

"Okay, now put me down," she softly demands.

I'd carry her up mountains if I needed to, but instead, I lower her to her feet and kiss her. With my hands holding her face and her fingers fisted in my shirt, we kiss like we always have. Like we can't get close enough fast enough. But I have the entire night to love this woman. I want her on every surface, in every room. We'll desecrate them all by building new memories in every one of them.

Halle pulls away first, taking a step backward to place her foot on the first stair.

"I don't know if I can make it to your room," I whisper, honest and breathless. I want her now. Here.

"Then let's not."

A half second passes before I understand her meaning. "Fuck, Sprint." My hands are back on her face as I devour her lips, thrusting my tongue forward and swiping into her mouth. Halle matches my eagerness, hungrily following my lead.

When I break the kiss to nibble at her jaw and suck at her neck, Halle slowly turns, showing me what she needs, inviting me to be reckless and wild right here on the staircase. With her back to my front, I press her forward and Halle lowers to her knees. Hastily, I unbuckle my belt and lower my jeans while Halle lifts the back of her nightgown and removes her panties.

"Want it fast and quick the first time?" I growl as I lower behind her. With her on her knees on a step above me, I have a nice view of how ripe she is, and I slick my tongue over her once just to taste her sweetness.

"Knox. Please."

I love how she's begging me, commanding me, and I don't want to make her wait. We've waited too long for one another.

With one hand on her hip and the other braced on a step higher than her shoulder, I slam into her. Halle yelps but presses back, drawing me deeper inside her.

Fire. Burn. Warmth. Respect.

Love.

Not enough words describe how I feel about her, but I say them anyway. "God, I fucking love you."

"I love you, too," she stammers around the rapid thrusting of my hips, driving my dick harder into her.

Halle reaches backward, her arm wrapping around my hip and her hand clutching at my backside like she doesn't want me to part from her body. She doesn't have to worry. I'll never leave her again.

I slip my hand from her hip to her clit and stroke her in quick, sharp circles, knowing how to trigger her. Knowing her body well at eighteen and learning it again at thirty-eight. She's bolder now. We both are, and I'm loving it. I love her.

"Never thought it'd be like this," I mutter, hammering into her as her fingernails dig into my ass. "Imagined it but didn't allow myself to believe it would be true."

"It's the truest thing I know," Halle whimpers, breathless and passionate.

"Gonna give me what's always been mine," I prompt her.

"Take it."

"Demanding little thing you've grown into, Sprint," I tease as her body is tightens.

Her breath coming sharper. Her fingers digging harder. She's so close and then she stills. And other than the clenching of her around my cock and the moisture dripping between us both, time stalls.

I'm exactly where I'm supposed to be. And so is she.

Home.

I jet off next like flint sparked against a rock.

After collapsing on the stairs for a minute to catch our breath, I pull back and Halle twists to take a seat on the step. We've made a bit of a mess, and I don't bother refastening my pants.

"Take a bath with me?" Her voice is small, hesitant, and I don't like the doubt. Maybe her dickhead ex never slipped into the tub with her, but I'll go anywhere she wants me to be. Like I told her outside, I'll go where she goes.

"Sounds perfect." I wince when I see how red her knees are from kneeling on the hardwood steps. Her scar stands out to me, angry and bright. I lean forward and kiss her there, asking, "You okay?"

With a soft smile, Halle stands and covers my cheek, smoothing her hand down to cup my chin. "I've never been better."

She takes the lead and I follow her to the bathroom in the main hallway as her bedroom bath only has a shower stall. Once inside the tight room, I reach around Halle for the faucet, allowing the water to heat. Halle tugs off her nightgown and I stare at her body.

"You're so beautiful, Sprint." With a shaky hand I reach out and palm one breast before lowering for the other to suck it into my mouth. Halle arches her back, forcing her closer to me. I place my hands on her ass and lift for her mouth, kissing her slower this time. I want her again.

"I could take you on the sink," I warn, muttering against her mouth, inching her backward for the countertop.

Halle chuckles. "How about in the tub?"

"Here. There. Everywhere. Sounds like a plan."

Halle checks the water. The sight of her from behind is just as tempting as her front, and I can't keep my hands off her. I coast my fingers over her ass and up her spine. She shivers as she stands before me and I clasp the back of her neck, gently tugging her to me. She twists only her head, and we kiss again, slow and deep.

"Get naked," she mutters against my lips.

"I like you demanding." I nip her lower lip and pull back to meet her eyes.

"I am not demanding," she pouts, reminding me of our first few encounters upon seeing one another.

"You're definitely demanding, but I'm here for all your commands." Stepping back, I make a show of slowly unsnapping the pearl snaps of my shirt. Lazily rolling the cotton over my shoulders and down my arms, I drop it to the floor and watch as Halle's eyes widen, and the blue sharpens.

Yeah, she fucking wants me.

She doesn't wait for me to work off my jeans. Instead, she dives in, tugging down my pants to remove them along with my socks and shoes. On her knees before me, she glances up at me and cups my balls.

"You put my dick anywhere near your mouth and we aren't making it into that tub."

Defiance sparks in her eyes. "Now who sounds demanding?" And tease that she is, she pumps my dick a few times then opens wide and sucks me between her lips.

I see stars after a few minutes, but I also see my future as it was always meant to be.

All Halle.

Chapter 40

[Halle]

In the morning, Knox tells me he'll be hanging out for the day. The auctioneer is due to arrive early but not too early that Knox and I don't spend a few minutes exploring one another again. I'll never have my fill of touching him, feeling his solid form beneath my hands, tasting him on my tongue.

In the quiet of the empty house, we don't speak but let our bodies do all the talking.

When we finally leave the bed, we shower separately, or we won't be presentable in time to meet the auction company employees.

The day is a whirlwind as the team divides the furniture into groups. The rapid-fire chatter of the auctioneer is like a nail gun piercing wood as piece by piece my grandmother and mother's belongings are sold off. With each item that leaves the yard—couches, chairs, hutches, dresses— a part of me exits as well. A moment in history is gone. A reprieve from the memories is in its place. The few pieces that remain bring me comfort and joy.

At the end of the day, I stand in the emptied front room. A sense of relief fills the vacant space.

"How are you feeling?" Knox asks, standing on the opposite side of the room. Anything that didn't sell we moved into the garage for now.

The slate is clean, as Art Simms might say.

"It's just a house." I shrug, having once heard that said. A structure with four walls, interior divisions, and empty spaces. It's what happens within those walls that determines if it's more. "But it has the potential to be a home."

The corner of Knox's mouth curls. "Our home?"

He isn't asking to move in immediately, just someday. And someday, he will, and we'll be the family we were always meant to be.

In response, I offer him a matching grin. One crooked and flirtatious and coy.

Knox tips his chin. "Meet me right there." He points to the middle of the room where a rumpled quilt lays in a heap on the hardwood floor. The command feels prophetic. Meet him in the middle, and the future is ours.

"Right there," I tease, pointing at the spot.

Knox smiles wider.

"You're so demanding," I remark, stepping toward the space, eager for us to come together. Knox rushes forward as well and we do meet in the middle. In the middle of our lives.

"I'll show you demanding," Knox huffs before kissing me soft and sweet, warning me with this first kiss that he'll never tell me what to do. He'll never interfere in my life, our lives, by making decisions for us without talking to me first. But as the kiss heats, he's also saying he'll command me in ways that will only bring me pleasure. He demands I love him every day.

As we lower to the floor, laughing a little as our older bodies fall rather than gracefully collapse, Knox gives me another wide grin, one accentuating his white teeth and the dark scruff around his lush mouth.

"I'm going to fuck you right here, Sprint, as a big fuck you to the history of this house. And you're going to be loud and reckless as I introduce you to our future."

I do as he says. With every touch and scream at the final release, I welcome what's next while on my back, but not meekly laying down.

Knox will stand beside me as I continue to stand back up.

As I continue to rebuild our lives, brick by brick.

+ + +

The following day, Knox rides with me to pick up the kids. We leave early so we can take another glider ride.

Jack might have given me stink-eyes over Knox's presence, but he kept his mouth shut, especially since he's brought Peggy with him to my home. We had discussed what happened with Tim at soccer camp. Jack's response was his personal life wasn't anyone's business, but we both know that isn't true for a person in the public eye, especially when that person has been so public about his personal business before. Our family had been a selling point for Jack's future.

"School, Halle," Jack mutters before we part ways for another two weeks.

"I'm getting there."

With the promise to Tim to pursue trying out for soccer, the answer should be evident but it's not. I still have Violet's emotional state to consider.

On Monday evening, Tim tries out for the soccer team. Parents aren't allowed on the sidelines. I have a feeling Knox is going to pace my yard instead. He sent endless texts throughout the day while he worked at Sylver Seed and Soil to organize an upcoming patio construction project. Final words of encouragement before I took Tim to the field.

Since I'll have two hours to wait out Tim's tryout, I make a stop of my own.

Being that it's August, the high school parking lot has a few more cars parked in it than the beginning of July when I first came here. I round the building and find the football field full of student-athletes, practicing for the upcoming season. I'll need to enroll the kids in school within the next few days which means final decisions need to be made.

But this evening I'm at the high school for me.

When I reach the running track that surrounds the field, I stride through the open chain-link fence entrance. With new running shoes on my feet, I take my first steps with intention. I'm not here to run. I won't be sprinting or hurdling any time soon. Or ever. But I can walk. I can take the steps to change my life. My health. My outlook. My future.

In the classic way we all learn this skill, I put one foot in front of the other, and circle the track.

Just like life, I go around and around.

+ + +

By the time I pick up Tim, I'm a sweaty mess. The tryouts involve a first cut and a second round, so we don't learn until late on Tuesday night that Tim made the team. Tim is ecstatic. Knox is elated as well, but it's Violet I watch for a reaction.

She's surprisingly quiet but offers Tim a warm hug and praise. "I knew you could do it."

Later, once Tim has finally settled down and Knox leaves even though neither of us want him to go, I'm passing Violet's room when she opens her bedroom door.

"Mom?"

"Yeah, baby." I pause and turn toward her. She looks so young while so grown up at the same time. Her hair is piled on her head in a messy bun and her face is lightly tan, emphasizing her freckles.

"Are you really selling grandma's house?"

Caught off guard by the question, I blink a few times. "I thought you wanted me to sell. Wanted us to move." Although living in Charles Town is off the table for me, we could potentially move closer to our old city.

"I do," she states but then her voice lowers. "But I also don't."

Stepping closer to her as she continues to lean on the open door, I softly ask, "What's going on?" Is she having a change of heart?

"It's kind of embarrassing that everyone knows my dad slept with my former teacher. I mean, I know she hasn't been my teacher for years, but she was Tim's teacher last year, and people talk." Violet stares at me like I'm unaware of rumors or gossip, when I'm very cognizant of what's been said about my children's previous teacher and my ex-husband. "Even though I'm starting high school, and not everyone at CTHS would know the story, it's still there."

"I'm sorry, honey. I didn't want that kind of pressure for you."

"I didn't want any of that for you either, Mom." Violet glances down at her sock-covered toes, drawing on the hardwood floors. Hesitantly, she looks up. "But you seem happier here. With Knox."

"Honey, Knox doesn't—"

"Mom, don't lie to me." Violet quietly chuckles, not deprecating but thoughtful. "Or yourself. He has everything to do with everything."

I don't even know how to interpret that, but Violet continues.

"You like him. A lot." Her tone is contemplative, as if questioning me while also pointing out a fact.

I love him and I'm not going to deny it. One way or another Knox Sylver is going to be in my life again. *Our lives*.

"He makes you smile," Violet adds, her own mouth curling in the corners.

Fighting a smile, I lose the battle and offer a goofy grin. "He does. And I do like him. Lots and lots. He's going to be in our lives, Violet."

Violet lowers her head, toeing the hardwood floor again. "And I'm okay if we stay in Sterling Falls."

"Really?" The question comes too quickly and too emphatic, but my heart is racing.

Slowly, Violet lifts her head and offers a timid smile, nodding her approval.

"What about Tim? Think he'll be okay staying?" I already know the answer. He just made the soccer team. He's made new friends, and he's made it known that Charles Town isn't his home anymore. But I want Violet's take.

"He's totally in the Knox fan club."

Again, with the fan club references. I snicker.

"He might be president." I wink at her, reaching out to tuck her hair around her ear. "But what about you?"

"I'm more Team Knox than Go Miss Montrock."

I let out a sharp laugh and stepping even closer to Violet, rubbing my hands over her soft cheeks and cupping her jaw.

"I could use a fresh start," she whispers.

"Me too, honey. Me too." Relief washes over me as I lean forward and press a kiss to her temple.

"What will you do here?" Violet asks as I pull back but still hold her face in my hands.

"I've been thinking a lot about that question since we first arrived, and I might have an answer now that we're staying."

Violet's brows lift, hearing the decisiveness of my tone.

"But first. There's someone I need to talk to."

Chapter 41

[Knox]

When Halle told me she was staying, I could hardly contain myself. I wanted to rush back to her house, scale the porch, and burst through her bedroom window. Instead, I settled on waiting until morning, sneaking over before my firehouse shift and kissing her senseless in the backyard. No more hiding behind the garage.

Two days later, Halle had even more news for me.

"I'm going to help Art with his fundraiser." Halle goes quiet for a second, watching me as we sit in the sturdy but ancient red cedar chairs on the patio. She doesn't have any living room furniture yet so outdoors is her main seating area for now. Thankfully, the firepit wards off the mountain chill of the August evening. Fall is already teasing the air at night while the days are still brutally warm.

"How did this come about?" I'm happy for her, but curious. Art isn't one who asks for help so the fundraiser fest he's hosting has been a surprise.

"I explained to him that I've worked on many fundraisers over the years. I have experience asking people for donations. I've also hosted dinners and parties, worked with caterers and bakers . . ." Halle paused with a chuckle. "At first, I told him maybe I sounded foolish. I should have written up a resumé."

Halle squints at the firepit and then turns in her seat to look at me. "But I haven't written one since college where it was mandatory for some next-level I didn't see myself taking at the time."

Halle's sense of failure is always going to linger within her but she's also miles away from that fall. She's stood up, moved forward, and now she's taking even bigger steps, both figuratively and literally. She told me about her walk earlier this week and another one she took the other night. She isn't going to run again but she's not afraid to walk instead.

"I bet Art got a good laugh out of you mentioning a resumé. He's still old school where your word and a handshake say more than a list of jobs on a paper."

Halle laughs. "He did say something similar to that. But what he really said was, 'I've been waiting for you to ask'." She softly smiles.

"To ask if you could help him?"

"To ask if I could be involved," Halle clarifies, her eyes glistening in the firelight. "He said there was a difference. It isn't *help* when it concerns your life. Your friends. Your family. It's love."

Halle swallows and rolls her shoulders. "Art reminded me, he's a friend. Asking for help can make someone feel weak. Asking to be involved makes someone feel powerful." Halle lifts a fist like Art might have done and I see my veteran friend and his quirky philosophy has rubbed off on Halle.

Halle chuckles and waves her hand to dismiss Art's rambles, but Art is insightful. "Anyway, I told him I'd make a donation to the overall fundraiser, financially backing some of the extras Art needs to pull off the fest, and in exchange, I'm a silent partner."

"Wow," I whisper. "He must really like you."

"He told me he knew a redhead once."

We both laugh.

"Have I told you I love you today?" I hold out my hand.

"Yes, but you can say it again anyway." She sheepishly smiles at me, taking my hand and kissing my knuckles, then beats me by saying, "I love you, too."

"You're too far away."

With a soft smile, Halle stands and then settles on my lap. With her side against my chest, I wrap my arms around her and press my lips to her head.

"You're really staying," I mutter to her hair. "You have a job. You have a home. And you have me."

Halle shifts to slip her arms around my neck. "It isn't always going to be easy, Knox. It isn't just me in this mix."

My gaze drops to her belly, and I cover her there with my palm. "Just hearing your kids call you mom warms my heart, Halle." I glance up at her. "Motherhood will be your greatest marathon."

I'm not melancholy over what I won't have with Halle. Violet and Tim are amazing. Our friendships—mine with the kids—are ones I'm excited to see nurtured and grow.

Halle cups my jaw and holds my gaze. "No more rewinds."

"No more pauses," I tell her.

Jostling her in my arms, I squeeze her tighter. "Love is hard; let's be the soft spots for each other, Sprint."

"Let's be the soft spots, Brick."

+ + +

Within a month, the kids have settled into their new school.

Some nights, Tim's middle school soccer games are almost as intense as professional ones.

Violet made the field hockey team with virtually no experience. As I told her when I saw her axe throwing the first time, she has exceptional eye-hand coordination. I didn't have a doubt she'd be great at anything that involves wielding a stick with a little aggression.

And Halle hosts ARTFest to support local artists and Art's Studio.

The lawn space near the studio is full of individual tents providing space for families to explore creativity and purchase wares. It's also teeming with people who want Halle's attention. She's become quite the popular prodigal-daughter-returned-home and I'm all for her getting the recognition she deserves; however, I need something from her myself.

Halle eyes me suspiciously when I cup her elbow and tell her I need a minute alone with her. Guiding her into the studio, I lead us to a bathroom off a short hallway.

Once inside the single room space, I lock the door and lean against it.

"What are you doing?"

"What I should have done the first time I saw you again." I cup her face and lean in, kissing her with awe, and love, and pride. I'm so fucking proud of her. For this day. For her changes. For who she was and who she is.

She kisses me back with equal intensity, leaning into me instantly and gripping my shirt like she can't get close enough fast enough.

Abruptly, she breaks the kiss, and I don't even mind because she's breathless when she says, "We probably shouldn't be in here. I'm working." Then she tugs me back to her for another powerful kiss, reminding us both that we *can* kiss one another. Because we're together again and nothing is going to separate us.

"That's right. My working girl," I tease. "Gonna be my sugar momma?"

Halle glares at me. Those blue eyes are electric and bright as she tries to be stern. "Don't ever say that to me again." However, she laughs.

All the rough edges of her from when we first reunited are now smoothed. Not polished. No brick is perfect.

A sharp knock on the bathroom door startles both of us. Halle smooths down her flowing dress and I adjust my jeans, tugging the front tails of my plaid shirt a little lower to disguise what she does to me.

Opening the door, Art mischievously glares at us. "I knew a redhead once."

I glance at Halle. "And she stole his heart."

Halle places her hand on my chest. "And she never plans to give it back."

"Good thing I don't have to run too far to catch the thief." I tug Halle against me and press another kiss to her head.

"Good thing you're in the bathroom because you two are making me nauseous," Art interjects, before laughing. "And as much as I hate to break up whatever you're doing, the mayor wants to meet Halle and talk to her about organizing another festival in town."

I chuckle while Halle and I exchange another glance. "Welcome to Sterling Falls, sweetheart."

Halle smiles wide. "It's good to be home."

Epilogue

October

"Ford?" The shock of seeing my brother again so soon cannot be contained.

Sebastian's wedding was only a week ago and our second-to-the youngest brother was home for the wedding. However, he was hardly present, holing up at a local bar upon his arrival and acting sour the remainder of the weekend despite the festivities.

"Hey." He runs a frustrated hand over his short hair, avoiding direct eye contact with me despite my surprise and concern. His tall, lean athletic build holds tension, like a coil wound too tight and ready to speedily unravel, whipping around in willy-nilly fashion.

We're gathered at Halle's house for a Halloween party slash open house to celebrate the updates to her place and officially mingle with the neighbors. After the fire across the street this summer, Halle is determined to know everyone on the boulevard. Violet and Tim have a few friends over as well and the house is filled with boisterous chaos as Halle leads everyone through old-fashioned Halloween games.

Apple bobbing. Bean bag tossing through a wooden cut-out pumpkin. Pin the face on the ghost.

Not certain that last one is a traditional activity, but Halle had fun coming up with ideas for the kids despite the aging of her children. There's enough candy here to send a diabetic into a sugar-induced coma, and not enough alcohol to numb the exuberance of teenagers.

However, as Halle and I volunteered to babysit Adara while Enya and Sebastian took a few days to celebrate their nuptials, I'm not indulging in hard cider yet. Being that *I am* Adara's favorite uncle, all my focus is on her.

Still, seeing my younger brother here again so soon is puzzling.

"Where are the girls?" Ford has three little ones.

"Violet nabbed them as soon as I entered." A timid smile graces Ford's stone-edged face. During the wedding activities, Violet designated herself in charge of Ford's miniature herd. His girls adore her.

Ford had been acting weird when he'd arrived for Sebastian's wedding. Even weirder as the weekend wore on. His wife was conspicuously absent then and I have a hunch she isn't present now either. I don't ask.

"Surprised to see you here so soon." He'd been invited to the party only a week ago but quickly declined. The air around him still stinks, a vapor that smells like *he couldn't get out of this town fast enough.* I recognize the stench. I'd been in a similar frame of mind when I exited all those years ago. However, nothing smells sweeter than Sterling Falls now that I'm back. And Halle is here.

With Adara in my arms, I glance up just as Halle walks through the back door.

"Are you hiding out here?" She's all tease as she saunters up to me, not ignoring my brother but not acknowledging him yet. Her gaze remains focused on me until she's close enough to swipe her hand over Adara's head. "She's so sweet."

"You're sweet," I whisper, leaning in to inhale her neck. She's wearing a long black dress and a pointed hat, making her the sexiest witch I've ever seen. She certainly has put a spell on me.

Halle leans down to kiss Adara's head. The baby is mesmerized by the flames of the fire pit, but her eyes are also drooping from my steady sway as I hold her in my arms.

As Halle lifts her head, she does a double-take, finally noticing my brother. "Ford?" Her tone is filled with the same surprise as mine had been. "What are you doing here?" Concern laces the question. She knows Ford rarely comes home. She also knows he's struggling with something. Something I'm certain he's spoke to Stone about but not the rest of us.

Ford shrugs his angular shoulder and glances at the fire pit again. "Just thought I'd come back home."

Home. He hardly called this place home, just like me, once upon a time.

But with his brows pinched and his concentration on the fire pit, my brother appears deeply puzzled about why he's here and what he called this place.

Halle glances at me and then back at Ford while her hand absentmindedly strokes over Adara's head. Somewhere I've lost the cap that compliments her pumpkin outfit.

"Well, we're happy to have you here. Can I get you a drink?"

Ford's head pops up at the suggestion. His mouth opens like he's about to accept the offer and then he closes his lips, bowing his head again. "Nah. I'm good for now."

Halle eyes me suspiciously once more, her brows pinching in question. I shake my head, not having any answers for Ford's presence.

"Okay. I need to get back inside before a popcorn brawl breaks out." Halle softly chuckles, thoroughly enjoying herself. She loves to host a party, and she's good at it, as evidenced last month when she ran Art's ARTFest. She raised fifteen thousand dollars for our local art teacher and friend. I think some of the funds might have come from Halle, but I didn't ask. She'll be hosting another festival in November, at the request of the mayor of Sterling Falls.

Halle tips up on her toes, kissing me too quickly before turning for the house. I long to follow her, but Adara likes it better out here where it's quiet from the chaos.

"You look like a lost puppy dog," Ford chuckles.

I gaze at him, breaking the spell of watching my girlfriend walk away from me.

"Best kind of lost," I mutter.

Ford's expression tightens as he peers at the dancing flames once more.

"Want to talk about it?"

"Not yet," Ford says, sighing heavily. He briefly looks at me and tips up his chin. "Why don't you give her to me? Go enjoy the party."

Eyes widened, I stare back at Ford, shocked once more by his offer. He's good with his girls although I have no idea how he handled the baby stage. I wasn't present when they were born. He didn't come home then either.

"I got her." I adjust Adara but I know this little pumpkin. She's going to wiggle her body back down to the crook of my elbow, dangling one arm over mine and leaning her head to the side. She's so stinkin' cute.

Ford holds out his hands. "Just give her to me. You look like you might piss yourself if you don't get to follow your girl."

"Well." I cough. "That's graphic."

"Considering you're dressed like a giant dog, I'd say it's appropriate."

Glancing down at my outfit, I chuckle, having forgotten that I'm wearing a head-to-toe onesie that makes me look like a giant Dalmatian. I had the costume on hand as last year I passed out candy from the firehouse.

Ford wiggles his fingers and I transfer Adara to his arms. "I'll be right back."

"Sure," Ford murmurs, lifting Adara to his nose, inhaling her baby scent before kissing her head and staring back at the firepit.

"Go get her," he says next, a little louder, like he'd tell a dog to fetch.

"Woof!" I bark out with a laugh and then rush for the house, finding Halle at the back of a pack of kids dancing to "Thriller" although they hardly know who Michael Jackson was. Violet is in the mix, laughing with her head tossed as she tries to teach the other kids the dance. Tim and his friends are suspiciously missing. He's a good kid but he's still a twelve-year-old hyped up on chocolate and tart candies.

For sixty seconds, though, I take in the scene before me. A house whose ceiling is decorated from corner to corner in black and orange crepe paper and an explosion of pumpkins. The music is loud. The laughter contagious. It's a party. But it's also a home.

Halle made this place festive and fun, and all her own. The new furniture has been pushed up against the freshly painted walls to provide open space, but the kids keep spilling into the yard. Adults linger on the edges of the front room, carrying on their own conversations. As my gaze travels around the room, I eventually lock on Halle who's looking at me. A soft smile grows on her beautiful face, bursting into a wide grin. She looks happier than she did months ago, and while I'd like to take credit for that smile, it's all Halle.

She lights up any room, making her the only person I see.

Slowly, I cross the floor like a cord tethering us together and she's reeling me toward her. Once I stand before her, she laughs, light and loud.

"Having a good time, Sprint?" I cup the back of her neck, needing to touch her despite the crowd. Violet and Tim have caught us kissing plenty of times over the past few months.

"The best." She chews her bottom lip, and I press my thumb to the lush swell, popping it free from her teeth.

"I know what would be better." My mouth on hers, me bobbing between her thighs with her knees wrapped tight to my head.

As if reading my mind, Halle laughs deeper, richer. Her hand lands on my chest. "Down, boy."

"Hmm. I want to go down." I let my gaze roam her body in that black dress. "Way down."

Halle leans into me, another giggle rumbling up her throat as her arms lazily wrap around my neck.

"Got a bone you want to show me?" Her brows wiggle and I'm the one to laugh next, hearty and ripe.

"Jesus." Without thought, I lean in for a kiss that's too quick but needed. I want to swallow her giddiness and revel in the curl of her mouth, expressing how happy she is.

I don't live with Halle. Yet. We date often. Have dinner every night together with the kids and have every other weekend to be wild and reckless with our bodies. In between those nights, we tease one another on the phone and sneak out to meet behind the garage, building up the anticipation until we can be alone.

Sex with Halle is even better than when we were teens, but it isn't that age or experience has perfected us. It's the love that never disappeared between us and somehow brought us right back here.

To Sterling Falls.
To Halle's house.
To one another.
"I love you," I mutter to her neck.
"I love you, too, Brick."

Thank you for taking the time to read Sterling Brick.

Please consider writing a review on major sales channels where ebooks and paperbacks are sold and discussed.

Want another seed of Knox and Halle?

Sterling Brick BONUS

Up next in Sterling Falls – single dad, baseball star in need of a nanny. *Sterling Streak*.

More by L.B. Dunbar

<u>Sterling Falls</u>
Seven siblings muddling their way through love over 40.
Sterling Heat
Sterling Brick
Sterling Streak

Parentmoon
When the mother of the groom goes head-to-head with the single father of the bride.

Holiday Hotties (Christmas novellas)
Holiday novellas certain to heat the season.
Scrooge-ish
Naughty-ish

Road Trips & Romance
Three sisters. Three destinations. All second chances at love over 40.
Hauling Ashe
Merging Wright
Rhode Trip

Lakeside Cottage
Four friends. Four summers. Shenanigans and love happen at the lake.
Living at 40
Loving at 40
Learning at 40
Letting Go at 40

The Silver Foxes of Blue Ridge
Small mountain town, silver foxes. Brothers seeking love over 40.
Silver Brewer
Silver Player
Silver Mayor
Silver Biker

Sexy Silver Foxes
When sexy silver foxes meet the feisty vixens of their dreams.
After Care

L.B. DUNBAR

Midlife Crisis
Restored Dreams
Second Chance
Wine&Dine

Collision novellas
A spin-off from After Care – the younger set/rock stars
Collide
Caught

The Sex Education of M.E.
The original sexy silver fox.
When a widowed professor decides she'd like to date again, and a local
fireman volunteers to give her lessons.

The Heart Collection
Small town, big hearts - stories of family and love.
Speak from the Heart
Read with your Heart
Look with your Heart
Fight from the Heart
View with your Heart

A Heart Collection Spin-off
The Heart Remembers

BOOKS IN OTHER AUTHOR WORLDS
Smartypants Romance (an imprint of Penny Reid)
Tales of the Winters sisters set in Green Valley.
Love in Due Time
Love in Deed
Love in a Pickle

The World of True North (an imprint of Sarina Bowen)
Welcome to Vermont! And the Busy Bean Café.
Cowboy
Studfinder

THE EARLY YEARS
The Legendary Rock Star Series
A classic tale with a modern twist of rockstar romance and suspense.

Paradise Stories
MMA romance. Two brothers. One fight.

The Island Duet
Intrigue and suspense. The island knows what you've done.

Modern Descendants – writing as elda lore
Magical realism. Modern myths of Greek gods.

About the Author

www.lbdunbar.com

L.B. Dunbar loves sexy silver foxes, second chances, and small towns. If you enjoy older characters in your romance reads, including a hero with a little silver in his scruff and a heroine rediscovering her worth, then welcome to romance for those over 40. L.B. Dunbar's signature works include women and men in their prime taking another turn at love and happily ever after. She's a *USA TODAY* Bestseller as well as #1 Bestseller on Amazon in Later in Life Romance with her Lakeside Cottage and Road Trips & Romance series. L.B. lives in Chicago with her own sexy silver fox.

To get all the scoop about the self-proclaimed queen of silver fox romance, join her on Facebook at Loving L.B. or receive her monthly newsletter, Love Notes.

+ + +

Connect with L.B. Dunbar

9 781956 337365